JAMES HARDCOURT

The Chastity Contract

Books 1-3 An Erotic Suspense - Tease, Denial and Chastity Cages

Edging Space
Publishing

Be careful what you wish for, lest it come true!

Aesop (Fables - 260BC)

Contents

Acknowledgement

To my incredible wife, the first to believe in me and my stories and who was excited to share them with the world.

You blow my mind.

I love you.

To the amazing team who've supported my writing from the very start. Thank you for your support, encouragement and eagle eyes!

To the remarkable friends and followers I've met through my blog, who've inspired, challenged and supported me.

You know who you are.

Even if I don't.

I can never thank you enough.

Preface

In a decade's time I'll either be looking back and thinking, 'This was the book that started it all' or 'Do you remember that time I wrote a book for you, darling?'.

Whichever it turns out to be, it's been a fun ride so far.

My wife, Jane and I, are kinky fuckers. A few years back we decided to share that online and have ended up running two of the biggest Tumblr blogs focused on our favourite kink, orgasm denial.

But it was only last year, as I whispered a fantasy to turn her on, that she challenged me to write it up properly as a short story.

I am a writer by trade, a storyteller even, but in the commercial world - a copywriter. Besides little captions on the blog, not a word of fiction has passed my fingertips since being forced to write some sorry story in middle school. It's been a bit of learning curve.

But that little fantasy, inspired by a recent Netflix twist on *Indecent Proposal*, turned not into some short story of a few thousand words, but an 100,000 word monster. And it's only getting going.

In form for the genre, I split the story so far into three novellas, but for the first time they have been put together in one volume, and that makes it large enough to now publish as a paperback as well as a bundled ebook.

To my surprise the book didn't turn out as pure erotica, but quickly developed some of the classic suspense tropes: mystery, intrigue and a growing sense of something not being quite right. Whether it's a love of cliffhangers or just I like finding every which way to mess with my characters, I don't know. But I have plotted out what's going to happen to poor Emma and Nate, and let me warn you now, I'm going to put them through the wringer. Will it turn out okay in the end? There's only one way to find out…

Aesop (whose *Fables* was the first book I fell in love with) was never more astute in his warning to us all: *'Be careful what you wish for, you might just get it'*

I

Book 1 - Entrapped

A Curious Question

'How much is your husband's cock worth?'

Emma stared at the message on her laptop and then laughed out loud. *I thought this one wasn't crazy.* 'What on earth are you talking about?' she typed back.

Instead of an answer she received another question. 'Would you want to lock him up long-term?'

At least she knew what that meant. She bit her lip and pondered the stranger's question. 'How long is long?' she replied.

'A year.'

Emma scrunched up her pretty, freckled face as she laughed again. The thought of just how crazy that would make her husband was an enjoyable fantasy, but a fantasy, nonetheless.

'I think—' she began to reply before the sitting room door opened. 'Be right back' she bashed out before closing the laptop lid and pushing it to the end of the sofa.

'Whatcha doin'?' Her husband, Nate, leaned against the door frame, folding his arms across his chest, the sleeves of the old t-shirt he was wearing stretching tight.

'Oh, just, you know, the blog. Blog stuff.' *That's kind of true.* Emma sat back on the sofa, legs crossed and patted the cushions next to her. 'Want to come watch something, have you finished for today?'

'Sounds like a good plan.' Nate dropped back onto the sofa next to her. 'Shelves are nearly finished.'

He smelled good. He'd been putting up some shelves in the spare bedroom

3

of their little semi-detached house. 'Nearly done?' said Emma. 'The sooner it's done the sooner you'll have your own office space.' *Even if it does mean it's no longer the nursery we hoped for.*

She pressed herself closer and breathed him in, loving the smell of hard work with his now ever-present musky hint of arousal. She hadn't even had to remind him to put the shelves up. *It's remarkable how much better he's got at doing all those jobs he used to put off, if only he'd learn to finish them.*

Nate grabbed the remote and pulled up Netflix on the TV. 'Anything you fancy?'

'Well now you mention it…' Emma leaned closer and slid her fingertips up the inside of Nate's jeans, until they tapped against the hard edge they found there. 'What a shame, it's such a turn on you being all rough and ready from the DIY.'

'Well that's easily fixed,' Nate said, letting out a frustrated grunt as his wife cupped her hand more firmly between his thighs.

Emma snuggled in, laying down on the sofa with her head on his leg. 'Oh baby, I really fancy sucking you right now.'

Nate stroked his fingers through her long, light brown hair. 'You're killing me you know.'

She rubbed her cheek against his thigh, not so accidentally bopping her head against his crotch. 'I know.'

After the ritual flicking through movie options they decided on a new film neither of them had seen. It looked from the trailer like it might have some steamy scenes and Emma wanted Nate buzzing before they went to bed. Her fingers stroked up and down his thigh to add to his frustration. 'Do you think it's essential to the plot she wears those super tight yoga pants?' Emma asked after they watched a few scenes.

Nate drew his fingers gently up her neck. 'Given how slow it is so far, I think it's their main tactic to keep us watching.'

'She does have a very nice bottom.' Emma turned more onto her back, looked up at her husband and slowly blinked her eyes. She tried to hide a smile, biting her lip as Nathan narrowed his gaze. She knew he was trying to figure out if this was a trap. It usually was.

'Not as nice as yours, my love.' Nate stretched his fingers to her tummy, stroking at the skin between her top and the summery skirt she had on. She arched her back a little so his fingers could slip under the waistband, but she wanted more. It used to be at this point she'd reward him for the right answer. Well any excuse for his cock in her mouth, really. But she couldn't right now, the key was upstairs. It frustrated her as much as him at times like this, but it did force her to be more demanding.

'Just how nice is my bottom?' she prompted, eyes glinting.

'Your perfect peach could launch a thousand ships?' He grinned, leaning further over and walking her skirt up with his fingers. The heel of his hand pushed against the soft mound hidden underneath as her pale thighs and simple cotton panties were slowly revealed.

Emma giggled. 'That's a very mixed metaphor.' She let out a little gasp as he wrapped his fist around the fabric of her panties and pulled, dragging them up into her and pulling her closer. He rubbed his fingertip against the taut fabric, scratching his short nails against the damp cotton right where she wanted him. She loved him like this. She could feel his desire, the way he touched, grabbed, pulled at her. His lust only stoked her own.

Let's see just how desperate he is. 'Actions speak louder than words, baby.' She wriggled around out of his grasp so her knees slipped off the sofa onto the ground. She leaned on the far end of the sofa, so her bottom and lifted skirt were in his direction. Emma looked over her shoulder, wiggling her arse at him. 'Do you remember when you'd just fuck me like this, any time you wanted?'

Nate growled and rolled towards her, grabbing hold of her knickers and pulling them down so her bare bottom was framed between them and her skirt. 'You are such a fucking tease.' He pushed his hand between the gap in her thighs, sliding his thumb between her wet lips and then inside her, fingers cupping her mound.

Emma gasped as she felt his thumb begin to rub inside her. She let out a little moan, 'I learnt from the best.' She opened her legs wider, giving him even more access.

Nate's middle finger pressed on her clit and she purred. She loved that, being held by her pussy, it made her feel so owned. He knelt on the floor too, moving behind her, kissing the curve of her buttocks, sucking, devouring—

'Ouch, no biting, naughty!' Emma laughed. She pouted as his thumb slipped out of her, but he began rubbing it over her labia, and then up, teasing it around her bottom. 'Oh sweetie, do you remember when you used to fuck there too? You took so long teaching me to like it, and now you can't. Isn't that ironic!' Her words turned into a yelp as his strong hand connected with her backside. 'Nathan Stevens, what are you doing?'

'You know what horny little teases get?' Nate's thumb stayed where it had landed, his thumb rubbing over her tight little bud. The look in his eyes made her tummy tumble.

'Is it a good spanking?' *Please, please let it be that.*

'Good guess. Clever girl.'

Emma grabbed a cushion and wrapped her arms around it, sinking her shoulders into the sofa and pushing her bottom up high with her knees still on the floor. She felt him stroking his fingers over her cheek, holding her breath as it lost contact. A pause. A moment of anticipation, and then the impact of his hand on her bottom. She bucked, her head pushing against the back of the sofa, and then the delicious sting. He stroked where he'd struck her, mixing the pleasure of his touch with the electric sensation of the spank. And then he delivered a second, harder, to the other cheek. She wanted more, staying quiet to provoke him.

The next two came with a satisfying sound, one to each cheek, before his warm hand slipped between her legs, kneading her pussy, grinding on her clit once more. She pushed back, wanting his thumb inside her again but she was rewarded with another two quick spanks. *It's been too long; I need this so badly.* She groaned as his fingers pushed inside her, roughly fucking her, curved so they ground on her g-spot. His mouth joined the mix, kissing gently where she was sure his handprints were already turning pink.

Emma felt her resistance crumbling. She'd worked so hard, keeping him denied, being the 'top' this time. But here, on her knees, being spanked and explored, was where she belonged, where she craved to be. She could just unlock him, let him take her, have his way with her.

6

She was about to tell him where she'd hidden the key upstairs when her laptop chimed. She paused for a moment, remembering the chat she'd been in the middle of earlier. *Saved by the bell.* She forced herself to push up onto her elbows and pulled the laptop nearer.

Nate's mouth left its important work for a moment. 'You're not going to answer that?'

Oh God I don't want to, but you told me this is better. 'Mhmmm,' Emma forced out. 'I was in the middle of an interesting conversation. Don't stop though.' Emma dared a look back over her shoulder and was rewarded with an amazed look on Nate's face. *You challenged me to blow your mind, this is your fault.* 'Edge me, honey, but don't let me cum. Not yet.' *Or at all...*

Emma squinted as she opened up the screen. As she'd hoped, 'Catherine' was back online.

'Damn I thought you were going to let me out then,' Nate said.

'I know you did, and it took all my willpower not to. So shush up and edge me.'

'Yes ma'am.' He chuckled. Emma didn't need to look behind him to know Nate probably just gave her a mock salute. The hard, final smack on her bottom was a surprise though and she cried out. It turned into a moan as his fingers slid back between her legs.

She watched as the three little dots flashed to show the other person was typing something.

'Hello are you still there?' Catherine sent.

'I am,' Emma typed, 'I thought some more about your question.'

'Good. And what did you conclude?'

Emma shut her eyes for a moment as Nate's mouth worked slowly with his fingers to take her closer to the edge. *Fuck, he is so good at that.* She turned her attention back to the chat. 'I love how caging his cock makes him, even now he's been all horny and pleasuring me.' *I won't mention the spanking, I don't think she'd approve.* 'But I get bored with it long term.'

'Bored, or tired?' Catherine asked.

'Okay, yes, maybe tired is better. It's hard being the one in charge, always having the pressure of whether to let him out. He always seems to find that

7

so easy compared to me.'

Emma could see her reply had been read. There was a pause before Catherine replied. 'What if I could help?'

'LOL.' Emma actually chuckled, that was her rule for typing LOL, she actually had to laugh out loud. 'Help, how?'

Most of the people who contacted Emma through her blog were ordinary folk, with extraordinary questions. But something about this Catherine was different. Their last few conversations had ended with Emma curious to hear what she'd say next. She wasn't disappointed.

'Let me ask you again, how much is your husband's cock worth?'

Emma stared at the words in the little chat box. 'I still don't know what that means' she typed back. She looked back over her shoulder. Nate's fingers were still doing their thing, but he'd rested his head on her back and was, she thought, eyeing the TV remote. 'Hey, Nate, sweetie?' she said in a sing-song voice.

'Mhmm?' He lifted his head and gave a big kiss on her bottom. His neatly bearded smile tickled her skin.

'How much is your cock worth?' Emma asked. She paused, waiting for the words to register.

'Huh? What do you mean?'

'Yeah, that's what I said, see?' Emma pointed to the laptop. Nate moved his hand to her back and knelt up, deliberately leaning over her, pushing himself against her. He kissed her neck in the spot that always made her tremble. 'Well hello up there,' Emma sighed. 'Fuck that makes me want you in me.'

'The feeling is very mutual.' Nate ground his shorts against Emma's bare bottom. 'Now what were you saying about my cock?' He read the chat up on the screen. '@catherineargent, well that's obviously a fake name. You do attract the nutters to your blog, you know that.'

Emma gave him a little push back. 'Hey, those *nutters* love me, and you, so shut up. And why's it obviously fake?'

'Catherine Argent, the author? She wrote several of those books I loaded onto your Kindle.'

'The cosy mystery ones?'

'No, you numpty. The other ones, the sexy ones. You probably didn't read them.' He let out a frustrated sigh. 'I don't understand how you can read and write all this hot stuff on your blog and then not enjoy reading it in a book.'

'You know me, honey. I like the pictures.' To prove her point Emma scrolled down the page until an animated image appeared. It was a little clip from some porn video, a 'gif' repeating on a loop. The predictably blonde, but admittedly cute actress was kneeling by a wall. Through a hole by her head slid an enormous erect penis. Her surprise seemed genuine, eyes and mouth opening wide. You could only guess what she would do next as the clip went back to repeat from the start.

'Hah, that's a cute one,' Nate said, one hand reaching under Emma's waist, pushing through the thin material of her skirt and rubbing between her legs.

Emma closed her eyes letting her mind drift as she felt his weight on top of her, his fingers underneath.

Nate was still watching the gif of the cute girl and the ever-reappearing cock. 'You do like your gloryhole pictures. Are you going to post it?'

She clicked a button below the gloryhole image and it moved to the middle of the screen, a new text box below it. She quickly typed 'Wow, it'd be tempting wouldn't it? That wouldn't fit in a cage. I wish hubby was this big.' And hit the button to post it.

'Wait, what?' cried Nate, only just registering what he'd read.

'Oh shut up, you love it.'

He really did. As much as she loved the creative effort of captioning these pictures, the true joy was Nate's reaction to each and every one.

He pushed her hair back and nibbled at her earlobe before whispering, 'I do love it. I still can't believe it some days. You blow my mind Mrs Stevens.' Emma smiled and avoided the obvious blowjob reference, which he'd probably been hoping for. Nate pressed his cheek to hers. Above his trimmed beard it was rough with his five o'clock shadow. 'I really want to fuck you right now.'

Emma pushed back into him again, feeling the seam of his shorts and the hardness beneath them. 'Mmmm, good. Why don't you then?' she teased.

'You know why not, meanie.' He reached under her hanging skirt and pushed his middle two fingers inside her, slowly fucking the tips in and out. 'Wouldn't my cock feel better than that? God, look how wet you are. My little bitch in heat.'

Emma smiled, she loved him calling her that. But if *she* was in heat, so was he, and she wanted to keep him that way. 'Your cock would feel so much better, baby. But, this "bitch" fancies something a bit… bigger. Go look in the dishwasher, you'll see what I mean.'

Nate laughed. 'The dishwasher, have you been putting our toys in there again?' He gave her another kiss in the nape of her neck and pushed himself up, wincing. 'You are making me very cramped you know.'

'In the best possible way. Make me a drink too please, surprise me. I seem to be getting dehydrated.'

Emma pulled her skirt back down over her bare bottom and gave her attention back to the computer.

'Are you still there?' had appeared in the chat without her noticing.

'Yes, sorry, got, distracted.'

It took a while but finally a reply from Catherine appeared. 'Okay. So, where were we?'

'You were going to explain the cryptic question about my husband's cock?'

'Yes. Sorry, I was being a bit melodramatic. I didn't mean to offend. I was just trying to get your attention.'

'Okay, you've got it. Explain please,' typed Emma.

'I love your blog. I love the ideas you have, the scenarios you paint, and the way you talk about your husband.' The indicator showed she was still typing. 'I really do have a proposition for you. I'm sorry, I shouldn't have tried to be so dramatic.'

'Are you really Catherine Argent? The author?' Emma typed.

'Yes. I really am.'

'Can you prove it?'

'Sure.' There was a pause again. 'Check the email address you use on the blog.'

Nate wandered back in, whistling, a rhubarb gin and tonic in one hand, and a freshly washed dildo in the other. 'I assume this is what you were after?' He waggled the skin coloured silicone dildo, it was remarkably realistic, if bigger than average, which is exactly why Emma fancied it. 'Still talking to crazy lady? I mean I say "lady", she's probably a 350lb guy in his mum's basement.'

'She says she can prove it,' Emma said. 'Oh is that for me?' She took the glass and had a sip. 'Yummy, you see, you're not *just* good for putting up shelves.' She giggled.

An email notification popped up: '1 new message - catherine@catherineargent.com'

Emma pushed herself up, clicking on the email. It looked genuine. 'Proof enough?' was the subject.

'Oh, I think she might actually be for real,' Emma said.

Nate sat on the sofa and took the G&T from her. He looked comical as he sipped it from one hand and held the dildo in the other. 'Seriously? What's she saying? What did she mean about my cock?'

'Never you mind, you have more important things to do.'

'Oh, is someone horny? That's what happens when you spend all evening putting captions on pictures of big cocks.'

Emma nodded. 'Very horny, but that's your fault. And they aren't *all* big cocks. There are lots of little cocks, mostly with chastity cages on them.' Emma grinned and pushed up from the sofa with a stretch. She turned, still on her knees and leaned in and gave Nate a kiss right on the seam of his shorts. 'However, there's only one cock in this room that isn't caged, and I want it. But wait a minute, my knees are a bit sore.' Emma stood up, stretching her legs and arms with a provocatively sexy sigh. She turned her back to Nate, hooked her thumbs under her skirt and slowly pulled her panties down until they dropped to the floor.

Nate purred his approval. 'You are so fucking sexy, you know that right?'

'Apparently so, but don't stop telling me.' She moved the laptop off the sofa and lay in its place on her back, one foot still on the floor, the other lifted to the back of the sofa.

At the other end of the sofa Nate laid the dildo down and took hold of her foot. He massaged his thumbs into it eliciting a groan of pleasure. 'Oh that feels so good, do that, for now. Actually...' She slowly pulled her skirt up like a curtain revealing a stage, the soft cotton ruffling up above the light hair of her pubes. She ran her hand through them, watching Nate, watching her. Her laptop pinged but she ignored it. The desire in her husband's eyes was what she cared about right now. She closed hers and sighed happily as her fingertips began making little circles on her clit while Nate massaged her foot. It reminded her of the image that had started all this.

To the Edge and Back Again

Emma had surprised herself a few years back. She'd never liked porn. It was all so fake and predictable. She'd rightfully protested that even the stuff Nate claimed was good quickly descended into gynaecological detail of things, going in and out of other things, until someone made a mess.

What she liked even less was how those videos made her feel. Those perfect women with their fake boobs and their complete lack of inhibition. How could she compete with that?

It turned out she didn't need to compete, she just needed to find a new perspective.

It was a Cosmo article that Nate found a few years earlier which set them on this adventure. '*Spice up your sex life with these 14 unmissable tips*' or some other clickbait. He'd unsubtly left it open on a tablet and finally got up the nerve to suggest they try some. Things like regular date nights had actually been great. Reluctantly she'd agreed to try the one about sending each other sexy images they found online. While most of the images she first saw didn't do much for her there were some that had captions on them, little stories, vignettes, that brought the image to life. Sometimes it might be the backstory, more often snippets of a conversation that gave tantalising glimpses into the story behind the picture.

The first time she tried writing some of her own the reaction from her husband convinced her she had a bit of a talent at it. She would never forget his first response, 'You just blew my fucking mind.' She decided she'd found a new calling. And then, much to her amazement, she discovered that not

13

only she was good at it, but the blog they used for it quickly gained a loyal following.

A couple of months into their shared sexy blog adventure Emma had stumbled across an image that had changed everything. It was a shot of a naked couple, the woman casually lying back on a sofa, drinking a glass of wine, while he rubbed her foot. 'Chastity play. Have you tried it?' the caption had read.

Emma had only ever linked chastity with nuns or Bible Belt teenagers making pledges. She hadn't understood how it related to this image. Until she saw it. Around the man's cock was a little steel cage. It was cute more than anything. But as Emma began to imagine the implications she'd felt a fire ignite inside her. The wine, the casual nakedness, the foot rub; everything was down to that cage he wore. Then she noticed a final detail. The woman's necklace, the only thing she wore, from it dangled a little key.

When she searched out a few similar images, and added her own captions, Nate's reaction had surprised them both. 'That is both terrifying and unreasonably hot. Are you kidding or shall we get one?'

When they found a cheap plastic cage for just a few pounds on eBay they both agreed it was worth it even as 'a bit of a laugh'. Much to her surprise, when he finally put it on, it was much more hot than funny. Much, much more. And he seemed to feel the same (it took him hours to get soft enough to put it on which should have been a clue).

That was a few years ago, but as popular as the blog had become, she often felt a bit of a fake. Before then, and still often now, Emma had been more 'vanilla' as kinky folk called it, or at least, classically submissive when it came to sex. Sometimes she still struggled to believe that her hot, mostly dominant husband wanted this. That he'd give up his pleasure for her. *One of these days I'm going to learn to really make the most of it.*

She stopped her reminiscing and opened her eyes, pleased to see Nate was still fixated between her legs as he massaged her other foot. Reaching down she took hold of the dildo from where he'd left it by the sofa. It was still warm from the dishwasher. She nestled the tip of it against her, pushing gently. She was so ready for it that the head of the big toy opened her up and slipped in with little effort. 'Oh God, that's what I need,' she said, truthfully, and to turn her husband on even more. As good as her foot massage felt, something was suddenly more pressing.

She opened her legs wider, pushing the tip deeper now, working the ridged tip against her g-spot. She kept watching him, taking such pleasure in his transfixed stare, as she took even more pleasure from the toy pushing deeper now inside her. *Time to get him more involved.*

'Fuck me, baby. Fuck me with it,' Emma said, leaving it half buried inside her while her fingers moved to play with her clit.

Nate slid one hand down her leg, frustratingly slowly, giving her foot a kiss before laying it down. He stroked the top of her thigh, ignoring the dildo, and brushing his thumb ever so lightly over her clit. 'Hand away then, princess.'

Emma pouted, but mostly because she knew he thought it was cute. She loved it when he reminded her that almost everything she knew about teasing, he'd taught her.

'Stop teasing me,' Emma complained. 'You know what I want.'

'Weren't you in the middle of an interesting chat?' he replied, playing with the end of the toy now, but just to twist it a little inside her.

'Oh goodness, I forgot!' She laughed, reaching down to the floor and lifting the laptop onto her tummy. She peeked up at her husband over the screen, hoping he'd take up the challenge of trying to distract her. He normally couldn't resist.

This was one of his kinks, teasing her, stimulating her while she was doing something else. Her best friend had once caught onto it when he made her cum during a call to her. Even remembering it was mortifying, although her pussy clenched at the memory. She let out a happy sigh as he began stroking it deeper and she tried to refocus on the screen hiding what he was doing.

Emma closed the email from Catherine and went back to the chat. It seemed she wasn't a patient woman.

'Hello'. 'Are you still there?'. 'Did you get it?'. Were just some of the messages.

Emma ignored her natural inclination to apologise and had to pause as Nate's fingers joined in playing. *Think you can distract me huh?* She read aloud as she typed, 'Hi Catherine, got the email, thank you. But what do you mean what's his cock worth?" she grinned up at him over the screen, 'it's not for sale. I'm extremely attached to it.'

'Not as attached as I am,' he said with a wink before disappearing down behind the laptop, nuzzling his mouth and nose into her thigh.

'Oh, that feels good,' said Emma, then she laughed.

'What's funny?' Nate moved his mouth up and kissed the cleft between her thigh and neatly trimmed mound. His tongue flicked out, tracing over her swollen clit.

'She just… oh damn, keep doing that. She just said I'm so attached to your cock I keep it locked up. It's true I suppose. Stop teasing me, I need more.' Emma closed her eyes and moaned as he closed his mouth around her clit, pushing the toy deep in her. He slowly drew the width of his tongue up her lips, taking his time. He knew how to drive her crazy. She arched, pushing into him, nearly letting the laptop slip off her tummy.

Nate paused again, 'What else is she saying? You've got me curious now.'

'And you've got me wet and horny. Did I tell you to stop?' Nate pushed her legs wider apart and Emma felt his mouth go to work again. 'Good boy,' she giggled.

She read back over Catherine's last messages. The indicator showing she was online had now gone. 'You're obviously busy but I'll email you my proposal now you know I'm really me,' it said. There was just a little peacock emoji after her last message. What's that stand for?

'Oh whoops,' Emma said, 'I think we pissed her off. She's gone.'

Emma shifted her legs as Nate's mouth combined with the dildo, its tip deep inside her. She felt the pleasure spreading down her legs and up her tummy. 'Oh babe, that feels so good.'

Nate's sucking slowed and he lifted his head. 'What does she mean "what is my cock worth"? Let me see the rest of what she said.'

'No,' Emma said, surprising him. 'Get your sexy face back down between my legs. She's going to email. I'll tell you what you need to know.' She smiled, proud of being so assertive, and its results.

Nate groaned. 'You are so hot when you're like this.' He kissed her right between the legs. 'I'm going to suck and lick you until you tell me what else your famous author friend was asking. No cumming for you until I find out.'

Maybe I'll just never tell you and you can never let me cum she wished, but said instead, 'How about we move off this sofa and get to bed?'

'Bed, already? Does that mean you're going to unlock me?' The look on his face was so adorable she already knew what the real answer was sure to be. 'Maybe, we'll see. Go shower, you're all sweaty from earlier. I'll be waiting.'

* * *

Emma's resolve had hardened a little by the time Nate sauntered into the bedroom. He was completely naked, well almost. She admired his body. It wasn't quite as buff as it had been when they'd got married but he still got to the gym a few times a week and to her he was the most beautiful man she could imagine.

What was between his legs made her catch her breath every time she saw it like this - the shiny metal cage encasing his cock. Just like that picture they'd seen a few years back. Despite both their initial arousal at him in that first cheap plastic cage neither of them had the slightest idea of the impact it was going to have.

Nate and Emma loved sex toys. She still had the little vibrator that he'd bought her as a 'joke' when they'd first started going out. She still blushed remembering him dragging her into that seedy old adult store around the corner from the Mexican restaurant they'd loved. Never in her life had she thought about going to a place like that. It turned out it was his first time too.

They'd both been rather shocked at the porn on display and found refuge in the small toys section. Emma had stared at the realistic dildos, asking Nate if men were really that big. It was his turn to blush. The most embarrassing moment had been when she'd asked what the strange wide but short toy was and Nate had laughed, explaining to her what a butt plug was. She hadn't believed him to begin with. She knew so much better now.

But the cage, the cage had been something different from the first moment he tried it on. A fire had ignited inside her, and his usual passion was suddenly under her control. It was intoxicating, for them both.

And so here he stood once again. It seemed so normal now. He didn't wear it all the time, there were weeks, and months where he was free. But she preferred him like this, her 'caged tiger'. The way it looked, the way it made him act.

Right now though, she wanted what was inside it even more. Emma had retrieved the key from its hiding place and it now dangled between her fingers. His eyes went from it to the sly little smile on her face. Throwing the cover back she revealed she was naked too, and she shuffled a little down the bed, lifting her knees and spreading her feet. She adored the fact she didn't have to say anything. Not just because it was so damn sexy, but because she still found it so hard to ask explicitly for what she wanted. Closing her eyes, she felt his lips on her shins. She had to fight back an apology for not shaving them and just shut up and let him get to work. She knew he didn't care. His hands gently pushed her knees wider apart and his kisses resumed, tickling her knee, then moving up her inner thigh. They became more passionate the closer to the apex they came. Harder, sucking at her skin, his tongue wet against her thigh. It traced a warm line that quickly cooled until it met her own wetness, swirling gently at her entrance. She felt him lick his tongue up slowly, tasting her, licking her until his mouth reached where she craved it so much.

Amazingly Emma hadn't been a fan of oral sex, well not receiving it, anyway. She'd fallen in love with sucking cock the first time she'd wrapped her lips around Nate's penis. But the reverse, him going down on her? As pleasurable as it was, she always felt a bit awkward; it was so intimate, so exposing. She was much more comfortable about giving it than receiving. Until she couldn't - until that cage around his cock gave her no option but to receive. Somehow that freed her up, it took away the guilt that she was just lying back and being selfish. And the awkwardness, that was dealt with by the pure desire that the chastity cage caused in her husband. He'd gone down on her before, and was pretty good at it, but something changed when he was locked up. Something wonderful. The way he went down on her, the passion he somehow poured into his ministrations on her clit and labia, it was so fucking hot.

'God you taste so good.' His muffled words broke her reverie. He said it so often now she actually started to believe him. Emma kept her eyes closed and ran her fingers over her breasts as Nate's mouth latched around her swollen clit. It was already so sensitive from his teasing earlier. She gripped her hard nipples between her fingers and thumbs as he began sucking.

She could cry from her arousal already, but she wanted more. *Make it worse* she wished, pulling hard at her nipples until her fingers slipped off before grabbing them and doing it over and over again. *Make it worse, make me hornier, don't let me cum.*

This was his fault.

When they'd met she'd been, well sexually naive is a nice way of putting it. They were both virgins, it was a bit of a fairy tale romance. But in one area she'd been far behind. Sex had been very taboo in her family and the liberal attitudes of his were a shock to her. But it went deeper than that. He'd been mentally exploring his fantasies for years; she'd never even masturbated.

He was wonderful about it. As they grew closer, as her trust for him had grown and their friendship had turned into more, he began to get her to open up about it. He shared his fantasies with her, and they began to shape hers too.

Most importantly he worked out her weakness. She couldn't resist a dare. So, he dared her to touch herself. To masturbate. To learn how good things felt. He bought her toys like the vibrator and then her first little dildo. He told her what he wanted to do with them while they were away from each other.

What he didn't tell her to do though, was climax. As she'd never masturbated, she'd never orgasmed. She remembered the look in his eyes when he'd first figured that out. 'You've never cum?' he'd whispered. She'd felt ashamed at being so innocent, but his next words transformed that, forever. 'That's so fucking hot, you have no idea.'

And so this became the central theme of their sexual exploration together. 'Edging' they discovered it was called. He did it a bit too, but the fact he'd cum so much as a teenage boy meant it was always so easy to revert to what he was used to.

For her though, an orgasm was something she'd never known. Somehow scary and forbidden, although that of course excited her too. His ideas for her, the tasks he set her, and the play they enjoyed together all centred around teasing her, edging her, denying her. And it transformed her. From naive little innocent to fully fledged kinkster. It caused her to delve deep into this new side of her and discover how much she loved the wider aspects of being told what to do by him, of submission, and more.

When he'd got down on one knee that day and asked if she'd be his wife his first whisper in her ear once she'd calmed down was, 'I'm going to give you your first orgasm on our wedding night.'

He kept his promise. In fact, he'd kept even more. With all the wonderful, kinky things to explore together they both agreed to save sex for that night too. Something her religious parents would no doubt have approved of, if it weren't for all the really kinky shit he was teaching her instead.

The deep irony of their current situation, that it was him who was regularly denied and whose orgasms were limited wasn't lost on either of them.

Back down between her legs Nate began working his magic. He'd mastered a combination of sucking and licking that meant he could relentlessly take her closer and closer to climax. But damn him, he could read her so well, the tiny movements she'd make, the noises, the tensing muscles. She didn't need to tell him when she was at the edge, about to climax, he knew. And so he kept her right there, right on the very edge of orgasm, utterly lost in pleasure, tortured by it. Her favourite place in the world. Her wonderland.

That's where he took her. She felt the world falling away as pleasure and need engulfed her. She began to beg. 'Please, oh god, darling, let me cum, it feels so good, let me cum, I need to cum.'

The words meant nothing. She knew it pleased him to hear her beg, and it was just so hot to say what she craved. But she loved knowing he would ignore her pleas, that nothing but their safeword would make him take notice of what she begged for in this moment. His mouth was unrelenting, devouring her clit, keeping her on the edge of the precipice but not letting her go over. It was utter torture; it was utterly beautiful.

As sometimes happened, she began to cry. Desperation, pleasure, frustration all merging together to give her some kind of release that the evil bastard between her legs wouldn't yet give her.

She used to be so embarrassed by it. She barely cared any more. It just brought back the words that had transformed the experience. 'Tears make the best lube' he'd whispered one day as he licked her salty cheeks clean. It wasn't true at all of course, but it was just so damn hot anyway. And it hadn't stopped him making her weep so much at times they'd actually tested the truth of it.

One thing had changed of course. The key dug into her palm as she clenched her hands against the duvet. In the blur of arousal she blurted out, 'I'll unlock you if you let me cum.' She didn't know if she meant it. She didn't know if she wanted it. And this was the confusion of the new dynamic the chastity cage brought. Before, it was just up to him. Now she had this new leverage. Some days she loved it, but right now she almost wished she didn't have it. She wanted to cum so much, and it had caught his attention. His sucking slowing slowed, easing back, lapping at her more gently, allowing her to catch her breath.

'Oh, will you?' He looked up, his beard wet with her juices. His eyes narrowed as he smiled. 'And what stops me from just taking it from you and fucking your brains out right now?'

His tiger was in full fury right now. His look sent a shiver down her spine.

'How about you unlock me and we'll see if we can fuck an orgasm out of this needy little cunt?'

Emma didn't need any more convincing. She threw the keys to him and he knelt up on the bed, legs apart, unlocking the cage in a swift motion.

21

His circumcised cock sprang out, the base of the cage acting as a cock ring, making his beautiful dick rise up harder and bigger with every beat of his heart.

'Turn over,' Nate commanded, stroking his cock slowly with a hand. Emma didn't want to stop looking at him but there was no arguing when he used that voice. 'Yes. Sir.' She rarely called him that nowadays, but it still felt so right when she did. She flipped over, biting her lip as she wrapped her arms into her soft pillow and pressed her cheek down into it.

His hands grabbed her hips, lifting her bottom up. He pushed her legs apart, kneeling in between them. His hand traced down to between her legs, and he slid two fingers inside her. 'God look how wet you are, you little slut.' His other hand came down on her bottom in a gentle smack. No matter how aroused she'd been by everything earlier, being treated like this was just taking her to another level.

'You want to cum, do you?' He ground his fingertips against her g-spot producing a different craving.

'Oh god, fuck me, please, fuck me!' she cried.

His fingers slipped out and Emma felt the head of his cock replace them, teasing the entrance to her. Automatically she tried to back onto it but his hand kept her in place, pushing her head and shoulders back down into the pillow. His palm opened her up even more and his thumb brushed over her now totally exposed arsehole, making her shudder. 'But fuck you where, my love?'

'Oh god, my pussy please, I want you in me.'

'But what kind of wife keeps her husband's cock locked up? Is she the kind who should get fucked in the ass if she's silly enough to let him out?'

'Please, just, oh god, anything. Let me cum, fuck me.'

'Well which is it baby, do you want to be fucked or to cum?' He bent over her more, the tip of his cock sinking in her a little deeper, and his hand reaching under starting to rub her clit, making her groan. 'Which would you pick, to be fucked, or to cum?'

'I, I don't know, you choose, please, Nate!'

'Good answer, my love, clever girl.' And with that he pushed, sinking his cock deep in her cunt. Emma cried out with pleasure as he stayed there, filling her, fingers quickly bringing her to the brink of orgasm, only for them to pull away just as she was about to go over.

He grabbed her hips again, holding her in place as he began to slowly slide the full length of his cock out to the entrance of her pussy and bury it hard right back in her. Over and over, building up speed. His hips were smacking against her buttocks as he pounded her harder and harder, driving her into the bed, taking out all his arousal and frustration on her, in her. It was divine. Nothing existed for them in that moment but him inside her, that most intimate of contact. He slowed, his hand again reaching under to pleasure her, igniting hope that she might get to cum. But she never knew. And she loved not knowing.

She could sense he was close to orgasm, from the way he was pacing himself, from how he breathed. It was exquisite, imagining that the pleasure she was feeling, the sensations her body was giving him, was about to take him over the edge. A primal urge to be filled with his seed overwhelmed her, the thought of his cum spurting deep inside, coating her, filling her brought her right to the brink of climax. 'Please, please I'm there, please baby, let me cum, fill me up, make me yours!' she cried out.

His fingers ground fast against her, his decision made as he thrust himself harder now, his breaths deep and shuddering. His cry of joy was what finally did it for her too. She felt him, thrusting, pumping his orgasm into her and her body arched, pulling him in, grinding against him as pleasure exploded inside her too, wave after wave of ecstasy, pure release, their climax perfectly shared.

'Wow.' He leaned over her, one hand on her shoulder, his cock half sliding out as he kissed her neck and nuzzled into her. He slowly pushed back in her; she could feel how full of him she was as his cock pushed it back up her.

'That was...' Emma paused, catching her breath. 'Yeah, wow.' She giggled. 'Umm, my knees hurt, can I lie down?'

'Of course, baby.' But instead of sliding out, he pushed in deep and then wrapped his arm around her midriff, rolling and lifting her so they both lay faces up with her on top of him. 'But I'm not done with you yet.'

Emma squealed with delight. 'You haven't had me like this for ages!' She wound her hands above her head and wrapped them behind his neck, just the way she used to. 'Bound to him' they called it. The rule was simple, if she took her hands down, he stopped. 'That was so amazing. We need to fuck more baby, I miss it.'

'I know, it's so good. But it would be easier if—' and he began to thrust his cock hard into her with each word, '— you didn't lock my cock up in a little cage.' He laughed and moved one hand to grab her breast as he began masturbating her with the other hand.

'You're right, but if it makes you fuck like that, well maybe quality over... Oh fuck, I'm going to cum!' she declared.

'Nu uh, no you don't.' Nate gave a short sharp smack to her mound, a tactic that almost always worked.

'Oh you bastard. I love you!'

He wrapped both arms tightly around her waist and started working her up and down on his cock. 'What a good little fuck puppet you make, baby. Maybe I'll just spurt in you again and leave you like this.' He arched his hips and somehow it made the sound of his cock fucking her cum-filled vagina so much louder. It was the most obscene sound, and turned her on even more given her current state of mind. She could feel it flowing out of her as he pulled his cock out and plunged it back in.

The base ring around his cock meant that he'd kept hard after his orgasm, something they took for granted when they first started having sex but wasn't always a sure thing five years into marriage. His cock swelled even more as plunged her down onto it. 'Is this what you need, my little slut wife? To be reminded that you're my fuck toy all over again? Your beautiful body dedicated to my pleasure?' He pressed his mouth against her ear, whispering as he slowed his thrusts. 'Do you think I don't see it, alongside the lust when you look at my caged cock? I see it my love. The envy. Wishing you could be so easily encased, so simply denied. You wish it was you, don't you?'

She couldn't think. She couldn't analyse what he was saying. Here, totally exposed, her arms bound around his neck, being fucked over and over, all she knew was that he knew her. 'Yes,' she whispered. 'Yes, yes, yes.'

She felt his hand move down, rubbing her once again. The heat of arousal from what his cock was doing burst into flames, consuming her. He felt her burn.

'Say it,' he whispered, 'say what you want, what you need, my perfect little denial slut.'

'Never let me cum,' Emma wailed as his fingers worked their magic. 'Keep me like this forever.'

'Maybe we'll have to get you fitted, my love. Finally get that pussy locked away in a custom fitted chastity belt.'

She let out a guttural groan, rising up against his fingers, but it turned into a high pitched whine as he stopped rubbing and just cupped her mound, squeezing it tightly, 'Imagine it, baby, steel keeping your needy little pussy all safe and sound. Not able to touch, locked away, like a good little denial slave.' He pulled her up, his cock finally sliding out, even more cum dripping out behind it, and wriggled, repositioning it. 'This is the only place I'd have to fuck, my little slut. Where princess, where would I fuck you?'

He pushed his rigid cock against her tight rosebud, the cum lubing him enough so that when she groaned, 'in my ass, Sir,' he pushed and it popped inside, her muscles clenching on him. 'Only in my ass,' she murmured again, sinking down into the fantasy, his fingers keeping her on the edge. 'Locked away. Anal only. Your denial slave.'

Emma writhed against him, squeezing herself around his cock, lubricated by the mix of her juices and his cum. 'Cum in me, cum in my ass,' she begged. And it was enough. Hearing her beg, feeling her squeeze on him. He groaned loudly, gripping her breast with his other hand, edging his wife as he emptied his balls in that secret, forbidden place.

Finally, his fingers slowed on her. His arms wrapped around her again, not in a hold this time, but in a loving embrace. 'Well we haven't done *that* in quite a while,' he said with a chuckle.

She let her head fall back past his shoulder. 'I forgot how much I love you there when you're denying me. You're still in my arse you know.' She laughed.

'Why do we say ass in the middle of things and arse now?' Nate chuckled.

Emma lifted herself off his cock with an unceremonious wiggle and turned around, so she was lying on him face to face. 'Well that's obvious. Most porn is American.' She grinned, kissing him. 'Why don't you go and wash that cock of yours and you can fuck me again.'

'Oh damn, I forgot how insatiable you are when you're denied,' laughed Nate.

'That's the whole point isn't it?' said Emma, pouting. 'I thought you love me like this.'

'Oh, I do, but my job is done here, your holes are filled and you're all horny and needy. It really is a shame chastity belts are so rubbish on women. I'd lock you up this instant.'

'I wish. Or, you could just make me cum! Or fuck me again. You can fuck my ass, arse, whatever, it's all warmed up for you now.' Emma wiggled on Nate and began kissing him again.

'You'd have to convince him; he thinks his job is done I'm afraid.' Nate nodded downwards.

Emma slipped off Nate to the side and looked at his shrinking cock. She laughed. 'Holy crap, how much cum was in your balls? It's like a proper mess down here, and half of it's still in my bum! Poor baby, you really must have been so desperate.' Emma started drawing shapes in the mess on Nate's tummy, leaving patterns in the short dark hair on his skin. 'Is it really bad that the thought of how full your balls were makes me want to lock you up again?'

'My god, I've created a monster. First you beg for me never to let you cum, and now you want my cock locked up too,' Nate complained.

'Best of both worlds, baby.' Emma kissed him again, and whispered in his ear, 'I'm only what you made me, this is entirely your fault.'

'It usually is, that's true. I think I better get in the shower,' Nate said.

'And I'll change the sheets. As usual the worst of the cumplosion is on my side. I swear you do it on purpose!'

Nate laughed, carefully getting up and grabbing a dirty t-shirt to catch the worst of the mess. He pulled the cage base ring off his now flaccid cock and tossed it onto the bed. Emma stared at it, her mind finally going back to her earlier conversation. *How much is that cock worth?* She looked up at him, her face alive with the afterglow of what he'd done to her. 'I love you very much, Mr Stevens.'

'I love you too.'

She watched his cock until he disappeared past the door. *How much is it worth? Everything.*

The Indecent Proposal

T rue to her word there was an email from Catherine waiting when Emma woke on Saturday morning. Nate was snoring gently next to her and she left him that way as she read through the email.

Dear Emma,

Here's the proposal I promised. But a little background first.

Your blog has been a wonderful source of inspiration to me and my husband along with some others. We found that chastity absolutely revitalised our sex life even in the autumnal years of our marriage. Sadly, winter came a little early, Henry passed last year, and in fact writing to you is something I've promised I'd do once my heart was a little lighter.

I know that this is going to sound a little strange, but there's a fantasy I've had for some time. I can't help but wonder what would happen to a couple like yourselves if someone else was in control of the man's chastity.

As I understand it he's often the dominant one, and I believe it, although I imagine you've grown in your own way to relish the power this all gives you.

Imagine if, for an entire year, you didn't have control of his cage keys either. That no matter how desperate he got, how horny, what he said, what he wanted, there was no escape?

How does that idea make you feel?

I for one would rather like to see what happened.

Now I know this sounds crazy, it IS, I agree. But this isn't just a fantasy, or it doesn't have to be. Why? Money. Money is a wonderful lubricant Emma. As you know I'm a successful author and I'm hoping that my money will help you make a decision you otherwise wouldn't.

So here's my question to you:

How much money would it take to let me control the keys to your husband's cock cage, and ensure he is kept denied for an entire year? I'm entirely open to your suggestions on how it would work, although I have some of my own non-negotiables too. And remember, when you decide your price, I am a frugal woman.

Kind regards,

Catherine Argent

She sat there not knowing how to process what she'd just read. Surely it was a joke, or a fantasy. Her heart was in her throat, and she felt that tell-tale tingle between her legs. Joke or not, Emma was aroused by the idea.

She slipped out of bed, pulled on a t-shirt and a soft pair of shorts, and made her way to the kitchen. As she walked down the stairs, she felt herself still leaking a little from the night before. It only made her more aware of the growing throb from her recently fucked pussy.

Her excitement was tempered a little by the pile of envelopes on the doormat. *More bills no doubt.* She stacked them up on the kitchen counter, trying to ignore the red lettering on some of them.

Flicking the coffee machine on she distracted herself by thinking about the email again. Should she even reply? Wasn't this just crazy? Emma remembered more of the night before, her nipples forming little peaks through her top. She thought about how wonderful Nate had been with her. But more than anything she remembered that key digging into her palm, the moment she'd had to decide whether to unlock him. It was the only point of the evening she'd not enjoyed.

She pulled out her phone and replied:

Hi Catherine, thank you for your message. I really don't know what to say. I'm assuming you're just joking, but I loved the message, so thank you. It's so nice to hear from other couples who have found chastity useful, I'm so very sorry for your loss.

Emma x

Once she'd got some coffee brewing, she couldn't help but reread

Catherine's email again, and as she found her fingers pressing the soft curve of her shorts without really thinking about it, imagining the scenario. She was about to slip them inside her shorts when she stopped. A reply had come through already.

'It's not a joke. Check the PayPal you set up for that toy sale last year. Regards, Catherine'

Impressed she'd even remembered about that little fundraiser they'd done, Emma eventually remembered the password to the anonymous PayPal account she'd set up and swore loudly when she saw it now had £365 sitting in it. It was emptied months ago.

The inbox lit up again:

Just a little goodwill gesture, to get yourselves a meal somewhere nice on me. I'm serious, very serious. So please, ask me any questions you wish, but if you're definitely not interested, I'd appreciate knowing sooner rather than later.

A meal! Good grief, they'd been on cheaper holidays. She didn't know what to do. This was beyond weird, it felt like one of her blog stories coming to life. Time to wake Nate.

'It's a joke, or a troll, it's got to be,' he assured her as he sipped his coffee.

'Well she gave us nearly £400 as a 'goodwill' gesture, so it's more than a joke!'

Nate paused, reading the email again. 'Is it just me, or is this kinda hot?'

'It's not just you, but it's bananas. We have no idea who this woman is.'

'At the very least have some fun with it. Relax. Message back. I want to find out what my cock is worth!'

Emma chuckled, 'You better hope it's not priced by the inch.'

'Hey!' Nate threw his pillow at her as she walked off to get her laptop.

Emma composed a message back to Catherine.

'I've spoken to my husband. I doubt we'd be interested but I must admit we are curious. Maybe you could tell us a bit more about what you're thinking, and what those non-negotiables are?

Thank you too for the donation, we're happy to send it back if this doesn't go anywhere, I mean it.

Emma

Once again it didn't take long for her inbox to get a reply. Looking at the length of the reply it obviously wasn't something she'd written spontaneously.

Hi Emma, thanks so much for considering it.

As you can imagine I've put some thought into this, and the following is how I'd expect it to work.

Your husband will be placed in an inescapable male chastity device, this requires him having a Prince Albert piercing (I don't believe he already has one). In that case I will pay for it and the cage.

On the last Friday of every month you will both attend a location of my choosing, at least at first this will be at my Berkshire estate. After a night together all expenses paid you will both attend a 'check-up' meeting that may take some or all of the Saturday.

Primarily this is to allow a full physical check-up and evaluation of his denied state. If his testicles are not found to be full enough at this time then there will be a financial penalty incurred of up to one half of the month's contractual agreement. It is your responsibility to ensure he's satisfactorily full.

We recognise that even while caged we cannot prevent your husband being made to ejaculate or even orgasm, so these check-ups are to encourage you to hold to the essence and purpose of this arrangement, that he be kept in a state of continued, unfulfilled arousal.

Failure to provide him in an aroused and full state for a second month will invalidate the contract and require full repayment of all monies paid and expenses incurred unless alternative arrangements can be agreed.

Your husband will be secured in a manner of my choosing for his check up and will be uncaged by our staff and fully inspected.

At this point you may be given some choices, choices that only you can make. Your husband will not be allowed to influence your decision. Some of those choices will come with rewards, others with penalties. You will not be forced to make any; they will be entirely optional.

You must however participate in the entire process and not leave before the full check-up has finished.

Under the terms of the agreement while under contract your husband will be subject to a broad variety of testing and investigation. During the unlock time I or those working on my behalf can do anything to him that does not leave any permanent damage. He can of course, stop proceedings at any time and forfeit the entire month's income or nullify the contract for repeated clause breaks.

Similarly, failure to attend one check-up will result in the loss of that entire month's contractual income. Failure to attend two results in all monies paid being rescinded due to breach of contract and become repayable within 14 days.

I hope all of that is clear, I'm open to discuss any of the specifics, but of course the one key element that would need clarity, is how much you would expect in return.

Why don't you have a talk with your husband, you're not committing to anything. Name your price, I think you'll find it an exciting process.

I look forward to hearing from you,

Catherine Argent

'Well shit,' Nate said when Emma went upstairs to read the terms on her laptop. 'She really isn't messing around. This is crazy, right?' He looked at his wife and she bit her lip.

'Yes, totally crazy. But, so freaking hot too, don't you think?' Emma confessed, pushing the laptop over the side and snuggling up to him. 'You know how much playing with this has already done for our love life.'

She traced her fingers down his chest, her bare legs hooking over his as she began to play with the bulge that had formed in his shorts. Nate gave a little moan in his throat. 'But seriously? Locking up my cock for an entire year? Are you actually considering this? Wouldn't you miss it?'

'Well yes, of course baby, I love your cock, but well, you've got so good with your mouth now, and your fingers were always magic.' She took his hand and placed it on her bare mons. 'And well, we could really do with some extra money. But most of all, honey,' she reached over and squeezed his rigid cock, 'the idea seems to have you excited too.'

Nate turned towards her, pressing his crotch against her thigh and switching hands, kneading between Emma's legs. 'But a full year. I'll be so desperate. You won't be able to fix it. All I'll be able to do. Is this.'

'Oh, not just that, honey. Let's not forget your talented mouth, and all the toys.' She pushed her hand inside his shorts gently tugging on his erection. 'Oh Nate, look how hard you are, and after last night too. Is it getting you all horny, baby, imagining it? Imagining being locked away with no way to get out?'

Nathan laughed. 'You seem sold on the idea already. Maybe I *should* let you cum, so you think a little more rationally and aren't ready to just sell off my cock to the highest bidder.'

She grinned at him then lifted her head to kiss him. 'That *is* the question isn't it baby. Just how much is it worth?'

She thought about his cock, inescapably caged, as his finger circled her clit, bringing her closer to an orgasm she hoped she wouldn't be allowed. She imagined his full balls, the desperation, desire to please, only getting more and more intense for a whole year.

She knew then what she was going to do. She lifted her phone, typing just a two word reply. 'We're interested.' Her thumb hovered over the send button.

Nathan rubbed her faster, kissing her neck, grinding his cock in her fist. She let him push her down this road, making her ever more desperate and horny. She wanted him like this too, and a promise came to her lips, 'Oh baby, you are so fucked.'

She hit send.

* * *

There wasn't an instant reply this time and by the time it came they were dressed and eating brunch on the small dining table in the corner of their sitting room. Catherine's reply was simply an acknowledgement and an offer to meet to discuss it further.

The invitation was for the following Friday for dinner at her home. They'd be picked up at 7pm, it would be about an hour's journey. It suggested they pack a few things in case they chose to stay over.

'Crikey, chauffeur driven too! I could get used to this!' joked Nate, pressing up against Emma, leaning over the dining room chair she was sitting on.

'I could get used to your cock being locked, so be careful what you wish for, darling,' she teased. 'Speaking of which, we should probably get in some more practise. Go and get the cage.'

'Oh come on, let's not. Don't we want to make the most of me being free?'

'That's a good point darling, but if you can't even manage a weekend in the cage, we shouldn't be thinking about much, much longer,' Emma teased.

Nate just let out a little frustrated moan and rubbed his thumbs into Emma's shoulders, massaging her. It didn't take long until his fingers slipped down and began to gently play with her nipples that quickly hardened under his touch.

Emma rubbed her cheek against his arm. 'Trying to change my mind, darling? I don't know if it's best to let you cum all week or just save it all up so we have another time like last night.'

'Oh I vote for option one,' Nate decided, standing and moving to the side of the chair. His cock was pressing obviously against the material of his trousers.

Emma noticed and nuzzled her face against his crotch. 'Of course you do, but just look at how hard the idea of not cumming makes you too.' She pulled down his zipper, undoing the button and tugging his jeans down. She planted little kisses against the straining cotton, nibbling with her lips at the most sensitive spot. 'Oh honey, if we do this it'll be steel here, not cotton. You won't be able to get this hard, all year. Can you imagine?' She tugged down the hem of his underpants, exposing the head of his cock. Nate moaned with pleasure as she sucked on his frenulum, licking, pulling, opening her mouth wide but not sucking his cock head in, not yet.'

'I wouldn't be able to do this, all year, baby? Not my mouth...' she finally wrapped her lips around the head of his cock and gave it a long, lazy suck. Emma slid her hand down between her legs, into her little shorts. 'And not in here either. Oh baby, I'd miss you so much.' She began to rub herself as she sucked, pulling his jockey shorts down around his thighs so she could take him deeper.

Nate's fingers slid through her hair, pulling her against him. She loved that, but she wanted to tease him even more.

'You're going to be so fucking horny, and you won't be able to do anything about it. Oh Nate, why did that make you get even harder?' She bobbed her head forwards and back, sometimes sucking hard, but sometimes barely touching him with her lips, just letting her tongue slide against his shaft. Her spare hand moved to cup his balls. 'Can you imagine how full these are going to get? That's what she wants isn't it. Your balls, big and full and achy. We're going to get paid to keep them that way. Isn't that so hot?' She gripped her hand around them more tightly, gently tugging as she sucked, her rubbing clearly bringing her close too.

He grabbed her head more tightly and she relaxed, opening up her throat the way she'd learnt. It wasn't the best angle, but she let him fuck her mouth, feeding on his desperation, torn between letting him cum and keeping him like this. She pulled back at last, when he was as close as she dared to let him get. 'When do I stop teasing you, Nate? When is enough, enough?' she moaned as she kissed his cock, beads of pre-cum oozing from it now. Those words had become a little ritual for them over the last year.

'Not till you've blown my fucking mind, my love,' he answered, adding his own twist. 'One of us cums now. You choose.' She beamed back at him, gripping his cock tighter, sucking on the tip as she looked up into his eyes.

Emma rubbed harder, making her choice. She came, hard, on her fingers, her mouth sucking carefully on his cock, the look of desperation at her choice only making the climax even better.

'I am so fucked,' he chuckled, taking a few deep breaths to bring himself under control.

'Yep, and you love it! Did I make a good choice?' She didn't wait for an answer. Emma pulled his pants back up and gave the ridge left showing a final kiss. 'I need another coffee. Go make me one darling, be a good boy.' She grinned and he growled down at her, then bent over and gave her a deep, passionate kiss, the taste of his cock shared between them.

Her eyes sparkled with an idea. 'I tell you what, if he's still that hard when you come back up with our coffees, you can do what you want to me. But if he isn't...' Emma made the noise of a lock clicking.

He paused, then decided to take the challenge, as though he had a choice. 'I really am fucked, what idiot taught you all this stuff?' He gave her biggest smile, all the more dazzling because she could see how aroused he was as he pulled up his jeans that still didn't cover his excitement.

'No touching' she yelled after him.

'As if I would,' he called back as he made his way to the kitchen.

Soon you won't be able to, not for a year. Her fingers slid back down between her legs; a few little rubs felt amazing. She began going faster, maybe she'd cum again before he brought the coffee. If not, it might be fun to let him catch her. She knew he wouldn't be hard when he got back, not without help. She could help lock him up, and then finish herself off, while he watched.

The more she thought about it the more this whole thing seemed like a great idea.

In Dominus Rex

T he big, black SUV pulled up outside their little terraced house at exactly 7pm. Nate and Emma drew a few impressed looks from some of their neighbours who were out in the warm summer evening. They hadn't known what to wear, and upon asking were simply told whatever they were comfortable in, which of course was no help at all.

So instead of a fancy meal out, some of the £365 was put to good use getting them both something new. Emma wore a dress that she hoped didn't look like it was trying too hard, but it was the nicest thing she'd worn for a long time and made her feel good. She admired Nate in his new outfit and was looking forward to getting him out of it when they got back home.

Despite the new clothes, they both felt nervous. They still didn't agree on whether Nate should have worn his cock cage underneath. After their fun at the start of the weekend, and his failure to win the 'keep hard making coffee' task, Emma had kept him in it a few days, and enjoyed exploring the fantasy of what the check-ups might involve. She'd been all for keeping him in it until tonight but Nate had made a compelling case, aided unfairly by his hand between her legs, and she'd reluctantly agreed not to put him in it for the mysterious meet up.

The disagreement was probably more due to nerves about tonight's dinner than anything but as they headed out it wasn't the entirely positive adventure she'd been imagining all week.

As the driver got out of the car Emma was pleased they'd made the effort with their outfits. He was dressed immaculately, a black suit and tie with a crisp white shirt, all of which looked awfully expensive, and almost definitely bespoke. He was a good 6'4" tall and the suit very effectively conveyed he was someone who took keeping fit seriously.

He smiled at them charmingly as he opened the car door. 'Emma, Nathan I presume? It's a pleasure to meet you, my name is Rex,' he said in a soft Irish accent. 'If you'd like to get in we'll be on our way.'

Emma returned his smile, wondering instantly if Rex was just a driver to the mysterious Catherine. She didn't tend to look at other men very often but there was no hiding the fact he was attractive in a rugged kind of way.

'If you stare any longer, we'll be late,' quipped Nate, with a hint of annoyance. He gave her bottom a bit of a bump to get her moving and nodded to Rex as he climbed in next to her.

'You'll find some chilled wine and glasses in the centre console,' Rex informed them as they began to drive. 'Please help yourselves, we'll be there in about an hour.'

The couple held hands in the back of the impressive car, not talking for a few minutes. But once Nate had opened the wine and they'd each enjoyed a glass of an excellent, chilled Chardonnay, they began to relax.

Emma tried to engage Rex in some conversation but his short replies and repeated suggestion to 'Ask Miss Argent about that' meant she soon gave up.

Emma leaned in to Nate, 'This is all feeling a bit too real right now. I can't believe we're going to see some stranger who wants to pay us to…' she just stopped saying what for as Nate grabbed her thigh, nodding towards the driver.

Emma was a couple of big glasses of wine in by now, and she was feeling a little naughty, so she continued, '…pay us to lock your cock up!' She laughed.

Rex didn't even look up, but she thought he might have smiled.

'Em! Oh my god, if this is how you're going to be we can just go home now!'

'Oh Nate, you can't be so shy. If you're serious about this, you have to relax and enjoy it a bit. I bet Rex doesn't mind, in fact she's probably locked his cock up too! Hey Rex, has Catherine locked up your cock too?'

This time he did look up into the rear-view mirror, and with a somewhat pained look on his face, simply said, 'Yes.'

'Oh my god, seriously?' said Emma, suddenly extremely interested.

'Yes.'

'How come, how long for? Oh, wow I've never met another man who's got a locked cock.'

Rex glanced up again into the mirror, and this time with a slight smile replied, 'You'll just have to ask her about that.'

Nate wasn't sure what to do with this new information. Emma, however, was starting to enjoy herself.

'Oh darling, isn't this something special. I'm with two men and it's actually my husband's cock that isn't locked.'

'I think this should be your last glass,' said Nate as she poured the last of the bottle into her outstretched hand.

'Worried by what I might say, darling? Or that my negoty..., nego..., bartering skills aren't up to scratch?'

'Yes, actually.'

Emma reached over and grabbed between her husband's legs, whispering into his crotch, 'Don't you worry little man, I'll get a good price for you.' She glanced up. Rex definitely smiled that time.

Suddenly emboldened by the wine and more turned on by knowing Rex's secret than she'd wanted to admit, Emma began nuzzling into Nate's neck. Her hand moved up his thigh and was massaging his balls through his new trousers.

'Emma, stop it!' Nate whispered.

'When was the last time we were in the back of a car like this,' she whispered back, her fingertips finding the zipper and slowly pulling it down. 'Oh look, someone's pleased to meet me.'

She leaned over and began kissing the thin material of his underwear against which his rapidly hardening cock was pressing. She could feel a little damp spot forming. She loved how much he produced that stuff now. She'd never given it much thought before they began all this chastity play.

Emma glanced again to make sure Rex's eyes were still on the road. They were, although she surprised herself thinking perhaps she wished they weren't. Then she reached in, pulling Nate's cock through the flies of the jockey shorts and slipped her mouth around it.

How she loved sucking his cock. This still surprised her sometimes. Nate had been her first, and before him she'd not really thought about it much. But from the very first time she'd felt him in her mouth she'd adored it.

This is what she'd miss most, she thought to herself as her tongue circled the head of him. Sex was beautifully intimate, she loved him inside her. But she'd cope without that. This though, the rush of power and submissiveness as she put all her effort into pleasuring him with her mouth. She couldn't imagine a whole year without it.

A stifled moan from Nate brought her back to what she was doing, and where. She didn't look up but imagined Rex watching them in the mirror, his caged cock straining, and she sunk her head down, down until Nate's cock pushed against the back of her throat. She held there, swallowing, stopping herself gagging. Sometimes that was enough to make Nate spurt. Not today though. He grabbed her hair, about to thrust, when she pulled all the way off.

'Nate! I spent ages on my hair.' She grinned, licking the saliva from her lips, her hand gripping his rigid cock. Now, now, be a good boy.' She slid her hand slowly up him, lubricated by her spit, and forced it back into his jockey shorts. 'More later,' she promised. Nate gave a frustrated moan as he zipped himself back up.

Emma squeezed his erection, stroking it through his trousers. She took Nate's hand and hitched her dress to her thighs. 'My turn.' He didn't need much more instruction. Stroking the bare skin above her stockings he played with the taut garter bands, taking his time for his fingers to reach their destination. Pressing against the thin lace of her panties the pad of his thumb pushed the material against her clit. Rubbing ever so slowly he leaned over and kissed her, making little circles between her legs as his mouth closed around hers. Rex watched, but neither of them noticed.

It didn't feel too long before they stopped at what looked to be some imposing security gates. A long drive up a tree-lined road before the sound of a gravel car park confirmed their arrival.

Rex got out of the car and opened Emma's door. She turned to Nate, straightening herself up and pulling out her lipstick. 'That journey went fast! Oh my, time to meet our potential benefactor.'

The Benefactor

While it wasn't a mansion, the house was simply beautiful. A classic Georgian manor house, perfectly symmetrical, with a big black door centred between the large white sash windows. It didn't look huge but Emma knew it would feel enormous inside as they crunched their way over the gravel to the already opening door.

Out of nowhere a loud, siren-like call sounded making both Nate and Emma jump. They both turned to see the dazzling purple and green display of a peacock, starring at them from the perfectly manicured lawn.

'They make good guard... birds, apparently.' A bright voice rang out. 'Certainly can't keep them quiet. Sorry about that.'

An unreasonably attractive woman had stepped out of the gloom. She'd have been nearly six feet tall without the heels, which added another five inches at least. Her blonde hair was brushed over to one side, falling over her shoulders in a style that reminded Emma of a 1950's pin up girl. Her skirt suit was anything but old-fashioned though, showing enough of her legs to make Emma instantly envious, and tight enough to leave little to the imagination. Perhaps this was a mistake. They could just be polite and leave soon.

'Welcome, Emma and Nathan, thank you so much for coming. I hope the journey wasn't too arduous,' she said in a well-spoken English accent, not really expecting an answer.

Emma reached out her hand, 'Lovely to meet you, Catherine.'

The lady laughed reaching out to shake her hand. 'Oh no, I apologise, there's no way you could know. I'm Elizabeth, Miss Argent's personal assistant. She's just finishing off a call, so she asked me to welcome you and keep you entertained.'

Nate just gave a little cough and Emma glared at him, warning him not to say anything stupid. *I could have known, how did I not think to Google her?*

Nate stepped up, 'Well thank you, Elizabeth, it's good to meet you, even under these strange circumstances.' He reached out his hand too but either she didn't see it or ignored it, as she turned around and led them into the house.

Somehow her not being Catherine made Emma relax a little, and she took Nate's outstretched hand in hers and they followed. Despite the beautiful wood-panelled hall both of their attention was focused on the very tight skirt and the perfect bottom swaying hypnotically in front of them as Elizabeth led through to a side-room.

Emma was still feeling the effects of the wine and mouthed to her husband, 'Oh my god that ass!' He grinned at her and it turned into a loving gaze. 'You're the best,' he mouthed back.

'You better believe it,' she whispered, her thoughts turning inward for a moment.

Emma had never been a very jealous woman. But one of the unexpected side-effects of exploring chastity play with Nate had been the almost complete eradication of any jealousy at all.

She hadn't realised how much it had worried her before. At mostly an unconscious level all those marketing messages had got to her - that she wasn't beautiful enough, busty enough, sexy enough. She used to get anxious when Nate was talking to an attractive woman, and when they'd first tried watching some porn together she'd nearly had a meltdown.

The cage had changed that in ways she still couldn't quite believe. She loved how it made him think about her all the time, want her, need her. It made her feel so secure knowing that he couldn't even get hard looking at another woman. In fact, she'd grown to quite enjoy the thought.

She still remembered the first time when they were sat in a little coffee shop and a stunningly attractive woman had served them. Why the girl was a barista and not a model Emma had no idea.

She'd waited until Nate was just drinking his coffee before she quietly commented, 'How hot was our barista!' He'd paused, not sure he'd heard her right, mouth full of coffee. She raised an eyebrow at him, leaned in and whispered, 'I'd totally do her.'

The fact the hot barista had to come over to help clean up the coffee he'd coughed all over the table was an unexpected bonus. Emma had secretly rubbed her foot against his caged cock as he tried not to stare. He failed, which she put to good use when they got home, rapidly, after that.

'Emma? Can I get you a drink?' offered Elizabeth, in a way that suggested she had already asked.

'Oh sorry, no thank you, I had plenty in the car. Maybe just some water?'

Emma's thoughts came back into focus as her hand gripped Nate's across the soft leather Chesterfield sofa Elizabeth had sat them in. She was feeling more nervous again. This big house, the beautiful assistant, the cock-locked chauffeur or whatever he was. This was outside their normal world, far outside it. What were they getting themselves into?

As if reading her mind, Nate turned to her while her water was getting poured and assured her, 'We're not committing to anything, just relax darling, let's try to have fun and enjoy a fancy meal with a woman who shares an interest with us, okay?'

'Alright, just don't let me drink much more please. I can't believe I just sucked you in the car!'

'I know, I'm already thinking about the journey home,' Nate chuckled.

Just as Elizabeth handed Emma her water a door at the other end of the room opened and a woman in a bright red flowy knee-length dress strode into the room, full of apologies.

'Dear Emma, dear Nathan, I'm so sorry to have kept you! I hope Elizabeth has been looking after you!'

'We'd barely even sat down,' said Nathan, standing, and pulling Emma up with him.

Catherine, for surely this was her, turned out to be far less physically imposing than her employees. In fact, she was short, petite; barely over five feet. But there was a vitality about her that meant her height became inconsequential. Besides the vibrant dress she was otherwise somewhat understated with her make-up and black kitten heels. The outstanding feature however was her red hair. Plausibly real, she had it cascading down and it bounced as she almost jogged across to them. She had a certain infectious energy as she closed the ground, ignoring Nathan's hand to instead wrap her arms around Emma.

'It's so good to meet you at last. I feel like I know you already from everything on your blog.'

She pushed herself back, and apologised again. 'I'm sorry, you have no idea who I am, a hug probably wasn't very appropriate, not yet at least.'

She turned to Nathan and shook his hand. 'So very proper, look at you both. You're even more attractive than I imagined.' Catherine raised her hand to Nathan's chin and lifted it, 'Oh his eyes are as lovely as you once described them, Emma. I do hope the green doesn't mean he gets too jealous.'

Nathan stepped back a little, jerking his chin from her grasp. 'My eyes are lovely?' He looked at his wife, 'Have you two been talking behind my back?'

Emma didn't know what to say. What was he suggesting? She was about to defend herself when Catherine stepped in.

'Oh Nathan, don't be so silly. She mentioned it on the blog last year, she was boasting about you, and I can see why.'

Nate muttered something under his breath and folded his arms.

'Now why don't the two of you sit back down. Elizabeth be a dear and get me some wine, and then you can have the rest of the evening off. I intend to look after these two myself.'

Elizabeth simply nodded and walked out, her heels tapping on the wooden floorboards. Emma noted she seemed to have a little less swagger when Catherine was around.

'Now I know this must all be so strange, but I just want to thank you for even agreeing to meet. I'm so pleased you didn't reject my little proposition outright. And even if it comes to nothing, I am delighted to meet two of my favourite people in person. I really have been inspired by your blog.'

She was interrupted by a loud peacock call again, just outside the window. 'How do you sleep with those things making that racket?' Nate asked.

'Oh, they tend to quieten down at night. They're a little pretentious, I know, but they're something of a personal motif.' Catherine motioned to the wall where there was a beautiful display of peacock feathers in a frame.'

'Seems a little cruel,' objected Nate.

Catherine smiled with her mouth but not her eyes. 'They don't have to die for you to pluck them out.'

Emma tried to de-escalate the conversation. 'Is there a reason why you've chosen them as your motif?'

'Yes.' Catherine paused. Was that the end of her answer? They didn't find out. Emma and Nate turned as Elizabeth's heels announced her return. Seeing her sideways on as she handed the glass of chilled wine to her boss made Emma envy more than her arse. She had the perfect figure. More than anything Emma wished Nate's cock was locked right now. That made everything right.

With little more than a nod Catherine dismissed her PA. One of Emma's favourite quotes came to mind, 'If you want to see the true measure of someone, watch how they treat their inferiors, not their equals.' She looked at Nate wondering if he was thinking of the same Harry Potter quote, but her guess was he was more likely imagining Elizabeth naked. *Men! The sooner I lock his cock back up the better!*

Emma turned back to catch a smile on Catherine's lips, a result of watching Nate's reaction. What was this woman up to?

'So what's this really all about, Catherine? I admit it's a hot fantasy but surely you want more than just to pay me for locking up Nate's cock for a year. What's in it for you?'

'I think I've explained that all quite clearly. 'If you want some deeper insight then I suppose it's that I find it deeply arousing to lock up a man's cock.'

Emma countered with a secret she thought might surprise Catherine. 'Isn't Rex enough for you?'

'Oh, he told you about his situation, did he? You really do like to get to the heart of things don't you Emma. Good, so do I. Rex is a delight, in more ways than one, but there's something very, selfish, about what I do with him. You Emma, are the difference here. What truly excites me is how all this might affect you. I've read everything you've written on your blog, multiple times, and you know what I see, potential. Potential for much more.'

'What if I don't want any more?' Emma said.

'If you didn't, you wouldn't be here, would you.'

Emma stayed quiet as she thought about that.

Rex made an appearance at the doorway. 'Dinner is served,' he announced.

'Oh, chauffeur and butler, your Rex is a man of many talents,' joked Nathan as they stood.

Catherine put her hand on Emma's shoulder and leaned in, whispering, 'Darling, you have no idea…'

The Prisoner's Dilemma

The dining room was an exquisite mix of old and new with dark, wood panelled walls lit by some very modern and clever ceiling lights over the polished oak table. At one end of the room hung a large, modern painting that somehow conveyed through its tones and curves that something very sexual was happening, somewhere. Emma couldn't keep her eyes off it.

Catherine indicated a seat on one side of the table to Emma and as Nate pushed Emma's seat in he looked over at another painting.

'Is that an original Jack Vettriano?' He asked, looking closer. 'I've never seen one in person.'

'It is, well spotted! He's a bit of a cliché I know, but behind every good cliché is some truth is what Henry used to say.'

They both turned to look at the painting of a woman facing away, wearing just a white corset, sat backwards on a chair, her legs spread. In between them stood a man, looking down at her, waistcoat covering his crisp white shirt, his hands, down, as though perhaps cupping her bare breasts.

'It's called "The Perfectionist". I took a fancy to it, so I bought it. Probably for far too much money.'

'How much did you pay for it?' Emma asked, somewhat impetuously.

'I like that you asked, Emma. We'll be talking money later so that's a good sign. I paid £150,000 for it.'

'What!' they both exclaimed, looking at it again. 'But you could get a signed print for £100,' Nate said.

'True, and I suppose my accountant would say it was an investment. But

47

really, I just like owning the originals.'

Catherine seated herself at the end of the table and indicated to Nate to sit at the place laid opposite to his wife. 'So, since we're talking money already, do you have a figure in mind for what we discussed?'

At a nod from Catherine, Rex came quietly into the room and started filling up a champagne flute for each of them.

'I'm not sure I should drink any more,' Emma said, but let him fill it up anyway. 'And no, not really, I mean we've thought about it but we still aren't sure if it's a good idea at all. We don't mean any offence, but we know nothing...'

'Let me interrupt you with one question that might help,' Catherine interjected. They both stayed quiet so she went on. 'If I offered you £10 million pounds to lock up Nate's cock for a year, would you both do it?'

'Ten million!' Nate almost shouted. He looked at his wife and they both nodded to each other. 'Yes, I think as long as the terms were acceptable, we'd do that.'

'Very good,' Catherine declared, and then with a smirk added, 'As Winston Churchill once said to a wealthy socialite to whom he made a similar offer. "We've established what kind of woman you are, now we're just haggling over price."'

Emma laughed nervously; Nate didn't seem so impressed. His dreams of becoming an instant millionaire disappearing as quickly as they'd arrived. They both sipped at their champagne.

'Anyway, let's leave those discussions to a little later and enjoy dinner, shall we?'

The smell of something delicious had been making Emma's tummy rumble for a while now. She turned at the sound of heels expecting Elizabeth to make another appearance, but it was someone new carrying the plates.

She was tall as well, heel assisted it seemed, but not nearly as stunning as Elizabeth, somewhat to Emma's relief. She didn't speak as she moved to everyone's side, laying down a beautiful dish of smoked salmon, beetroot and some other vegetable Emma couldn't identify.

'Thank you, Alexandra, please let Jenny know it looks wonderful.'

'Jenny's, your cook?' Nate asked.

'Yes,' confirmed Catherine. 'And Alex here is my little house elf, doing everything else around here. I don't know what I'd do without her.'

'Thank you, Miss,' mumbled Alexandra before heading back out. Emma watched her go, her smart black and white housemaid's outfit looking not too out of place in the wood-panelled setting.

'Please, dig in,' Catherine encouraged. 'Jenny has put together quite the menu for your visit.'

And so it turned out, five extraordinary courses, some of the best either of them had ever eaten, accompanied by some of the tastiest wines they'd ever drunk too. The meal passed surprisingly quickly, with not even a mention of cock or cages or anything but pleasant conversation.

Catherine explained how she'd brought some wealth to her marriage to Henry, but he'd really been the one who'd invested it wisely over the years. When her writing career had taken off he'd done the same with the earnings from that. When he'd died, on top of all the returns on investment, his life insurance meant she'd never have to worry about money again.

After they finished the most delicious chocolate dessert paired with a pudding wine Catherine led them through to a drawing room where Alexandra was already serving coffee on a table set between two facing sofas.

'Please, take a seat. I hope you enjoyed the meal, but this is the part I've been most looking forward to,' said Catherine.

Feeling very full and more than a little tipsy, Emma and Nate sat themselves down on the sofa facing the one Catherine had just planted herself in.

So, you've read my terms, did you have any questions?

Emma tried to recall the points she'd been thinking about all week. One came straight to mind. 'Does he really have to be pierced, it seems a bit brutal. You said there'd be no lasting damage.' Nate grunted his approval at the question.

'That's a good point, Emma. But you both know how these cages are. While it may be true that Nate never 'cheats' the temptation to do so under

49

these circumstances, and the length of time involved, means it's much more of a risk, don't you agree?'

'Yes, I suppose so,' Emma said.

'What's more, haven't I read you're both intrigued by the idea?'

'Yes, but it's a different thing considering it for real,' Nate replied.

'This is real, Nathan. This isn't one of your fantasies. That's what makes it so exciting, don't you think? Me, this woman you've just met, having complete control over your cock, so neither you nor your wife can enjoy it for such a long time.

'Imagine how horny you're going to get, and stay, Nathan,' Catherine continued. 'Imagine how passionate he's going to be with his mouth, Emma. Imagine what it'll be like, to truly be locked in chastity.'

Catherine leaned in across the coffee table. 'Are you hard, Nate? Is your body betraying how you really feel about this already?' She looked at Emma, who looked down at her husband's lap, and reached over.

'It seems he is,' Emma confirmed. She didn't take her hand away, but gently squeezed.

Catherine smiled, and looked over her shoulder. 'Rex, come over here.' He stepped silently from a corner where they hadn't even noticed him, coming to stand next to Emma.

'Have you seen one, a piercing - not on a screen, in real life?' Catherine asked.

'No.'

'Would you like to?'

Emma felt her husband's cock twitch hard in her hand, it was all the confirmation she needed. 'Yes, please.'

Catherine looked to Rex and nodded. Without any hesitation or show, Rex pulled down the zipper on his suit trousers, reached in, and extracted his caged cock.

'Oh. My. God' Emma said.

'Fuck,' said Nate.

Despite seeing countless photos and videos, the sight of this big, caged cock, right there next to her took Emma's breath away. She immediately felt the visceral thrill that any penis nicely caged up now gave her, but this one was just a different animal altogether. It was completely filling the largest cage either of them had seen, the bars elegantly curved downwards past a pair of large, shaved, clearly full testicles. Even in its caged state it was bigger than Nate's cock when he was fully erect.

There was almost nothing to show of his piercing save for a curved piece that entered his flesh just near the tip and exited his urethra.

'How does he pee with that there?'

'Sitting down,' laughed Catherine. 'Poor Rex's biggest problem is sometimes the whole cage hits the bottom of the bowl. I had to get that custom made, as you can imagine. Even getting him in that thing takes considerable effort. It's a good thing he doesn't get out often, isn't it Rex?'

He stayed silent. Apparently, she didn't expect a reply.

'You want to hold it?' Catherine offered, 'Have a better look?'

Emma turned to her husband. His cock was still rigid under his trousers. She took his silence as approval.

'Okay then. I've never touched someone else's.'

'It's just research, you're examining it, right?'

Emma tentatively reached out, 'I guess so.' Her hand was shaking a little as her heart raced. This thing was so different from Nate's. How could two penises be so incredibly different? Curiosity overcame her anxiety. She cupped her hand around the warm metal and flesh. She couldn't quite get her fingers around it.

She turned back to Nate. 'It's so big! Have you ever seen one this big in real life?'

Nate shook his head, his eyes transfixed as he watched his wife handling this caged monster.

She got a little braver, knowing her husband had a secret kink that was undoubtedly coming into play here. 'It's so much bigger than yours, baby. I can't even get my fingers around it and it's not even hard.'

Nate let out a little groan of aroused frustration. She knew she was hitting him right where it made him ache.

'Can you imagine how big he'd be out of this thing? Bigger than our big dildo I reckon.'

'Geronimo?' Catherine asked, with a grin. She really did know the blog well. Emma laughed.

'Yes, big old Geronimo. I feared it at first, but, well you've read our accounts. I didn't think I'd ever be able to cum just from sex. Apparently, size does matter.'

'It certainly does. Yet another lie men tell to make them feel better about themselves,' Catherine observed.

Emma stroked her fingers down the bars of Rex's cage. He seemed to be struggling a little, beginning to bulge.

Catherine chuckled. 'Poor Rex, I don't let him out much at all. I think he's relishing the attention.' Her eyes sparkled as she watched. 'It does seem a bit unfair though, Emma.'

'How's that?'

'I've shown you mine.' Catherine stood up and walked over next to Nate. 'It'd be rude if you didn't show me yours.'

Emma laughed again. The wine from dinner was certainly helping. She stroked the hot skin under her fingers. 'Go on baby, show her,' she encouraged her husband.

'Don't I get a say in this?' complained Nate.

'Well you aren't going to for a whole year, Nathan. You realise that, yes?' said Catherine. 'What's in your pants becomes essentially my property. I think I have a right to inspect the goods before purchase, wouldn't you say?'

'But...'

'Nathan, if you can't even handle this we might as well stop now. Are you serious about this, or not?'

He stood up, mirroring Rex on his wife's other side, and started to fumble with his zipper. 'I'm not, as big as...'

'As Rex?' Catherine finished. 'Oh Nathan, I know that, your wife isn't exactly subtle with her teasing on the blog now is she. That turns you on doesn't it. Don't worry, I know that good things come in small packages. Now... let me see.'

Nate sat on the arm of the sofa, Emma watching him carefully. If they wanted to do this, this would be the least of what he could hope for in their check-up sessions. He made his decision, quickly pulling down his trousers and his underwear around his thighs.

Catherine tapped her fingertips together. 'Aww precious little thing! It *is* excited isn't it. It's not *that* small Emma, I'd imagined it was some kind of micro-penis from the way you tease him. It's really quite attractive.' Catherine turned to her and winked. 'If only it were bigger, huh Emma?'

'If only,' Emma teased with a big smile. Rex snorted. She dug a nail into him.

This was less strange than she thought it would be. The wine definitely helped but if they were going to take the offer then hubby would have to learn to be a bit resilient. Catherine looked at her. 'Can I touch it too?' she asked.

Emma gave it a moment's thought and surprised herself with the answer. 'No, I don't think so, not until you've paid for it.'

Catherine laughed, 'Oh so that's how it is, I understand, but I did have a question in that case. She turned to Emma. 'Has he been locked this week?'

'Yes, actually, well for most of it. I let him out yesterday.'

Catherine directed her next question to Nate. 'Nathan, when did you last cum?'

'What?' said Emma. 'I told you, I've had him locked this week.' Nate however, stayed quiet, and didn't make eye contact with either of them.

Catherine explained, 'I asked because those balls don't look very full. You see Emma, while you've enjoyed some of the benefits of keeping your husband chaste, I'd suggest you haven't seen the half of it. Most men it seems, no matter how much attention and pleasure we share with them, cannot keep their hands off their cocks.'

She turned to him, 'Nathan, are you an honest man?' Catherine asked.
'I like to think so.'
'When did you last cum?' she repeated.
Emma began, 'it was last week, as I said I've locked him...'
'Yesterday,' admitted Nathan.
Emma blushed, forgetting all about what was in her hand and frowning

at her husband. 'What? Yesterday? You're kidding? After I unlocked you, you couldn't even manage a day?'

Nathan looked embarrassed, and was about to make an excuse when Catherine stepped in.

'You see Emma, they just can't help themselves. You may think you're getting all the advantages of his arousal and desire but the moment you give them a chance, they selfishly waste it. I saw it with my own husband. Sadly, too late. By the time I'd worked out what he really needed, he'd begun to get ill.'

Emma started putting the pieces together. 'So, that's why you want this? Why you've made this offer?'

'Yes, at least in part. I didn't ever get to see the full difference it could make. Something I always regretted. I want to see, and make sure others like me don't miss out. So, what do you say, ready to start negotiating?'

With a nod from Catherine, Rex put himself away, and deliberately mimicking her, Emma turned to her husband, glanced at his empty balls and gave the same nod. *The sooner it's locked up the better.*

Emma sat right in the middle of the sofa, facing Catherine. She looked straight in her eyes. 'How much for my husband's cock?'

'How much do you want?' she replied.

Money Talks

Emma glanced towards the door, thinking back to the painting on the wall.

'£150,000. If you can spend that much on a single painting, then it's at least what my husband's cock is worth.' Emma sat back, heart racing, trying to look as though she knew what she was doing.

'That's a lot of money. £12,500 a month. I told you before, Emma, I'm a frugal woman. I can tell you right now, that's much more than I'm willing to spend.'

'You were talking in the millions earlier,' Nate objected.

'I was, and it was to prove a point - your cock, your chastity, is for sale, well, at least for rent. Now be quiet Nathan, the women are talking.' Nathan folded his arms and sank back on the sofa. He looked just about ready to leave but the money talk was just too interesting.

Emma asked, 'So, what are you prepared to pay, Catherine?'

She paused for a moment. 'Three thousand pounds a month sounds like a fair price to me. That would pay your mortgage, all your bills, and even give you a little extra. You'd be a kept woman, Emma, for a whole year. Wouldn't have to work if you didn't want to. All for the price of your husband's chastity.'

Nate bristled. 'One, how do you know what our bills are? And two, that's not enough.'

Catherine turned to him with a dismissive look. 'It was just a guess, Nathan. It's not hard to figure out what your little house would be worth. And secondly, I'm talking to Emma.'

'No, I agree,' said Emma, 'it's not enough. That's a fifth of what I asked for.'

'More like a quarter actually,' Catherine replied. 'Okay, so give me a more reasonable figure.'

'I think there's somewhere in the middle we can meet but I have more questions. Mostly about these check-ups. They seem to give you free reign to do pretty much anything. What are they going to involve?'

Catherine explained again that they were to ensure the two of them were keeping to the essence of the arrangement, that as much as possible Nathan was being kept denied, aroused and with full and aching balls as proof of it.

'But you need to understand, Emma, this is just as much for you as for me. I want to free you from the pressure you'll feel to ease Nathan from his arousal, his discomfort. It's what I'm sure you'd want as a good, loving wife. But I want to see what happens beyond that, what happens to him, and to you.'

'I guess I understand that, but a whole day for it? What's actually going to happen?'

'Ah well, that is yet to be determined. It really depends on how things are going, and will be tailored to you both once I get to know you better.'

'Tailored, how?' Emma leaned in, this is the part she'd been most curious about.

'The check-up isn't just something physical. It's to understand what the experience is doing to you both, how perhaps it's changing you. I want to find ways to test that, to explore it. I really don't know quite what it will look like yet.' Catherine paused for a moment. 'Here's an idea. I talked about those sessions having a chance for reward, or penalty. That was to give me some options on how well I think you've been doing. But, how about we add some financial incentives too?'

'Go on,' Emma said.

'How about, we agree that you could increase the amount you get from this, a lot, if you make certain choices. How would a possible income of at least £300,000 sound?'

Emma and Nathan looked at each other with wide eyes. That was far more than they'd hoped for.

'That's £25,000 a month,' Emma calculated.

'Yes, but not guaranteed. But we could start with a base rate of £5,000 a month. So you can have some stability. But I warn you, if you want the chance to increase it, you'll also have the chance to reduce it.'

'All this is optional, though right? We can do nothing and still get £5,000 a month?' Nate asked.

'Yes, that's right, just turn up to the check-ups, satisfy me that you've been chaste, and you'll still get that.'

The couple asked for a minute to talk, which Catherine gave them as she went to mix some more drinks.

She returned, putting a whiskey in front of Nathan and an espresso Martini in front of Emma, 'Try that, I think you'll like it'.

'How's this enforced?' Nate asked, sipping the excellent booze. 'I assume you have a contract of some kind?'

Catherine went over to the sideboard and picked up a sheaf of papers. 'I do indeed, it's right here. I've tried to make it as plain language as I can, but if you have any questions, just ask.'

Emma and Nate began to scan through the contract but before they had a chance to raise any questions Catherine sat on the table in front of them, leaned back on her hands and folded one leg over the other.

'I have one last offer for you, an incentive. To get things moving. If you sign the contract this weekend, before you head home, I'll throw in the Vettriano painting when you complete the 12 months."

They both did the maths, that'd mean even if they did nothing the offer had just grown from a guaranteed £60,000 to about £200,000 plus maybe the same again. This was more than either of them had imagined.

'I'll leave you to think about it. But it's getting late. Why don't you stay the night, give you more time to read the contract and think it all over? I need it signed before you leave if you want the bonus. Let's say, 4pm latest on Sunday. A deadline always focuses the mind.' Catherine looked up at the painting. 'I'm rather fond of it to tell you the truth.'

She walked to the door, and Alexandra was there, handing her a small gift bag. She turned back to face the two of them. 'Oh I nearly forgot. Emma, this is something for, well both of you I suppose.'

Emma stood and went over to her. Catherine handed her the pretty little bag with ribbon handles. She spoke softly, so Nathan couldn't hear. 'It's a cage for him, a very expensive one. It would please me to know he's caged while in my house. Do you think you could manage that for me?'

Emma smiled, looking back at her husband, his confession still fresh in her mind. 'Oh yes, I think that can be arranged.'

'How about I pick up the key in the morning, give you both a taste of how it is to not have it?' Catherine suggested, watching Emma carefully.

'Hmm, I'm not sure about that.'

'You can always ask for it back, until you sign the contract,' Catherine added.

Emma thought for a moment, and then nodded. 'Well in that case, sure, good idea. I'll break the news to him upstairs.'

Catherine smiled and then spoke more loudly. 'Thank you again for considering this. I think it'll be wonderful fun if you decide to do it, but either way it's been lovely meeting you both. Alexandra will show you to your room if you'd like some privacy.'

The Path to Ruin

Alexandra wasn't very chatty as she led them through the entrance hall and up the sweeping curved stairs. Their room was halfway down a corridor that led off the landing. She opened the door and showed them that their bags had been put in the walk-in wardrobe.

'Thank you, Alexandra,' said Emma, 'or is it Alex?'

'Alexandra,' the housekeeper replied quietly. 'Is there anything else you need?'

'Only advice on what to think of your crazy employer,' Nathan joked.

Alexandra looked awkward; an obvious, nervous gulp was all she offered. She walked back to the door, pausing for a moment. 'I'm, I'm sorry, I really can't help you there.' She paused and looked at the little gift bag Emma had put on the bed. 'Don't forget your gift.' It felt like even saying that had cost her something. She shut the door and left them to admire the room.

The bedroom was stunning. Big and beautifully decorated, with high ceilings and an enormous bed. Emma jumped straight onto it but Nathan was a bit less enthusiastic. He stood by the big sash window, looking out over the extensive gardens, the sun setting on the fields beyond them.

'Oh honey, don't let Catherine rattle you,' Emma said. 'She's just fucking with you. You know how it works, you do it enough with me.'

'It's not the same though. I love you. I have your best interests in mind. I'm not sure I believe what she's saying about her motives.'

'Three hundred, *thousand* pounds!' Emma reminded him.

'It could be much less.'

'It could be even more. And it was what, at least sixty guaranteed, even if we don't take up on any of her optional extras? That's like winning a big game show. It's life-changing, baby, we'd pay off all our debts and more.'

Nathan turned back to her. 'Our student loans you mean?'

Emma seemed at a bit of a loss for words. 'Yeah, yes, sure... them,' she finally said.

Nathan came over to her and sat himself on the bed. 'You're right. We'll read the contract and make sure we're not being stupid. But it is a lot of money. And, as much as I don't want to admit it, the whole idea is so hot.'

'So, freaking hot,' Emma agreed enthusiastically, reaching over and pulling Nathan back to lie next to her. She turned to face him, and he did the same. 'So, do we need to talk about something?'

Nathan's face paled a little. 'Umm, about me...?'

Emma just laughed. 'No, although I'm not letting that go. I was thinking of something... bigger.'

Nathan's eyes widened. 'Rex's cock.'

'Rex's *massive* cock, oh my god! Can you believe it? How big must that thing be out of the cage.'

'I'm almost scared to think about it.' Nate laughed.

Emma pushed him onto his back and straddled him, grinding herself on his crotch. 'Oh, I'm not scared to think about it.' She gave him the naughtiest wink. 'It weighed so much in my hand. What was it like to see me, fondling it?'

'I can't even put it into words. Although, well you saw the reaction when you made me show her! That was mean by the way. Although I loved you not letting her touch it.'

Emma stopped grinding and took on a more pensive expression. 'I won't have that option if we sign the contract though. I don't like the thought of your cock... being hers.'

'That's just bullshit. She can't legally own my cock, whatever the contract says. It's always going to be yours, I promise my love.'

'Awww, really? Well in that case, I should probably do something with it while I'm still able to.' She wriggled back and slipped down onto the floor while Nate hung his lower legs over the end of the bed and propped himself up on his elbows, grinning.

Emma undid his trousers, yanking them down around his ankles and his jockey shorts with them. 'I'm glad to see someone's pleased to see me.' She wrapped her hand around Nate's growing cock, squeezing it, enjoying how it felt getting bigger in her hand. 'Oh darling, do you realise, we won't be able to do this much longer. He won't be able to even get hard.' She looked up, 'that thought seems to get you even harder.'

Emma pushed herself up on his knees and pulled her dress over her head, nearly managing to make it look sexy, but ruining it when the waistband got stuck on her breasts. With a few more tugs she managed to get it off while Nate wisely kept quiet. She slipped her bra off much more successfully, the pale breasts she was rightfully proud of catching all of Nate's attention. She sank down again. 'Now, where was I?' She squeezed her breasts together with her upper arms as she took hold of Nate's cock with one hand and his balls with the other, massaging them.

Slowly rubbing her thumb against the underside of his cock head she decided to try a little interrogation. It was a technique he had used against her with devastating effect earlier in their marriage, bringing her close to the edge of orgasm, then teasing her, questioning her, making her spill the secret fantasies she never thought she'd tell even him. And if that wasn't enough, with her drastically lowered inhibitions, he'd plant new ones, whispering ideas she'd never even thought of, making her want things, need things done to her he was only too happy to make a reality. Her thumb rubbed the trickle of slippery pre-cum that leaked out of him, a plan formulating in her mind. *You taught me so well, darling.*

'So, forgetting about the money, baby, what do you think of the whole idea? Still think it's freaking hot?' Emma asked.

'I seem to recall those were your words, but,' Nate paused to let out a little moan as Emma began licking where her thumb had been, 'but, fuck, yes so freaking hot.' His breathing became more ragged as he watched his wife licking and sucking on his erection.

She knelt up a little higher, going back to just her hand slowly stroking him, letting him gaze at her breasts. She loved that they still had the power to mesmerise him. They always had. She recalled the first time, a few months into dating, where he'd persuaded her to let him see them. She'd been shy, but hadn't really understood the appeal. They were just... breasts. And then she saw the look on his face. The wonder, the adoration. As he'd touched, kissed, worshipped them, the way she felt about them, and her body, had changed forever.

Of course that had faded as they'd gone on to explore so much more. But they had never completely lost their impact, and these last few years, exploring chastity, keeping him aroused, had reignited that original passion.

His pre-cum was flowing more freely now and she leaned forwards, pushing his cock against her sternum, and squeezing her breasts around it. They were just big enough to perfectly encase him. Emma rose up a little on her heels and then sunk back down, slowly fucking him between her breasts. It was a move that always held a special place in her heart. It was the first way she'd ever made him cum. His enduring adoration of her breasts, along with her edging-inspired curiosity about porn, had led her to develop a mild obsession with the idea of the 'tit wank'.

It had been the first 'scene' she'd planned and brought to life. They had taken their time getting physical, the mind games taking precedence. They spent months just making out, letting fingers slowly explore further. Her edging and denial meant there was plenty of grinding, and rubbing, but it was all through clothing for a surprisingly long time.

Just as she planned though, only a week after he'd put a ring on her finger, she surprised him, kneeling down beside his bed at university, undoing her shirt to reveal she'd left her bra off. When she'd finally managed to get his cock out she wrapped her breasts around it, already lubed and ready to go, and just like now, had wanked him between them. To both their surprise he'd lost control, she'd watched him cum that first time, fascinated at what lay beyond all the teasing they'd given each other. Feeling him spurt was something of a shock. His warm, copious cum, splashed across her neck, chest and breasts with a cry of pleasure. She hadn't known what possessed her, but the look of amazement on his face when she'd dipped a finger in and brought it to her mouth. 'You taste good,' she'd told him. A line from her fantasies she'd never thought she'd actually bring to life.

She knew better now, how to read him, how to ensure he didn't climax until she wanted him to. 'I wish I'd known about cock cages before we were married,' she said. 'I'd have locked your cock up whenever you were away from me. Maybe I'd have made you wear it at our wedding, the key nestled between my tits just like your cock is now. Can you imagine it baby, how our wedding night would have been? Licking me to orgasm after orgasm while your little virgin cock dripped in expectation of finally fucking my virgin pussy.

'Oh Nate, it's like I get a second chance now. An entire year, just like our engagement, a year of licking and loving and cumming while you stay all locked up for me. I have to be honest, my love, right now, the money's just a bonus. I'd let Catherine lock you up for nothing if she asked. What about you though, would you?'

He collapsed back onto the bed with a frustrated groan. 'You are being so mean. Fuck my life, why did I ever introduce you to this?'

'It's okay baby, she won't even know how much it turns you on. How much you want this to happen. You can use the excuse of the money, I will too. But just tell me, I want to hear it. How hot is it knowing you can't get out. Knowing all your sweet words, all your persuasion, all your charm, mean nothing, as I won't even have the key?'

'I plead the fifth,' Nate replied.

'This is England, baby, the Fifth Amendment doesn't apply here. I could stop though, if you don't want to answer.' Emma paused stroking her tits around his cock.

'Okay, okay, I'd do it for you even without the money,' Nate confessed.

'Oh babe, that's so sweet of you to do it for me. But that's not the question. Do you, my darling, dominant, husband, want your cock locked up for an entire year?' Emma let his cock slip from between her breasts but caught it in her hand, bending in to begin sucking on the tip of it. She'd let him stew on the question while she encouraged him to be honest. She knew just what a mindfuck this was, she was loving it.

Finally, he sat back up on his elbows. She lifted her eyes to meet his. 'Yes,'

Nate said.

'Yes, what?' she asked, her lips playing over his cock head.

'Yes, I want to see what happens if I'm locked up and you don't have the key.'

'Mhmmm,' Emma murmured. 'Is it just… curiosity? Or are there other reasons you should be locked up?' She could barely contain herself. Watching him like this, having him in this headspace was always such a thrill. 'Why don't you give me three *big* reasons why this is best?' She perched her elbow on his thigh and leaned her chin on her hand as her other kept stroking him, keeping him on edge.

Nate thought for a moment, and she saw in his face the decision just to go for it. 'One,' he started, 'I'm a better husband when I'm locked up, when I don't cum. I think more about what you need, I want to please you, pleasure you. I am more helpful. It makes me a better man.'

Emma lovingly gazed at him. 'That, Mr Stevens, is a bloody good first answer. Tell me more about how you want to pleasure me.'

'I, I want to cuddle you. I want to kiss you more. I want to rub you, edge you, make you cum. I want to lick you all the fucking time. I want to spend my nights between your legs showing you how much I love you.'

Emma's eyes glistened as her heart swelled with even more love for this man. 'I want that too, so, so much.' She quietly replied.

'Two,' Nate continued, 'as much as I hate admitting it, I want what Catherine wants. I want to see who you become when I'm locked up and can't persuade you to unlock me, because you don't have the key. This has been such an amazing journey already and seeing how else you could grow is very exciting.'

'I like that. I want that too, even if I'm nervous about it,' Emma said.

'Good. Hmm, three, I don't know.' He scrunched his mouth up as he thought about it.

Emma raised her head off her hand and grinned. 'Err, well I did ask for *big* reasons.' She made a fist and just left her thumb and forefinger open, a few inches apart.

'Oh, come on, you're pulling that card now? You want me to say that?'

'From how hard your cock just got,' Emma replied, 'it's not just me. Say it.'
Nate sighed, rolling his eyes and with a wry smile said 'Three, my cock…

'Little cock,' Emma interrupted.

'For fuck's sake, you're being so mean! Okay, my *little* cock deserves to be
locked up so I can focus on fucking you with big cocks that make you cum.'

Emma went back to sucking Nathan's straining dick before kissing the
shaft again. 'I mean if Rex's monster gets locked up this little fella should be
under maximum lockdown.'

Nate fell back on the bed again with a frustrated growl. 'If you're this
mean now, what are you going to be like when you don't even have the key?
You were only saying last week you wish you were denied.'

'Oh, but I *am* being denied, darling. I won't get to rub you, or suck you,
or…' she stood to her feet and stroked her fingers down to between her legs,
making it clear what she was thinking. 'Maybe you should go shower. I'll
put on something cute.'

She walked over to her suitcase, turning back to look at him still lying
on the bed, his cock standing up like a flagpole. 'Don't take too long baby,
it's getting late and it's been a long day. You don't want me getting tired do
you?' That got him moving. 'No cheating in the shower,' she called after
him.

* * *

Emma was sitting on the end of the bed when he came out. She was dressed
in one of her favourite sets of lingerie. It was a cute black basque which had
little pink bows at the hips and between the built-in push up bra. It made
absolutely the most of her boobs. She was leaning back on one hand, and
the other was rubbing the thin material of the matching black thong. She
didn't stop as she looked up at him. 'Your turn on the floor, babe,' she said,
spreading her legs wider.

Nate didn't argue. He came over to her, dropping the towel wrapped
around his waist. His cock was just in front of her but she held off the
temptation to play with it. It wasn't erect, just in the middle ground of being

bigger. For her plan to work she needed to keep it that way.

Nate stayed standing for a little bit, clearly hoping she would suck or play with him, but she patted her mound and he rolled his eyes, going down onto one knee at first. It was Emma's turn to lie back as he began kissing her thighs, moving slowly. She checked her little gold watch that he'd given them for their fifth anniversary last year. 'Don't take too long, darling, or Cinderella might turn back into the maid at midnight.'

'Maids are hot too, well some of them,' he replied between kisses. But the encouragement worked. Emma moaned as his mouth found her clit, licking and sucking at her. She wanted to tease him, to tell him how this was all he was going to be able to do all year. How his caged up cock wouldn't get any release, it would just be her. But she stayed quiet. She knew how hard that would get him, and she didn't want that, not yet. 'Oh my god you are so good at that, it feels amazing. Get me ready baby, get me ready for your cock.' Emma reached down and took hold of both his hands which had been resting on her thighs. She loved the connection it gave them, but that wasn't her main reason. She didn't want him playing with himself.

She took her gamble. 'Stand up, I need you in me.' Nate looked a bit sheepish, but stood up slowly. Sure enough he was a bit harder than before but his focus was always so completely on her when giving cunnilingus it was common for him to need a bit of a hand afterwards. She felt a little mean playing this trick on him, but she knew how hot it would be too.

'Oh dear, baby,' Emma said, 'don't you want to fuck me?' She fluttered her eyelids to let him know she was teasing.

'It's not that and you know it,' he said, jumping onto the bed next to her. 'As you said it's been a long day and he just needs a little help.'

'Oh, I know what might help,' Emma declared, reaching over to get the little gift bag from where she'd left it by the bed. *This is going perfectly so far.*

She reached into the bag and it made a metallic jangle. When she withdrew it she held a metallic ring. It was actually two rings joined up with a short bar jutting out from one side. 'Maybe a cock ring would help get him to full attention?' She twirled it between her fingers.

Nate looked at it closely. 'Oh wow, is that a Mature Metal cage? Those are literally the best you can buy.'

Emma laughed. 'I cannot believe you're such a chastity geek now you know what brand this is from the ring! Get over here.' With a practised hand she quickly pulled his balls through the hoop and gripped his rapidly growing cock with her hand. This was always a challenge, although easier than it had been to start. When they'd got their very first, cheap plastic cock cage their initial attempts to even get it on failed because he was getting so hard at the idea. That really should have clued them in to how powerful it was going to be.

Now though, she was a seasoned pro. Once his balls were through she bent his cock around and pushed it through the little gap left in the ring. She had to be quick. All the prodding and gripping and pushing along with the restrictive ring meant his cock was about to surge to full size; something she never got tired of seeing. She managed to get his cock head through and with a bit of effort push the rest after it. Sure enough, up it shot, rising with every heartbeat. 'There we go, isn't that better,' she declared with a big smile. She couldn't resist him anymore, and she didn't have to. Gripping his rigid cock like a handle, she pulled him closer. *That's more like it.* She sunk her mouth around the hot, swollen head, tasting him.

'Oh yes, that's so good. Please baby, make me cum, let me cum. I want to fuck you.' Nate grabbed her hair and pushed himself deeper into her mouth. She loved him like this, desperate, primal. She didn't plan to waste it.

Emma slid her mouth back, just kissing the tip of his cock, circling it with her tongue. 'So, which is it you want, to fuck me, or to cum?'

'Both?' Nate asked, hopefully.

'Nu uh,' Emma said, rubbing her lips over his cock as she shook her head. 'Pick one.' She went back to sucking, a big smile on her face that he couldn't even see. She glanced at her watch, twenty minutes to midnight, that was about perfect.

After a long pause, he gave his answer. 'I want to be in you, more than anything.'

Goddamn he makes teasing him hard when he stays stuff like that. 'Good choice,' she told him, sitting back up and moving herself up the bed. 'How do you want me?' She winked at him.

'Just the way you are. You're perfect.'

Damn you Nathan Stevens your charming words are ruining my resolve! Emma said nothing, but lay back, feet on the bed with her knees just six inches apart. Her gaze moved from his cock to his eyes as he ate her up with them. She relished it, beckoning him with her finger. It was a bit of a cliché but she didn't care at that point. Nate climbed onto the bed, hands first, then on his knees, prowling up like a lion assessing its prey. He pushed himself up on her knees, then spread them wider, his cock jutting out towards her. His hands fell to the bed again as he moved even closer. She battled her two sides, one wanting him to ravage her, the other wanting to drive him even wilder. As he began kissing her pushed up cleavage she made her choice, and reminded him of his. 'Remember, you chose to fuck, not to cum.'

Nate just growled an agreement into her neck.

'I want you to fuck me. Own me. Show me who I belong to.' She forced the next words out, 'but don't cum. Not yet. Last until the stroke of midnight, and then, then you can fill me up just the way you want to.' *There, I said it, now it's up to him.*

Nate moved his kisses up to her mouth, kissing them gently, his nose rubbing against hers. 'Okay. And if I can't last that long?'

Emma bit her lip, the licked his lips, whispering, 'Then pull out. Ruin it on me, all over me. And clean up the mess you make.'

He didn't reply with words. His mouth was hard on hers, his tongue pushing into her, urgently, desperately, and then with no hesitation he plunged his cock into her, pushing her down into the bed. She cried out into his mouth. No space left for clever words, for any plans. Just him, in her, taking her. His cock thrust again and again as he wound his arm around behind her, pulling himself in, trying to get even deeper. Emma's legs wrapped around his back, squeezing him close, resenting even the moments their bodies weren't completely pressed against each other.

She felt him shudder, he quickly pulled back, panting. 'Oh fuck that was close,' he exclaimed. She laughed, trying to pull him back in with her feet, lifting herself up as he raised higher.

She wanted to cry out, 'Fuck me, cum in me, fill me up,' but she held herself back, staring into his eyes with pure lust, daring him to just forget it all and pump her full of his cum. He'd lifted as high as he could with her clinging on and she managed to get the tip of him back in her.

'You are insanely hot, I love you so much,' he told her.

Damn him, now I don't want to cheat. She relaxed a little, sinking back to the bed. His body followed her down. He'd calmed down enough for him to start rubbing against her, laying his shaft between her lips, taking control again, masturbating her against his cockhead. 'Oh, that feels really good,' she gasped. He pressed himself harder, grinding himself against her clit. 'Don't stop, don't stop that seriously I'm going to…'

As she climaxed he pulled back from her clit, and fucked her violently, dragging her orgasm from her clit down inside her. All the emotion, all the passion of the last few hours rose up inside her exploding in a primal shout. 'Don't stop, don't stop,' she cried, scared by her own emotions but not wanting it to end. At her prompting Nate shoved his hand behind her back, grasping her shoulder and dragging her down onto his cock, driving himself as deep as he could go.

'Oh fuck, oh fuck,' he yelled. She felt his body arch as her pussy kept clenching down on him, her orgasm coming to an end as his began. She could feel the sudden wetness inside, but then, to her amazement, he pulled back, and she looked down, his cock raised above her mound, spurt after spurt of his cum jetting out across her pussy and even up her tummy. Her view was blocked as he dropped his head onto her shoulder, He let out a cry of desperate frustration that sent shivers down her spine. He kept his body lifted above hers as she felt the last few spurts of hot wetness splatter on her skin. Nate heaved a few deep sighs then raised his head, looking at her, shaking it with a deep chuckle. 'We are fucking crazy, you know that?'

Emma gazed with adoration at this incredible man, her love igniting her need. 'I know. That was just, fuck. I didn't think you'd ruin it. That's so hot I might die.'

Nate gently kissed her lips, she could feel his smile. *What's he thinking?*

'If you think that's hot…' he left the ending unfinished as he began kissing down her neck and across her breasts and then made his way down below the bottom of the basque. Emma watched with amazement as he looked up at her, stuck out his tongue and lapped it right up the highest spurt of his cum on her abdomen.

'That tickles,' she squealed instinctively. He laughed but didn't stop, moving further down, to where it didn't tickle. To where it felt incredible. Emma dropped her head back and listened as her husband went down on her cum drenched pussy, tenderly sucking her clit as he cleaned her. *This might be the hottest thing he's ever done.* To her surprise emotions overwhelmed her. As Nate's mouth brought her close to another orgasm tears started rolling down her cheeks. 'I love you so much,' she sobbed, his hand snaking up to find hers, recognising what was happening and giving her just what she needed. She clung onto his fingers, her others grabbing hold of his hair, not to push him down, but just to hold him, to feel him, to make sure he was real.

He stayed quiet, making love to her with his mouth, sucking in her aching, needy clitoris and lapping at it with his tongue; pleasuring her among the mess he'd left. His fingers pushed in her, sandwiching her clit and g-spot, sucking and grinding and rubbing until she shattered under his touch, falling down into an orgasm that brought all her emotions with it. Tumbling down, reaching for him, needing him to catch her. And he did. Somehow he was around her, holding her as she shook with the intensity of it all. His arms, protecting her, keeping her safe.

She stayed there, held in his arms, his weight pressing down, making her secure. She could feel his breath on her cheek, carrying the musk of the semen that must be coating his beard. 'Kiss me,' she whispered.

'But I'm—'

She leaned up, finding his mouth, feeling the wetness on her face. At that moment she wanted it all over her. To be coated inside and out with him. She recalled the deep, frustrated groans he'd made as he'd pumped out his ruined orgasm over her sex. Kissing his mouth, his beard, she tasted him, licking, sucking at him before returning to his mouth. From somewhere down the hall she heard a grandfather clock chime. She smiled, opening her eyes at last. 'You can cum now.' She giggled.

'Well give me a few minutes, it was only a ruin.' Nate grinned, his beard still shiny from his endeavours.

'It was, wasn't it. Oh baby, are you going to be all horny again? In that case—' Emma rolled to her side taking Nate with her, leaning over him and grabbing the gift bag from the bedside table. She tipped out the contents on the bed, ignoring a little piece of paper that fell out and grabbing the cage. It would fit perfectly onto the ring that was already secure around Nate's cock and balls.

'Oh my god that's small' exclaimed Nate when he saw it.

'Isn't it, but it's so beautiful, and so light.' Emma was already wriggling down the bed and quickly took hold of Nate's only just flaccid cock, pushing it into the cage and sliding it onto the bar that stuck out from the ring. She picked up the strange key, its head fitting snugly into the unusual screw that was half done up on the shank of the cage. 'Oh, that's different from usual,' she commented, quickly working out how it tightened up the security screw. 'Oh baby, doesn't he like it in there, he's already trying to escape.'

True enough, Nate's cock was already trying to grow, but in such a small cage it had nowhere to go, simply pulsing angrily against the still cool surgical steel. 'You're so hot when you're mean,' Nate confessed, writhing his hips but to no avail. 'Don't you want to suck me again, let me fuck you again?' he pleaded.

'Oh I do, I do,' Emma said, pressing herself up against him again. 'But I want you like this, all horny and desperate, even more.' She paused, leaning in to whisper, 'I hope you like it too, I'm giving the key to Catherine in the morning.'

'Fuck.'

She kissed him on his nose. 'You're all sticky, and so am I. See if you can convince me to change my mind in the shower before we sleep.'

She slid off the bed, wiggling her bottom as she undid the basque, letting it drop to the ground as she walked to the bathroom. Nate sighed, adjusting the already tight cage to no avail, and got up and followed her, pausing to throw back the duvet ready for when they returned.

71

Neither of them saw the little piece of paper that had fallen from the gift bag as it fluttered to the ground behind him. It dropped, face down, under the bed, no one reading what was scrawled hastily across it:

'Nothing is as it seems. Be careful what you wish for. Get out while you can!!!'

Enticed

To the amazing team who've supported my writing from the very start. Thank you for your support, encouragement and eagle eyes!

Look at the peacock; it's beautiful if you look at it from the front. But if you look at it from behind, you discover the truth...

Pope Francis

II

Book 2 - Enticed

Breakfast in Bed

N ate woke up first. His hands went to the aching throb between his legs as he looked around the grand bedroom and across to his wife, Emma, still curled up in the heavy duvet.

No matter how often he slept in a cage, his cock always seemed to forget at about 6 am and attempt to get hard. He was used to it now, and usually, a squirt of lube around the base was all he needed to manage it. But today there was no lube on hand to ease his discomfort.

The events of the previous evening must have come to mind, as his cock seemed intent on breaking itself out of its new prison. Nate slid his hand down, cupping the small cage, tugging on it trying to relieve the pressure. After a bit of readjustment, he settled back down, nearly getting back to sleep but the piercing cry of a peacock began, an alarm even more effective than morning wood. 'Bloody stupid bird,' Nate muttered.

Emma stirred beside him. She turned, snuggling into him. 'You okay baby?' She nuzzled her mouth against his shoulder and put an arm over his chest.

'Yes thanks, honey, just, tight, and horny.'

Emma opened her eyes a crack and looked around as the rising sun started to filter through the curtains.

'Oh so it wasn't a dream,' she said. 'I wasn't sure when I woke up. It could so easily have just all been in my head.'

'Trust me, it's very real,' Nate replied, 'And this cage is definitely smaller than the one at home.'

'Oh sweetheart, your poor little cock all caged and soon I won't have the key to it. Can you imagine?' She slid her hand down and pushed Nate's out the way, wrapping her fingers around the warm steel and hot flesh that was pressing through the gaps. 'It feels so different. Not the cage, I mean, but not being able to get it out. It makes me want it even more. God, I've never wanted to give you a blowjob more than this moment.'

'Don't say that,' whined Nate. 'It's not lubed at all, this hurts.'

'Oh dear, is me squeezing it making it worse too? I can stop.' Emma moved her head up onto Nate's bare chest, her lips perched just next to his nipple. 'I still can't believe we're thinking about giving up the key for a whole year. Twelve whole months. Are we crazy?'

'Yes, completely crazy. Oh fuck, a whole year, I don't know if I can do it.'

'That's okay baby, I'm here to help you. Plus, you don't have much choice, do you? I'm not giving you the key and soon I won't even be able to if I wanted to. Isn't that what makes it so hot?' Emma's tongue lazily flicked at Nate's nipple, causing him to instantly moan, a sound that conveyed pleasure with frustration and pain that instantly turned Emma on.

'I mean,' she continued, 'it's all got to be about me now. Just like in all those captions and fantasies we read.' She paused, taking a moment to suck on his nipple and her hand on his chest rubbing the other one, making him groan again. 'I wonder how many times I'm going to cum while you can't,' she said. 'You know what, let's make a start now.' She pulled back the duvet a little and slipped her hand from Nate's chest to the top of his head, pushing ever so gently downwards to signal what she wanted.

'Oh fuck, you are so hot,' he whispered and turned on his side towards her. He kissed her deeply on the mouth before starting to move down, planting little kisses down her neck, which always made her shudder. Emma's moans began as he latched his mouth around her nipple, sucking for a moment. He pushed his knee between her legs, and then the other beside it. He kissed her breast tenderly a few more times before moving to the other and kissing around her hardened nipple, teasing her.

Emma's moans grew louder as he sucked her nipple into his mouth, his hand moving down between her legs as his knees pushed her thighs wider apart. He slipped a finger inside her, she was already so wet. 'Oh God, I want to fuck you so much right now.'

'I know darling, but you can't, not for a whole year,' she said with a teasing tone. 'No pussy for you, no cock for me. Just lots of fingers, and toys, and mouths. Suck me.'

She pushed his head more forcefully now and he slid his legs down, sinking under the duvet. Emma spread her legs wider, bringing her knees up so she was exposed and open to his mouth. She moaned out loud as his lips found her clit. She always forgot just how good it felt, it was a surprise every time.

She was overwhelmed by the thought of his cock, locked away, sold, forcing him to pleasure only her. She grabbed his head with both hands and pulled him in, one foot hooking behind his neck. Nate took it as a signal and pushed his tongue inside her, the tip of his nose grinding against her clit. Then Emma grabbed his hair in her fist and ground herself against him, she was desperate for more, for everything he could give her. His lips closed around her clit again, sucking her rhythmically as his tongue flicked over the tip of it. He knew exactly what felt best.

'Oh fuck, don't stop,' she told him, arching her back, pulling him against her. His hand curled around her leg and her fingers found it, interlocking as her other hand kept his face pressed against her sex.

'Make me cum,' she told him, suddenly so bold, feeling powerful and in charge. 'Only I cum now,' she added, the last word turning into a moan of pleasure as Nate's mouth took her into a powerful orgasm that made her shake and clutch at his hair.

He backed off, tongue gently flicking over her clit as the last waves of it subsided. He gave a frustrated little moan and kissed her thighs a few times.

'Aww sweetie, don't be frustrated. Look how well it makes you go down on me when your cock is all locked up. When you stay this horny it just makes you want to keep on giving me orgasms, doesn't it baby?'

'Mhmm, you know it does, but I'd rather...'

'I know darling, but you can't, so — I don't think I'm done.' She tapped her mound, wet with his saliva and her juices. 'Make me cum again, please.' She grinned at him before shutting her eyes and laying her head back. *This might be the best decision I've made in a long time,* she thought as his mouth began its work once more.

'When did *you* turn into such a pillow princess? Aren't you going to miss being able to suck me or a good hard fucking? What happened to my hot, submissive, wife who is never happier than on her knees or over mine?' He licked teasingly around her clit, just not quite on it, his soft tongue exploring up and down the crease of her thighs.

'Oh I will, I'll miss it terribly I'm sure. But - oh fuck, yes just there, that's good - but your mouth doing that will make it bearable, darling. And the thousands of pounds we'll be getting each month for your poor little willy to be incarcerated will also help. Oh fuck, are you edging me on purpose you bastard, let me go over.'

She grabbed his hair, trying to push his face that little bit harder between her legs that would let her cum, but he was too strong. 'Okay, I'm going to miss it, I'm going to miss it. Please let me cum...Sir?' She looked down, grinning, raising her eyebrows. His beautiful eyes gazing back up at her, his beard clamped firmly on her mons. He smiled, sucking that little bit harder, both of them holding eye contact as she shuddered and groaned with another orgasm.

* * *

A little later the two of them were curled up, Nate's caged cock pushing gently between the top of Emma's thighs. There was a knock on the door.

'Come in,' he yelled at the door as both of them sat up and covered themselves a bit more.

Catherine strode in. She was wearing a flowing floral pantsuit and some elegant heels that were tall enough to effectively mask her petite stature. 'Good morning both of you, I hope you slept well. Nathan? Any trouble down there?'

'Nothing I couldn't handle, thank you.'

She sidled up to the bed, perching herself on the corner and leaning on the elegant wooden footboard. 'Now, you probably read the contract last night, and saw that before this all begins I need you both to have a medical.'

Nate and Emma looked at each other and pulled a face. They'd got so busy with each other in the fancy bedroom that the contract had just lain, unread, on the side table.

'I've organised that for this morning.' She leaned towards them. 'While you're doing that I do have a little request. You're free to say no, but I promise you it'll be worth it. I'd like to keep it a surprise, but again, if you'd rather not...'

'What is it you want Catherine?' Nate sat up straight in the bed. She gave him a cold stare before turning back to Emma and putting on a big smile.

'Would you be so kind as to give Rex permission to enter your house?'

Nate shook his head. 'No, absolutely not. Isn't locking me up enough? Why would you need to go into our house?'

'Nathan, if you want out, just say. You're both entering into this willingly and for a considerable reward. But let's not lose sight of what it's really about, having fun! Isn't that why you wanted this, the thrill of losing control, for real?'

Nathan huffed a grumpy agreement.

'Why *do* you want to go into our house?' Emma asked.

'Three reasons. Firstly I know you only planned to be out for the evening so your cat, Mr Titmus isn't it, will need feeding.'

'Oh my God, I completely forgot about the cat,' exclaimed Emma, suddenly grateful. 'Thank you, Catherine.'

'You're welcome. Secondly,' Catherine continued, 'the medicals will take some time, and there are a few more things to sort out after that, so I wondered if you'd be willing to make a weekend of it? I'm having a little dinner party tonight and you'd be welcome to attend, or just have some time to yourselves.'

'Oh, a dinner party?' Emma's eyes went wide and she sat up in the bed.

'What's the third?' Nate interrupted before his wife got carried away.

'Well, I wanted to treat you to some fun things, extra gifts. Please, let me make it a surprise,' Catherine pleaded.

'We've been somewhat surprised already,' Emma said. 'What kind of things are we talking about?'

'Some fun things for the bedroom, is that enough detail?'

Emma looked to Nate who just shrugged. 'Yep, okay, go for it,' Emma said.

Ever since Nate had bought Emma her first vibrator she'd begun to develop a passion for sex toys. Most of the stuff they had was pretty cheap. She was keen to see just what this rich eccentric might get them.

'Wonderful. And you'll stay? You're welcome to make yourself at home. I can schedule something exciting for tomorrow if you're able to stay the whole weekend?'

The two of them looked at each other, taking each other's hands.

'What the hell, let's make a weekend of it,' Nate confirmed.

'Oh fabulous, thank you. I thought you might enjoy breakfast in bed. Alexandra will bring it up shortly. After that Elizabeth will escort you over to the medical. It's just over there,' Catherine pointed out of the window. 'I've had the stables and barn converted, it's quite lovely.'

She stood. 'I'll leave you two to it. I believe there was something I was to look after?' She raised her eyebrows at Emma.

'Oh yes, gosh, there was.' Emma turned and searched the bedside cabinet drawer, trying not to let the sheet drop that she was holding over her breasts. 'Here it is.' She turned back, the single key to the cage around her husband's cock dangling from her fingers. Emma looked at her husband as she held it out, his eyes were transfixed on it as Catherine reached out her palm in front of him. Emma laid it down, still keeping hold of the ring it was attached to. There was a moment of silence as she watched him bite his lip, and take a deep breath in. She let it go.

'Excellent,' said Catherine. 'I'll be sure to keep it somewhere very safe, I promise.' A genuine smile of satisfaction spread across her face as she closed her fist around the key and slipped it into a pocket.

As soon as Catherine was out of the door Emma was bouncing up and down. 'A dinner party, and breakfast in bed. Room service! I could get used to this. Oh my goodness what am I going to wear?'

Nate chuckled. 'Your red dress from last night was gorgeous, why wouldn't you wear that?'

'But I wore that yesterday! Oh honestly, you have no idea.' She grinned at her husband, kneeling up in bed and straddling him. 'I don't have your ke-ey, I don't have your ke-ey' she sang, putting her hands on his shoulders.

'We are insane, you know that. We barely know anything about her.'

'She is rich and wants to give us money for something we find hot anyway. What more do we need to know?' Before he could object she leaned forward and kissed him, her tongue in his mouth, grinding her still damp mound back and forth over the little cage enclosing his cock.

'Oh Nate, you have no idea how this feels. It's like a burden's been lifted. I can enjoy all the benefits of how horny and loving you're going to be without the pressure of being in charge.'

Nate pushed back a bit. 'I didn't realise it was such a burden.'

'Oh don't be like that, you know what I mean. You're the dominant one really.'

'I don't feel very dominant right now.'

'Okay but you are, it's how you are. And isn't this the craziest, hottest thing? Even if it's just for this weekend. Don't try to tell me it isn't, I can feel how hard you are in that thing.' Emma wiggled her hips, reaching down, manoeuvring his caged flesh to her wet entrance. She sank down on him, so just the tip of the cage was able to push into her.

'Oh fuck,' Nate whispered. 'It's so tight, I can barely feel you.'

'But you can, can't you baby? Can't you feel how wet I am, how needy my little hole is for you? It's so frustrating.' She leaned in, her fingers rubbing at his hard nipples. 'It's like I'm being denied too. And you know how much that turns me on.'

'Oh my God, I'm so fucking horny already.'

'And it's only going to get worse. Oh baby, imagine how good it'd feel, to just sink your cock, balls deep in me now. You're barely in, and that's all you'll be able to get, all year.' She leaned back and beamed.

Nate shook his head, 'You're fucking loving this aren't you.'

'So much!'

A knock on the door interrupted her teasing. 'Breakfast. Can I come in?'

'Just a minute,' Emma squeaked, jumping off Nate and the bed to fetch a dressing gown. 'Come in.'

Nate just pulled the sheet over himself as the door opened and Alexandra carried a tray into the room, dressed as before in the quintessential maid outfit. It was a bit of a cliche, even if her looks didn't match the usual fantasy. She paused, staring at Emma who was making her way back to the bed, and then Nate - not his eyes, but the bulge between his legs clearly visible under the bedsheet.

'Hello,' asked Nate, getting her attention. 'Can we have it over here?'

Alexandra stayed where she was. 'Yes, of course. Did you...?'

'Did we what?' Emma slipped into the bed next to her husband. Alexandra looked down, gave a little resigned snort, and tottered over in her heels, placing the tray in the middle of the bed. 'Never mind. If you need anything else let me know.'

She backed up a step, bent over from the waist and picked something off the floor, tucking it away.

'We will, thank you,' said Nate, his attention quickly moving to the delicious cooked breakfast in front of them. Emma noticed a flash of irritation on the maid's face, it didn't make her any prettier. She soon forgot about it as the irresistible smell of cooked bacon took over any other thoughts and they tucked into breakfast.

A Most Unusual Medical

A call to their room informed them Elizabeth was ready to take them over for the medical. They quickly got dressed and met her in the hallway. They were led downstairs and through the house, via something of a maze of wood-panelled corridors. They emerged from a heavy set of doors into another gravelled area, the bright sunshine causing them all to squint.

Elizabeth seemed keen to talk as she led them over to a side-building that was signed as 'The Stables'. It had been converted into something more useful. She engaged Emma in conversation, while Nate dragged back a little behind them. She knew exactly why but now he was locked back in a tight little cage Emma was more than happy for him to inflict pain on himself.

'So have you decided to take the deal already?' the PA asked.

Emma felt like there was a little bit of judgement in her tone and got a bit defensive. 'You know about it then? It's the chance of a lifetime. She's even offered us one of her paintings if we move quickly.'

'She did?' Elizabeth sounded surprised. 'Which one? Not the Vettriano?'

'Yes actually, supposedly it's worth £150,000.'

'If not more, to her,' Elisabeth mused. 'God, she must really want you two - like you both, I mean,' she corrected herself.

Before Emma could question her phrasing they'd arrived at the large double doors of 'The Stables'. Elizabeth knocked and the door was opened by someone who was very obviously a nurse. Emma heard Nate's intake of breath as he caught up to them and paused.

Emma looked her up and down. *Oh good, another unreasonably attractive woman to contend with. At least this one's shorter than me.* Though the nurse would be classed as petite, there was a confidence, and solidity to her that stood out despite the ultra-feminine uniform. While the outfit she was wearing wasn't completely unprofessional, it was certainly navigating the boundary between work attire and roleplay costume very skillfully.

The scooped neckline showed off a fair bit of the nurse's olive skin. It teased the tops of her pert bosom, lifted and pushed together by some magic bra no doubt, to produce a cleavage that would comfortably hold a lot of medical devices.

The uniform was plain white except for red piping around the hems of the short sleeves and, most compellingly, the zip that formed a bold red line right down the front of it. The little zip dangled teasingly between her breasts, not quite drawn up to the top. Even Emma felt a compulsion to pull it, she could only grin at how it must affect her husband.

'Hello, I'm Nurse Englemann.' She spoke in a soft accent, English wasn't her first language Emma guessed. 'Call me Mené if you'd prefer.' She reached out her hand, to Nate first this time. As the nurse stepped forward Emma noticed the tight dress ride up her thighs even higher. She looked up at Nate, who actually managed to look Mené only in the face as he shook her hand. *Good boy,* Emma thought, *easier when your cock's tight in a cage isn't it.*

Mené turned and gave a very warm smile to Emma, shaking her hand too.

'Men-ay, was it?' said Emma, sounding it out. She grinned, looking up. 'The hat, the hat's a nice touch.' Emma chuckled, staring at the little matching nurse's cap, perched on top of the long curls of her almost black hair.

'I know, isn't it. It is like one I had as a child. As you might guess, the uniform was provided. I get to keep it though! Even the heels!' The nurse did a little spin, she was clearly enjoying herself. Emma liked her immediately.

'I'll leave you in Nurse Englemann's capable hands, have fun,' Elizabeth told them before twirling away, her heels crunching over the gravel. This time Nate didn't do so well, his gaze lingering on her bottom for far too long. Emma gave him a dirty look when he finally glanced back.

Mené took Emma's hand, 'Come in, come in, we have lots to do! Welcome to the clinic!' She let go and spread her arms. 'Isn't it adorable. I think it's temporary but it's all very professional looking.'

'You haven't been here before?' Nate asked.

'No, my first day here. I was travelling around Europe when I got offered this.

'Ah yes, I noticed your accent' Emma said.

'Right. I'm taking time out to travel. I demobilised in January, I was a nurse, in the Israeli army.'

'Oh wow, that's so cool!' *Damn, a military nurse, Catherine isn't messing around.* 'Mené is Hebrew?'

'Hmm… Aramaic and Greek. My parents were history teachers. At least it's unique. I'm lucky it's not Belshazzar or something.' She laughed, twirling again and heading inside.

Mené led them through the pristine white clinic area. On one wall was a large internal window which just had a curtain on the other side. There were very authentic looking examination tables and chairs, and a little administration area which they walked over to. Emma and Nate sat on one side of the desk while she elegantly seated herself opposite.

Emma couldn't help thinking of this petite woman running around with a big rifle. There was something very sexy about that.

'Welcome both of you, I'm your nurse, and here to carry out a medical. I understand you're both here expecting that.' Her accent sounded a little like French as she read off a clipboard, sometimes looking up.

'We will be joined by Doctor Hastings a little later.' She caught Emma's eye and fanned her face, mouthing 'So hot' to her with a conspiratorial smirk.

Emma sniggered and Nate looked up from apparently being lost day-dreaming about red zippers, having missed the exchange.

Mené scanned down the page and turned over to the next, revealing a long list of questions and data boxes. 'This is a very extensive medical, wow. You're both aware of how intimate some of this gets?' She looked at them both, less jokey now.

Nate replied, 'Yes, we can guess.' He took Emma's hand. 'It's fine, whatever you need, we're up for it.'

'Excellent.' Mené beamed. 'Me too, this is a bit different from my last job. As long as you're both happy then I think it should be fun.'

'I have some questions for you both, and then hopefully Doctor Handso… Hastings will be with us and we can do some other tests'. Mené beamed another cheeky grin at Emma. 'Of course, everything here is confidential, just shared between ourselves and your… sponsor.'

'Huh, of course, I wouldn't expect anything less,' said Nathan.

Mené worked through some of their basic details, any existing or previous conditions. It all seemed very humdrum until she turned over the page.

'Number of sexual partners. Is this something you are okay discussing in front of each other?'

Nathan laughed. Emma smiled, 'Yes, it's not a problem, very easy in fact. One.' She squeezed her husband's knee.

'One.' Nathan said too, putting his hand on hers.

'You are so cute,' declared Mené. 'Sorry, not very professional, but that is so nice.'

'Thank you,' said Nate. 'We think so too'.

Mené moved to fill in a column of boxes. 'And how often do you have sex?'

'Umm, a lot?' answered Emma, looking at Nate.

'What kind of sex do you mean?' he said.

Mené laughed and scanned down the page, 'That, is an excellent question. Apparently, we have options.'

'Okay, how many times in the last month have you had, 'penis in vagina' sex. Eugh, could there be a less sexy way to describe it?' she complained. She looked at them both with narrowed eyes. 'How often do you fuck?' Something about the accent made it sound ten times hotter.

Emma thought back, 'Fucking… three times I think'

'Three? In a month?' Mené asked, double-checking. 'That doesn't sound a lot'

'Keep working through the list,' suggested Nate.

'Okay, fellatio – blow jobs?'

Emma looked pleased with this one, '15, at least'. She winked at Nate.

'Okay, that's more like it. Handjobs, you on him?'

'Probably about 20?' she looked to Nate who nodded.

'Wow, okay, I see why 'a lot' now. Who's a lucky boy,' she smiled at Nate. It suddenly hit home that he was about to get a medical from this very attractive, sexually open nurse. The realisation made his cage very uncomfortable.

'Okay, so Emma now. How many manual orgasms, from Nate?

'Wait are you asking about sex, or orgasms?'

'That's a good point. Sex, 'manual sex'. How do you say it?' She stuck two fingers up in the air with a few thrusts, 'finger-banging?' She looked pleased with her language knowledge.

Emma laughed at the description, and said, 'Oh maybe 20, 25.'

Mené wrote it down. 'My goodness. How do you two have time for anything else? What about cunnilingus?'

Emma looked up to think about it and inadvertently let out a little moan that surprised everyone including herself. 'Oh, I'm sorry, God, err, 10, 12 probably.'

Mené looked impressed. 'Damn, you're going to have to tell me where I find a man like him.'

Nate looked like the cat who'd got the cream.

It didn't last for long as she asked, 'Okay, so yes, now, orgasms, how many orgasms do you have a month, Emma?'

'Oh, that's hard to guess. Like maybe, 100.'

'One, hundred? Nate gives you 100 orgasms a month?' Mené put the clipboard down. 'Seriously? What is your secret? Can I...' Mené put her hand up in the air over the desk.

Emma laughed loudly, realising what she was after, leaned forward, high-fiving her new favourite nurse.

Mené coughed and straightened her dress, grinning, 'So unprofessional' she joked. 'How about you Nate, how many orgasms?'

His answer took long enough for her to stop and look up. Nate bit his lip, looking as though he was unsure. 'Errm, three I think?' Blushing a little he turned to Emma.

'I'm pretty sure it was six.' She looked at Mené. 'But half of those were ruined orgasms, are we including those?'

Mené pulled a confused face. 'What the hell is a ruined orgasm?' She looked at her sheet. 'Well damn, look at that, ruined orgasms are next. I really should have read this more carefully. That still doesn't answer my question.'

'Darling, would you like to explain to the lovely nurse what a ruined orgasm is, and why I give you them?'

Nathan looked pained, both emotionally, and physically. 'Umm, well. It's when you go over the point of no return, so you start cumming, well, ejaculating more importantly. But then, you stop.'

'So, it all pumps out but you don't get stimulated?' Mené was absolutely fascinated. 'But why would you do that, that's when it feels best, yes?'

Nate nodded. 'God yes, always when it would feel the best. It's to stop that, and I don't know, it's hard to explain.'

Emma chimed in. 'No, it isn't, it keeps him much hornier. You know how guys are after they cum? Lose all interest, fall asleep as soon as you let them? If you ruin it, they stay horny, and interested, and get back to being very attentive much faster.'

Mené smacked the table with her hand. 'How have I never heard about this before, this is so good. Although, my lovers would not have been pleased about it. You are just the perfect husband, giving up your pleasure for your wife.'

'You have no idea,' muttered Nate.

'Okay. Three orgasms, and three ruined. I am curious. Only a few boxes left. Anal sex - frequency?'

'None,' Emma said, a little less confidently.

'None this month?' The nurse looked up.

'Not for a while' said Nate.

'Okay then,' said Mené, moving on. 'And last of all, masturbation. Nathan, don't be embarrassed, we're all friends here.'

'Zero.'

Mené stopped and looked at him again. 'Really, you don't masturbate?'

'He wishes,' giggled Emma.

Nate just shook his head as Mené looked at them both with fascination. 'There is something here I don't know about, I'm so curious!'

'Mhmm,' agreed Emma. 'Don't worry, you'll find out soon.' She was clearly enjoying herself now. She looked at her husband trying to cope with the upheaval of physical and emotional experiences he was going through. As much as she had sympathy for him, she knew, deep down, he was loving this.

Mené started to stand and then looked down at the sheet. 'Oh sorry, one more, Emma, masturbation for you?'

Nate's gaze was straight back on her. She smiled whimsically to herself, knowing what she was about to say was going to make things even worse.

'Hmm, now let me count.' Her heart was racing as she enjoyed her husband's undivided attention. She made a little thing of bobbing her head back and forth, and moving her fingers around, adding up.

'Honestly, I'm not sure, but 15, 20 orgasms perhaps.'

'What!' said Nathan. 'That many?'

'Oh yes baby, I've had lots to think about this week, haven't I. And you know how horny you get me.'

'How long have you two been married?' Mené asked. 'It's not on the sheet, I'm just curious.'

'Six years in August,' Nate told her.

'This might be unprofessional but whatever you have happening you are 'serious goals' as they say.'

'Well thank you Mené, that's lovely of you to say,' Emma said, 'And if it's time for our physicals, then you're about to find out just what the secret is, or part of it anyway. I have to say, I think I'm more excited about your reaction than my dear husband's.'

Mené stood. 'In that case, let us start. If you could both go through there and change into some gowns. Doctor Hastings should be arriving shortly.'

The couple went into the small changing room and bathroom. Nate wrapped his arms around his wife, and hugged her, letting out the little frustrated moan that always got her horny. 'Looks like you're having fun.' He whispered in her ear, the hug turning into more of a feel-up.

'Mhmm, I certainly am, isn't she fabulous! How about you honey? Been thinking about how that hot little nurse is about to discover your secret? She's either a great actor or she has no idea.'

'Yeah, I don't think she knows. I…I'm a bit overwhelmed, honestly. This mix of extreme arousal along with anxiety. You're going to look after me, right?' He pulled her in close, holding on tight.

'Of course I am, baby. If this is too much, we can just stop, go home. I'm serious.'

He hugged her even harder before kissing her neck, then her ear. 'Don't you fucking dare, my love. Overwhelm me. I mean it. Remember our safewords?' She nodded. 'Unless I use those you feel free to go for it, you hear me?' She nodded again. His hands moved to her buttons, undressing her as he whispered. 'I love you, I trust you, we need to make the most of this crazy, incredible opportunity. You realise we're getting paid for this!' He unclasped her bra, grabbing her breasts as though he was holding on for his life. 'So what are you going to do, my love. When is enough, enough?'

'Not till I've blown your fucking mind,' she whispered back.

A polite knock on the door from Mené brought them back to reality. 'When you are ready, Doctor Hastings is arriving.'

They hurriedly stripped down. Emma stopped Nate from putting the robe on with a touch. And pressed her naked body against his, her hand cupping his caged cock and balls. 'You are so hot, Mr Stevens. I'd let you do anything to me right now if this wasn't all caged up.'

'Is that supposed to help, you wicked woman,' he said with adoration in his eyes.

'Nope, just making it worse! Come on then,' she said, slipping on the gown, 'let's go live out a medical fantasy. I hear the doctor is super hot!' She stood by the door, her gown barely done up.

'What!' exclaimed Nate, 'he's what? Oh shit, fuck my life.' Looking down he pointed at his cock, bulging in its cage, 'Do not let me down, little man.' He followed his wife out. Nurse Englemann was bending over getting something out of a low cupboard. Emma looked at her, then grinned. 'You're so fucked' she mouthed as Mené stood up.

'Welcome back Nathan. Can I ask you to stand on these scales for me.' She noted down his weight, and then his height as she had just for Emma.

'Okay, that's great. Can I get you to sit on this examination table now. This is where it's going to get quite intimate.'

Emma bit her finger in anticipation. They'd played around with this as a shared fantasy for a long time. Seeing it come to life was enthralling.

'Please lift your gown for me, Nathan.'

He hesitated, of course he did. Emma decided to help. 'Oh please, let me.' She stepped up, glancing from her husband's face to Mené's. She didn't know which she wanted to watch more. She decided on the nurse. Drawing the gown slowly up to tease every last moment out of it she watched Mené's eyes open wide and her mouth form a perfect 'O'.

'Oh my God,' she exclaimed. 'I've heard about these, but never seen one! Now I understand. That. Is. So. Cool. How does it work, is that where the… Oh… I am stupid. The instructions make sense now. Look, it says it here, "Ring for the keys". I thought they meant the keys for a cupboard. I am sorry, I can't get your measurements while you're tucked away in there. Give me one moment.'

Mené virtually skipped over to the phone on the wall, which was pretty impressive in five-inch heels. Emma took a seat right next to him so she could whisper to Nathan. 'You're about to get your cock checked out by a chastity nurse, my darling husband. Is it going to make me proud?'

'It's nearly breaking the cage already if you hadn't noticed'

'Oh, I doubt that, hubby. Isn't titanium even stronger than your steel one? Gosh, look at her.' Emma nodded to Mené who was waiting on the phone. 'Is it just me who keeps wanting to pull down that little red zip?' She nuzzled her mouth against his ear.

Nate groaned, grabbing his caged cock to readjust it.

'Now, now, be good. Let's get you sitting on those hands please, we don't want them getting in the way, baby.'

Nate reluctantly moved them under his bottom as Emma continued whispering. 'What do you think she's going to do to you, my love? Measure you I'm sure. Are you going to get as big as you can for me? Look at her. I bet she's played with some big cocks in her time. Do you think she'll say anything about yours, how you, measure up?'

'Aren't you jealous?' Nate tried to retaliate.

'Nope, not in the slightest. It's my cock, well, it's on loan to some crazy woman but it's mine and I'm loving watching this happen to it. Plus isn't she adorable? I don't think I've ever meant it more when I say –' she watched Mené walk back to them, call completed, '– I'd totally do her.'

Nathan groaned, pushing his head back, and arching his back a little.

'Having fun?' Mené said. 'Apologies for the delay, I hadn't quite grasped the…nature of the situation. Doctor Hastings is on his way with the key. While we wait, Emma, tell me. How long have you been locking up your husband's penis?'

The two women discussed how they'd got started with it all a few years ago, and how it had brought all kinds of benefits. Nate just lay there as they talked about him like they were old friends discussing the weather. Well, apart from the peels of laughter and Mené's genuine amazement at how it had changed their love life.

'Don't you miss the, you know, fucking though? I know I would,' said the nurse.

'Well, you didn't quite cover all the options in your questions earlier,' Emma told her.

'I didn't? What did I miss?'

Emma leaned right over Nate's half-naked body and whispered into Mené's ear. The nurse burst into laughter. 'You're kidding! Who wears it, you or him?'

Emma shrugged, 'Both, but him wearing it, over the cage, is my favourite. Always hard, pick what size you want, and the way he fucks me… like a caged tiger. It's crazy. And none of this 'one and done'. Oh no, he keeps going for as long as I need. It's actually got him much fitter!'

'This is amazing, it's like "pick your own penis". I had a girlfriend I used one with but not much. I can see why you'd like it though. Wow. How big do you go?'

Emma bit her lip and raised her hands, slowly making them wider apart until Mené's eyes opened wide. 'That big! I had a lover that size and he nearly split me in two!'

'Yeah, I know it took me time to work up to it but wow, sometimes nothing else will do. Did you break up with him because of it? You're kinda teeny after all,' Emma asked.

'No, no, like you say, you get used to it. Then, you need it, right? No, the asshole was fucking my friend too.'

'Oh no, I'm so sorry.'

'I know, stupid guy. We could have shared. Instead, I lost a big cock *and* my friend.'

'Okay, wow. That's so outside my realm of experience.'

'And don't you ever regret that,' advised Mené. 'What you have, it's so special. I mean it. And this,' she pointed to his caged cock, 'is so fucking hot I cannot even say. If I'd known about these things I could have caged that asshole up and saved all the problems.'

The Chastity Nurse

Their little conversation stopped as the door to the clinic opened and in walked a life-size television doctor. Well, that's what Emma assumed, as no man deserved to be that beautiful and smart enough to practise medicine.

Six foot and a few inches, the blond demi-god strode into the room with barely a glance at the unusual sight on the table. 'Nurse Englemann, good to see you again. And you must be Emma. Catherine's told me all about you. It's a pleasure to meet you. And Nathan, don't get up, and don't worry, it's nothing I haven't seen before. Catherine and I go back a long way.'

Feeling slightly giddy Emma reached out her hand and shook his. She turned to Mené and mouthed 'wow'.

Mené coughed, 'I told you' and both of them giggled. Emma realised she'd held his soft, large hand for uncomfortably long and let it go. She put her hand down on the table to steady herself and only to grab poor Nate's cock cage.

'Oh God, sorry darling. Anyway, wasn't the point to get some keys?' She smiled a cheeky smile at the doctor.

'It is indeed,' he confirmed. 'However, there's a rule I'm afraid. Catherine was very clear. I'm afraid we can't unlock the cage unless your husband's hands are restrained.

Finally, Nate spoke up. 'What the hell, where was that in the contract?'

'It was honey, in Catherine's original email, remember?'

'Shit, yes, I remember. This is ridiculous, do they really think I can't keep my hands off my cock.'

Doctor Hastings spoke up, 'I've been told if you still want to stop this you're welcome to. But you know what you'll lose?'

'God, how many times does she need to remind us? Okay, fine, fine, tie me up, whatever.'

'Thank you, I'm sorry if it's frustrating. Catherine does love her little rules. The restraints are on the chair, if you'd like to move across for me.

For the first time they looked properly at the chair that was by the big glass window. It was an authentic gynaecological chair, in an attractive aquamarine. That didn't stop it being scary, with its stirrups and Velcro restraints. He was going to be properly helpless in that thing. Nate covered himself up and reluctantly swung his legs down, walking to the chair and jumping a little when he sat on the cold plasticky surface. Mené and Emma walked over together. The two already looked as thick as thieves.

'See baby,' Emma began, 'this is what we have to go through for lots of check-ups. Welcome to my life.' She gave him a little kiss on his cheek. 'This is still so hot. Go with it.'

Mené tapped one of the padded stirrups. 'Your calf goes up here, Nate. Thank you, and the other one. Emma? Can you help me tie him up.'

'Oh yes please!' she said, beaming. Nate's eyes showed a mix of fear and arousal as the two women tightened up the wide straps around his legs, and then did the same with his arms.

'Give a wiggle, honey. Is that all secure?' Emma stepped back. She looked at her husband, bound in the chair, escape was clearly futile. He was truly helpless. She bit her lip, this was way sexier than it should be. She remembered his words earlier, and stepped between his legs, folding the gown up, giving his caged cock nowhere to hide. She cupped it in her hand, stroking the little strips of exposed skin.

'I love you, baby, are you going to make me proud?' She looked to Mené, who'd picked up a tape measure. 'You're going to measure him right?' The nurse nodded. 'Oh darling, are you going to get as big as you can for me? I don't want my new friend here laughing at your little dicklet.'

Emma saw Mené make eyes at Doctor Hastings. *Yeah, that's right, I am a piece of work, you better believe it.*

She turned to the doctor. 'May I unlock him?'

'I'm sorry Emma, Catherine…'

'Okay, okay, the rules. Bah.' She turned back to her husband, leaned over and kissed the tip of his cage. It was very wet with his pre-cum. 'Miss you already.'

She stepped back, her fingers running along his tied up leg, tickling his bare foot. 'Oh honey, I'm going to have to let the super hot, military-trained, nurse get your cock out, I hope that's okay?'

'Unless you want me to do it?' offered Doctor Hastings, finally seeming to warm up a bit and join in the fun.

Nate regained the power of speech. 'No, no, really, Nurse Englemann would be - good.'

Mené turned and took the offered key from the doctor. Stepping up to where Emma had just been, between his legs. 'Well this is a first. Let's see what we've got here shall we.' She pulled out a pair of medical gloves from a little pocket and snapped them onto her hands. 'Let us get to work.'

She wrapped her fingers around the warm cage. Lifting it up, looking underneath, inspecting it from every angle. 'This is so cool,' she said to no one in particular. 'Does it hurt, what's it like to be in it?'

Emma watched the two of them, feeling strangely detached. It was like the porn clips or gifs she'd watched so often with Nate, but this was real. It was her husband getting his caged cock fondled by the beautiful nurse. A complex mix of emotions flowed through her. She tried to make sense of them. Jealousy for sure, envy that it wasn't her doing this to him, but all that was far outweighed by a strange joy at seeing this deep-seated fantasy come to life. It was more than arousal. It was an intoxicating cocktail of nerves, excitement and visceral pleasure.

As she watched Mené take the key and start to inspect the cage she had to hold herself from leaping forward, intervening. She gripped the table behind her with both hands, wishing she was tied up to, that would make this a lot easier.

Nate struggled with his helplessness too. But he couldn't do anything about it. The experience of being restrained like this made everything so much more intense. Just knowing this woman could do anything she wanted to him must be an overpowering sensation.

Nurse Mené repeated the question, 'Nathan? Does it hurt?'

'Yes, sometimes. Not very often now, it was worse at first. I guess my cock has got used to it, but sometimes, waking me up, trying to escape, or when a super hot nurse is playing with it, yeah.'

Mené turned to Emma, 'He is so cute! Was he always like this, or is this thing magic?' She waggled the cage again.

'He was always cute but, well anything's cuter when it's wrapped up, right?' Emma smiled.

'Hmm, yes, well, let's see what we have under the wrapping. I do have some work to do, some measurements.' She located the keyhole at the top of the lock, sliding the small metal key into it and twisting it. When it didn't open she looked a little confused.

'The whole lock slides out, with the key, like a tumbler,' Emma explained.

Nurse Englemann tugged gently on the key and sure enough, the entire locking mechanism slid out smoothly. 'Oh, that's clever!'

As soon as the cage was unlocked Nate let out a groan of relief. The force of his erection pushed the front of the cage off the base, lifting it as his cock began to finally be allowed to grow.

'That is so cute,' declared Mené. 'It's like a little hat now! Wow, it really does keep you down, doesn't it. Let's free it up properly.' She took hold of the cage portion and slid it off the head of Nate's cock. Strands of precum dangled between his skin and the metal. 'Is this lube or...'

'No, it's precum. He leaks it most of the time,' Emma said. 'It's pretty hot, how it used to be my panties that'd get damp, now it's him too!'

Mené turned her attention to the ring encasing Nate's cock and balls. 'How does this come off?' She turned to Doctor Hastings.

'It doesn't, not with that design,' he informed her. 'You have to wait for the patient to become flaccid before removal.'

'It works like a cock ring though,' Emma added. 'It helps keep him hard. You can move that bit with the lock, out of the way though, just give it a twist, that's what I do.'

'Best toy ever,' Mené said to herself, giving the ring a 90-degree twist. 'Okay, let's see how you measure up.' She checked the paperwork. "Unassisted length and girth". That's what he's reaching now?'

She checked with the doctor, he nodded. 'It'd be better without the ring but as Emma said, removal of that isn't an option right now.'

The nurse picked up the measuring tape and placed the cold little metal tab on the tip of Nate's cock, pulling it down the top of it to where it met the base.

'Wait, wait,' said Nate, 'you measure it from underneath surely?' He looked from the nurse to his wife, who just shrugged her shoulders.

'That's what you told me,' she said back to him. 'You're in the hands of an expert now.'

'Think about it, Nathan,' Mené said as she leaned in to read the numbers. 'If you're fucking your beautiful wife here, this is how deep you go. Hmm, yes 13 centimetres.'

'Five and an eighth inches,' the doctor added to the notes.

'Oh my God, you always said you were six inches baby, you're only just five.' Emma looked genuinely surprised.

'It gets bigger than that, I promise!' Nate wailed.

Emma stepped up close to Mené, and asked in a soft voice, 'How does it compare to the ones you've known, nurse?'

Mené wrapped her fingers right around his cock in a fist. She turned to Emma, biting her lip and grinning. 'I have not had a boyfriend I could just wrap my fingers around. I'm sorry Emma, it is small. No wonder you want to lock him up.' She gave her a wicked wink that Nathan couldn't see.

Emma played along. 'I didn't think he was six inches, but he always insisted he was. You really aren't supposed to be able to get your hand around them?'

Mené acted up even more. 'No, not for a *real* cock anyway. I think I could just about for my first boyfriend but we were only teens, his cock got way bigger. Even then, it started off larger than this.'

Emma could see the effect their words were having on her husband. He was almost speechless, he managed to stutter out, 'But it does get bigger, please...'

Mené ignored him and measured around the circumference. '9cm around. Hmm, I thought it'd be less.'

Doctor Hastings stepped forward. 'Emma, as fun as this is, I'm running a bit short on time. There's another room next door. Do you think you could join me? We need to give you a quick medical too as I think you know.'

'Aww, can't I stay? Having Nate like this is so much fun.'

'I'm afraid not, but we'll be right next door. He isn't going anywhere.' He flashed her a dazzling smile.

'All right then.' Emma walked over to Nate and kissed him on the cheek. 'I'll leave you in Mené's capable hands. Be a good boy.'

'No, Emma, don't go, please.'

'It's okay baby, I'm just going to be next door with an unbelievably handsome doctor while you're helplessly bound in here.' She leaned in and whispered, 'It appears I need some education about cock size. I saw a big bulge in his pants. I bet he's bigger than six inches. Maybe I'll find out.'

With that, she gave him a big, deep kiss on the mouth and brushed her fingers across his nipples. 'He is all yours,' she said to Mené.

Emma walked briskly across the room, stealing a last glance at her bound husband, and went through the door with the doctor following after. They rounded the corner and stopped on the other side of the big glass one-way window. 'We can see them, but they can't see us,' he explained.

'Oh fun! It's like an interrogation. Can we hear them?'

'We can,' said the doctor, flicking a switch. The sound came through immediately.

Mené stepped up to Nate. 'Alone at last, Nathan. Are you enjoying yourself, I am. This is the best job I've ever had. I guess I better perform if I'm going to keep it. Hmm, maximum size - that shouldn't take long.'

She reached over for a large jar and pumped a few shots of a thick white lubricant into her gloved hands.

'This might be a little cold, but I'm sure it'll warm up soon.'

She gently stroked the lubricant cream over his pulsing cock, teasing it with her fingers. Nate groaned, throwing his head back. 'Please, I need more.'

'Oh don't worry, I think I've got a good idea what you need. Lucky Emma, in that room all alone with that handsome doctor. She's having some kind of medical too, isn't she? I wonder what that involves. Did you see how turned on she is by all this, Nate? I hope she doesn't do anything she regrets.

He just shook his head, 'She wouldn't, I know her.'

'Yes, I'm sure you're right. But what about the medical, do you think he's touching her, like I am you? Maybe she's in there right now, spreading her legs, letting the gorgeous man slide his fingers…'

'No, no, no. You're wicked. I thought you were nice, Mené.'

'That's Nurse Englemann to you, Nathan. You're the one tied down and completely at my mercy, I'd be careful how you speak to me. I mean, I could do… anything.'

She slid her hand down his shaft and wrapped her fingers around his balls, beginning to roughly massage them as her other hand stroked increasingly fast up and down his cock. 'Or maybe the doctor is the one lying back,' she mused, 'his big cock out, and she is stroking it just like this. But it needs two hands I bet, not like yours.'

Doctor Handsome

'She is good!' exclaimed Emma, peering through the glass and listening to what was being said.

'I know, isn't she,' Doctor Hastings replied. 'I have to say I'm very impressed. I only met her for the first time this morning, I thought she might be a bit of a gamble. Anyway, I didn't just bring you in here to spy on him, as much fun as that is. I do need to give you a quick once over if that's okay.' He patted the examination table.

'I have a question,' Emma said as she hopped up. 'How big is an average penis?'

'Five to seven inches, it depends on which country, but that's average.'

'So he is average, he wasn't lying?' Emma lay back on the inclined table.

'He's on the lower end but yes.'

'Why do you think he gets so turned on being teased about it, Doctor Hastings?'

'I don't have a lot to go on, but from what I know Nate is quite an alpha male, his natural tendency is dominance?'

'You mean despite him being tied up in there and agreeing to cage his cock for a year, yes, I'd say so.'

'Well, in that case, I'd guess that it's one of the few things he can't do much about. That gives him a thrill, but also means it carries no burden that there's more he could be doing. It's like a shortcut past the part of him that always wants to be in control. It's very common and strangely unrelated to actual size. The same is true for some women, did you know that?'

'They want bigger cocks?' said Emma, laughing.

101

'No that's a different thing altogether.' He grinned. 'No for many women it's their breast size, they fetishise it just the same way as men do their penis size. As much as they'd never admit it, the idea of being restricted or even punished for having small breasts arouses them.'

'I have never heard that.' She glanced down at her own body. 'But okay, I can believe that. So, I'm okay teasing him about it? Not doing any harm?'

'None at all, he seems very resilient. I expect Catherine has far worse to throw at him than you can come up with so teasing him sometimes is good practice.' He put a cuff around her arm. 'I'm just going to test your blood pressure. Hopefully, Mené's doing the same next door.' They looked through the window. Mené was bent leaning over Nate, wrapping the pressure cuff around his arm. It appeared the zipper on her dress had finally 'slipped' as the view down her top was apparently irresistible to her husband.

He could have shut his eyes... as if.

After a few basic questions and checks, all the while watching her husband ogle the nurse next door, Emma had an idea, 'Doctor?'

'Please, call me Graham.'

'Okay, Graham, He can't see in here at all right?'

'No, it's one way.'

'But are there speakers, could he hear?'

'Yes, I think so.' The doctor checked around the curtains and found the relevant switch. 'Here it is.'

'Are we nearly done, with my medical?' Emma asked.

'A few more things but yes, nearly, why?'

Emma bit her lip and gave a wicked smile, beckoning him closer.

* * *

'Hmmm, your blood pressure is high Nathan, why might that be?' asked Mené, her breasts pushed up his chest and abdomen squishing against his bare, full balls.

From the way she skipped about, she appeared to be having the time of her life. She noted down the reading with a comment beside it about 'unusual circumstances' and a little smiley face.

'Okay, that's almost all the measurements done. Just one more, or well, as many as possible, according to the instructions.'

'Hmm? What do you mean, what are you measuring?' asked Nate in a delirious voice.

'I'll give you a clue Nathan, it is measured in millilitres.' She cupped his balls with her gloved hand. 'Volume.'

His head snapped up. 'Oh my God, really?'

'Apparently so, let me just read the full instructions.' She slowly scanned down what seemed to be a lengthy description. 'Hmm, okay, yes. Oh great, I know what that is now. Oh, wow, I've never tried that before. Hah, I bet he won't, oh well, that's only optional.' She looked up with a beaming smile. 'Oh Nathan, you are in trouble. I'd apologise in advance but I suspect I'm going to love this. I think my future boyfriends are going to hate what you've taught me today.'

She fetched a stack of little plastic beakers, put them on a wheeled table, and then paused, went over to the desk, and fetched out a small packet from her own bag. She put that on the table, hefting the large bottle of lube onto it, and wheeled it over.

Finally, she fetched a stool that was against the wall, put it on the floor between Nathan's spread legs, and sat on it.

'Okay, ready Nathan? Do you need any water?' He shook his head. His cock was rigid, the cock cage ring keeping it bigger and harder than it had been in a long time. He was desperate for release, and clearly figured this might be his best chance, especially while Emma was out of the room.

Mené lubed her hand again, rubbed them together to warm it a little, and reached out, stroking her hand softly from the tip to the base, letting the thick lube soften on his hot skin.

'Oh, you are so hard now. What a shame Emma isn't here to see. I don't think you're much bigger though, just harder. Does this feel good, Nathan? Have you guessed what I'm going to measure next?'

'My cum?' he said with hope in his voice.

'Your semen volume, yes, clever you. It says I have to milk it out of you and measure how much you produce. I have these little cups to catch it in, which might be a challenge. Your balls really feel full now, I'm quite intrigued how much we'll get out of them.'

Nathan moaned as her hand strokes got faster, topping each one with a little twist on his cock head. Mené's voice dropped low so Emma could barely hear through the speaker 'So is this what she does, Nathan, all those many handjobs she gives you, just leaving you full, no satisfying orgasm at the end?'

'Yes, yes, most of them, some of them.'

'While you make her cum, isn't that frustrating?'

He mumbled agreement but was struggling to express himself as her relentless strokes took him closer to what he craved.

Suddenly she stopped, gripping his cock a bit harder with her hand. 'Wait, wait. You said you two were the only ones who… Nathan, am I only the second girl ever to give you a handjob?'

He raised his head, nodding. His breath was coming in ragged bursts now. 'Please, don't, stop.'

'I feel so special. It's a shame Emma's not here, she would love this. Maybe she's watching though, they can see through there if they want I think.' She gave another dozen long, squeezing strokes, massaging his full balls with her spare gloved hand.

'So that means… only your wife has given you blowjobs too? This is so cute. It really makes me want to suck you, isn't that bad.' She moved her mouth closer as she began stroking again to his rising groans.

'It'd be so unprofessional, Nathan. Sucking on your cock until you cum. I guess I could just spit it in the cup.'

Nate just stared at the nurse, utterly transfixed, every stroke was keeping him near the edge now. Either she was doing it by accident or she knew exactly what she was doing.

There was a click from somewhere above them and some white noise before a low moan came through into the room.

Mené slowed her stroking, looking around. 'Did you hear something?' she asked him.

'You're sure he can't see through?' came a voice from speakers above them. 'If he's going to let her then I don't see why I can't. Let me see it.'

Mené seemed to genuinely blush a little. 'Was that Emma? Oh damn, they were watching, that's so embarrassing.' She straightened up and began stroking more vigorously.

Nathan meanwhile was straining in his bonds trying to look over his shoulder through the mirrored glass.

'Oh my God, you said you were above average, that's big, Doctor, no question,' came the slightly metallic tones of his wife. There was a male chuckle. 'Mené thinks you're really cute, you know, and she hasn't even seen this magnificent cock. It's so big! It's really okay if I...?'

Mené made a gasp. 'Nathan, oh my God, did you hear that? She's playing with his dick, what a lucky girl! He is so dreamy!' Mené stroked him even faster as slurping and sucking sounds started over the intercom. Nathan bucked in the chair, trying to get himself free. He had no chance.

Mené kept up her relentless stroking. 'Wow, she is really going for it! What a lucky doc.' The nurse appeared quite flushed from what she was hearing. She kept stroking as she heard a noise behind her, turning to see and only just stopping herself from laughing out loud.

Doctor Hastings stood there at the end of the room, out of Nathan's line of sight. He was fully clothed, his finger to his lips, a big grin on his face. Mené grinned back at him, her strokes growing stronger. *This is such a mean trick, I love it.* She watched him slip quietly out of the main exit. Nathan, as was clearly the plan, hadn't noticed at all.

Emma's voice grew louder over the intercom. 'Oh doctor, sucking you isn't enough! I'm so wet, please, fuck me, I need to feel a real cock inside me.'

Mené leaned in to the completely oblivious Nate. 'Oh my goodness, you got even harder listening to them, that's so bad. Don't you hear what's going on in there? She's about to get her first feel of a real cock. She's never going to want to go back, Nate, not once she knows how it should feel.'

Nathan closed his eyes, unable to process anything, worn out from struggling. The insistent pleasure from Mené's hand was bringing him closer now, as he listened to his wife next door.

Mené took the opportunity to beam a big smile at the window, assuming she could be seen, and waved an enthusiastic thumbs up.

A loud moan came through the speakers. 'Oh fuck, you're so big, please, go slow. Ohhhhhh it's so deep, yes, yes, oh my God that's so good. Harder, fuck me harder Doctor!'

Trying hard not to laugh Mené reached over and grabbed a cup, she could tell he was close. Unseen the women worked in partnership.

'Yes, yes, oh fuck I'm going to cum, make me cum on your massive dong.'

Mené couldn't help but laugh but Nathan was so close and past caring he didn't even notice.

As his wife pretended to climax, he did for real. He let out an animalistic cry as his semen jetted out into the waiting cup. His yell of pleasure turned to begging misery as Mené followed the instructions, stopping all stroking as soon as he began to ejaculate. She slid her hand down to the base, just holding it in place to catch everything he squirted out. And how it squirted, jet after jet. She couldn't believe it, and had to concentrate not to spill any from the little cup.

She was so focused on it in fact that she didn't notice Emma saunter in, fully clothed, until she gently put a hand on her shoulder, giving a squeeze. She slid her fingers up her husband's sweat-soaked arm and ran her fingers through his hair. He opened his eyes and looked at her calm, dressed demeanour. 'Wha? But?'

'The doctor left a while back. That was just me having some fun, by myself. I told you, I'd blow your fucking mind, you big idiot. Did I succeed?'

Nathan nodded his head, a sigh of relief and frustration issuing from him. 'That was, insane. I love you.'

'I love you too, numpty.'

'You two are adorable!' Mené announced again. 'Did I do good, Emma?'

'You were amazing, even if you lost it at the end. Although I laughed at "massive dong" too. Oh is that what he produced, what volume?'

Mené carefully lifted up the considerably full measuring cup. 'Hmmm, 17ml, wow that is a lot. I think that's about five times average. For real. I wonder if ruining makes a difference.'

Emma patted her husband on the head. 'You see baby, you do have some bigger than average things'. Both the women laughed. Nate looked quite pleased despite himself.

'Can I get out now please?' he asked.

'Not quite yet,' Mené replied.

'What, really?' They both looked at her.

'Yes. I have to measure - total - volume. Everything in there. Ready to go again?' She looked down at his now limp cock. 'Hmm, it seems not. Emma, can you help?'

'Oh, can I touch his—'

'No, but maybe, encourage him?' Mené suggested.

Emma looked pleased to be involved and leaned over Nate from the side. Her fingers slid under the top of the gown and started playing with his nipples. She planted her mouth on his and started giving him a hard, deep kiss.

'That is the ticket,' said Mené, copying something she must have heard on TV, as he immediately began to get erect. She wasted no time lubing her hand and beginning to stimulate him. Nate let out a little groan into his wife's mouth as she continued to play with his nipples and the nurse masturbated him with her gloved hand.

'Wow, does he get this hard this quickly if you let him cum properly?' said Mené.

Emma turned from the kiss towards her and shook her head. 'Nu-uh, it's amazing, isn't it. I love ruining him for that reason among others.'

'Oh, what others?'

'The best is the little frustrated cries he makes as it ruins. Oh God, so, so sexy. And then just watching it pump out is so freaking hot too. Ohh but you know what else is? A dribble ruin. Oh, oh, let's do that!'

'Teach me, oh queen of ruins.' Mené took a little bow and brought her mouth dangerously close to his cock. She looked up and gave a naughty smile to Emma.

'I really thought you were going to suck him earlier, you know. That's what made me decide to drive him crazy.'

'I'm sorry. I got carried away. Not very professional.' Mené paused, making Nate groan as the stroking stopped. 'How did it make you feel?'

'Jealous, angry—aroused.' Emma glanced at her husband. He was staying very quiet even though his short shallow breaths gave away just what state *his* arousal was in. She looked back to Mené and signalled for her to resume.

Pressing her mouth to his ear she whispered so Mené could hear, 'Did you hope the sexy nurse would suck your little cock, baby? Is that what you were hoping? Aren't my blowjobs enough for you? I guess they aren't now. You won't feel the inside of my mouth for a whole year, have you thought about that? My soft tongue stroking your cock head, my warm lips buried deep down your shaft. A. Whole. Year.'

Nathan whimpered, he pressed his head harder to Emma's mouth as the only way he could get closer.

'I bet if I asked her, she'd suck you, even if she's used to much bigger cocks. It might be the last time you feel any mouth. Do you want that baby, do you want me to ask her to give you a blowjob?'

Nate paused, then gently shook his head. 'No my love, you're worth waiting for,' he whispered.

A little sniff from Mené made them both look at her, she was wiping away a tear as she continued to stroke him. 'You are *killing* me. Oh my God. I can't believe I'm crying!' She began to stroke hard and fast as if to show she was focused on the job and Emma saw he was getting close. Nate opened his mouth, about to groan when Emma said, 'Stop!'

Mené immediately slid her hand to the base, waiting for further instructions.

'No, no, no, please!' cried Nate.

'Just give it a minute,' said Emma, her head tilted, watching. Nate's cock throbbed, a fresh bead of pre-cum formed at the end and trickled down the shaft. 'Okay, ten more hard fast strokes then stop again.'

Mené obeyed, getting the idea. Each stroke caused Nate to arch his back and groan. 'Please, *fuck please!*'

'I did this for a couple of hours once. He nearly passed out. Okay again, grip him really tight.'

Mené's lubed hand stroked up and down. She counted under her breath, stopping at ten again. Again, nothing happened and she was about to resume when Emma stopped her. 'Wait, wait, watch!'

Nathan bucked, 'No, nooooooo!' he sobbed. And his cock jerked gently in Mené's hand, and to her amazement, a stream of thick white semen began dribbling out in a steady flow down the shaft and over Mené's gloved fingers.

'Oh no, the cup,' she remembered and leaned over, pulling one near and catching most of what was still spilling out of him. 'Where is this coming from, I can't believe there is more.' She shook her head in astonishment as she caught the last of the flow and wiped what she could off her glove.

'Is that all of it?' She set the cup next to the first.

'Only one way to find out,' smiled Emma, another plan forming in her mind. 'Wank him again, start now, hard.'

'Isn't he sensitive now? I've been thrown across a bed for keeping going.' Mené laughed.

'Yep, but *this* guy is tied down. Here's another new term for you to learn, "Post Orgasm Torture", or "P.O.T." it's called. Stroking even when they are super sensitive. It's crazy stuff. Really go for it, don't hold back. Let's see how secure those bonds are.'

A sadistic smile spread across the nurse's face. 'Okay then!' Mené started stroking Nate's cock before it had shrunk to much and instantly he was screaming blue murder. 'Aiy yi yi yi! No, oh God no, it's so sensitive. I can't handle it.'

'For some reason, he turns into a Mexican singer when I do this to him.' Emma laughed. 'Harder, go on, especially working the head.'

Mené followed the instructions, looking at Emma with new eyes. 'You are a bit scary, you know that?' She was laughing too. 'Do you do this to him often?' she said loudly over his ongoing cries.

'Only as a punishment, if he cums without permission, or lies to me. He lied to you earlier you know.'

'He did?' said Mené, seeming to enjoy it more now she had an excuse.

'That's awful, what about?'

'He said he hadn't masturbated this month. He did, just on Thursday when I let him out early.'

'Oh Nathan, you are naughty,' Mené teased. 'Lying and masturbating? No wonder Emma keeps you locked up. This is the least of what you deserve.' She stroked him harder and faster, working out exactly what made him convulse the most. Despite him straining at the bonds with all his strength he was helpless to do anything to stop the overwhelming sensations.

Mené tugged hard at what was still an only semi-hard cock. 'Is this really going to make him cum again?'

'Sometimes, if he hardens at all, get the cup ready.'

'I thought I knew everything there was to know about sex. I love being wrong. Oh he's hardening up. He'll cum again? That's like multiple orgasms. I thought only we did those.' She reached over for the third measuring cup and sure enough his cock spurted out a small amount of very thick cum into the cup.

'Again, where is this stuff stored? Did he just make it?' Mené wondered. 'They don't teach this in nursing school.'

'I have no idea. We'll have to ask the doctor.'

'Is that it, can I get any more out of him?'

'If you edge him long enough, but each one gets harder, my record is five I think. Which was disappointing, he gave me 13 ruined ones once. For Halloween.'

'Wait what, ruined orgasms are for us too?'

'You better believe it.' Emma gave a wicked grin.

'I have to try this later.'

Nate let out an exhausted laugh. 'Okay, I'm done, if even hearing that doesn't turn me on. Can I please get out now?'

Emma confirmed, 'You won't get more than a drop out, he's done.'

Mené shook her hand. 'Phew, I'm glad to hear that, my arm is worn out. Okay, let's get him out.'

'I think you've forgotten something,' said Emma, pointing at the cock cage lying on the table.

'Oh wow, that would have got me in trouble, thank you.'

'Emma,' complained Nate, 'whose side are you on?'

'Hmm, that's a good question. If I had to answer–' She stood and sauntered over to Mené, dangling the cage from her fingers, and dropping it into the nurse's hand, '–I'd probably say it'd be wise to be on the side of the sexy nurse who has control of your cock cage key.'

Mené giggled, rotating the cage trying to work out how to fit it back on.

'Those two prongs fit in the holes in the ring,' Emma explained, stepping behind the nurse and sliding her hand over Mené's to guide her.

'Ahh yes, okay and the lock slides back in there.'

'That's right. You should lock it fast though.' She slipped her other hand around Mené's waist.

'Oh, why's that?' Mené fumbled with the lock a little before sliding it slowly into place. Emma put her head on Mené's shoulder.

'I am so, fucking, horny. Watching him, tied up, with you, stroking him. I can't even process it.' She paused, looking at Nate, and whispered to Mené so that he could hear, ' I'm so wet. I was worried the handsome doctor was going to give me an internal. I think I'd have come all over his fingers.'

'Emma, oh my God!' shouted Nate, starting to strain at his bonds with some renewed strength.

She completely ignored him, a wicked smile on her lips as she whispered to Mené. 'I just need some cock, you know? The thought of Nate locked up for a year is driving me crazy and it's just the first day. Watching you lock it back up is making me so desperate.'

Mené played along. 'Oh really. Just how desperate?'

Emma whispered something in her ear.

'Oh gosh.' Mené turned her head so she was nose to nose with Emma. 'Would I be your first?' she tilted her head a little so their lips were almost touching.

'Mhmm.' She paused a little, feeling Mené's breath, cool on her wet lips, and gave a little smirk, nodding her head to her husband. 'Well, at least the first, that *he* knows about.'

'What?' shouted Nate. Both of the women collapsed into laughter.

Emma reached out and gave the steel cage a little wiggle. 'I'm just teasing you, darling, it's not fair Mené got to have all the fun.'

'I love you, and hate you right now. Can I please get out now?'

They both kept chuckling as they undid the straps and let Nathan carefully get himself down. He gave a tired hug to his wife and sat down on a plastic chair.

'Well, that was something else. Thank you Mené, as crazy as that was, you were amazing. I still can't believe it really happened.'

'I couldn't mean it more when I say it was my pleasure.' Nurse Mené gave a little curtsey and pulled off her latex gloves with a snap.

* * *

Nathan spent a good while in the clinic's shower before coming out dressed and looking a little less exhausted. He glanced at his wife, who was sitting up close to Mené, speaking in hushed tones, but with the occasional giggle.

'No, how did that fit?' his wife suddenly exclaimed, breaking the hushed conversation.

'You can never have too much lube,' laughed Mené, patting her hand. The nurse turned and smiled at Nate, giving him a little wink. 'How is our patient, feeling drained?'

Emma chortled. 'I can't believe that just happened. You know you just made one of our major fantasies come to life?'

'Yes, really, that was incredible, thank you,' added Nate.

Mené flapped her hands at them. 'No, no, thank you! I have learnt so much. It was the nicest introduction to something new. I just need you to go now so I can deal with how horny it got me.'

'Oh my goodness, you are too much.' Emma grabbed her hand and squeezed it.

Mené's face fell a little. 'I am?'

'No, she's joking, it's just a thing we say. You were amazing. As Emma said, we have talked about the idea of a chastity nurse for so long, and you made it real. I can't believe it.'

'Oh a chastity nurse, is that what I am? I like the sound of that. Is it just men I look after?' She laid her hand on her leg.

Emma felt the blush starting from where Mené's hand lay, all the way up her leg to start a distinct tingle, and then her face following in the heat. 'I mean, I...'

'You like this too I think. To not be allowed?'

'Yes,' admitted Emma. 'I love it.'

'I don't think I would like it,' Mené declared. 'But these ruined orgasms have me very curious. I liked the noises you made, Nathan. They got me very horny.'

Emma and Nate exchanged glances, grinning at this woman unlike any they'd ever met. Emma coughed. 'That's, very good to know.'

'Yes thank you, but I'm starving,' Nate said, 'Did Catherine say there's food?'

The girls stood and hugged each other. 'I'm sure I will see you both soon,' Mené said. 'I didn't expect to learn so much today, or have so much fun. You've got my number, so if you need anything...'

Both of them looked at Nate and then back to each other, and ended the hug with a kiss on the lips that went on long enough for Nate to start feeling uncomfortable. 'Err, bye then Mené, umm, thanks I guess?'

The girls broke apart, laughing again.

A Cock Casting

After their medicals, the two wandered the elegant gardens a little before returning to the house. A simple buffet lunch was laid out and Alexandra was on hand to get them some drinks. Elizabeth caught up with them as they were just about finished. 'Catherine told you about some admin that needs doing?'

'Yeah,' said Nate, standing up from the table. 'Shall we do it now?'

Elizabeth chuckled. 'Umm, no, you'll want some privacy for this.'

Emma was suddenly interested, 'Oh, really? What is it?'

'Oh, I shouldn't spoil the surprise. It's kinda cute though. I need to get some things and umm, change. How about I'll come up to your room in an hour?'

Nate stood up. 'Sure, see you then.' Elizabeth nodded and headed off, they both watched her go.

'She has to change? It'll take her half an hour to peel that dress off. What admin could mean she has to *change*? Nate!' she smacked his arm, 'stop staring! You just came four times.'

'Four ruins,' he corrected her, 'by a chastity nurse, while my wife blew my mind. You can't blame me for still being horny.'

'No, but I can for looking where you shouldn't. Maybe I should ask Catherine if she has a spiked cage?'

'You wouldn't!'

'Don't tempt me, mister.' She grinned, then pointed her two fingers at Nate's eyes, and then at her own bottom. 'Keep 'em right here,' she called as she sauntered off, wiggling her bottom in some attempt to look at least a

114

bit like Elizabeth's perfect rump.

* * *

Almost exactly an hour later there was a knock on their bedroom door. Emma had taken the opportunity to have a shower too and they were both lying on the big bed, checking their phones. 'Come in,' they shouted in unison. 'Jinx,' Emma added, laughing. She needn't have bothered, the outfit Elizabeth had changed into would have probably rendered him speechless anyway.

What she was wearing was technically a suit, but it stretched the concept to the very limit. It was as though a pinstripe suit and a corset had got together and produced very elegant offspring. The perfect tailoring ended below the shoulders, leaving them and her arms bare. But it was the shaped cups lifting and exaggerating her already ample breasts that was the real party stopper. It ended like a little waistcoat, matched perfectly by a pinstripe mini-skirt that was perhaps only 1cm off being pornographic.

Emma saw Nate's reaction and knew just what other impact it would be having. 'Oh I *love* your suit! I've never seen anything like it? How can something be so sexy and so professional?'

'Thank you,' Elizabeth replied, seeming a little taken off guard, swinging a simple white paper bag by the ribbon handles.

'I wish I had boobs like yours. I'd wear stuff like that all the time.'

'They're a blessing and a curse,' Elizabeth replied, looking at Emma curiously.

Emma sat up straighter, 'They give you a bad back?'

'Something like that.'

'I bet Nate wishes I had boobs like yours' She put her head on his shoulder. Nate started to splutter a response but Emma continued, 'but he always says anything more than a handful is a waste.' She kissed him on the cheek. 'What do you really think, hubby dear, if you had to choose?'

'Emma, what has got into you?' Nate leaned back a bit, giving her a 'shut up now' glare.

115

'Well not you, darling,' Emma grinned back.

They both looked at Elizabeth in surprise when she gave a genuine laugh. 'My husband used to say the same. "A handful is perfect".'

Emma glanced at Elizabeth's bare ring finger but didn't dare ask about the past tense, so she asked something else. 'Oh you, you know, got implants?'

Elizabeth's face fell again. 'Yes. It's a long story. Anyway,' she said as she lifted a white gift bag, 'did Catherine tell you about the something I had to do¿

'Nothing more than "admin".' Nate answered.

'Well, "admin" might be a bit of a stretch.' She emptied out the contents of the bag on the bed.

'Is that what I think it is?' Emma jumped up and picked up the heavy cardboard tube that had fallen on the bed. 'It is, it is – Nate, it's a Clone-a-Willy kit!'

Nate's curiosity got the better of him, he pushed himself forward. 'This, is your admin? You want to...'

'Get a cast of your penis, yes.'

'Just why do you need a cast of my cock?'

'Well, it's going to be locked up for a long time,' Elizabeth explained. 'Catherine doesn't want to be liable for any claims that its confinement leads to lasting...impairment.'

Emma gave a warm laugh. 'You want to prove it didn't shrink.'

'We want to prove it didn't shrink.' Elizabeth couldn't help responding with a smile.

'This is the best weekend ever,' Emma declared. A thought struck her, 'but he's locked up?'

Elizabeth slipped her fingers into the tailored pocket on the side of the corset-suit and took out a key. That got Nate's attention. Emma sat by him, tube in her hand. 'Just who's supposed to be doing this?'

Catherine's PA took the tube from her and twisted it open, emptying out the contents on the bed. It was a strange variety of items; a clear plastic cylinder, a bag of powder, and some other bits and pieces. 'Well, really it's supposed to be me. But I'll be honest with you, I have no desire to be pushing your husband's cock into this. If you can keep it secret, I'm more than happy for you to do it. But, please, promise you won't tell Catherine.'

'No, of course we won't. Are you going to stay?'

'I really should but, maybe if I forgot something in my office and had to go and get it? Oh actually, I did forget something. I believe we need some boiling water. I'll just go and fetch it.' She dropped the key onto the bed where Emma and Nate both stared at it. 'I won't be *that* long.' Elizabeth turned on her heels and disappeared out of the door.

'Oh this is perfect, just before we lock up you, I get to clone your willy.' Emma bounced around in delight before grabbing the instructions.

'Ohhh, that means, you need to get me hard,' Nate realised.

'Yes sirree, what a result huh! Get your pants off, we need to make the most of this.'

They both suddenly felt like naughty, horny teens as they pulled his trousers off. Emma fumbled with the key before slotting it in place and pulling out the lock. The cage was off and Nate sighed with the pleasure of being free. 'That has never felt better,' he said.

'Oh, challenge accepted. I bet I can make it feel much better.' Emma grabbed her still damp towel from the end of the bed and gave him a quick clean up. 'Ring off too?'

'No, it'll help it stay hard in that thing.' Nate nodded at the tube. 'How's it work?'

Emma didn't answer as she slipped off the end of the bed onto her knees. Grabbing his hardening cock by the base she wrapped her lips around it, sucking, nuzzling. 'Hmmm?' she murmured, not looking up.

'Fuck, never mind, you keep doing that, I'll read the—oh God that feels so good.' Nate tried reading the instructions but it wasn't easy as Emma's head bobbed up and down. 'Damn we do need hot water, Elizabeth was right'

Emma lifted her head, her hand taking over from her mouth. 'This is so cool, I've always wanted one of these. I wonder if...'

'Do you really need to talk now, baby?' Nate slid his hand into her wavy hair and then gave her a gentle downward push.

'I'll suck you again in a minute you big lunk. I wonder if I could ask for a copy of your cock to play with while you're all locked up. How cool would that be?'

'I—I'm really not sure. Cool, I guess, maybe a bit weird?'

'Nah, it's great, it means I won't miss this fella quite as much.' With a wink she started sucking the tip of his cock again, flicking her tongue over the most sensitive bits underneath.

'Hot water coming in,' announced Elizabeth with a knock on the door. To Nate's surprise, Emma didn't instantly stop sucking his cock. She pushed down on it a few times, taking it right to the back of her throat, making him groan involuntarily.

'Err, don't mind me, I'll just put this here.' Elizabeth made a determined effort to look in other directions. She put down a steaming jug of water on the floor and a plastic mixing bowl on the bed beside them.

Emma knelt back up with a deliberately loud slurp. Her hand went straight back to Nate's cock, slippery with her saliva, and she didn't even pause a beat as she kept on stroking him. 'Thank you for the water.'

Elizabeth headed back to the door, not looking around, 'I'll, I'll stand outside. That stuff sets very fast. I made one once, so as soon as you mix it, pour it in the tube and push it on.'

A thank you was barely out of Emma's mouth before it was full of Nate's cock again. She paused, lifting her head. 'Did you just get harder when she walked in?'

'I totally did,' Nate confessed. 'And you know why? Because you didn't stop. You are so amazing. What happened to that innocent vanilla girl I married?'

'You let her lock your dick up. You better get mixing,' She nodded to the bowl and got back to sucking on the head of Nate's cock while her hand worked up and down the shaft.

Nate awkwardly reached over, picked up the bowl and bag of powder, read the instructions on the bag and finally figured out how to open it despite the wonderful distraction. 'Oh gosh I'm close already baby, but—I need 400ml of that water, can you pour it in that measure?'

Emma stopped again and gripped his cock hard in her hand while she poured out about the right amount of water.

Nate handed her the spatula. 'Hey if I hold the bowl can you mix?'

'This is literally like rubbing my tummy and patting my head,' Emma giggled. 'Oh, it's just like Plaster of Paris. I think that's ready, where's it going?'

Nate grabbed the tube. 'In here I think, I'll pour it in.'

Emma continued stroking Nate's cock to keep it hard while she tried to hold the tube that Nate had given her, steady. 'That's it, it's not quite full though is that right?'

'Eureka darling, don't forget Archimedes,' said Nate, showing off his geeky history knowledge.

'Oh yes, your cock will displace it, this could get messy. There, do you think you're hard enough?' She gave a few more hard strokes but her saliva was starting to dry out, making it more difficult.

'I think so, I'm so close though, I don't think I could handle much more. Let's go for it.' He swung his legs back over the side of the bed and pushed the tip of his cock into the warm clay-like mix.

'Close huh,' said Emma, 'maybe if it sets fast enough I'll be able to make you cum.'

'But we're not allowed are we?'

'So? How are they going to know? I'll just swallow the evidence.' She gave him a naughty grin and pushed the tube on hard, some of the mix spilt out and dripped on the floor.

'Oh God, don't say that, just the thought is going to make me—oh no, no, no!' he cried.

'Nate, don't cum, not in the tube.' Emma looked genuinely upset but it was too late. Her husband jerked his hips and with a groan, he shuddered.

'I told you I was close, oh no, I so wanted you to do it.' He let out a frustrated little sob. 'A ruin in a plastic tube wasn't quite what I'd imagined. It's probably ruined the moulding too.' He chuckled, 'I wonder what it'll look like?'

A knock on the door interrupted them. 'How are you getting on in there?' Elizabeth asked through the door.

'We're pretty much done; it's just setting,' Emma said.

Elizabeth peeked through a gap in the door, her mouth stretching into a big grin when she saw the tube pushed between Nate's legs. 'That'll be quite the Christmas tree ornament.'

'It might even have a bit at the top to hang it off,' Emma whispered to Nate.

Elizabeth came back in. 'I can do the rest of it. The silicone needs pouring in once it's set hard.'

Emma handed over the tube. 'Ummm, it might need a wash out first.'

Elizabeth looked quizzical and then clicked. 'Oh, really? That was quick.' She bit her lip, staving off a smile.

'It's been a stimulating day,' objected Nate.

'Yes, I can imagine.' She nodded over to the cage lying on the bed. 'I'm afraid you have to...'

'Cage him up?' finished Emma. 'Probably for the best with you in that outfit.'

Elizabeth went a little red. 'It wasn't my choice.'

It was Emma's turn to pinken a little. 'I'm sorry, I didn't mean... I can imagine working for Catherine isn't easy.'

'You'd be right.' She turned her head away.

Emma stood. 'Elizabeth. Or, what do you prefer, Lizzie?'

'I hate Lizzie.' She turned back. 'Liz though, Liz is fine.'

Emma went up to her. 'You can call me Em if you want.' She took her hand, 'Liz, are we crazy doing this? Is there anything you can tell us?'

'Just, just read the contract *very* carefully. And, be careful what you wish for. These things they... can take on a life of their own. Think about what's really important.'

'We will, we promise,' said Nate.

Elizabeth kept hold of Emma's hand, and looked down at Nate, and then at her. She made a twisted little smile, 'Do you want a hand putting the cage back on, Em?'

'Do I ever!' They helped each other kneel down either side of Nate's legs. 'It's so strange, before yesterday no one had ever seen this besides me. Now it feels almost normal, especially after watching Mené at work.'

'She is quite something, isn't she. Instantly likeable, and yet somehow terrifying. I was rather proud when I found her. We've offered her the apartment above the Stables so she's going to use this place as a base to explore the UK.'

'Can I get you ladies anything while you're having a chat, a cup of tea perhaps?' Nate interrupted.

Elizabeth laughed. 'He's cute. It's a shame his dick isn't bigger.' She looked at Emma, biting her lips and raising her eyebrows to check if she should continue.

'I know huh. I had no idea what I was missing until we tried the big strap-on.'

'Oh but it's not the same.' Elizabeth grinned as they both watched his cock start to swell. 'There's nothing like that soft hardness of a really big dick. Feeling its warmth, and girth inside you. Knowing that being in you feels just as good to him.'

'I can only imagine.' Emma nodded at Nate's cock. 'Oh dear, I don't think he's going to fit in the cage now.'

'Oh no, was it something I said?'

'Well yes, either that, or the view right down your top.'

'Surely he wouldn't look.' Elizabeth made a shocked gasp.

Emma chuckled. 'I can barely stop *myself* looking, to be fair. And I don't mind actually, well not if he's caged.'

Elizabeth picked up the small steel device. 'I guess you better get it back on then.'

Emma paused, looked up at Nate who didn't seem to know what to think or where to look. 'I guess so. Give me a hand will you?' Nate just made a whimper.

They both giggled as they wrestled his cock into the little cage, chatting away as they did it. 'How was the medical?'

Emma squeezed Nate's leg, 'It was very productive.' She kissed him on the knee and went back to pushing the cage down on his erect cock, determined to make it fit and ignoring his frustrated moans. 'So about tonight, this dinner party. Any surprises we should be aware of?'

'You'll find it quite eye-opening, I expect. It's quite the group. Let's just say, all of them share a similar interest. I think Catherine is very excited to show you off. You're very much the guest of honour.'

'Oh really. Why?' Emma concentrated on the cage for a moment. 'There we go.' She declared with satisfaction as the key turned in the cock cage lock.

'Well, the group is called the Chastity WAGS, if that gives you a clue.'

'As in Wives and Girlfriends?' asked Nate, trying to readjust the cage. 'Like footballers?'

'Exactly. An interesting mix. And Emma, they *all* read your blog, religiously.'

Emma didn't know what to say. She received a lot of messages through to the blog but no one knew it was her writing it. The idea of facing a whole group of women who read it was a bit scary.

Elizabeth noticed her pause and reached out to touch Emma's arm. 'Honestly, you're going to feel like a celebrity tonight. And the outfits should help, I picked them out myself. I assume you haven't checked the wardrobe?'

'Outfits?' Emma jumped up and slid the mirrored door open. 'Oh wow! Look at the dresses.'

'And matching heels', added Elizabeth, pushing herself up off the floor.

'Heels!'

The PA laughed. 'I'll leave you to see what you like best. Catherine is giving you any one you want as a gift.' She paused at the door. 'But just one, they're very expensive, okay?'

'Yes, yes, thank you so much,' Emma said into the wardrobe, gasps of excitement warning Nate he was about to be treated to a fashion parade.

Emma was already half-naked before he had come to have a look. 'Oh Nate, they are amazing. Four different dresses. Four!' she exclaimed. 'Here help me into this.' Emma was trying to figure out which way round a poppy red dress went. She finally slipped her arm through the right hole, leaving one shoulder bare and the other trailing a waterfall of colour down to the ground.

'Damn, you look like a Grecian goddess.' Nate's eyes ate her up in the dress, her bare shoulder matched by a split right up to her thigh on the same side. She did a spin and the train over her other shoulder swished around behind her.

'Isn't it amazing, it's called an asymmetric dress. I didn't see who...' she checked the hanger. 'Elie Saab, God, he's famous. This must cost thousands. Oh, it has matching shoes. Jimmy Choo, are you kidding me?' Emma tore off the box lid and squealed at the red suede strappy sandals inside. She slipped them on, wrapping the fine suede band up her ankle, and then sat to do the other foot.

When she stood it somehow transformed her pose and the dress.

'Damn,' said Nate. 'You look amazing. My lady in red.' He grinned.

'How about a lady in white?' Emma carefully took the dress off, laid it on the bed and went over to have a look at the long white gown. This time she checked the label. 'No fucking way. Stella McCartney. Wait—' She held the dress in front of her looking in the long mirror on the inside of the wardrobe.

'Nathan...'

He immediately looked at her, she hardly ever called him that. 'What is it, honey?'

'Umm, this is the dress Meghan Markle wore to her wedding reception. I'm not even kidding.' She easily slipped it on, moving to Nate to have the white halter neck collar done up.

'That is extraordinary.' He stepped back, admiring the view. 'I love it, although, yeah, kind of wedding day vibes about it.' He stepped up to her, wrapping his arms around. 'Remember what you wore? You looked amazing, even if it wasn't what Meghan Markle wore. You'll always be my princess.'

'Aww, thanks, baby. I don't know about wedding day vibes, all this white feels more like the virgin's sacrifice. Catherine's clearly had all this planned. You heard they all read the blog?'

'Yes, and that you're like a celebrity. Stop worrying about it, it'll be fun.

We can always head back to our room if we don't like it. Honestly, I'm exhausted already, I'd much rather be resting but I want to see my wife in celeb mode! Now, what's the third dress?'

Nate went to the wardrobe and pulled out a very sparkly beige mini-dress. 'Naeem Kahn,' he read. 'Never heard of him, or her,' he added. 'Kinda cool though. Try it on.'

Emma carefully removed the white creation and hung it back up before pulling on the dress over her head. 'Wow, this is amazing. Imagine this on the dancefloor.'

'Or a stripper's pole,' said Nate.

'Oh really, is that how you think of me?' Emma paced up to him, catwalk style, one foot crossing the other. 'Would you care for a dance?'

Nate slipped his hands around her waist, the sequined fringes covering his fingers. 'I mean, that's very kind of you, but my wife, I don't think she'd approve.'

'Oh don't you worry about that mister, Emma told me all about you. And your–' she slid her hand down to his caged cock, '–little fella.'

'Ouch.'

She looked at herself in the full-length mirror, smoothing down the sides. 'I'm not going to wear a stripper dress to the posh dinner, if that's okay with you?'

'You look incredible in it. You know that right? How does anyone with less than perfect boobs wear this stuff though?'

'Awww, are you calling my boobs perfect?' Emma wrapped her arms around the hem of the dress and lifted it straight off and onto the bed. Then put her arms around Nate and pressed against him.

'Always.'

She kissed him on the nose before returning to the wardrobe. 'Let's try the last one, I liked the colour a lot.'

Emma pulled out a teal dress with small white vines running down the sides. 'It's far less showy than the other ones, not even a bare shoulder.' Emma looked at the label. '"Oscar de la Renta", not someone I know but famous no doubt. Oh, I love the material, I think it's wool.' She slipped it on. 'Gosh, you could even wear a bra under this, how conservative. Zip me up, honey.' She spun her back to him. 'What do you think?'

'It's beautiful. Really suits you, and brings out the green in your eyes. You could actually wear that in normal life too. Let me Google it, I wonder if he's a famous designer too.' Nate whipped out his phone and in a few seconds his eyes went wide. 'I found it, although we may need to rethink wearing it in normal life. Oh my God, most of our cars cost less than that dress.' He showed her the picture on the screen.

'£4,370, how is that even, what? I don't know if I like it more or less because of that. Okay, how does it look?'

Nate sized it up as she spun around. 'Are there heels for that one too? Try it with them on if so.'

Emma found the shoebox that had been with the dress. 'Oh yes, Jimmy Choo's again, white ones this time. They're pretty, although I might need a hand with the laces again, I think, yes, they go around a few times. There we go. How's that?' Emma stood on the slightly lower heels, and gave a comfortable twirl.

'You look fabulous, darling, absolutely fabulous even.' Nate grinned. 'You look incredible in those other two, serious movie star stuff, but I think this is my favourite. It's much more, you.'

'I agree, and a bargain at a tenth of the price. I'm glad I'm not paying. I don't even want to know how much the shoes are. All I'm going to be worrying about is spilling something on the dress all night, you realise that?'

'Oh, the burden of having designer clothes. We could just go in jeans, cause a ruckus?'

'Hmmm,' Emma pretended to think about it. 'Nope, I think I'll cope. But what about you, I assume you've got something in your wardrobe?'

Nate went over and checked. 'Just one option for me apparently, oh it's a nice, probably very expensive, dinner jacket. That's handy, I don't think I fit in the one we had as students anymore.'

'Oh I do love you in a DJ, put it on, put it on,' insisted Emma.

'I'll go shower first.'

'Okay honey.' Emma was quickly distracted, gazing at herself in the mirror.

She stroked her hands down the dress, feeling the tiny white vine leaves carefully sewn down both sides. It was without a doubt the most beautiful thing she had ever owned. She couldn't believe it was hers to keep. She looked at the other two dresses with a little regret. They were gorgeous too, but they just weren't her. They were more suited to walking down a red carpet, *or apparently a royal wedding* Emma thought.

Weariness from all the day's excitement suddenly struck her. Emma took off the dress so she wouldn't crumple it, and undid the laces on the new shoes, taking a moment to admire them before laying them beside her. *What a crazy 24 hours.* She thought back over the negotiations yesterday, and then the medical this morning. Her mind went to the thought of Mené, in her outrageous little nurse's uniform, draining him over and over. Her hands found themselves between her legs as she explored the ache it all caused there. Her fingers slipped inside her panties as she pictured the tight cage around him even now and maybe even the ring that was going to make his cage inescapable.

Her feet slid up towards her bottom as she spread her legs wider, pressing harder, rubbing faster. Poor Nate, he'd not feel this for so long. All the orgasms were for her now, every, single, one. With a sharp intake of breath, she took herself over the edge, writhing against her fingers, her other hand squeezing at her breast. She didn't stop, she pushed through the sensitivity, circling her clit with wider circles before she could press hard again, this time, teasing herself, getting close, riding the edge. How she loved this feeling.

* * *

Early on in their relationship Nate would keep her like this – edging her, whispering fantasies into her ear. She'd been so frustrated at first. She'd never orgasmed before they got together but after he'd first made her climax she had quickly learnt to love cumming. Who wouldn't? But as good as orgasms were, being edged, being denied, was even better. The constant sexual high it put her on, the thrill of not being allowed to do what she wanted even when she went home from seeing him. The hotness of his refusals when she got to the point of begging. It got to a point where she hoped he wouldn't say yes, which he knew of course.

And it was just the start, the gateway to so many other things. She still adored edging as she sucked him. Orgasm denial had taken her from reluctant about even the idea of oral sex to being a deep throating, cum swallowing, queen of blowjobs.

How ironic, and hot, that the situation was reversed now. All the restrictions on him, the frustration, the arousal, the constant ache. The fact she loved it herself made denying him easier. She knew its power, she was a true believer - a denial slut. And now even unlocking his cage was out of her hands. She revelled in the freedom it would give her from having to make the choice. And with him locked, she knew she'd enjoy being selfish, orgasms just for her, not even an option for her poor, desperate hubby. For a whole year.

She came again, hard, thinking of it, only just aware the shower had stopped. For a moment she considered letting him catch her, but she liked her little secret edges and orgasms. She was delighted with his reaction when she'd told Mené about it earlier. So instead she snuggled her head back into the pillow and shut her eyes. A little nap before dinner would do them both good.

* * *

She woke to the sound of a phone alarm slowly getting louder. It was Nate's, and as usual, it woke her first. She reached over and turned it off before it got annoying. His naked body stirred next to her but he didn't wake. They had 45 minutes to get ready, she was grateful he'd thought about setting an alarm. Her eyes were drawn to his cock. It really was a small cage. She liked that.

Emma wondered how it would be to suck his cock with a Prince Albert piercing. Probably a bit weird, but they could normally be taken out. It was the idea of it inside her that she was most curious about. Would it really make that much of a difference? She'd never orgasmed just from Nate being in her, it always took his fingers or a vibe to take her over. But from what Rex had said, it really could happen. The thought was getting her horny again, but she didn't have time to play. Nate would only need five minutes to get dressed. She could leave him resting a bit longer and get ready herself. She stood, running her fingers over her beautiful new dress, and carefully put it back on before heading to the bathroom to get her make-up right for this evening.

30 minutes later she emerged, hair and makeup done, and gave Nate a gentle shake. 'Honey, we have the party in a little bit, sorry to wake you, but you need to get ready.'

Nate shook himself awake and took the pills and water she held out to him. 'Thanks honey.' He opened his eyes wide to wake himself up a bit more and looked his wife up and down. 'Wow baby, you look so lovely in that, I'm going to be the proudest guy at the party.'

'And I will be the proudest wife. Now get that hot DJ on, I want to see you in it.'

Nate dressed quickly, popping to the bathroom to wet and brush his hair before he put the jacket on. 'How do I look?'

'So hot, you know I can't resist you dressed up like that. Remember the winter prom at uni?'

'How could I forget. I couldn't believe it when you snuck under the table!' He grinned, and winced a little as his cock remembered too.

'What a shame I can't reenact it. Although, we have five minutes. At least one of us can get warmed up before the party.' Emma sat on the edge of the bed, her heeled feet just touching the floor, and lifted her dress. To Nate's obvious delight she'd not put any panties on yet. Clearly she'd been planning this.

Without another word he came over, running his fingers up her bare legs, sinking down, his lips replacing them, kissing up her thigh until he reached her mound. Emma felt a surge of pleasure shoot up her as he closed his lips around her already waiting clitoris. Sucking and flicking with his tongue the way that drove her crazy, she grabbed his hair, not caring about messing it up.

'Oh God, Nate, you're so good at that. I just want you there all night.'

He mumbled something in response. 'What?' Emma asked.

Nate lifted his head, 'But I'm hungry now', he protested with a big smile.

Emma swatted his head, 'Then eat me, mister'. He didn't hesitate, a couple of fingers sliding easily inside her as the pleasure resumed. He sucked and kissed and licked her, driving her closer to another orgasm. Emma held her breathing steady, determined to make it last. She reached a decision, 'Don't let me cum, edge me baby, set me on fire and keep me that way.'

She thought she could feel his smile on her cheeks as his fingers worked inside, but holding their pace, sucking, fingering, he knew just what to do.

A knock on the door caused them both to pause. Emma looked at her husband, between her legs, and whispered to him. 'Don't stop.'

'Really?' Nate asked, truly surprised.

'Don't stop,' she said again, then in a loud voice. 'Come in.'

The door opened and Elizabeth came in. She stopped, looking at Nate kneeling by the bed, his mouth busy on Emma's mons. 'Well, good evening,' she said, with a grin.

'Hello Elizabeth, is it time for the party?' Emma asked, trying to act nonchalant.

'It is, indeed. Guests are just arriving, so when you're ready…'

Feeling very bold Emma slid her fingers through her husband's hair and pushed him harder between her legs. 'Great,' she said trying not to moan. Nate was working hard to make her cum, probably deciding two could play at this game.

'I think,' Elizabeth said, 'you're going to enjoy this party. I'll tell Catherine you'll be coming, soon.'

'Sounds perfect,' was all Emma could reply, pushing her head back into the bed, trying hard not to lose the battle between her legs. She heard the door close and laughed. 'You are so naughty,' she scolded Nate. 'You wanted to make me cum in front of her didn't you.'

'Mhmm,' Nate murmured between her legs, then with a final few sucks lifted up. 'I have a question.'

'Yes?' answered Emma, slipping her fingers down to keep rubbing right in front of his face.

'Who are you and what have you done with my wife?' he laughed, his fingers still stroking inside her. 'Do you want to cum, or shall we go to the party with you well edged and horny as fuck.'

'You choose,' she said softly, stroking her fingers down his cheek.

'Horny as fuck it is.' He gave a final kiss on the fine hair covering her mound. 'I'm going to go and clean up. My beard is a bit wet.'

Emma laughed and hunted around for where she'd left her panties. She pulled up the sexy lacy thong that matched the bra she was wearing. *These are going to be ruined by the end of the evening.*

She checked her make up as Nate came back in, looking very smart. He slipped on the well-fitting jacket and offered her a hand, pulling her up and giving her a kiss. Despite the wash, his beard still smelt of sex. 'Let's go meet the ravening hordes shall we Mrs Stevens?'

'We can't just stay here and you make me cum all night?'

'As good as that sounds, I think I'd fall asleep between your legs. I'm tired. Let's get this over with. You can always jill off with me cuddled up, although I'd have thought earlier was enough for you.'

Emma turned to him in surprise. 'How did you know about that?'

'I was watching in the bathroom mirror. Plus I can usually tell, you always act too innocent when I come in afterwards, it's adorable.'

'Well, a girl has needs, plus you told me it's super hot,' Emma said.

'Oh, it is, it was a painful shower, and worth every moment.' He pressed his mouth to her ear in a way that always sent a shiver up her spine. 'But I prefer you like this, well edged, with that dangerous, horny look in your eye. Let's go make an impression.'

He took her hand and they walked together to the landing. The buzz of conversation rose from downstairs, mixed with the clink of glasses. The distinctive pop of a champagne cork made Emma turn to Nate at the top of the stairs. 'Oh dear baby, seems I'll be horny *and* tipsy, your poor cock really is going to miss out tonight.' She entwined her fingers with his and they walked down the stairs together.

The Dinner Party

As Nate and Emma rounded the bottom of the stairs Catherine immediately spotted them. 'Our special guests have deemed to show themselves. Everyone, can I introduce Emma and Nathan.'

It seemed to be about a dozen guests, suddenly swarming around them, shaking hands, saying how much they loved the blog, how good it was to meet them.

The men were all in well fitting-dinner jackets. But with her £4,000 dress on, Emma felt, not under-dressed, if anything, over. It seemed like the women were all trying to outdo themselves in how little they could wear. The outfits were all stunning, but very little was left to the imagination. Some were incredibly short little black dresses, others had plunging necklines that somehow magically concealed their breasts. Others covered more, but were so close-fitting that every curve was on show.

Nate snatched a moment in between pleasantries to whisper to Emma, 'Apparently, the dress code is "as little as possible"'. Emma giggled.

'Emma, darling, Nate. So kind of you to join us. Welcome to the gathering of the Chastity WAGS. We're so happy to have you with us. It was Danielle's idea for a name, isn't it fun!' Catherine put her arm around Emma, her voice dropping, but not much. 'They're all caged, obviously. It's become a bit of a game to see just how revealing the outfits can be - to tease the men. See if you can spot which of them have spikes in tonight, that's always fun.' Catherine put her hand in the curve of Emma's back, rubbing the fabric of the teal dress. 'A lovely choice, really makes you stand out from the rest of them.'

Catherine herself was much more dressed up than they'd seen her before. A very elegant black dress that went to her knees, plus patent black leather heels, with the trademark Louboutin red sole. Her hair was very styled too, dead straight down in a blunt bob, curling into the gem-filled necklace around her throat.

'You look lovely too,' said Emma, before being pulled away to meet the only black couple in attendance, Danielle and Duncan. Danielle was in a bright, red bodycon dress that hugged every curve, showing off her amazing physique. As they chatted it turned out Danielle was a professional women's football player. Duncan had been a professional player too, but injury took him out of action so now he looked after their two young kids while she focused on her career.

They both looked very happy, and delighted to be at the dinner. But there was something going on Emma couldn't put her finger on. Every so often as they talked, Danielle would lose focus for a few seconds and have to snap herself back into it.

Emma looked at Danielle's dress and curves with hidden envy. *I shouldn't have given up hockey so soon.* She shook it off, remembering that all the men here had little devices that would keep them very focused on pleasing their wives, her husband included.

A tap on her arm interrupted her thoughts. A quiet voice said, 'Can I just say how excited we are to meet you. Your blog has meant everything to us.' It belonged to Helen, who had an enduringly youthful look that meant while she looked in her early 50's, she might be considerably older. She was holding hands with her husband, Rob, who just nodded in agreement.

Over another glass of champagne, they explained to Emma and Nate how their marriage had been on the rocks. They didn't go into detail but the sheepish look from Rob suggested it was his fault. 'But now our marriage has never been better,' Helen said, whispering so only Emma could hear, 'And the sex, oh my, thank you, thank you.'

'Dinner is served,' rumbled a deep voice from one of the waiters. Emma couldn't help looking at him, he was gorgeous. All of them in fact, two male waiters, both tall, one black, one white, who both looked like they spent any time not serving food in the gym. They barely fitted in their crisp white shirts.

And the two women, equally stunning. One a busty blonde who reminded Emma of Elizabeth a little bit, the other a petite but beautiful woman of Asian descent by the look of her. The tight black and white skirts and tops they wore would normally have been the focus of all the men's attention, but compared to most of what the female guests were wearing they looked positively modest. *Oh the wonders of cock cages* thought Emma, taking Nate's hand and squeezing it as they followed the rest through to a grand dining room.

* * *

Catherine seated them opposite each other at the top of the table, with her taking the seat at the end. Next to them were two women they hadn't met yet. Katie seemed the youngest of the group, only mid-twenties, with shoulder-length dirty blonde hair who won the prize for the tiniest outfit of the night - a clingy black and white patterned slip dress that Emma thought would be more suited for the bedroom than a dinner party. She quickly confessed it was her and her new husband, Kyle's, first party like this.

It emerged she was here on the invitation of Fiona, who was sat opposite, next to Nate. Probably in her late-thirties, her obviously dyed dark red hair tumbled down her back, to what was possibly the most extreme dress at the table. It was a shiny black strapless mini-dress that looked more than anything like latex. It wasn't stretched flat though, instead it was ruched all over making it look far more elegant than it had any right to be.

'Do you like it?' Fiona said, noticing Emma looking at the dress. 'It's quite something isn't it. A complete bitch to put on, I can tell you.'

Emma laughed. 'Is it latex? I've only tried wearing that once and it didn't end well.'

Nathan began laughing too. 'Oh my God, I remember that, I had to rescue you from the changing room. Her arms were stuck trying to put it on.'

Fiona smiled, 'Yes it is, but thankfully this has a zip. Even then, lots of talc needed and thank goodness I don't have big boobs.' She looked pointedly across at Katie, whose youthful cleavage was not just on display but quite magnificently self-supporting. She was oblivious to the stares as she looked at Emma with a somewhat awed expression.

Emma turned towards her. 'Hello, Katie was it? How long have you and your husband been married?'

'Kyle, umm, nearly a year. It's our anniversary next month. I just want to say how much I adore your blog, I've read it all, several times.' She looked across the table with a big innocent smile. 'Actually it was Fiona who introduced me to it.'

'Oh wow, well thank you. It's lovely to actually, you know, meet people who enjoy it. So, you've been enjoying chastity as newlyweds?'

Katie laughed. 'Oh longer! Three years now.'

That got Emma's interest. The questions spilled out of her, 'So you caged him while you were engaged? I've always imagined that. What was it like? Wasn't it hard? What did you do for your honeymoon?'

'It's been so great,' Katie replied. 'I was so shy about everything. Fiona here ran a Pilates class in the village we live in, and she introduced me, well us, to the idea.'

'What did Kyle think of that?'

'It was his fault really. I wanted to save myself for marriage. I know it's old fashioned but it's how I was brought up. Kyle was really pressuring me, saying now we were engaged we can have sex. I burst into tears after one class with Fiona, and explained why, and then, well it all happened.'

Fiona chipped in. 'I told him if he loved her, she was worth waiting for. And isn't she just.'

Emma had to agree. Katie was extraordinarily beautiful. A complete natural girl next door beauty. She could understand too why Kyle hadn't wanted to wait.

'Didn't he keep pressuring you to unlock him though, how did you deal with that?'

Katie looked up at Fiona and bit her lip. 'I didn't have the key, so that made it easy. Fiona even helped with monthly check-ups so he couldn't complain he was sore, it was such a burden off my mind.'

Did she now, thought Emma, eyeing up the latex dressed woman opposite. *I bet she just loved having a young man all locked up.*

Katie continued in hushed tones, 'And he started doing all kinds of things to me, being so helpful, and other things too.' She leaned in and whispered, 'Sexual things, you know.'

Emma laughed quietly. 'Yes, I can guess. Well aren't you lucky to discover it so early. But what about the honeymoon, did you let him out. It wasn't like all those captions where you decided to keep him locked up?'

'Of course I let him out. The whole honeymoon.' She replied. 'Well, at least once a day.' Emma looked at her, surprised. 'I even let him cum. Once, you know, inside me. So we're properly married.'

Emma looked across at Fiona, clearly delighted in her little protege's work. She turned, and saw Catherine with a similar look of pride as she watched Fiona. *So that's where it's all coming from. That's no surprise.*

She brought her attention back to Katie. 'Just the once huh, didn't you like it?'

'It's nice, but it's so messy, even after he cleaned it up. Plus Fiona gave us the best wedding present. It's a copy of his, you know, willy. But it's bigger. And no mess. We make love with that a lot.'

'Katie, how many times have you let him out since the honeymoon?' Emma asked, a suspicion growing in her mind.

'Let him out? Never. I don't have the keys. We thought it would be better if Fiona looked after them. I'm allowed them again for our anniversary though.'

'And tonight,' interjected Catherine.

'Oh yes, I almost forgot. That's what got Kyle to agree to come along. But what do I need them for?' Katie looked to Fiona for an answer.

Fiona smirked. 'You'll find out soon, dear heart, don't you worry, it's a fun surprise.'

'I love surprises!' Katie bobbed up and down, fake clapping her hands. Emma rolled her eyes. She was like a little puppy. It was clear Fiona had a tight hold of her leash.

Poor Kyle, he looks the least keen to be here. That might explain why. Emma could only imagine the frustration of having this perfect little wife running around with him unable to reap the benefits. 'So what are your favourite things about chastity so far, Katie?'

'Oh well, there's you know, all the stuff he does to me. I have to have an orgasm every day, Fiona says, it's good for me. Oh and I love not wearing clothes around the house. I used to be such a prude,' she confided. 'And soon Fiona's promised to teach me some special things that will make it all even more fun.'

'That's... nice of her,' said Emma. From the way Fiona couldn't take her eyes off the young wife next to her Emma began to have her suspicions of just what 'special things' Fiona might have in mind. *Poor Kyle, I bet he regrets trying to jump the gun.*

Conversations were put on hold as bread was served by the unreasonably good-looking waiting staff. Emma noticed Nate's eyes wandering as the blonde waitress leaned across to pour some wine. *He's getting over those ruined orgasms then.* She gave him a gentle kick under the table and it brought him out of his reverie. Unfortunately, he started talking with Fiona next to him, which she wasn't sure was an improvement.

Food was quickly brought out. The smoked salmon and salmon mouse looked and smelled delicious. Katie had started tucking into hers next to Emma when a tinging on Catherine's glass made her put the half-eaten slice of toast down without anyone noticing.

'I'd like to thank you all for being here,' Catherine began. 'It's especially lovely to have Katie and Kyle here for the first time, guests of Fiona and David.' A polite murmur went around the table. 'Most of all of course, I want to extend a big welcome to our special guests, Emma and Nathan.' The murmur turned into applause. Emma and Nate both acknowledged it with a bit of an embarrassed wave. 'Emma, Nathan, your words have inspired us all. It's an honour to have you with us, and we look forward to all our time together.'

All our time together huh, thought Emma. *Given how the last two days have been I'm no less nervous about that.*

Emma felt she should say something given Catherine's expectant look. She looked around the room at them all. 'Thank you, everyone. It's lovely, and a huge surprise, to be here. It's amazing to meet other couples for whom chastity has had such an impact.' She looked at Nate, he was grinning, no doubt at her 'for whom'. She ignored him and went on. 'It seems incredible we could have been an encouragement to you. We can't wait to hear all your stories and get to know you better. If you have any questions, well, we're here all evening.'

She let out a nervous breath, turning to Catherine. 'I hope that was okay?'

'It was lovely, dear. Well done. And actually, I had a question. It's been quite a day for you and we haven't had time to catch up. How are you getting on?'

Emma fed back how the day had gone. She could hardly believe it herself. She looked at Nate opposite while she spoke. His cock had a cage around it, and this woman next to her had control of the keys. She refocused on Catherine, who was listening politely while scanning the table with her eyes. 'Why are you really doing this, with Nate and me?'

'I told you, I see potential in you. I mean it. Even more now I've seen you in action. I heard about your little act in the Stables this morning. Poor Nate, do you think he thought it was real?'

'From the way he reacted, yes, I think so.'

'And how did that make you feel?' Catherine asked.

'Very naughty, very turned on,' replied Emma, so only Catherine could hear.

Catherine placed her hand next to Emma's and lightly stroked the side of it. 'And tell me, what turned you on more. Imagining that gorgeous doctor's cock, fucking you, or watching your husband get masturbated by a very cute nurse?'

Emma chose not to be intimidated by her and replied. 'Oh the nurse, definitely.'

'Oh really. The way you sounded you had me convinced you were thinking of both.'

How did she know how I sounded? Emma noted. 'Well, you know, he was cute but I didn't actually see his cock. I was very fixed on what was happening to Nate's.'

'Oh it doesn't disappoint, I can assure you. He's the complete package.'

'I'm surprised you haven't pierced and caged it then. That does seem to be what you like doing to ones you admire.'

Catherine laughed and sipped her wine. 'Yes, I supposed I do.' She lifted her eyebrows. 'Who says I haven't?'

Emma laughed and decided to dig deeper. 'What about poor Rex. Do you ever let him out?'

'Only for special occasions. It's very tricky getting it back in. Maybe–', she paused for thought, 'Maybe tonight might count as a special occasion. Would you like that?'

Emma's heart raced at the thought of seeing that giant cock unlocked. She nodded, biting her lip. Over the last day, she had found her thoughts turning to Rex's caged cock more than a few times. In all the pictures she'd seen online since they'd discovered chastity play, she'd never seen one that size. The thought of it aroused both her curiosity and, well, other bits.

The conversation was paused by the waiting staff clearing away the plates while the main course was brought in. It was announced as venison with Dauphinoise potatoes. Emma smiled at Nate who tucked in voraciously. He didn't seem to be tiring yet.

'How does it feel, knowing I own your husband's cock?' Catherine looked up from the piece of meat she'd just skewered with her fork.

Catherine's question caught Emma completely off guard. She put down the slice of venison that was halfway to her mouth and said, 'Firstly, we haven't agreed to anything yet. And if we do, you just control it. I still own it. I'd be letting you borrow, well rent, it for a while.'

Catherine smirked at her response, 'Go on'.

'Secondly, it's very exciting for us both. I'm looking forward to not having the choice of unlocking him. It's not something we've ever tried. Somehow the idea of getting money for it, I don't know, it makes it even naughtier.'

'I'm very glad to hear that. What are you looking forward to most?' Catherine asked.

'How horny he gets, all the orgasms for me, I don't know. Actually no, it's the freedom. I've felt it even today. I love him caged, but I find being the one in control of the key surprisingly hard work. It's been a breath of fresh air.'

'That's very good to hear, just what I hoped.' A waiter topped up Emma's drink, and with a nod from Catherine, went around to Nathan too. Somehow he managed to knock it over though. Apologising profusely he brought him a fresh glass, already filled which Nathan got to drinking straight away.

Emma leaned in closer to Catherine. 'I'm excited but nervous about the check-ups too. Can you tell me any more about what they will involve? Will Mené be doing them?'

'Would you like that?' asked Catherine. 'Did you like the way she treated Nate?'

'Yes. She was lovely, and funny and yeah, I liked her a lot.'

'Consider it done then. She can take the lead on the check-ups. Now, don't let your food get cold, eat up.' Catherine brought a tiny square of venison up to her mouth and chewed on it delicately.

Emma took the chance to be quiet for a while. The conversations, and wine, were flowing around the table. Nate was holding up his end of the chat with Fiona but beginning to flag from the look of him. He returned her gaze and gave her a subtle half-lidded wink. Further down the table, she noticed Danielle slumped down into her chair a little, her focus on her husband opposite. Emma guessed why that might be and craned forward to see Duncan reacting to whatever it was she was doing with her foot under the table. *If Nate was a bit closer this would be a great time to play caged footsie.*

Catherine noticed Emma observing the black couple at the other end of the table. She brought out her phone, the first time Emma had seen her with one. It was the latest iPhone, she guessed. Catherine turned the phone to face Emma, and there was a slider on the screen with Danielle's name at the top above the ten on the sliding scale. 'Watch this.' Catherine pushed the slider from zero to one on the screen and Danielle's head immediately whipped around to look at them.

Emma was puzzled. Then it struck her what it might be controlling. 'Is it, a remote vibe?'

'Clever girl aren't you. Yes it is. Keep watching.' She gave Danielle a little wave with her fingers, and with the other hand slid the slider to four.

Immediately Danielle gripped the table with both hands, her breathing ragged. Catherine gently slid the slider back down, and then back up again, four or five times. Each time Danielle arched her back, trying her best to hide it. What she couldn't hide though were her nipples. They'd shot up like bullets, obvious to all through the revealing red dress.

'How powerful is that thing, that's amazing,' said Emma.

'Oh it's not *that* powerful, the battery has to last. It's mostly because she's very sensitive. She hasn't cum in a while.'

'Is she in chastity too?' Emma asked.

'Not as such. Female belts are so awkward. But this works much the same. You know whatever the cause, the vagina clenches during orgasm. Well, the toy inside her, it's called an Oestrus, monitors for that. And can tell if it's removed too. So, no easy way to cheat.'

'That's clever. But it vibrates too?'

Catherine just nodded her head towards Danielle, swiping her fingers on the phone. Before Emma could look she heard a stifled cry from the athlete. Everyone stared. From what she could fathom most of them weren't sure what was going on but Fiona looked straight back at Catherine's phone. 'You must tell me where you get those,' she said to Catherine but looked across the table to where Katie was still trying to see what was going on further down. 'Remind me, how long do the batteries last?'

'A month if used judiciously. It depends if the counter-climax measures kick in.' Catherine replied.

'Counter what?' It seemed Fiona was as clueless about it as Emma.

'Oh, a new feature. Maybe I'll show you later. We really must be getting on. Let's get dessert out.'

Emma had another question. 'What about Duncan, why's he caged?'

'All men are better caged, darling. I learnt that from you. If you want to know, they have a similar arrangement to the two of you. Only she's the one "under contract". It didn't take long to convince her to cage him up once we got started.'

Emma glanced again up the table. Danielle was gripping the table still, clearly using all her willpower to hold back whatever Catherine's device was doing to her. Emma had imagined it was simply to avoid embarrassment that she was resisting the toy's vibrations. But from the sound of it, something worse than humiliation might be involved. She looked again at the phone on the table. 'CCM: On' was written in red beside the scale. *Counter Climax Measures - what the hell could that be?*

To everyone's relief, but particularly Danielle's, Catherine slid the dial down, not to zero, but to two. As Danielle visibly relaxed, conversation resumed and the last bits of the food were quickly eaten as Catherine pressed the waiting staff to move things on.

Emma stayed quiet as the plates were taken away. She barely even noticed Nate trying not to stare at the waitresses' tops. It did seem they were doing it on purpose. His eyelids were starting to droop.

She stared back down at Danielle. *So she's the one who's under Catherine's control, and her husband has got caged up as part of it.* Emma wasn't sure what that meant for her. She thought she'd be safe from Catherine's games but it seemed partners could get caught up in it all too. *That's a worrying thought.*

The sharp smell of lime brought her out of her reveries. In front of her had been placed a delicately stacked cake, a very light green custard in between each thin layer of sponge, cut into a perfect square and then topped with what looked like swiss meringue.

How did Catherine know this was her favourite? Emma was sure she'd not mentioned it on the blog.

'To finish we have Key Lime Icebox Cake. I had the key limes flown over, so I hope you enjoy it.'

Emma sliced off a corner with her cake fork and tried to elegantly get it to her mouth. She failed at the last hurdle, it just smelled too good. She closed her eyes in pleasure as the soft custard battled with the sharp lime juice all across her taste buds. 'Oh my God, this is heavenly.'

'I'm so glad you like it.' Catherine paused. 'I wonder what else we'll find you like over the coming months.'

Emma noticed she barely touched her dessert. She looked over at Nate who'd finished his even before Emma. He was eyeing up Catherine's. Emma prayed he wouldn't be so rude as to offer to finish hers.

'Catherine...' Nate started.

Oh no, Nate if you embarrass me I'm going to kill you.

'Thank you so much for this wonderful dinner. It was absolutely delicious.'

Good boy, I knew you wouldn't let me down.

Nate continued, 'I'm pretty exhausted from everything today, as I'm sure you can imagine. I think I'm going to head up and get some rest. I hope that's okay.'

Emma looked at Nate, giving him a pout that was trying to convey a mix of sadness he was feeling so wiped out and a bit of regret at leaving so soon. 'Do you want me to come up with you, baby?'

'No darling. Everyone's here to see you. I'm still not feeling one hundred per cent.' He gave her a tired grin. 'You stay and have fun, I'll have a lie-down. Maybe I'll come down later. But just message me if you need me, okay?'

'Alright, I will, I promise.' Emma replied. As he rose he said his goodbyes to those he'd been talking with, and walking around the top of the table, he put his hand on Catherine's shoulder as he said thank you again. Emma noticed her recoil just a tiny amount at his touch. But perhaps she'd just not expected it. Catherine accepted his thanks with a polite smile and then turned back to talk with Fiona as Nate came around to Emma.

'Have fun darling, and don't do anything I wouldn't do. I'm just upstairs if you need me, okay? He kissed her on the cheek, 'Watch out for that Fiona, she's a man-eater.'

I don't think it's men she wants to eat, Emma thought. But didn't say anything. Instead, she turned and kissed Nate on the cheek. 'I love you, I'll be good, I promise.'

Nate kissed her back, then whispered in her ear. 'I know, but you don't have to be too good. Just tell me all about it later. I wish I could stay but, I'm about to fall asleep in the Key Lime Pie.' He looked pointedly at Catherine's leftovers. 'Do you think if I asked her...'

'Nathan Stevens don't you dare. Get your gorgeous arse to bed and I'll come join you later. I love you.'

With a final kiss and a wave to the rest of the room Nate headed through the big wooden doors. Emma watched him go, wondering if she should join him. Looking around the room there was a growing air of expectancy. Something was about to happen. She needed to find out what.

The Queue for the Loo

When Nate left, Emma and a few others took the opportunity to take a bathroom break. A couple more scattered to other bathrooms but she found herself waiting outside the one by the hallway with Danielle. Perhaps it was her imagination, but Emma thought she could hear a gentle buzzing. For sure Danielle was having a hard time concentrating. *Oh, that explains how she was earlier.* Her nipples were still rigidly poking the tight red fabric. There was a slight tremble if you looked closely.

'Are you okay?' Emma asked, not quite sure what to say.

'I'm fine, just, it doesn't matter,' Danielle replied.

'She told me, Catherine. About the phone thing.' Emma risked being honest.

'Fucking Catherine, of course she did.' Danielle shook her head, leaning heavily on the corner of a wooden plant pot stand. 'Did, did you see it, the app?'

'Yes, why?' asked Emma.

'What level did it go up to? Did you see?' Danielle had a desperate look in her eye.

'Ten, it went up to ten, for sure.'

'That was one hundred per cent, she put it on as high as it goes?' Danielle asked.

'Oh, no sorry, I see what you mean. No, the scale went up to ten. She only put the slider up to, four, maybe five actually.'

'Oh my fucking God. That was only fifty per cent earlier? I thought it

144

might be all it could do. Oh shit, oh shit, oh shit.' She grabbed Emma's arm. 'Was there, an on-off switch, something about climaxes maybe?'

'Yes, she talked about that. The Counter-Climax Measures.' She took Danielle's hand in hers. 'What does it do exactly?'

Danielle's eyes began to tear up. She turned her back against the wall and sank down to the floor, her dress pulling up against the wooden panel so her pretty matching red knickers were visible too. 'You know those dog collars, the ones that shock them, to make them behave?'

'Yeah, but aren't they illegal now?'

'Too fucking right they are. Disgusting to do that to a stupid animal. Although what does that make me?' Danielle started to weep, folding her arms across her knees and pressing her head down on them.

Emma crouched down beside her, putting it all together. 'Are you telling me it gives you electric shocks if you orgasm?' Danielle just nodded her head on her arms, crying harder now. 'That's barbaric! Why would you let her...' Emma trailed off, thinking about what Nate and she were considering. He was in bed now, her cage around his cock. All because Catherine wanted it. 'She's giving you money to do this?'

Danielle nodded again.'It's not just the shocks, that's just her sadistic twist. We're trapped, we can't get out, it would ruin us.'

Before she could say any more the door opened and to Emma's surprise the maid, Alexandra, stepped out, nearly tripping over Danielle's legs. 'Oh I'm so sorry,' she muttered before dashing off.

Probably isn't supposed to be using this one, thought Emma. She put her hand on Danielle's shoulder. 'Do you want to use the bathroom first?'

Danielle shook her head. 'No, you go, thank you, Emma.' She looked up, mascara smears around her big brown eyes. 'I really do love your blog. I hope you and Nate, well, you know.'

Emma didn't know, but she didn't want to ask, with Danielle in this state. Maybe she could corner her later. Anyway, she really needed to pee. She stood and went inside the loo. To her surprise, it was beautifully decorated. Unlike the stuffy old wood panels of the hall it was tiled with sparkling turquoise and had a very funky mirror that was backlit somehow. She would have stopped to admire it for longer but her bladder was insisting she had other priorities. Lifting her dress and pulling down her panties in one move she had to stop herself as she nearly sat on the bare ceramic bowl. *Alexandra must have left it up after cleaning it.* She flicked the seat down, but had to wait, dancing around with her dress lifted and panties around her knees as the lid made an annoyingly slow descent.

'Bloody self-closing lids, hurry up!' she said to the toilet. But she didn't want to risk getting her beautiful dress messy so she waited and finally, oh joy, could pee.

As she wiped, her fingers lingered between her legs. She thought about Danielle, having something in there. She'd often considered buying a remote-controlled vibe. She thought it would be fun if Nate could control it, maybe out at a restaurant. But what Danielle was going through was anything but fun. *That Catherine, what a psycho. We are going to have to be very careful.*

After quickly tidying up and washing her hands she pushed the door open. Danielle was nowhere to be seen. Emma looked at the stairs, thinking of Nate up there. She just wanted to go and tell him everything he'd missed. But that would be rude, and you don't want to be rude to a psycho. Maybe some more wine would help. Conveniently she returned to the dining room just as the couple she hadn't met yet, Zoe and Jeremy, had taken it upon themselves to get some more bubbly. He seemed a timid, skinny little thing, in contrast to his voluptuous wife, who also had more than enough personality for both of them, it seemed.

'Bubbly, get your bubbly 'ere,' she shouted, as Jeremy, popped a cork across the room.

Emma raised her hand, then pulled it down. She wasn't in class. 'Actually yes, that would be lovely, thank you.'

Since she'd been gone Fiona had shifted up to take Nate's empty place next to Catherine. Preferring to avoid another conversation she popped herself in Fiona's previous chair.

'Oh Zoe, do that thing you do,' urged Fiona. She nudged Emma, 'You've got to watch this, it's her party trick.'

Zoe pretended not to want to do whatever it was. She didn't fool anyone. With a few more shouts of encouragement she stood and sauntered over to the bottle as Jeremy opened it with a pop. She carefully took it from him and then placed it on the end of the table, looking around and picking up a pair of ice tongs. 'Oh gentlemen, who's going to be the lucky one tonight I wonder?' she said. She stroked her spare hand slowly up and down the top of the bottle, a predatory look in her eyes. Emma looked around too. Every man was fixated on her, on her hand, she could imagine why. Jeremy looked to be in some serious pain. How long was it since he'd felt his wife's hand do that to him.

Katie whispered, 'It's not much of a party trick, anyone can wank a bottle.' Emma was about to agree when Zoe took the tongs and knocked them hard several times against the side of the bottle. To her astonishment, the champagne surged out of the top. 'Okay that's cool,' said Kyle. The bubbles cascaded over her fingers then to oohs and ahhs Zoe slid her mouth right down over the frothing hole and started giving the champagne a blowjob, a very impressive one. She drank down the bubbles and licked up the sides of the bottle in a way that got all of the men undoubtedly tight in their cages.

'That's a good party trick,' Emma said to Katie. 'Look at her husband.' Katie looked at Jeremy, who was now gripping the top of a chair with both hands, a pained expression obvious. 'I wonder when she last did that to him.' Emma chuckled.

Catherine slid down next to Emma and put her arm around her shoulder in a very familiar fashion. 'Just a few years ago she wouldn't say boo to a goose. Quite the transformation don't you think?'

'Remarkable,' Emma replied, trying not to shrug her arm off her shoulders. 'Jeremy doesn't seem to share your enthusiasm though.'

'Oh, that's because he's got spikes on. He objected to her taking another boyfriend.'

'Wait what?' Emma asked. *Another* boyfriend?'

'Men have been doing it behind our backs for years, Emma. At least she has the decency to tell him.'

'You know we're not into that, at all, don't you Catherine.' Emma turned, using the opportunity to pull away from her arm.

'Yes, yes, of course. We all read the blog.' Catherine patted Emma's knee and stood. 'Gentlemen, I think it's time for you to withdraw next door. We'll join you in a while.'

The men all suddenly perked up and formed an orderly queue out of the door. Kyle sat where he was, not sure what to do. Catherine patted him on the cheek. 'You too Kyle. Who knows, maybe you'll get lucky tonight.'

Clearly oblivious to the exact meaning, even the hint of something happening was more than enough for Kyle to leap up and jog around the table to join the other men as they left.

'Where's he going?' Katie asked in a nervous little voice. Fiona moved to sit next to her, her hand resting on Katie's bare thigh, giving it a little squeeze. 'Don't you worry, princess. I told you, it's a surprise. The night is just beginning, are you ready for some fun?'

The trigger words of surprise and fun were apparently enough to wipe any concerns from Katie's head. She jiggled up and down again and Emma watched Fiona gazing down her top. *I bet she picked that out for her* Emma thought, before realising she was wearing something Catherine had picked out for her. She picked up the champagne, toying with it in her hands. *To drink, or to sleep, that is the question.* Just as she was deciding to go get the hell out of here and cuddle up with Nate, Danielle came back in the room. She caught Emma's eye and gave a sigh of relief, a veiled look of hatred saved for Catherine next to her.

'Oh Danielle,' said Catherine. 'So good to have you back. If we're all here, let's finish off this champagne and we can head through too. Katie, Emma, I think you're going to love what's next door.'

Fuck it, I can always leave once I find out. Emma downed the champagne in a couple of glugs and handed it out to 'bottle blower' Zoe who was pouring it out. The waiting staff seemed to have disappeared. After a few minutes, Elizabeth popped her head through the door. Emma wondered where she'd been all evening. 'They're ready for you,' she told Catherine. With that, they all stood, and followed her out. *This is going to get weird, I can feel it in my bones.*

The Chastity W.A.G.S.

Catherine led the women down the corridor to another room that Emma hadn't been in before. Elizabeth was already there, holding the heavy wooden door open. She stood, leaning her back against it, looking more like a hooker than personal assistant. She'd changed from the corset-suit of earlier. Unlike the elegance of everyone else, her outfit looked cheap. *Cheap and slutty, what an odd choice.* It was a grey metallic mini-dress, tight with a scoop neckline that barely kept her breasts from falling out. She didn't catch anyone's eye as they entered, following them in and closing the doors with a heavy thunk.

It was a large, but strange room. At the end by the door were four large upholstered grey sofas plus a few matching armchairs arrayed around the three walls. The wooden floor was covered in the centre by a large and luxurious rug, that left only a small gap between it and the furniture. A square coffee table sat in the middle of the rug, its feet buried in the fabric. Emma had never seen a rug or carpet so deep, it was a good ten centimetres. No wonder Elizabeth had struggled across it. But that wasn't what made the room so strange.

Some four metres into the room was a curtain, stretching from one side to the other. It reminded Emma of an intimate little playhouse she'd once been to at the top of a fancy pub in Richmond. That had only seated a couple of dozen people, which had been awkward as the play they'd gone to see had been terrible, but she couldn't get up the nerve to leave with so few other patrons. The grey curtains complemented the rug, but the obvious question was what was on the other side.

'If you'd like to take a seat, ladies, we can begin.' Catherine sat in the single armchair on the rear wall, taking central place – the queen seated upon her throne.

Emma saw Fiona making a beeline for Katie, but managed to grab the young woman's hand and tug her towards the sofa next to Catherine's chair. She dropped down next to Danielle, who gave her a welcoming smile. Fiona did not look pleased. Emma tried to hide a grin as she listened to Katie asking what this was all about. 'I have no idea, I'm in the same boat as you. I guess we're about to find out.'

Elizabeth was the only one left standing and Emma took a moment to review what she was wearing. While she was surrounded by women in incredibly revealing outfits, Elizabeth stood out as just plain slutty. She struggled to cross the rug with her matching grey high heels on, but she persisted, and she stopped in the centre of the room, holding onto one of the curtains for support. She looked to Catherine, waiting for permission for something.

Catherine ignored her and looked around the room. 'Ladies, I hope you enjoyed dinner. Thank you again for joining me tonight. This is, remarkably, our tenth meeting of the Chastity WAGS.' A little 'ohhh' went around the room. 'This is of course what the evening has really become about over time. As always, everything we share here is in the strictest confidence. Ever since my dear husband passed, knowing that I'm able to share the joys and benefits of this wonderful experience with you has given me something to look forward to. So, my beautiful WAGS, who will go first and share their chastity blessings?'

The one lady in the group Emma hadn't yet spoken to raised her hand. 'Ah yes, Helen, thank you, how have things been with Rob since we last met?'

Helen was the eldest in the group and had hardly said a word at dinner, so Emma was surprised she'd volunteered. She guessed she was in her mid-sixties, although she looked amazing on it. Her unashamedly grey hair was cut in a neat bob and her little black dress was more formal than most, and a little longer, but she was radiating sexiness that made Emma smile.

Helen stood. Her voice trembled a little as she started to speak, but she soon found her confidence as she gave her report. 'It's actually our own anniversary this month, so I thought I'd go first today. A whole year of exploring chastity. I really can't believe it. What a year it's been.' She turned to face Emma. 'Emma, can I just say a huge thank you to you now. I've actually written to you a few times on the blog and you've been so helpful. I can honestly say, with your help, and Catherine's of course, you've saved my marriage.'

Emma's mind went into overdrive as she tried to think which messages Helen might be referring to. She got so many from older couples that she couldn't be sure which it would be.

Helen continued, 'As some of you will know, our marriage, our sex life, any romance, was dead just a year ago. Honestly it had been for a long time. I love Rob but nothing of that original spark was there any more. It was only really the thought of the embarrassment of telling our family and friends and church that we were getting divorced that stopped us going further. That was until Catherine, bless her, came alongside and despite my initial ridicule, suggested what we are all here to celebrate. Locking up his cock.'

A little cheer went around the room.

'I followed Catherine's, and Emma's, ideas on how to introduce it. To my wonderment, even that first conversation got Rob hard. He'd been struggling with erectile dysfunction for some time, or so I thought. I interrogated him using some of those questions Emma came up with—' She paused and clasped her hands together in thanks.

Everyone around the room nodded and smiled at Emma. *This is surreal, is my blog really having such an impact?*

Helen continued, '—I discovered that he had been masturbating nearly daily, throughout our entire marriage.' Tuts of disapproval and murmurs of sympathy came from all sides. 'No wonder he'd had no energy for me, he was wasting it all into a tissue, and addicted to pornography.'

Emma was utterly fascinated. *This is like some kind of Alcoholics Anonymous meeting.*

'Honestly caging him was a huge relief to him. I was finally saving him from himself. He is transformed back into the man I knew he truly was.

151

Romantic, charming, attentive. My friends can't believe it. They've asked what my secret is.' Helen paused, a naughty smile lighting up her face. 'Six of them know now, my entire ladies Bible study group.' Catherine laughed out loud, the first honest laugh Emma had heard from her. 'Three of them have tried it, and given their and my reports, I think the rest will too.' The room broke into clapping and congratulations.

'Tell us about the sex,' Zoe yelled. Everyone laughed.

Helen fidgeted but took a deep breath and continued. 'It's still incredible. He'd never, you know, gone down on me, before all this.'

Katie gave Emma an amazed look. *You have no idea how good you have it, sweetie.* She patted her hand.

Helen went on, 'This month we tried, you know, him licking back there. Who knew that felt so good?'

'All of us now,' Fiona chortled.

Helen laughed too and sat back down. Catherine thanked her and asked if anyone else would like to share. Her gaze rested on Zoe, who seemed to finally notice.

Zoe stood up, supporting herself on the arm of the chair. 'Oops, I think I drank a bit too much of the champagne.' She let out a little burp. 'It's been an interesting couple of months since we last met. Jeremy had been all on board with me sleeping with some bulls, but when I wanted one as a boyfriend he'd become most objectionable.' She turned and picked up her half-full glass of bubbly, taking a few sips.

Katie turned to Catherine, 'A boyfriend? How can she have a boyfriend if she's married?'

Emma frowned, 'Sounds like cuckolding, having sex with another man, and sometimes even a relationship.'

'I don't have to do that do I? It would break Kyle's heart.'

Emma felt a sudden flood of empathy for the nubile but naive girl beside her. 'No, you never need to do that. Nate and I would never, I don't think it's a good idea.'

Zoe continued after finishing her glass. 'So as you all suggested, we've tried the spiked cage this time around. It hasn't stopped him complaining, but at least now he's complaining about the spikes and not my boyfriend.'

Catherine laughed loudly next to them, Fiona too. The others seemed to join in as though it were expected. Katie stayed quiet, and so did Elizabeth, who seemed to wince at the comment.

Catherine spoke up, 'So are you going to let him out of the spikes tonight?'

'Well I dunno,' replied Zoe. 'Let's see what everyone thinks later'

Some of the other women started chanting, 'Spikes, spikes.' Zoe laughed and managed to sit herself down without falling over.

'Would anyone else like to speak? Emma, would you like to say something, perhaps share what you did today?'

Emma didn't feel like sharing. It was clear Catherine wanted the others to know about the arrangement. *I'm not your little pet.* 'Actually, I have a question. What's behind the curtain?'

Catherine didn't look pleased but with a glance at her watch she decided to move things on. She put on a smile and took back control of proceedings. 'What a good question. Shall we show her, girls?'

Gloryholes Galore

With a nod to Elizabeth, the curtains were drawn back along rails hidden in the ceiling. What they revealed was an upholstered wall, a darker grey than the curtains. Katie gasped, others laughed, and despite her misgivings, Emma felt herself clench at what was on display.

Along the wall at regular intervals were holes of about 6 inches in diameter. Beautifully upholstered, a little leather ring of padding around each one. Eight holes in total, spaced evenly along, a few feet between each.

Through seven of them hung cocks, caged cocks. It was a set of gloryholes. Beautifully upholstered gloryholes.

'Holy shit is that Kyle's cock,' exclaimed Katie. 'That's so cool.'

Emma's eyes scanned along the row. The black one was obviously Duncan's. It defied the cliche in that it wasn't anything beyond average in size, although it did look pretty snug in the cage that was a new design to Emma, a mix of bars and a flat plate at the top and surrounding it.

The spiked cage must be Jeremy's. It looked very uncomfortable. It was a small cage, maybe three inches long, but the small triangular spikes protruded from every bar and ring. Even a set of them pressing into the head of his cock. *No wonder he complained.*

The next cock looked like it belonged to an older guy, so Helen's husband, Rob was her guess. It was pretty average, not quite fitting the cage that was an attractive set of bars curving down tightly over his balls.

Beside that was a tiny little cage. It had a solid metal cap with just a few holes in the middle that made it look like a steel pepper pot. The cock inside it was clearly squashed in. Emma couldn't imagine how uncomfortable that must be, not much better than the spikes. She guessed it belonged to Dave, Fiona's husband. A cursory glance from Fiona suggested she was right.

That meant the next one was probably Kyle's. Katie's direction of gaze confirmed it. Emma thought she recognised it as a 'Jail Bird'. One of the expensive custom cages that was raved about in the forums she'd visited. It was attractive, but most noticeable were his balls beneath it. While most of them, apart from Rob's, had obviously full balls, poor Kyle's were as full as any Emma had ever seen. She could only imagine a whole year's pent up frustration, just how achy and sensitive they must be. With a bit of a shock, she realised that was just what they'd signed up Nate for.

'Do you ever give him any release, let him cum?' Emma asked Katie.

Katie looked puzzled. 'How would I do that, his cock is caged up?'

'There are lots of ways. I talk about them on the blog.'

'Oh, are they the big articles? I don't read those much. I like the pictures best.'

You can lead a horse to water but you can't make her drink. Poor Kyle.

Emma's thoughts were interrupted by Catherine standing. 'Ladies, let's unlock shall we.'

As the women stood, all removing keys from necklaces or purses, or in Fiona's case, an anklet.

There were still two cocks unaccounted for though. The first was easy to guess. She'd seen it only the day before. Rex's enormous cock hung through the hole. It dwarfed any of the others, made them all seem small, even the larger of the rest of the set. Even in steel, it looked magnificent. As the other women went up to unlock their respective cocks Catherine didn't make a move to do the same to it.

Similarly, Katie didn't move from beside Emma. *She doesn't have the key* Emma remembered. 'You should go and get your key,' Emma emphasised the last bit, 'from Fiona. Imagine how happy it would make Kyle to let him out.'

'Are you sure that's okay?' Katie asked.

'Yes, definitely. You can do whatever you want to him, okay? It's your cock to have fun with.' Emma leaned in, 'Why don't you give him a blowjob, I bet that would make his year.'

Katie looked unsure. 'I've always thought it looked fun but I've never been able to. I don't know what to do.'

'You've watched it in porn, haven't you?'

'Yes, they look so sexy but I can't put him down my throat like that can I?' Katie rubbed her throat with her fingers.

'You don't have to do that. Just kiss and lick the head of him, and stroke the rest with your hand. He'll adore it, I promise.'

'If you're sure it's okay?'

'It's more than okay, I promise, and I'm the expert,' Emma declared. 'Now go and get your keys, and suck your husband's cock!'

Katie jumped up and went straight over to Fiona who pulled the key out with clear reluctance. She gave an angry glance at Emma as she dumped it into Fiona's hand. Katie, seemingly oblivious, bounced on the deep carpet over to Kyle's cock. It jumped at her touch. This was going to be as much a surprise for him as her it seemed.

As Katie remembered how to unlock it the other cocks were being uncaged. Fiona appeared to not even want to touch Dave's cock, dropping the cage to the ground and stalking back to her chair without looking again at Emma. Looking at his uncaged cock Emma was amazed. How it possibly fit in that tiny cage was hard to understand. It seemed to keep on expanding. Not getting erect as much as simply rediscovering its true size. It still hung down, but was perhaps five times the size it must have been when compressed.

Rob's older cock was making a valiant effort at getting hard, but not being very successful. It bounced as it throbbed a little. Emma found herself wishing for it to grow, a desire it seemed Helen shared as she gazed at it from back in her seat.

In contrast was Jeremy's cock. The red welts from the spikes were evident along the shaft, but it didn't seem to care. It stood up hard and proud, jutting into the air like a flag pole. A short flag pole. It was perhaps a little under five inches in length. Not much below the average, but nothing to write home about.

Duncan's cock, however, was another matter altogether. Apparently he was a grower, not a shower. He wasn't huge, but his big black cock grew magnificently once uncaged. He wasn't circumcised, unlike most of the men barring Dave it seemed. But as he grew the glistening pink head of his cock emerged from his foreskin like a turtle out of his shell. Emma found herself quite fascinated. She glanced at Danielle and saw an untamed look of lust in his wife's eyes, and remembered why that was quite so intense. Danielle bucked in her seat, her focus shifting to Catherine. Sure enough, Catherine had her phone out. Danielle trembled as Emma watched Catherine push the slider up on her phone, to a little beyond what it had been earlier. She locked the phone and put it back down.

All this had distracted Emma from the real mystery. A thought made her heart race. She looked at the seventh, mystery cock. It couldn't be Nate's, could it? If so it had been put in a very different cage. This one was unlike the rest. No bars. Just a solid metal tube that pushed the cock down, and to some extent the balls with it. Compared to most of the others one other feature stood out. The lack of any hair whatsoever. All the others seemed shaved or at least neatly trimmed, but everything on show there was completely hairless and smooth. *Who the hell does that belong to?* Emma looked around. All the women besides Katie had returned to their seats. Danielle glanced at the mystery cock but as far as Emma could tell that was just curiosity. Her eyes were straight back to her husbands while her hand tightly gripped the sofa's fabric arm.

Katie had finally unlocked Kyle and Emma wasn't sure if she'd ever seen a penis get hard so fast. It literally sprung to life. It was an attractive cock too, a bit above average in size, but just very, pretty. It reminded her of Nate's, although he was a bit smaller. Her mind went to him sleeping upstairs. She was feeling a bit of regret that he wasn't there too as Katie started to kiss and fondle Kyle's steely hard erection.

Fiona intervened. 'Katie, come back here, princess. Catherine has something she wants to say.'

Katie looked about to object, and Kyle seemed to certainly protest, pushing himself even further through the hole as she stopped touching. She came back to her seat next to Emma. 'You can have more fun soon I'm sure. Let's see what happens next.' Emma's curiosity had got the better of her. Whatever weird stuff this lot were into, right here was a fantasy come true. She was eager to know how it worked.

'Ladies, as has become the tradition, you can now make the case for why your husband should be the one to get the big reward.'

Danielle was the first to make her case. She said how romantic and loving Duncan had been since he was caged up, and that it had made a huge difference to their home life. Since he'd been dropped by the club he played for, the third time for them, he'd begun to help with their two young kids and seriously talk about whether Danielle's football career might be the one that takes precedence.

Emma was impressed. She couldn't imagine what it must be like to have your dreams shattered like that. There would be a lot of pride to get over to consider letting your wife succeed where you hadn't.

Helen made a similar case about Rob being transformed in terms of romance and shyly reminded everyone of the things he was doing now. *They are so cute,* Emma decided. Zoe said that she was more interested in a punishment than a reward, and Fiona didn't even bother speaking on behalf of Rob. That left Katie to speak, she looked from Fiona's scowl to Emma.

'May I speak on someone's behalf?' Emma asked.

'I don't see why not,' Catherine said.

'I'd like to nominate Kyle. Well, more Katie I suppose. She's just told me she's never given him a blowjob, and I think she'd really like to try it, wouldn't you?'

'Oh yes, yes please' Katie begged.

'That doesn't mean he has to cum,' argued Fiona, giving Emma a hateful glare.

Emma ignored her look.'The poor boy hasn't even had a ruin since their honeymoon nearly a year ago. Is there a better reason to let him?'

'But it's almost their anniversary, I'm sure Katie would like to wait until then.' Fiona offered in a final bid to keep Kyle from cumming. Katie didn't look at all convinced. Emma leapt on her doubt.

'Katie, would you like to give your husband a blowjob and make him cum?'

'Oh yes, please, if that's really okay?' Her innocent enthusiasm won the day. It was decided that Kyle would get the grand prize, and Rob and Duncan would both get ruined orgasms.

'Can I do it now? What do you recommend?' Katie asked the room but focused on Emma.

A sly smile appeared on Catherine's face, 'Why don't you show her, Emma?'.

Both Katie and Emma didn't know how to respond. Kyle's cock really was beautiful, and sticking out from the wall like that it was so erotic, and also safely impersonal. This was something Nate had teased her about for so long. Emma thought about the fact she wouldn't be able to suck Nate at all while the piercing healed, or even perhaps the whole year. *Would he mind, if I did? I don't know.* Something felt wrong about it, especially with him absent. *Maybe if he was here, if he was watching and I did it to drive him wild.* She remembered how the threat of Mené with her lips around him had inspired her this morning. It had got her completely crazy.

Emma looked again at Kyle's cock; hard, throbbing, desperate. She was so torn. She'd love to suck it, to make the fantasy come true, and to show Katie just what the perfect blowjob should be. But without Nate here, it just felt wrong. She came up with an alternative.

'Perhaps, I'll show you with my hands, and you use your mouth?' she suggested to Katie. The little puppy seemed to like that idea. She sprang back to the hole and sank down on her knees, her breasts straining against the thin material of her top. The scene was like one of Emma's captions come to life. *If only Kyle could see her too, I think he'd pop without a single suck.*

Katie hovered there, looking over at Emma for her to take the lead. As she stood, so did Helen and Danielle, the latter had her husband's cock in her mouth before Emma even got to the wall. She watched the beautiful woman down on her knees, sucking her husband as though her life depended on it. Her lithe, athletic body barely concealed by the dress and all the sexier for it. She splayed her hands against the wall, as though trying to get as close to Duncan as she could. She was pressing her face right to the wall, easily taking his length down her throat, rolling her head in a figure of eight to pleasure him. *Doesn't she need to breathe? Wow, she's got skills.*

Catherine made a polite cough. Danielle froze, nose to the wall. Emma could see the outline of Duncan's cock pressing her throat out. 'Danielle, remember the deal. Only one of you can climax.' Danielle slowly pulled out, his long cock dripping her thick, bubbly saliva over her chin and top.

'Please Catherine, have mercy. We all agreed he could have a ruin.'

'And he can, as long as you don't orgasm first.' Catherine unlocked her phone and slid her thumb right up the screen.

Danielle cried out, grabbing everyone's attention who hadn't already been watching. She dived back to Duncan's cock, wanking it with her hand, sucking on the tip. She was struggling to do even that, her body arching, every muscle tense. 'No, please no, don't make me–' but it was too late. She yelled as all the pent up arousal from God knows how long surged through her body. Danielle clung onto her husband's cock with both hands as though it was saving her from being washed away in a flood. Her orgasm went on, and on. Emma had never heard noises like it. Deep, sobbing, gasping moans. On the floor her dress went a dark scarlet as she gushed squirt after squirt.

'Oh my God did she just wet herself?' Katie whispered.

'No, I mean, probably not, you know how women can ejaculate?' Emma quietly explained. Katie looked completely baffled. 'Squirting, you've seen it in porn, surely?' Katie just shook her head. 'Okay well, it's not pee, mostly. It's complicated, but it's normal, I promise.'

Danielle's climax seemed to have finished. She knelt there, her hands still locked around her husband's rigid cock, her head bowed below them as though praying to some phallic idol. She heaved in breaths, sobbing quietly as she let them out. Emma looked at Catherine. She was utterly focused on Danielle, her thumb resting on the phone's screen. Her eyes were wide, taking every moment in. She watched her slowly slide her thumb back up the screen once more, and heard Danielle cry out in pleasure once more. *You love to pull the puppet strings, don't you Catherine.*

Emma looked back at Danielle, her mouth was back around her husband's cock, sucking, stroking her hands. Emma realised her own heart was racing. This was unlike anything she'd ever seen. Part of her felt sorry for Danielle, but another part envied her. The idea of that toy, out of her control, buried inside her. Emma realised how deeply aroused watching this had made her. She wanted to walk over, kneel by Danielle, hug her, feel her moving against her husband. But Katie's voice brought her back to the task in hand. She had another cock to touch, to caress. This was it, this was real. She wished again Nate was here. Not just for his support, but because deep down she wanted to suck every cock stuck through the wall. And maybe if he was here, she'd feel okay about it. But holding one was enough. For now.

She stepped up to where the beautiful young woman waited on her knees, glancing back to Catherine who was now watching them with interest. *I won't be your puppet, not today.* She turned back to Katie who gave her a big, excited smile. 'So, you want to learn how to suck your husband's cock?'

Emma leaned on the wall with one hand so she could undo her heels. Unwittingly she bent over and realised the tip of Kyle's cock was just inches from her mouth. The urge to slide her lips around it was overwhelming. Her mouth actually watered at the thought, and that wasn't all that was getting wet. She stayed there, fiddling with the strap on her shoe, masochistically enjoying tormenting herself with the thought of sucking it. She glanced at Katie, kneeling below, looking up with her soft brown eyes, her full lips a little open in anticipation. *Oh, Kyle, I'm going to make up for what you had taken away.*

Flicking the first shoe off she stood again to swap feet. With a cheeky smile to Katie, she wrapped her fingers around Kyle's cock and used it to balance on. 'Sorry Katie, I needed a railing,' Emma joked. Katie laughed, not aware of just what a significant moment this was for Emma. *I have my hand wrapped around another man's cock.* Once again Emma wished Nate was there, this would be blowing his mind.

With the other shoe removed Emma sunk her feet into the rug, and then lowered herself down to her knees, still holding onto Kyle. 'I love that men come with a handle, don't you?' Katie giggled and nodded. She couldn't take her eyes off her husband's cock, Emma could see desire building in her eyes. 'Okay, so the key to a good blowjob is it's not all about your mouth, okay? You see this bit here,' Emma indicated his frenulum under his cock head. 'That is the most sensitive bit, kind of like your clit, and you know how good that feels. But the whole head, all of this bit, feels amazing in your mouth.'

Emma looked around the room and found Elizabeth who was standing over by the empty gloryhole watching proceedings. She was lost in thought as it took a couple of calls from Emma to get her attention. 'Hey Liz, have we got any lube?' Elizabeth nodded and picked out a couple of white bottles from a basket in the corner and brought them over. She handed them to Emma with a sigh. 'Liz, is everything okay?'

'It doesn't matter.' She glanced at Catherine behind her then back to Emma. 'You're doing a great job,' she said in a hushed tone. 'Don't worry about us.'

Emma looked at the two bottles. One was a water-based lube, the other silicone. 'You know the difference between these?' She asked Katie, really getting into teacher mode now. Katie shook her head. 'Water-based is great for things inside you, maybe Kyle puts some on the strap on? But if you use it in the air, it dries out fast and gets sticky. That's where this stuff, silicone lube comes in. It's amazing. Try this, stroke his cock now, with your hand, just try, copy me.'

Emma took a deep breath and focused on Kyle's cock. She slipped her dry hand around the base and gave it a gentle stroke up to the head and back down again. Just the extra inch it had over Nate's made it feel so different. She felt it get even harder in her hand, her thumb caressing the underside as it reached the tip. 'Can I have a go now?' Katie interrupted.

'Yes, yes of course. So just nice smooth strokes. See how the skin travels with your hand if you hold it tighter? That's okay, that feels nice for them too. But not nearly so nice as with this.' Emma dripped a small amount of the clear silicone lube along the top of his cock and had Katie rub it all around before she started stroking again.

'Oh that feels so sexy, all slidey and soft and hard at the same time,' Katie exclaimed. 'Does it feel good for him?'

'Yes honey, it feels amazing, I promise. Now it's all slippery, here, let me show you.' Emma could have just told her but wanted another chance to play. She wrapped her hand around his shaft and slid it up and down, this time she went higher, her hand encasing his swollen cock head, giving it a twist in her palm before she slid back down. Kyle pushed against the hole every time. 'See how he likes that?'

'I can, I can. Can I have a go again?'

Emma reluctantly let go. Teaching this beautiful young woman how to do this was incredibly sexy, but everything inside Emma was screaming for her to just rub and suck this cock until it explodes. Watching Katie do it was sweet torture. She was a fast learner though, Emma had to give her that. Without any prompting she was trying different speeds of stroke, just playing with the tip, even rubbing the underside with her thumb with a bit of squeeze, watching his precum flow out. 'Why does it do that, what's it leaking?' Katie asked.

'That's precum. When he's really turned on his cock produces it, it's actually natural lube, see for yourself, rub it in.'

'Oh it's all slippery too, that's so cool!' Katie made her finger and thumb into a ring and pushed it back and forth over the ridge of his cock head. 'You know what that makes me think about?'

'I can guess,' replied Emma. 'Did you like it when he made love to you?'

'It hurt a little bit but yes, I loved it. And now it doesn't hurt at all with the strap-on. I wish we could do it more properly.'

'Why can't you?' asked Emma, keeping her voice low. She didn't want Fiona to overhear this part of the conversation.

'Fiona said I shouldn't, that he won't learn to be a good husband if I let him.'

'I think Kyle has learnt to be a very good husband and loves you very much. If you want it, and he does, I think—' Emma leaned in and whispered in Katie's ear, '—you should let him fuck your brains out as much as you want.'

'Really?' Katie whispered back. 'I'd love that so much. Thank you.'

'You're welcome, but let's focus on learning to blow his mind with your mouth first, shall we?' Katie giggled and nodded. Emma took the opportunity to replace Katie's hand with her own again. From the way it was jerking she thought Kyle wasn't far off cumming and so she just held it, letting him calm down while she explained.

'Unlike in most porn, a great blowjob is not about getting it as far down your throat as you can. Although Danielle did that amazingly didn't she.' She looked back over to the corner where Danielle was still on her knees. She looked exhausted, but happy, and sated, stroking, kissing, and gently sucking her husband's cock.

'So don't worry about that today. What we are going to do is stroke with your hand, and then use your mouth on the head and tip. Kiss it, lick it, and suck it. Try not to get your teeth on it too much though, it's very sensitive.'

'How do I avoid that? Fiona says I have big teeth.' Emma looked over, Fiona was ignoring them all now, talking quietly with Catherine.

'You have beautiful teeth, ignore her.' *She's really messing with this poor girl. I bet she is hating watching every second of this. Good.* 'It's easy, just wrap your lips over them like this.' Emma said.

'Do you want to show me, it's okay, you can, I don't mind.'

Yes, yes, yes! 'No honey, he's your husband, he'd want it to be you I'm sure.' Emma looked around again. 'Oh look, see what Helen's doing? That's how it's done.

Helen noticed them both looking at her and pulled back, still stroking her husband. 'Look how hard he's got,' she said, waggling him up and down. 'I think he's about to blow, do you want to see?' Without waiting for a reply she started stroking his cock faster, sucking him into her mouth again. Watching this elegant older woman having such fun made Emma feel all warm inside.

Some of this is messed up but some of this is awesome she decided. She watched as Helen expertly pulled her hand and mouth away and moved to the side. Nothing happened for a few seconds, Emma thought she'd mistimed it. But just as Helen began to move her hand back, Rob's cock twitched a few times and thick white cum began pouring from the end with barely a squirt. It just flowed out.

'A perfect ruin, Helen, well done,' said Catherine from behind them. Elizabeth came over with a towel and mopped up what she could from the rug.

Emma turned back to Katie. 'Okay, you get the idea, hands, and mouth. Start slow, with teasing licking. Yes, that's it, right under there. Try sucking a bit on it and flicking your tongue at the same time.'

Katie struggled to get the technique, so Emma took her finger, 'Like this.' She slipped Katie's finger into her mouth and gently sucked on it, while the tip of her tongue flicked over the pad.

'That tickles, but okay, I get it.'

Kyle's cock swelled even more as Katie's mouth started pleasuring it. Emma stayed close, adding a little more lube, but mostly just leaning in, watching from inches away as this gorgeous girl sucked her husband's perfect cock. It was making Emma insanely aroused. She could feel her panties were nothing but a saturated mess now. This wasn't like porn. If it were porn she could slide her hand down between her legs and cum. This was better, and so much worse. She looked over to Danielle, who was slumped with her back against the wall, eyes shut now. *I wish I had one of those things inside me right now.*

Emma refocused her attention on Katie. From the way Kyle's cock was jerking and absolutely rigid she guessed he was close to cumming. She had a very definite lesson for Katie now.

'Okay, you are doing so well, he's loving this, I think he's about to cum. So just slow down a little, keep him on the edge, it feels amazing.' Katie bobbed her head, really enjoying herself now, eyes closed, stroking, tasting him. She was clearly a convert to the joys of giving a blowjob.

'So when he cums, Katie, he's going to pump out all that cum, and there's going to be lots of it because you've teased him and sucked him so well.'

Katie opened an eye, looking to Emma for guidance.

'You're going to have a choice,' Emma continued. 'You could pull away, so it all shoots out on the floor, like Helen did, but still stroking with your hand. But I think what would make Kyle happy is if you kept sucking, so it felt extra good. But that means it would go in your mouth, do you want to try that?'

Katie slid her mouth off him somewhat reluctantly. *This girl's a natural-born cocksucker. That makes two of us.*

'What do I do with it then though? What does it taste like?'

'It's nice, I like Nate's anyway. It's weird, kind of fizzy on your tongue.'

'Like popping candy?' Katie's eyes lit up.

'Umm, not quite like that but still cool.'

Katie pouted a little but went back to sucking the tip of Kyle's cock as she listened.

'As for what you do with it. Well, you have two choices there, spit it out,' Emma pressed her mouth to Katie's ear, and whispered in a low, sexy voice, 'or swallow it down, right into your tummy.'

Emma guessed how much Fiona would hate that, and it made her want to do it all the more. She refocused her sexual energy from Kyle's cock, to Katie's mind. 'You're doing that so well honey, isn't it the sexiest thing, sucking him; down on your knees, his beautiful cock in your mouth and hand? What a good wife, you're doing so well. I love doing this to Nate, even though I lock him up, I love sucking his cock.'

Emma breathed in the scent of Katie's hair, and perfume and the sexual musk Kyle was releasing. She felt almost drunk on it all. 'Suck him deeper, feel him fill your mouth. Imagine him spurting, showing how sexy you are, how good you make him feel. Are you going to let him cum in your mouth?'

Katie bobbed her head and sucked and slurped more hungrily than ever. Emma slid her hand up Katie's back, under her hair, scratching her nails gently up her scalp. She groaned in pleasure at the simple sensation, and Emma took the chance to push, push her deeper onto her husband's shaft. Katie moaned as his cock filled her mouth. She was so into this now. Emma clutched her hair gently in her hand and pulled back, sliding Katie's mouth to the tip, and then pushing again, fucking her against her husband's cock. She whispered in her ear as it brushed past her lips. 'Good girl, fuck him with your mouth. Imagine how good he's going to feel between your legs too. That's it, own him, control him, love him with this. Isn't this the best?'

Katie barely responded, she was completely in the zone, under the control of Emma's hand, sucking and fucking him with her mouth. Emma didn't dare look away, trying not to think that everyone was probably watching. 'I love doing this to Nate, you're being such a good wife now, well done, I'm so proud of you. He's going to cum soon, are you ready?'

Katie nodded, both her hands stroking, holding onto Kyle now.

'You know what really good wives do, Katie? Good wives swallow. They suck their husband's beautiful cocks and swallow what he gives them. Do you want to be a good wife? Do you want his cum in your tummy? It will make him so happy to know you did that.' Katie bobbed her head again. 'Good girl, faster then suck harder, show him how much you love his cock.'

With a final push at the gloryhole Kyle erupted into his first orgasm in nearly a year. Emma massaged Katie's neck, feeling her throat tightening with every big swallow. 'Keep sucking, keep swallowing, there will be lots.' Katie faithfully kept her mouth there, trying to swallow it all but after a few more gulps she choked a little and pulled back, a big grin on her face, laughing.

'Oh my God, there's so much!' Another squirt jetted across her cheek and she laughed even louder.

Emma joined in laughing. 'Keep rubbing him at least.'

Without prompting Katie put her lips back around him and stroked him, sucking eagerly as his cum dripped off her chin onto her cleavage. Without hesitation, she swallowed the rest of it down, and only stopped when a round of applause took Emma and Katie out of the moment.

'We have a new blowjob queen!' announced Danielle, clapping loudest of all.

Katie looked suddenly shy, but felt the cum on her cheek and chin, and wiped it off with her finger. She stared at it, smiled, and popped her finger in her mouth and sucked it clean. 'I like how he tastes,' she declared. 'I like blowjobs, a lot. Thank you, Emma, that was so great!' She leaned in and kissed her right on the mouth, taking Emma by surprise. Katie's mouth didn't pull away. Emma's just stayed there, it must have only been a fraction of a second, but it was long enough to taste... to taste Kyle on her lips.

Thoughts of kissing her hard and deep flashed across her mind, wanting to taste more. Her heart pounded in her chest, but she pursed her lips, making a big kiss sound, and pulled back.

Fiona was the first thing she saw as everything came back into focus. Never had she seen such hate directed at her. A chill went down her spine. *Oh shit, I've made an enemy there.*

Helen, Zoe and a weary Danielle distracted her, coming around to congratulate Katie and Emma. 'Wasn't she great?' Emma encouraged.

'Hell yeah girl, you looked like a pro,' said Danielle, rubbing her already messed up hair.

Despite what that might imply Katie seemed happy with the compliment. 'Danielle, can you teach me to do that deep throat thing you did, that looked so cool!'

'Sure I can sweetie, any time. It's really not as hard as some say it is.'

'Does it make everyone cum like you did? I didn't know a blowjob could do that.'

Everyone paused, and then started laughing, even Danielle. She put a hand on Katie's shoulder, 'Oh honey, maybe Emma can explain it to you later.'

Katie looked a little confused but joined in the laughter. Danielle leaned over and whispered in Emma's ear. 'You were amazing, a complete godsend. When you get the chance we need to talk.' She cast a glance over to Catherine who was quickly walking over.

Catherine smiled around the room. 'Well done everyone, well done. Another successful night.'

Lizzie's Secret

Emma began to pick herself up from the floor. Her legs were a bit achy from kneeling for so long, but the deep carpet had made it more comfortable than it could have been.

Catherine approached. 'Seeing you in action was quite a revelation. It appears your ideas translate well from the written word to something more substantial.'

'Apparently so.' Emma looked over to Fiona, who was the only one who'd stayed in her seat. 'Fiona doesn't seem too pleased.'

'Don't you worry about her.' Catherine stepped right up and took her hand, helping her to her feet, and pulling her in close. She raised her eyebrows, 'I'm the one you should worry about.' She gave Emma a slow wink that reminded her more of Ka from the Jungle Book than anything else.

'Yes, so I see. I'm intrigued to see *you* in action, to tell you the truth.'

'Oh, I promise, it won't be long. Not now I have your husband's cock under lock and key.' There was a power coming from this woman that scared and excited Emma in equal measure.

The others started to depart. The remaining unlocked cocks were done back up. Emma looked at Dave's, the only one that had remained completely untouched all evening. She felt sad for him, but also a little tingle when she imagined just how frustrating that must be.

Fiona handed over her key to Elizabeth, apparently instructing her to lock Dave back up. *She can't even be bothered to do that.* Elizabeth knelt and locked him back up with surprising tenderness. Her eyes, however, were mostly somewhere else, the two cocks at the end of the room that hadn't

169

even been released.

'That's Rex's, right?' Emma asked, nodding over to the big cage.

'Yes, isn't it magnificent? I like to have the biggest cock in the room, even if it isn't undone.'

'Whose is the other one?'

'Isn't that a mystery,' said Catherine. 'I do like mysteries.' She looked over to where Elizabeth was finishing locking up Dave. 'Although, I think you're about to get a clue.'

The rest of the women exchanged goodnights with the two of them and it wasn't long until only Catherine, Emma and Elizabeth remained. All the husband's cocks had been withdrawn, only the two caged ones remained.

Emma watched with interest as Elizabeth came over to Catherine, fidgeting, waiting for Catherine to acknowledge her. She leaned in and said something quietly to her boss.

'How much do you want them? Show me,' Catherine replied.

Looking down at her feet, the PA slipped off the straps to her long dress, and let it fall to the ground. She avoided Emma's stare and looked to her employer.

'More.'

Elizabeth hung her head again, and reached behind her, unhooking her bra, and removing that too. Her large breasts stayed in place as if by magic. They were so obviously fake. Emma was surprised, she'd wondered if they were natural, she didn't seem the type to get them.

Once again Elizabeth paused. 'Must I?' she asked.

'Yes.'

She hooked her fingers through the waistband of the matching panties and slid them down too, kicking them off her heels. Emma couldn't help staring. Elizabeth was completely bare, *that's pretty common nowadays,* she thought. Nate loved it when she occasionally did it for him. With the blonde hair, big boobs and curves she reminded Emma more than anything of a Barbie Doll. Emma glimpsed something catch the light down between her legs. *Oh does she have a clit ring? Barbie doesn't have those.* Emma had sometimes considered getting a clit hood piercing. Now Nate was getting done, maybe she'd be brave enough to get something to match.

'More.' Catherine extended her foot forward a few inches.

Elizabeth sighed and dropped down onto all fours. She crawled over to Catherine's foot and began to kiss her shoe.

What the hell is going on? I thought she was her PA.

As she knelt at her boss's feet Emma's eyes were drawn to Elizabeth's back. Right in the middle of her left shoulder blade was a vibrant tattoo, iridescent blues, greens and oranges, like an eye. *Another peacock feather, what on earth?* 'What a beautiful tattoo. There seems to be a theme of peacocks around here.' Emma turned to Catherine who showed no reaction to what was going on at her feet.

'Yes, I decided I needed an emblem some time back. Elizabeth here inspired my thinking, in fact.'

Phew. I thought for a minute she'd made her get that. 'You said there was some meaning to it?' She looked down again, it was unnerving to see a naked woman at their feet especially with Catherine completely ignoring that fact. Elizabeth's breasts swayed as she kissed Catherine's shoe, brushing forward and back over the carpet.

'Are you a fan of mythology, Emma?'

'Not really, that's more Nate's thing.' She looked back at Catherine, trying not to freak out at Elizabeth's continued subservience. She could hardly believe it was the same woman who had been so intimidating yesterday.

'I see. Well Hera, Zeus's wife, Queen of the Gods, has a peacock as her sigil.'

'Is there a reason?'

'Of course.' Catherine switched the foot in front of her PA as nonchalantly as though she was just shifting her stance. 'Zeus was a rogue. Fucking anything he could put his cock in. Hera caught him one day trying to take another mistress, Io, after whom the moon is named. It was a major betrayal as Io was Hera's chief priestess.'

'And peacocks feature how?'

'Well to hide his affair, Zeus turned Io into a cow. Very fitting if you ask me. Hera knew something was up and demanded the cow as a present.

171

He couldn't refuse of course, and so poor Io got stuck as a cow, tied to a tree, guarded by Hera's loyal servant, Argus.' Catherine lowered her hands to her dress, and without looking down, lifted the hem of it to above her knees. After a moment's pause, Elizabeth's kisses began climbing up her shins. Emma watched as they rose, above her knees, kissing the stockinged thighs of her boss just below the hemline.

Holy shit, this is insane. What if she lifts it all the way... Emma tried to stay cool, not letting on how freaked out this was all getting her. There was something about this story, it wasn't a coincidence it was being told. 'Argus, the one with the ship?'

Catherine laughed, but a fire burned in her eyes. 'No, that's Argos, Argus was the 'all-seeing' - faithful servant of Hera, with one hundred eyes. Only half of them ever closed so Zeus couldn't steal back his beloved heifer.' She did it, she lifted her dress to her waist. Emma tried not to look but could see that Elizabeth's head was straight between Catherine's legs, nuzzling and kissing her there. Catherine showed no reaction at all. No arousal, nothing.

Fuck me, what is going on here? Then a thought clicked. 'One hundred eyes? Like... like a peacock tail!' She forgot the weirdness of the moment as she smiled at working out the connection.

'Indeed, very good Emma. I didn't think you were stupid. Zeus sent Hermes to lull Argus to sleep and kill him. It's said that she took his eyes and gifted them the peacock, so he'd never be forgotten.'

Emma finally looked down. There was Elizabeth, naked and on her knees, her face pressed firmly between Catherine's legs, kissing her mound and thighs without ceasing. 'And the cow?' she asked, trying to figure out what all this meant.

'The cow—' Catherine laughed, finally acknowledging Elizabeth by sliding her fingers through her hair, pressing her on harder. '—the cow suffered. Hera sent a gadfly to sting her without ceasing. Perhaps she still wanders in torment today.' She grabbed Elizabeth's hair and pushed her back, her dress dropping back down. Out of somewhere, she fished a gold chain, a key dangling at the end of it.

She dropped it on the floor next to her PA. Elizabeth grabbed it, looked up to see Catherine give a dismissive nod, and she scurried over on all fours to the mystery caged cock.

'Wait, who *is* that?' asked Emma, mystified. 'Does Elizabeth have a husband here?'

'It's a story for another time, perhaps.' Catherine replied. 'Lizzie, five minutes, that's it.'

Elizabeth knelt in front of it, and from her clenched hand lifted the key to the lock of the cage. There was also a gold ring dangling from the other end of the chain. Elizabeth had some trouble undoing the padlock. She even looked back to Catherine, who just shrugged with a cold smile. 'Maybe it's rusted up, wouldn't that be sad.'

Finally, the key turned, the lock was removed, and the tiny cage dismantled. To Emma's surprise, the cock didn't show the slightest inclination to grow. Elizabeth caressed it, kissed it, began tugging on it, but still without any result.

'Please, baby, please,' she whispered to the wall, seemingly oblivious to them watching. She sucked the cock into her mouth, tugging back with her head but none of her efforts seemed to have the desired effect.

Elizabeth turned to Catherine with anger in her eyes. 'What have you done?' she asked her.

A spark of fire ignited in Catherine's face too. 'It wasn't what I did, you'd do well to remember that.' She looked at her watch. 'You have three more minutes.'

Elizabeth refocused her efforts on the cock, pulling at it, sucking it. At last, it seemed to start to respond. She jerked, fingers tight, pulling it back and forth. Yes, it was finally starting to get hard. Catherine started laughing, amused by her desperation.

Elizabeth stood, still pulling at it, now only semi-flaccid. Turning she pressed her bottom to the hole. From where Emma was standing she could see that she was trying, and failing, to push the cock into her arse, but it just wasn't hard enough. *It's never going to get in there, why wouldn't she...* Emma's gaze moved from behind to in front, her hand covering her mouth as she audibly gasped.

Emma stared in disbelief as she began to cry with desperation, but it wasn't the tears that had shocked her. As Elizabeth pushed herself back against the wall, her silicone filled breasts swinging back and forth, her labia were visible clearly for the first time. They were closed tight, but not naturally. A set of small rings pierced either side of her lips, from top to bottom, each pair sealed shut with a tiny silver padlock.

Emma looked to Catherine for some kind of explanation but she was laughing, watching the spectacle. 'Time's up,' she announced. 'Oh dear Lizzie, didn't he get it up? That was part of the problem in the first place. Cage it back up, and get dressed, you're embarrassing yourself.'

Emma was trying to process what she'd seen. The Danielle stuff had been crazy enough earlier. But what on earth was going on with Elizabeth? She couldn't get what she'd seen out of her head. The idea of being sealed shut like that. It was so terrible, it was so… She felt her body respond, despite all the insanity. She imagined what it would be like to be closed up like that. *No, this is madness. Stop thinking about it.*

She forced her gaze to Rex's cock, still jutting from the wall, caged in steel. *Who knows what Catherine is capable of. Maybe we should just get out now, while we can.*

Elizabeth had managed to lock up the other cock and it too was gone. She'd had pulled her panties back on but didn't bother with her bra or dress. She virtually threw the key back into Catherine's purse, seeming to hold herself back from saying anything.

Before Emma had a chance to ask about what she just saw Catherine stopped her. 'I'm sure you have questions, but they'll have to wait for another time I'm afraid. It's late, I'm going to bed. I suggest you do the same.' She paused. 'Unless that is—' Catherine fished out another key, '—you'd like some alone time with Rex? He hasn't been out in months you know.'

Emma's mind dropped into a vortex of emotions. She couldn't remember the last time she'd been this horny. Helping Katie, and watching Danielle, and just the whole fucking gloryhole fantasy come true had left her almost high with arousal. The craziness of what she'd just seen with Elizabeth had left her emotions in turmoil. But the thought of unlocking that truly massive cock, and having her way with it through a gloryhole was beyond tempting.

She took a deep breath. Somehow she found the willpower to answer. 'No. It's been a very long day, I should get to bed too.' She went over to pick up her discarded heels, opting to just carry them. Her eyes were drawn back to Rex as she imagined stretching her mouth wide to fit it in. How it would feel, stroking its full length with both hands until it came hard, just like Kyle's had. She finally dragged her eyes away from it and walked to the door. pausing to turn.' Thank you, Catherine, that was an extraordinary experience, I guess.'

'Just the first of many I hope.' She put Rex's key back in her bag and closed it. Emma's eyes went one last time to his cock. *I must be good, I must be good.* She walked out as elegantly as she could before she dashed upstairs, only just remembering to quietly open the door so not to disturb Nate.

* * *

Nate was fast asleep, lying on top of the duvet as he often did. She paused at the end of the bed, wanting to wake him, tell him all about what happened, what she saw.

But another ache, an irresistible need throbbed between her legs. It was even more pressing. She carefully took off the dress, hung it up, then scattered her underwear across the floor on the way to the bathroom.

As the hot water cascaded down her body her fingers hungrily sought to satisfy the need that had nearly overwhelmed her this evening. She was so aroused, hardly needing to rub before she was right on the edge. As she'd just watched Danielle attempt, she tried to hold herself there, resisting the climax, tormenting herself as she recalled all that happened.

She imagined being Danielle, deep throating Duncan as she came, knowing it meant he couldn't. She smiled as she remembered Katie's kiss, sharing the taste of her first blowjob. She thought about all those cocks, hanging through the wall. She imagined everyone watching her sucking and servicing every one of them, whatever was in Danielle getting her closer and closer with every orgasm she dished out. She opened her mouth, imagining it stretching around Rex's monster cock, trying to hold back, to be a good girl, to give them all orgasms before she came.

But the need won out, she turned her face into the flow of water as she went over the edge, imagining it was their climaxes, splattering on her body, on her face, just like Kyle had on Katie. But it was all of them, every cock, aimed at her, tugged and sucked to climax, and last of all Rex's, a never ended jet of his pleasure dragged out of him coating her in his seed.

She finished rubbing at last, not wanting the orgasm to ever end, but like all good things, it did. And with the drop came the confusion. Thoughts of Danielle, and Katie, but most of all, Elizabeth. Her situation, what she'd had done. It was terrifying, and unnervingly arousing, even now.

She dried herself off and went out to Nate, kissing him, waking him enough to get him under the duvet so she could snuggle up, arm wrapped around his chest.

The sharp, almost painful need between her legs had been suppressed. But not stopped. Something had awakened in her tonight, and it wanted more.

Book 3 – Encased

To the remarkable friends I've met through Tumblr, who've inspired, challenged and supported me.

You know who you are.

Even if I don't.

I can never thank you enough.

Men are so simple and yield so readily to the desires of the moment that he who will trick will always find another who will suffer to be tricked.

Niccolo Machiavelli

III

Book 3 - Encased

The Morning After

Emma woke, curled around Nate. She nuzzled her face against his arm, breathing him in. He stirred a little as she pressed herself up against him, conjuring last night's events into a sexy blur between reality and a dream.

But it wasn't a dream. It was a fantasy come to life. *Oh, wake up Nate, I have so much to tell you.* Her arousal spiralled up inside her as she recalled more of last night's events. Emma carefully slid the hand that wasn't wrapped around her husband down, cupping herself, squeezing. She'd cum several times in the shower last night. *How can I be this horny?* Her middle finger pressed in, pushing the thin, damp material of her panties between her lips. She let out a tiny gasp. It felt amazing already.

Out of habit she considered waking Nate with a blowjob, only to remember not only was his cock caged, but she didn't have the key. It was the first moment of true desperation, of wanting, needing him out, but not being able to do anything about it.

It only made her hornier.

She took a few deep breaths and forced herself to dwell on the emotions she was feeling. His cock, locked away by another woman. She had to make a choice, to let it frustrate and annoy her, or to decide it was hot as hell. She remembered Danielle, climaxing, sucking desperately on her husband, Duncan. Then Kyle's beautiful cock, and the pleasure she helped cute little Katie bring it. Thinking about it all again brought her quickly to the edge, just a few more rubs and she'd climax.

'I know what you're doing,' Nate whispered in a sing-song voice, followed by a chuckle.

'Oh my God, how long have you been awake?' Emma pressed her face into his shoulder, hiding.

'Long enough. You were about to cum, weren't you?'

'Yeff,' came a muffled reply.

'Don't you dare, but keep rubbing, keep on the edge, and tell me all about last night, what did I miss?'

Emma snuggled up, her hand slowly working between her legs as she told him about the crazy events of the night before. He kept interrupting to clarify points, or just to make her tell him again.

'So Catherine made Danielle cum over and over while sucking Duncan's cock, in front of you all? Wow.'

'I know, it was so crazy but so fucking hot. Honestly baby, the thought of that remote-controlled vibrator, inside her, out of her control. Keeping her under control...' She gave a deep-throated groan, 'It's so fucked up but I can't stop thinking about it. She squirted so much too. Katie thought it was pee.'

'Fuck,' was Nate's accurate summary. The conversation moved to Katie and Kyle.

'She'd never given him a blowjob? That's mad. But I suppose if Fiona's contrived to keep him locked up all the time, it makes sense.' He nuzzled his nose against her, his voice dropping low with arousal. 'So you were right there, telling her what to do? I'm not sure my cock can handle picturing this – but don't stop.'

Should I mention I stroked him? She held that back as a surprise for later but told him about the kiss with Katie afterwards. Nate just went quiet for a while, shifting uncomfortably in the bed. 'Okay, ouch, that mental picture hurt down below.'

She cupped his caged cock, it was pushing out, straining, hot in her hand, trying to get hard. She rubbed herself more quickly, letting out a little moan into his ear, building up her bravery to share the next revelation. She bit his earlobe and licked it. 'I could taste his cum on her lips.'

Nate's head snapped to her, his eyes wide in amazement. 'You are fucking killing me. Oh my God, how did I miss this?'

Emma cooled him off a bit by telling him about Fiona's venomous reaction. 'Yeah she has "predator" written all over her,' Nate agreed. 'Sounds like you messed up her plans. I'm proud of you.'

'If she's a predator, what does that make Catherine? You wait until you hear about Elizabeth.' She told him all about the slutty outfit and the mystery cock, waiting until the end to share the big reveal - what she saw between Liz's legs.

Nathan was suitably shocked. 'Her pussy is closed up with piercings, are you sure? I know people do it but it sounds extreme.'

'Uh honey, we're planning to pierce your cock soon, remember. *Extreme* seems to be the norm around here.' Emma cupped his balls, they were hot and tight in her hand and the cage was slippery with Nate's frustration. 'Can you imagine it, totally secure? No way to pull out, no way to cheat. Fuck, why is that *so* hot?'

'I'm dying here, you know. But thinking about that, I better go shower and enjoy it not being sore.'

Emma kissed him on the cheek, and deliberately rubbed herself harder, her hand banging on his thigh. 'And if you hear me yelling, you'll know why.'

'I love you, horny girl. Try not to cum.' Nate carefully swung his feet over the edge of the bed and stood. 'But don't try too hard.'

'Thank you, kind sir, I'll do my best. Maybe I'll have a few, depending on how long you take. Now go wash, I want you all presentable.'

The bathroom door shut with a clunk and she heard the shower begin. Emma wondered if she should go and join him, but it was just so comfy in bed. Instead, she rolled over onto her tummy and brought her knees up, spreading them apart, her bottom pushing the duvet up high. All the fingers of her right hand rubbed now, hard against her clit, sliding over her wet pussy lips. She loved this position, how exposed she felt, how desperate it made her. She buried her face into the pillow. The effort of breathing through it always helped her stave off her climax for longer. She was going to edge like this until he found her, she decided. And then, she was going to cum on his cute fucking face.

A thump on the wall behind the bed made her lift her head up. There was another a few seconds later. And again, settling into a rhythmic pattern of thuds against the wall. The distinctive sound of someone getting fucked, hard. Emma imagined it, just the other side of the wall, someone getting pounded. She resumed rubbing, imagining it. She lifted her shoulders and reached out, touching the wall. She could feel it, the slight vibration of each thrust. Propped against the wall she could move her fingers back between her legs. Silently she rubbed, and sure enough, she could just hear moans of pleasure through the wall. They grew in intensity, the pounding coming faster.

Emma rubbed harder as the sounds of sex from the next room grew even louder. *God, I wish I had my toys right now.* The intensity of a vibe on her clit would be perfect, or the look on Nate's face as he found her using a dildo, on display like this. It wouldn't be the first time.

Emma looked around. What could she fuck? It was going to have to be the old faithful, a hairbrush handle. She grabbed hers from the side of the bed.

The wooden handle was curved into a series of bumps. *They know exactly what they're doing when they design these.* She cast the duvet aside and leaned forward again, excited at the thought of Nate finding her like this. As she slipped the cool brush down between her legs she began rubbing the bumpy handle over her swollen clit. She remembered when her best friend first confessed to her what she did with her brush. Emma had been scandalised, and then thought of little else in bed for the next few months. As she slipped the rounded tip inside her she remembered her first time, Nate convincing her to try it as they sexted each other. Nearly stopping as it stung so much, but the promise of pleasure being just enough to keep her going. From that night on, her brush and she became the best and most intimate of friends. *My hairbrush with benefits.*

Listening to the rapid thumps of the bed head next door, the cries of pleasure, Emma buried the brush in her, only managing a few hard strokes before the woman next door climaxed. The female cries of pleasure soon joined by a male voice, before it went silent.

Emma imagined how good Nate would feel right now. She revelled in how desperate listening to the other couple made her. It was going to be so frustrating to not have access to his cock. Her resolve held to decide it was hot. She let it turn her on. The truth was, as much as she loved locking up Nate's cock, she was the real 'denial slut'. All those early times with the brush, she never came. All she'd ever done was edge herself, over and over.

It was only with Nate she'd ever been brave enough to go over. He gave her her first orgasm. As much as she'd loved it, it still didn't compare to being on the edge, to being like this. Her thoughts were irresistibly drawn to Danielle, to that device inside her. To the 'counter climax measures'. Emma pushed her face back in the pillow, imagining it in her, helpless to do anything to stop it. Suffering whatever stimulation was forced on her, but punished for cumming. The thought drove her crazy. She plunged the brush handle in and out, all thoughts of Nate discovering her forgotten until she heard the door open. She put on a show, groaning into the pillow, spreading her legs wider, reaching up with her other hand to pull open her cheeks to give him the best view.

'Ahhhm, sorry, I did knock,' Mené said, in her distinctive Israeli accent.

An Unusual Inspection

Emma whipped around and tried to drag the duvet over herself but got caught up and ended up in a tangle, only half covered. 'Oh my God, oh my God. I'm so sorry I thought you were Nate.' She finally dragged the cover over herself and wrapped it around her body like a burial shroud, hoping she'd sink down into the ground.

'Yes, sorry Emma, I knocked first, I promise.' Mené was in the same incredible nurse's uniform as the day before, but her face was even less professional, barely able to hold in the giggles.

Emma broke first, her peal of laughter letting out some of the embarrassment. 'Well that's my medical covered then, I think you saw everything just then.'

'Yep, but it's all honey,' Mené flapped her hands at her. 'I can officially give you a pass.' She walked to the corner of the bed as Emma struggled to sit up against the headboard.

'A pass, is that all I get?'

'That's true. You get a distinction. I can give my sincere medical opinion. You have a grade-A tushie.'

'Well, thank you.'

Mené stepped up closer, her voice dropping a little. 'And excellent brush technique. A little bit old school.'

'Old school works sometimes,' quipped Emma, 'when you have nothing else at hand.'

'Oh my, yes. A girl never forgets her first brush handle.'

Both of them chuckled. Emma was amazed how quickly this Israeli, ex-military, nurse had made her feel at ease, after what must count as one of the most embarrassing things she'd ever done. She tried to straighten up. *Oh shit, the brush is still in me.* She felt it slowly start to slide out of her. It was infuriatingly arousing and she couldn't do a damn thing about it.

'Can I sit?' asked Mené, perching herself on the edge of the bed without waiting for a reply. 'Again, so sorry about that. Well, not that sorry, that was hot.'

'Are you allowed to say that, Nurse Englemann? It's not very professional.' Emma grinned.

'I think after wanking your husband off yesterday most hope of staying professional has gone bye-bye.'

'Good riddance,' declared Emma. The brush moved some more and began to poke into her in a less than pleasant spot. 'Speaking of which, excuse me for a moment.' She reached under the cover and slipped the rest of the brush out.

Mené giggled. 'Brush problems?'

'You know it.'

'Don't let me stop you.'

'You didn't before,' Emma quipped.

Mené crossed her legs, the short hem of her tight uniform sliding up her toned thighs. 'No, that was naughty wasn't it. You just seemed so into it I didn't want to interrupt.'

'You are so thoughtful. Wait, how long were you watching for?' Mené simply bit back a grin and lifted her eyebrows. Emma looked up, 'You're not wearing the hat today, I loved the hat.'

'I know, but it was bad enough having to walk through the house wearing this. I think I might have given an old man a heart attack.'

'There are worse ways to go.'

Mené paused. 'Oh wait, maybe he was wearing a cock cage, that would explain it. Do all the men here have to wear them?'

Emma thought about last night, all the caged cocks arrayed through the wall. 'Pretty much, yeah. As far as I've seen. Oh, apart from Doctor Handsome.'

'That we know of.' Mené gave an exaggerated wink and Emma giggled. 'I was imagining him last night with one on,' the nurse confessed.

'Oh, were you now, tell me more.'

'As you know you, how would you say it, summoned my curiosity yesterday.'

'Piqued it.' Emma suggested.

'Piqued, is that a word? I like that. You piqued my curiosity about ruined orgasms. So in the name of science I was trying it out. Let's say Doctor Hastings and his unfeasibly large, but caged cock, were immensely helpful in my research.'

'Wait, just to be clear, for real or in your head.'

'In my head, sadly.' Mené confirmed. 'But he wasn't alone.' Mené looked straight at Emma, her tongue poking out to wet her lips. Her dark eyebrows gave a cute little double jump that gave Emma the clear impression that she, or Nate, or maybe both were in her head too. 'Speaking of which, where is your husband?'

'He's in the shower. But hold on, did you try a ruined orgasm?'

'I stopped like you described, but then it seemed like such a waste, so I went back to finishing it off.'

'You missed the best bit, or the worst bit. It's complicated.' Emma laughed.

The door to the bathroom opened and Nate was just doing up a towel as he pushed through, oblivious to Mené's presence. 'Fuck I'm so horny, or this cage is just extra tight.'

'Why don't we have a professional have a look.' Emma suggested. Nate froze, looking up at the scantily clad nurse perched on the end of the bed.

'Hello,' was all he managed to sputter out.

'Allo Nathan,' said Mené, her Israeli accent almost sounding French, and even sexier for it. 'I was asked to drop in and see how you're getting on. To assess how the cage is.'

'It's definitely tight. But I think it's okay.' He stayed frozen to the spot.

'Perhaps I can have a look.'

Emma recalled all the things this beautiful nurse had done to him yesterday, and bet he was thinking the same. 'Mené?' Emma beckoned her closer. They both leaned in and Emma turned away from Nate as though she had something secret to share. Instead, hidden from Nate, she reached over and took hold of the red zip that ran all the way down the front of the uniform. She tugged it down a few inches, the fabric springing open to display Mené's pert, pressed together cleavage. 'It is warm in here, don't you think?'

'That's entirely your fault,' Mené replied, leaving the zip where it was and standing, turning on her heels and walking around to Nate. She reached into a side pocket and drew out a thin black plastic ring that uncoiled in her hand. 'I'm afraid I'm going to have to tie you up again, Mr Stevens. I do apologise, but the rules are I can't unlock you unless...' She didn't finish her sentence as she was looking around the room. 'Ah yes, there it is.'

She walked over to beside the mirror where for the first time Emma noticed a small black steel ring some seven feet up the wall. Mené smacked the black plastic strip into the palm of her hand. 'These are just temporary cuffs, neat aren't they. We used to use these in the army. A lot.'

Nathan hadn't moved. Emma wiggled herself off the bed, pulling the bedsheet with her. 'Come on darling, it *is* a small cage. If I can't get you out it's only wise to make sure everything's okay in there.'

'This is not how I imagined my day starting.' Nate took a deep breath and followed Mené to the edge of the room.'

'Just think of it as good practise, darling. We're having some kind of check-up every month as part of this contract. I keep imagining what those might involve.' She shuffled over to join the two of them.

With a grin at Emma, Mené pushed one end of the thick cable tie through a hole in its middle, making a wide loop. 'Can you slip a hand through this for me?' Nate obliged, still holding his towel with the other hand.

Emma stepped nearer, trying to keep the sheet in place. She wanted to see every detail of this. Watching Nate slip that cuff on had her heart racing again.

Mené pulled the first one tight enough so he couldn't slip out. 'Now the tricky bit. Nate, can you reach up and put it through the loop?' She turned to Emma, 'I normally have a couple of huge guys to help me with this bit.'

Emma didn't even want to think about what possible context that might be. Nate managed to put the other end through the loop, his towel nearly slipping off before his spare hand grabbed it.

Mené looked up 'I'm going to need a chair for this bit.'

'Let me get it,' Emma volunteered. 'I'll just put something on first.'

'Don't feel you have to on my behalf', said Mené. 'It's nothing I haven't seen before.' She sent a dazzling grin Emma's way.

Emma paused. *Fuck it, let's have some fun.* She dropped the sheet, walking around to grab the chair by the desk, completely naked, followed by Nate's wide-eyed gaze. 'Here you go,' she said, dragging the chair to the wall in front of her husband. 'Is there anything else I can do?'

Mené looked at the expensive upholstery on the chair. She paused, looking at Emma's naked body, and seeing the potential. 'I'd need to take my heels off to climb on there. You don't suppose you could do the other cuff up?'

Emma reached the same conclusion with a grin. 'It'd be my pleasure.' She held the back of the chair and climbed up, feeling a bit strange doing this naked, but excited about how she hoped this was about to work out. She put a hand on Nate's shoulder to help her balance on the deep padded cushion. 'Other hand please, baby.' Nate let go of the towel and put his hand in Emma's. As she stood fully she lifted his hand, and pressed forward.

'Oh you are joking.' Nate laughed. Emma's breasts were pressed right against his face as she looped the plastic around his hand.

She deliberately took her time, her erect nipples brushing across his cheek, then his lips. She just managed to get the plastic tip through the hole of the cuffs when she felt his mouth open around her nipple and give it a suck. 'Nathan, behave yourself, you naughty boy,' she scolded, laughing. She pulled her breast back and he gave a frustrated moan. Somehow her other breast found itself pressed against his mouth as she slowly, click by click, pulled the cuff secure. Sure enough, his mouth opened again, and she gently sighed as his mouth caressed her nipple.

With a polite cough, and a giggle, Mené brought her back into focus, thanked her, and helped her back down. She moved the chair to the side and it caught the towel, unfastening it at last. It dropped around Nathan's bare feet.

Emma stood, naked, next to her husband who was naked too, besides the cock cage. As fantasy fulfilling as seeing him restrained yesterday had been, this was somehow more erotic. Simply tied up against the wall in what felt like a hotel room, nothing but some plastic around his wrists but completely at her mercy. *I've got to get some of those cuffs for my handbag.*

Mené walked over to the door, opening a small white leather bag she must have left there before surprising Emma earlier. The memory and thrill of that moment of discovery made her pussy clench again. She slipped one arm around Nathan's back and went up on her toes, whispering in his ear. 'She caught me, earlier. I was waiting for you, on all fours, fucking myself. I thought she was you. She watched a while before I noticed.'

Nate turned his head to her, 'You're kidding me! How long for?'

'Long enough,' replied Mené, still digging around in the bag.

'How long was it?' asked Emma, genuinely curious.

Mené stood, a key swinging in her hand, and walked back towards them both. She paused, leaning in close to them, their heavy breaths mingling for a moment. 'Long enough to dampen my panties.' She put her empty hand on his chest and sank down to her knees, leaving Nate and Emma looking at each other with wide eyes. At the same moment they both burst into laughter.

'Mené, we officially love you. I hope you know that,' Nate declared.

'The feeling is mutual,' she said, looking up at them, crouched steadily on her heels. 'Now let's get this little guy out and see how he's getting on.'

'Hey,' objected Nate. 'Not so much of the little.'

Emma kissed him on the lips and stepped back. 'Oh baby, trust me, after what I saw last night, "little" is more than fair.'

Mené had unlocked him and was taking off even the ring of the cage as though she was a practised hand. 'Oh what happened last night?' she asked, not looking up.

Emma stepped back and sat back on the bed, legs crossed, feeling sexy as hell. As she watched Mené methodically examining Nate's penis, something that was strangely normal already, she told her all about the gloryholes, and the other guests.

'You helped her give her husband his first blowjob?' Mené asked, struggling to make sure she understood. She elegantly stood from the crouch and sat by Emma on the bed, crossing her legs in the same pose. There they sat, Emma stark naked, and Mené in an outfit that was already borderline pornographic, Nate didn't seem to know where to look.

'Yeah, I gave her advice, and—' she looked up at Nate, helplessly tied to the wall, listening to her every word,'—and stroked him while she sucked him.'

'Wait what, you jerked him off? You didn't tell me that!' Nate exclaimed.

'I know baby, I was saving it for when you weren't locked up. I thought hearing it might break something.' She stared at his cock, free at last, the ring from the cock cage making it grow even faster, every beat of his heart displaying his arousal more prominently.

'Did he have a nice cock?' Mené asked.

'Oh yeah, it was really nice. Like Nate's actually.' Emma looked back up at her husband who was obviously pleased with her answer. 'Only, bigger, you know, a proper length.'

'Oh, so about average then?' teased Mené, looking at Nate too.

Nate's eyes darkened showing how aroused their words made him. His cock kept growing, rising up high, veins standing out now.

Emma giggled. She was having so much fun. 'I've never held another cock, so that was a new experience.' She fell back on the bed, half turning towards Mené, propping her head up on her arm. Mené copied the pose facing her again.

'So did you make him cum?' Mené asked.

'No, I let Katie do all that by the end, she was a natural. I did help though. I slipped my fingers behind her head and fucked his cock with her face.'

'Oh fuck that's so hot. I love it when a guy does that to me.'

'Nate's done it a few times but it always makes me gag when it hits my throat though.'

'You know the best way to do that?' Mené asked. She sat back up and spun around without waiting for a reply. She lay back down so her head hung back over the edge of the bed, towards the wall Nate was tied to. Her long black curls cascaded down the side of the bed as she demonstrated. 'Like this, he can grab the back of your head and just throat fuck you in a straight line. Much comfier.'

Emma thought 'comfy' was probably a relative term but she spun around, remembering that she was naked for a moment then forgetting about it as she laid her head back and giggled. 'Oh, everything is upside down. Hello, Nate's upside-down cock, you don't look pleased to see me from this angle'. She laughed again and Mené joined in.

'So wait, if he's fucking you like this, aren't his balls...'

Mené laughed even harder. 'Yeah, it's not the prettiest view.'

Emma looked at her upside-down husband. 'Oh baby, would you like to face fuck me right now?'

'Both of you are wicked teases, I hope you know that. Fucking evil, both of you.' Despite his words, Nate couldn't stop smiling. His cock was almost totally erect.

The girls kept giggling as the blood went to their heads. Mené turned to Emma. 'There's a toy in my bag if you want me to demonstrate.'

Emma sat up. 'Head rush! Woah.' She skittered over to Mené's nurse bag. 'There's loads of stuff in here.' She pulled out a dildo, but also a ball gag. Emma looked up to Nate, 'What was that about us being wicked teases, darling?'

She danced over to Nate who'd resolutely shut his mouth. 'Oh baby, open up.' She rubbed the end of the dildo on his nipples. 'Unless you'd like a blindfold too, sweetie?'

Nate reluctantly opened his mouth and gave her a wicked stare. 'Good boy,' Emma said, slipping in the ball gag and doing it up loosely behind. 'Now the girls can talk without interruption.' She kissed his cheek before she jumped back onto the bed and laid back next to a red-faced Mené who seemed to have also got the giggles. Emma handed her the pink silicone dildo. 'You wanted this?'

'Why thank you, that's most kind,' said Mené, copying Emma's English accent. 'What was this for again?' she asked in her normal voice. She waggled the dildo. 'Oh yes, so like this.' Mené leaned her head right back and slid the six-inch toy into her mouth, easily sliding it in and out.

Emma watched with fascination. 'That's so cool, I can see it right down your throat. I see what you mean, it's all a straight line. Let me try.' She looked up at Nate with a smile before lying back. 'This makes you feel all dizzy,' she declared, head dropping back and taking the dildo in her hand. She tentatively sucked on it and pushed it deeper. She gagged a little bit but soon managed to fuck it a few times. 'Wat wiz weesier' she said, dildo still half in her mouth.

'What?' laughed Mené, processing it for a moment. 'Oh yes, it is easier, I told you.'

Emma coughed a bit. 'But I still want to gag.'

'I know a magic trick for that,' exclaimed the nurse. Try this. Get your left hand and put the thumb in the fist, and squeeze it as hard as you can.'

'Really? Okay.' Emma copied the instructions as Mete counted to five.

'Now, keep it there, and put your right-hand first finger on your chin.'

'You're making this up!'

'I'm not. Trust me. One, two, three, four, five.' She counted again. 'Okay now last of all, that bit of skin between your left thumb and first finger. Squeeze that with your other finger and thumb. As hard as you can.' She counted one last time to five.

'This is insane, how could this possibly do something?' Emma did it anyway.

'Stick your fingers, in your mouth.'

Emma looked sceptical as she pushed her first two fingers to the back of her throat. Her eyes opened wide as she pulled them straight out. 'What the fuck! How, what? How can that work?' She grabbed the dildo and laid down, sliding it in her mouth and into her throat, her eyes watering a little but without any gagging at all.

'See. I told you,' Mené said. 'It's *very* useful for big cocks.' She looked up at Nate and poked her tongue out.

Emma slid the dildo out. 'If only you weren't tied up, hubby, I'd let you do fuck my face and cum down my throat.'

'I would too,' added Mené.

'Mené!' Emma feigned shock. They faced each other, both still upside-down and laughing.

Mené's big brown eyes went a little darker. 'You wouldn't like to see that?'

Emma coughed a little, glad her already red face was hiding her blushes.

Nate shook his head. His rigid cock told them both the effect they were having on him.

Mené kept her head hanging back and tried an English accent again. 'You know you're naked, don't you, Emma. And we only met yesterday. That's very rude.' She giggled some more. 'It's a good thing you're so hot.'

'I'm not hot, you're hot. Do you know how incredibly you look in that uniform?'

'It's so good, isn't it. I—' Mené paused then admitted,'—I kept it on when I tried that thing last night.'

'You know I'm always going to think of you edging in that outfit now?' Emma laughed.

'Yes. And so is Nate,' replied Mené.

'You are so bad,' Emma pretended to scold her.

'Well, it's only inspired by you.'

Emma smacked the dildo into the palm of her hand like a police baton. 'I blame the horniness. I honestly haven't been this horny in forever. Nate wouldn't let me cum this morning while I told him all about last night.'

'Oh really. I'd let you, you know, while you told me all about it.' Mené dared Emma with her eyes.

'You *are* so kind. I do wonder though. What it'd be like edging with my head hanging over the bed like this.'

'I got fucked a few times with my head hanging over like this, it was great.'

'Is there anything you haven't done?' Emma asked.

'I've not found a man, or woman, I want to spend my life with.' Mené told her, taking hold of her hand on the bed. 'Someone who I'd give everything up for like you have. You are inspiring.'

'Mené!' Emma held her hand even tighter. 'If nothing else comes of this madness, meeting you makes it all worth it.'

'That reminds me.' Mené wiggled further off the bed, put her hands on the floor and elegantly flipped her legs over her head to end up on her knees.

'Holy shit, that was so cool,' Emma laughed.

'You can thank years of gymnastic competitions.' She stepped over to Nate, whose cock was in full display mode. 'Okay Nate, let's just see how he's doing now something seems to have got him hard.' She pulled a small tape from another pocket and measured him. 'Well what do you know, he is a little bigger today. That cage can't be doing any harm.'

Mené sat back on the bed by Emma, who had shifted back so her head wasn't off the edge any more. 'So, you were going to tell me about last night.'

'Wasn't I supposed to cum while I did that?' Emma giggled.

Picking up the dildo from the bed Mené handed it to Emma. 'Don't let me stop you. That's better than a brush handle.'

Wow, do I actually do this? She looked back at her husband, tied to the wall, cock jutting up, helpless. *I guess I might just let him enjoy being uncaged a bit longer.* She turned to face Mené who was lying back beside her. 'That is so kind. But I'd feel bad, you know if it was just me.'

'Well, that's easily solved.' Mené grinned, climbing up onto the bed and lying back besides Emma. A squeak of disbelief came from Nate's gagged mouth as Mené wiggled her panties down and kicked them off her legs over her head. They all watched them sail through the air and, miraculously, land on Nate's erection.

Emma gasped. 'No way! You did not do that on purpose.'

Mené laughed. 'Hoopla! Is that a thing here too?' Emma nodded. 'So what do I win?'

'All the juicy details from last night?'

'Deal. Heads back? You wanted to try?'

Emma gave a little nod and lay back, her heart racing. She looked up at her husband as she slid her fingers down between her legs, starting to rub gently, knowing Mené was doing the same. She took the dildo, gave it a few thrusts in her mouth again and watched Nate's eyes follow it down to where she made it disappear between her legs. A few strokes and she calmed her breathing. 'So, where was I?' She turned to face Mené whose eyes had dilated with the pleasure she was giving herself.

'Ummm, wasn't there a dinner party?' Mené eyes closed for a moment, her lips parting, before she refocused on Emma.

'Oh yes. Let me start at the beginning. So, when we left you...' Emma shared all of the previous day's adventures with her new friend. They soon got too dizzy with their heads down, but shifted in, laughing, sharing, rubbing. At some point Emma decided it was unfair Mené got to stay clothed, so she helped her out of the uniform, all the while watching Nate's reaction.

By the time she got to the story of Lizzie's mystery cock and piercings they were both too horny to discuss it seriously. Emma leaned in and whispered out of Nate's earshot. 'I really need to pee, but let's tease him. Come with me to the bathroom.' Mené paused, then played along, speaking loudly, 'Won't he mind?'

'What can he do about it, he's all tied up.'

'Okay then if you really want to. They both got up slowly from the bed, Nate's eyes glued to their every movement. Emma stepped up to her husband, taking Mené's hand. 'We're going to go take a shower, baby. Sorry you can't join us.' She slipped her other hand around her husband's cock. 'Oh darling, how much precum have you made, you're dripping.' She slid her hand up and down his shaft, just a few times. 'Oh Nate, if only I was allowed to make you cum. But I'm sure that would break the rules, so just shout if you need anything.' She reached up and popped the gag out. It didn't make a difference. He was speechless.

'Hurry up.' Mené pulled on Emma's hand and dragged her into the bathroom, both of them laughing. Emma waved with her slick fingers at Nate before the door was pulled mostly closed, leaving him, hanging.

* * *

Inside the bathroom, Mené rushed to the loo. 'I'm desperate to pee too you know. You snooze, you lose.' She sat without any inhibition, starting to pee. Emma wasn't sure where to look. Mené laughed. 'You've just been masturbating on the bed next to me and now you're shy of me peeing?'

'It's not quite the same,' argued Emma.

'You English, you're so kinky but so prudish at the same time.'

'I blame the *Carry On* movies'

Mené took her bra off in a quick move and hung it on a rail. 'The what?'

'Never mind. Too strange to try and explain,' Emma said.

Mené reached into the shower and turned on the water. 'You know what he thinks we're doing in here don't you?'

'Uh-huh. I can imagine.' Emma nodded, a big smile forming as she thought about the mindfuck she was giving him. *Screw Catherine, I'm the boss at this.* 'Oh Mené!' she cried out, hiding her laughter.

'Oh fuck yeah that feels so good,' Mené yelled above the water, giggling.

'Oh yes, you do that so much better than Nate.' Emma replied, trying to outdo her, laughing too.

Mené nodded to the shower. 'I need to clean up—'she paused,'—and cum. You want to join me?'

'Yes. But no, I really need to pee, I wasn't kidding and I shouldn't. What we did was perfect.' Emma went and sat on the loo, holding on until Mené got in the shower.

She half stepped in, leaving her head around the edge of the curtain. 'You aren't going to cum?' Mené asked. Her expression softened. 'We could, you know...'

Emma shook her head, struggling to hold back from peeing. 'It's better this way. I like not cumming. I like feeling like this. You should try it.'

'Maybe I'll try another ruin, but no promises.' Her head popped in behind the curtain and with a sigh, Emma finally felt able to pee.

She jumped a little when Mené shouted from behind the curtain. 'Oh God, I'm cumming, oh yes Emma like that with your mouth.' Both of them couldn't help laughing at that. Mené went quieter then. It felt strange knowing what she was doing, different when Nate wasn't there. Suddenly Mené shouted out, 'Ben-Zonna. Why would you do that, why would you ruin it?'

Emma laughed. 'So you did it this time?'

'You are crazy, you know that.' Mené stuck her head around the curtain. 'That is awful. I'm supposed to feel good after cumming.'

'Give it ten minutes.' Emma grinned.

'What happens in ten minutes?'

A knock on the bathroom door interrupted her reply. Emma jumped up and poked her head out. Catherine was walking back to the middle of the bedroom, a bemused look on her face as she looked at Nate, naked, bound and gagged on the wall. His cock was rapidly shrinking.

'It's good to see you restrained him for his check-up, I suppose,' she said. Her eyes wandered over to the uniform on the bed. 'I don't suppose Nurse Englemann is with you, Emma?'

'Yes, she was just, I mean...'

Mené walked past her neatly wrapped in a towel. 'Oh hello, Mrs Argent. I apologise. The check-up got a little messy and Emma kindly let me use her shower. But I can report all is well. The cock cage isn't doing any harm.'

'Good, good. I came to invite Emma and Nathan down to a late breakfast. It seems everyone,' Catherine looked at the three of them, 'well most of the guests, had a lie-in. Mené. Once you're dressed. Feel free to join us.'

'Thank you.' Mené dropped her towel without the slightest hesitation and slipped on her panties before going hunting for her bra back in the bathroom. Catherine walked up to Nate and wrapped her hand around his cock, glancing at it.

Emma was more shocked by this than anything that had happened so far. Her instinct was to scream at her. As if reading her mind Catherine looked up. 'Just inspecting it pre-purchase. Did you want to say something?'

Emma looked up at Nate's face. His eyes were scrunched up in concentration. She guessed what he was trying to prevent. Looking down it seems it wasn't working. Nate's cock was growing in Catherine's hand. Emma felt a bit sick. After all the fun they'd had this morning this, witch, had to come in and spoil the whole thing.

She stepped up to Catherine, looking quite the spectacle, naked to Catherine's elegant outfit, pushing into her personal space. 'I don't know what your game is yet Catherine but let's get one thing clear. We're letting you have some control that you're going to pay us handsomely for.'

Catherine returned her tirade with a cool gaze. She moved her hand to Nate's balls and squeezed, hard. He winced. 'Legally, I'll be able to do what I want to this,' She reminded them of the contract's wording. She squeezed harder, making Nate grunt. 'If you can't handle that, just tell me. I'll find someone else to give my money to. No?'

With a final tug, she let go and walked to the door. She turned to look at Emma. 'See you at breakfast. Don't let the croissants get cold.'

Emma ran over to Nate, 'Are you okay honey, did she hurt you?'

'No, no I'm fine.' He bit his lip, looking a little embarrassed. Emma looked down.

'Nathan! For fucks sake, that got you hard? I was battling for control of your dick you know.'

'I know, I know, and it was so hot. *You* were so hot. Oh God, I want to fuck you so hard right now.' His cock was jutting up like an iron rod. Emma was tempted to just climb up on him then and there.

'You two are the single most adorable couple I have ever met.' Mené zipped up the uniform in a flourish. She walked over to Nate via her bag and reached up to cut open the plastic cuffs with some scissors. 'She wouldn't let me fuck her in the shower, just so you know.' She patted him on the cheek as he carefully lowered his arms and rubbed his wrists.

'Yeah I kind of guessed,' grinned Nate. 'It was insanely hot but she's never that loud for real.'

Mené gave him a wink and patted his behind. 'With you maybe, chastity boy. Trust me. Just say the word and I'll make her louder than you knew she could get.'

'Oh my God you two, what are you like?' Emma looked at Nate's straining cock that was just stood up between them all. 'How are we going to get *that* back in a cage. And as for you Mené...' Emma stopped what she was going to say and looked up at the clock on the wall and grinned. 'Oh, that explains it.'

The other two looked at her, 'Huh?'.

'She ruined her orgasm in the shower.' She looked at Nate.

'Oh, I see. So she actually, you know, in there?' Nate nodded to the bathroom door, Emma nodded back. 'Did you?' he asked Emma.

'Nope and I'm horny as fuck so we seriously need to cage you back up before I lose my self-control.'

'So wait,' interrupted Mené, her hand unconsciously pressing between her legs. 'You get this horny, this fast, after a ruined orgasm? That's insane.'

'Yep, often worse than before. Welcome to our world. Ask me about the "denial high" over breakfast. Speaking of which I'm starving and despite her being a bitch I really want Catherine's warm croissants. So how are we going to solve this problem?' She pointed to Nate's only slightly less erect cock.

'Oh, that's easy, you get dressed, I'll get my magic pack.' Mené went over to her bag and came back with a hand-sized white plastic pack of some kind of gel. She bent the bag until there was a snapping sound, and then shook it. 'Instant ice pack, clever huh.' She slapped it under Nate's cock making him yell from the cold. 'Let's get you back in your little cage.'

'Are you ever going to stop teasing me about my cock size?' he complained to them both.

Mené grinned, picking up the chastity ring and slipping it over his rapidly shrinking cock. 'Not now I've seen how hard it gets you, no.' She raised her spare hand up just as Emma walked by on her way to the wardrobe. Emma high-fived her and kept going. 'I was told this morning someone asked for me to be in charge of your check-ups all year long.'

'That'd be me,' said Emma, pulling on her dress.

'So it seems like you better get used to having my hand around your dick, Mr Stevens.' She expertly pulled his balls through the cock ring and slid the cage on, pushing it firmly so that Nate's shrinking cock was forced into the little space. 'Oh Emma, could you get the key from my pocket, my hands are full.'

Emma waltzed over and stood behind Mené, sliding her hands seductively around Mené's waist. 'Where did you say it was?'

'You two are unstoppable.' Nate's cock was trying to break back out. 'I thought you were starving.'

'I am, baby, but do you think they could bring room service? Mené and I are *so* horny. You know you're the best at dealing with that, my love.'

Mené laughed heartily as Emma brought out the key. 'You do it' Mené told her. Emma slipped around the side, knelt down, and more serious now, slid the lock into the cage and closed it.

'I wonder when that will be open next.' She gave the cage a kiss. She looked up through Mené's arms to Nate. 'I love you.'

He was about to reply when Mené broke the spell. 'I know, and it's only been a day? Now I don't know what to say.'

'That makes a first,' laughed Nate, giving Emma a tender stroke on her cheek. 'Damn I'm ravenous too. Who knew being tied up gets you so hungry.'

'I did,' Mené said, matter of factly. Nate and Emma looked at her, then at each other and grinned.

Nate hunted around for a shirt and some trousers while the girls quickly put on some lipstick. They were waiting by the door as he pulled his socks on.

'Hurry up darling, the croissants, the croissants,' Emma teased.

'I'm more in the mood for a baguette,' Mené joked.

Emma laughed. 'Are you making big cock jokes again, Mené?'

'I am, who knew it could be so fun.'

'I guess I could unlock Rex, his dick is enormous, more than enough to share.' She slipped her hand into Mené's. 'Catherine offered me the key last night.' Emma pranced out the door with Mené following.

'What?' shouted Nate after them, still trying to get his shoes on. 'She did what?' He raced down the corridor after them, hopping mostly on the one shoe he'd tied up, following their laughter.

Breakfast and Boys' Talk

When he caught up with them, Emma and Mené were already scouting out the breakfast items laid out on the side of the large dining room. No one was actually sitting at the table, everyone had opted to take their food through to the beautiful conservatory that looked out over the grounds.

Emma carried her selection of pastries and coffee through and spied Katie sitting next to Kyle on a wicker sofa, mostly empty plates in front of them. She signalled over to Nate, who was still stacking croissants onto a plate and headed over to where they were sat.

Emma put her plate down and dropped into the comfy cushions of the sofa opposite them. 'Well hello, you two. Kyle, nice to see *more* of you this morning.'

Katie giggled. Kyle looked a little embarrassed but also much more relaxed than he had at dinner the night before. 'So how are you two this morning?' Emma asked.

Katie gave a shy smile and slid her arm through Kyle's. 'We didn't get much sleep.'

No wonder Kyle looks so much more relaxed. 'Is that right?'

'I kept the key last night, and unlocked him as soon as we got to bed and oh I just wanted to suck him forever.' Katie looked down shyly. 'I kept thinking about your hand on the back of my head. It made me go deeper. I definitely want Danielle to show me that thing.'

'What thing?' asked Kyle, shifting in his seat.

Emma looked down and could see his hard-on clearly outlined in his trousers. *She didn't lock him back up. Hah, that'll mess up Fiona's plans.* 'So how was it Kyle, being able to watch her do it this time?'

'The second most beautiful thing I've ever seen.' He smiled.

Katie blushed, and nuzzled into him, looking down and seeing his arousal too. Emma knew that look in her eyes. 'The second, what was the first?'

Kyle leaned forward a little, giving his quiet confession. 'Her face, when she, you know, from me just being in her.'

Emma beamed. 'Katie, you came from making love?'

Katie nodded happily, 'Three times.'

'That's so great, what a lucky girl. Although Kyle does have a beautiful cock, so I'm not surprised.'

It was Kyle's turn to blush, which Emma found similarly adorable. She looked at the two of them, happy and horny and found her anger growing at Fiona's selfish schemes to keep them apart.

Nate came over and joined them, plopping himself down and only just managing not to drop any of the croissants piled in a heap on his plate. 'Good morning.'

'Good morning.' Katie smiled at him and then continued, 'I kept Kyle out and he was so hard again in the morning and he wanted to be in me again and we made love so much. I've been silly not doing it more haven't I?'

Kyle pointed at Emma with both hands. 'You, are the boss.'

Emma grinned at Nate. 'I am the boss, apparently!'

'This comes as no surprise,' said Nate shoving half a croissant in his mouth just as Emma decided to make a cheeky introduction. 'Darling, you remember Katie and Kyle. I held his cock while Katie learnt to blow him last night.'

Just as Emma had hoped Nate couldn't help gazing down and seeing the large outline of Kyle's unlocked cock. He coughed out flakes of croissant and had to drink some water.

Kyle seemed surprised. 'It wasn't just *your* hands?' he asked Katie.

'No, Pumpkin,' said Katie. Nate and Emma exchanged a grin over the nickname. 'I told you she helped me.'

'When you said helped, I didn't realise it meant—'

'You are the big cock Emma jerked off last night?' Everyone turned to the new voice. Having listened in, Mené perched on the arm of the sofa next to Katie and popped a last bit of pastry into her mouth, grinning. Kyle could not take his eyes off her. 'Katie and Kyle, right?

Emma introduced her. 'This is Nurse Englemann — Mené. Yes, she really is a nurse, not a strip-o-gram.'

'A strip-o-what?' asked Mené, sucking a bit of chocolate off the end of her finger rather more seductively than she needed to.

'A stripper, you know, but they come to your house,' explained Nate.

'Oh okay. I tried that once, in a club though.' Mené said nonchalantly.

'You worked as a stripper?' Emma asked, turning to face her.

'Oh no, it wasn't a job, I was at a club and it looked fun. It was with that guy, you know, the one with the massive—'

'What was it like?' Katie's voice got everyone's attention. She was clearly enthralled by the idea. All her attention was on Mené.

'It was great. I've done them for a partner before but doing it up there on a stage, in front of a few dozen people was quite different. A bit scary but so sexy.'

'What were you wearing? I want to picture it.'

Oh my, look whose secret fantasy we've stumbled upon. Emma took a gamble. 'Katie, if Mené showed you how to strip, would you like that?' She looked up to Mené who was running her tongue over her teeth, seeming to like the suggestion.

'Oh would you, would you, would you? I'd love that so much.' Katie was bouncing up and down in her seat.

Mené intervened. 'Oh, but I bet Emma can strip too. I couldn't do it without her.' She looked at Emma with a delighted grin.

Emma shook her head. *I really should have anticipated that.*

Katie's face turned from a smile to a pout. 'When though, we're going home after lunch.'

Emma looked up at Mené and then put a hand on Nate's leg, squeezing and running her hand up his thigh. 'Well, I mean lunch isn't for a while. Of course, the boys would have to agree.' She looked at Kyle, whose eyes kept flicking between the three women like a kid at a pick-and-mix sweet stall.

Nate leaned in and said to her quietly, 'Where's my wife gone, and who are you?' He kissed Emma on the ear. 'You're so fucking hot.'

'Aren't I. It seems this whole thing is having quite the effect on me. Let's see if I can blow your mind. Again.' She squeezed his thigh as he let out a little frustrated moan. 'Nate's in. Kyle, would you like us to teach your wife to strip for you.'

Katie spun around to him and grabbed his hand. 'Please baby, please let them.'

Kyle might not be the brightest spark in the box but he just nodded his head. 'If it would make you happy, Kookoo.'

Katie jumped up, pulling on Nate's arm. 'Come on, we don't have long.'

Emma looked at the baggy t-shirt Katie was wearing. 'Katie, why don't you and Mené quickly go to your room and get ready. I'll bring the boys up in a little while?'

Katie was up off like Tigger on speed, grabbing Mené's hand. Laughing she pulled her along.

'I think she liked that idea,' Nate said. He turned to Kyle, 'Did you know that was a fantasy for her?'

'Is that why she likes it so much?' Kyle was still staring after them.

Emma tapped him on the knee, trying to avoid looking at his cock outlined even larger through his thin trousers, and failing. 'You two seriously need to start reading the articles on my blog.'

Nate had his own question for Kyle. 'So how was it on the other side of the wall?'

He seemed happy to talk about it. 'It was weird. We all had to take our pants off and then a kind of wide belt held us tight against the hole. Some of the guys even had their hands cuffed up but I didn't have to.'

Emma remembered how Nate looked this morning, bound against the wall. The thought of him the same way, but just his cock exposed gave her a familiar tingle. A sudden thought made her snap out of it. 'Oh honey, we still haven't read the contract properly. Did you look at it last night?'

'No, sorry baby, I just fell straight asleep. You don't want to now, right?'

Nate's eyes went to the doorway Katie and Mené had just left through. Emma shook her head and rolled her eyes as he looked back at her. 'I mean, umm, it's been such a long time since you did that for me. Remember that time on honeymoon.' He laughed.

'It wasn't funny, I was trying to be sexy. I didn't think that curtain pole would break so easily. Anyway, as long as we read the contract after lunch, okay?'

Emma's phone vibrated. "Rdy. Rm 114 nxt yrs. Bring heels.'

'Okay boys, let's head up. It seems you're just next door to us.' A light dawned in her eyes. 'Oh, *you're* next door to us.'

* * *

Emma left the boys standing at the door to their bedroom while she went to find heels.

She could still hear them talking. 'I can't believe your wife jerked me off last night,' said Kyle quietly.

That's quite the conversation starter. She glanced at Nate and rolled her eyes.

'No. I'm still processing that,' Nate tactfully answered.

'She's really hot. You're so lucky,' continued Kyle. Emma couldn't help having a little flush of happiness hearing someone else tell her husband that.

'Thank you? But Katie's gorgeous, you're a lucky guy too.'

'Oh yeah, yeah I know but Emma. I guess I just like older women.'

What the fuck, how old do you think we are? She returned Nate's wide-eyed expression before opening the wardrobe to get the heels.

'Okay. I'm sure she'd be happy to hear that?' she heard Nate reply.

'You think I should tell her?'

I'm right here dude, I can hear you. Damn, and I thought Katie was the bimbo. Emma grabbed the shoes, closed the wardrobe harder than necessary, and sat on the bed, pretending not to be listening.

Nate was a bit sterner with the younger guy. 'Maybe, you know, focus on *your* wife? You want her to feel good right?' Emma looked up at her husband with a proud smile, slipping the first of the shoes on.

'I made her cum all night. With my dick too. That makes her feel good.' Kyle reached down and seemingly unaware, started playing with the head of his cock through his trousers.

Emma pulled a face. *Eww, does he know he's doing that? I guess he hasn't had access for a while but that's still weird.*

Nate hadn't noticed. 'Kyle—'

'Mate, I bet Emma is amazing in bed,' Kyle interrupted, not even attempting to whisper.

'Kyle.' Nate forced him to make eye contact. 'Sex is one thing, but a woman needs more. Romance, cute stuff, compliments. Do you tell Katie how beautiful she is?'

'Fiona said it's best to show love with actions. Making her cum mostly.'

Fiona's got her claws into you too, has she. Emma stood, the heels making her feel significantly taller. She looked at the men. Well, one man. The other, a boy still fondling himself. Nate had noticed.

'Kyle,' Nate said, putting his hand on his shoulder. 'Firstly, dude, stop playing with your dick, especially while talking about my wife.' Kyle pulled his hand away, but stuck it back in his pocket where Emma suspected he wrapped his hand right back around it. 'Secondly, Fiona is wrong. Those things are all incredibly important.'

'Why would she say it then?'

Emma walked over to them both, not saying what she was thinking. *Because Fiona wants to fuck your wife and turn you into a chaste cuckold.*

'I don't know. But trust me,' Nate wrapped his arm around Emma and pulled her in close, 'Emma loves sex but she needs to hear me tell her how good she looks, that I love her, be romantic, be helpful. Don't you baby?' He kissed her on the cheek and whispered. 'He's something else isn't he.'

'Mhmm,' she whispered. 'You're doing great.' Emma turned to Kyle. 'Have you ever heard of the Five Love Languages?'

'Was that a movie?'

'No it's a book. You know what, I'll send you a YouTube video later.' She looked down at the gorgeous sexy shoes, and their contrast to the dress she was wearing. 'Give me one more minute, boys.'

She went back to the wardrobe and pulled out the sparkly mini-dress that she hadn't picked the night before. *I know Liz said I can have just the one dress but it can't do any harm.* She quickly wriggled out of what she was wearing and slipped it on, going back and opening the door. The wide eyes that greeted her confirming her decision. 'This was still in the wardrobe. You said I looked like a stripper.' She winked at Nate but he was looking at Kyle's stunned reaction.

Emma bit both her lips together in amusement. 'What do you think Kyle?'

'Sexier than anything.' His mouth was hanging open.

'Now, now Kyle,' said Nate. 'The rule is your wife is always the sexiest woman in the room. Always remember that.' Emma put her arm around Nate and gave him a squeeze.

'But Katie isn't in the room,' he objected.

Emma laid a hand on his arm. 'That wasn't Nate's point. It's about making Katie always feel the most special.' Emma noticed Kyle's arm was moving up and down under her hand. She put one hand through Nate's arm, the other through Kyle's. 'Let's go teach Katie some new moves.' She led them both down the corridor to the next bedroom.

Stripped Bare

Emma deliberately pulled Kyle's hand out of his pocket when removing her arm before knocking politely on the door. She was fairly sure he'd kept on fondling. The door was opened a few inches. 'What's the password?' asked Mené in a heavier accent than normal.

Emma paused for a moment. 'Nurses are naughty?'

The door didn't open. 'True but not the password.'

Nate had a go. 'Shalom aleichem'.

'Impressive knowledge Mr Stevens. But no.'

'Abracadabra?' offered Kyle.

Mené giggled. 'Oh honey, did you mean open sesame?'

Kyle went a bit red. 'Yeah, that one.'

'Nope. Emma, your turn.'

Emma put her hands on her hips and did a spin around in the corridor. 'Is it "I have a five-thousand-pound stripper dress on, wanna see?"'

Mené stuck her head through properly. 'It wasn't but it is now. Seriously, five thousand?'

Emma twisted side to side and the tassels swung around, glittering in the light. Mené cooed and reached out, 'Can I touch?'

'No touching!' laughed Kyle, stepping in the way. 'You know the rules in a strip club.'

'Oh is that right?' said Mené. 'I think you'll find this is a girls' club, and we set the rules.'

Emma nodded in agreement. 'That's right, and the first rule is, boys are only allowed in their underpants. You can keep your shorts on but trousers off.'

'What?' complained Nate. But Kyle had started stripping off without even questioning it.

Emma looked at him with surprise. *Someone's used to following orders. Gosh, Fiona, what have you been doing with these two?* 'We can just let Kyle watch if you prefer, babes?' She patted Nate on the bottom and he quickly got to stripping too, right there in the corridor. He was soon down to his boxers, and Kyle, to his noticeably tight, and full, jockey shorts. Mené opened up the door with a laugh and let them in. 'What *was* the password?' Emma asked.

'I had no idea, I just wanted to see what your filthy mind came up with. Did I mention I read your blog last night? When I was, you know...' Mené gave her best dirty wink.

'You did not,' said Emma, walking in behind the boys. 'Which bits did you read?'

'All of it, a few times.'

'A few times? But that would have taken all day.'

'Yes! As soon as that medical was done. Found Nate's too.' Mené looked pleased with herself. 'Where do you think I read about ruined orgasms for women?'

'I guess I figured you'd just worked it out.' Emma glanced at the boys, waiting for them in their underpants. 'So, what did you think? About the female orgasm denial stuff?' Emma bit her lip, trying to look indifferent.

Mené leaned in and put her mouth right on Emma's ear. 'I think, that you're the real, what was it — "denial slut" yes? And as much as you like locking up Nate's cock, you wish it was you.'

Emma was stunned. She'd known Mené for a little less than 24 hours and she'd already figured that out. She didn't get a chance to respond, Mené was already marching over to the boys in her heels, full military nurse mode engaged.

'Alright boys, get your *nates* on the bed. It's showtime!'

They correctly guessed it meant their bottoms, and sat down, as far as they could from each other, at the end of the big four-poster bed.

'Wait, wait,' said Emma. 'Are you saying "Nate" means bottom in Hebrew?'

'Nates, but yep. You are married to "bottom". Isn't it perfect? He does have a very cute one.' She didn't wait for a response. 'Oh Katie…' Mené called to the bathroom door, '…our guests have arrived'.

All eyes turned towards the door where a shapely leg slid through followed by a hand that stroked up and down the door frame.

'She's off to a great start,' announced Mené. 'Gentleman, welcome to the strip club. Please greet, Katie.' Kyle wolf-whistled and Nate clapped as she walked in wearing the same sheer slip dress as she had worn last night. This time she had a bra underneath it but otherwise, she looked as sexy and well made-up as she had last night.

Emma sidled up to Mené. 'How did you get her looking like that so fast?'

'She's like a make-up diva, it was all her. Apart from the glitter, that was my idea. Wait till you see where we put that.'

Emma watched Katie strut across the floor towards them. 'I'm not sure we can teach her much. Do you get the feeling—'

'That she's been practising this forever? Yes.' Mené finished her thought. She looked at the bed, 'Kyle, no touching,' she suddenly shouted, 'If I see you playing with your cock again it's going back in its cage for the rest of the day. Is that clear?' Kyle jerked his hand away guiltily. 'Hands behind you, you too Nate.' The boys leaned back with both hands on the bed. 'If those hands come back up you're going in there and missing out.' Mené pointed to the bathroom.

'Yes, Nurse.' Nate grinned. Kyle nodded.

Katie had squeezed up alongside Emma and put her hand around her waist. 'You look amazing, Katie. How did you do your make-up so fast?'

'A lot of YouTube tutorials and practise.' She smiled. 'Do you really like it?'

'You look so sexy.' Emma turned to Kyle. Leaning back on his arms made his cock stand up in a rigid arch, stretching the thin material all the way to his waistband. Emma stared at it for a moment, feeling her arousal grow as she remembered the night before.

When she raised her gaze, she found Kyle was staring at her. Not her face though. He was undressing her with his eyes without a hint of subtlety. She didn't really know how to process that. She usually dressed quite modestly, except for private time with Nate. To have this, obviously very aroused, virtual stranger, staring at her so lustfully was an odd experience. The last time she remembered it was at a school swimming lesson. As one of the first to develop breasts in her year she got a lot of attention from the boys. Just like then, she kind of liked it but didn't know what to do about it. *The fact he's staring at me and not his wife is the big issue here.* 'Hey Kyle, doesn't she look beautiful?'

'Huh, what?' He glanced over at Katie and smiled. 'Yeah, she looks great.' Kyle's eyes went straight back to Emma's tits.

She looked over to Nate, wondering if he'd noticed what was going on. Apparently not, because all he could seem to look at was Katie's boobs bouncing up and down as she ran about excitedly. *Fucking men. At least he has a cage on his cock.* Mené returned her look of exasperation — seeming to have taken in everything going on and explaining it all away with a simple shrug. *I guess if you are used to screwing around this isn't all so weird.*

Lady Marmalade started blaring out of the TV. Katie put her phone back down. 'My stripper mix' she explained with a beaming white smile. She began clicking her fingers in time with the music and in perfect sync with one of the singers. She paced across the room to the bedpost next to Nate.

Mené stepped out of her way, grinning at Emma 'Holy shit' she mouthed.

Katie put her heeled foot up on the bed right between Nate's legs. She had good aim because Nate did nothing but stare at the hot little wannabe stripper. Kyle had finally peeled his eyes off Emma and was looking at his wife with some amazement.

'Voulez-vous coucher avec moi?' Katie started singing in a pretty voice as she spread her leg and leaned back off the bedpost, squeezing her bra with her spare hand. Mené started dancing along, swinging her shoulders back and forth. *She really is bendy, damn.* As the chorus ended Katie spun away from the bed and grabbed the padded stool from the dressing table.

Katie planted her bottom on the stool in time with the music, legs spread wide as the rap bit of the song kicked off. She had everyone's attention as she began grinding back and forth on it, her hand holding onto the front like a cowboy trying to stay on a bull. Somewhat to Emma's consternation, her eyes were fixed right on Nate as she humped herself back and forth. To Emma's relief, he broke his gaze with her and looked to her. 'Wow,' he mouthed. *At least he still remembers I'm here.*

Mené had clearly had enough of being on the side-lines. She moved into the middle of the room, high five-ing Katie like a wrestling tag team.

Mené turned away from the boys, slowly bending down, her hands sliding down her long legs until her hands pressed flat on the floor. Even more impressive given the five-inch heels she wore so easily. Emma watched with amusement as the boys' eyes followed her down, then zipped straight back to the same place. Her pose had completely lifted her short dress hem up high and left her tiny white thong all that kept it from being an almost gynaecological pose.

As Christina Aguilera took over the song, Mené wiggled her bottom and slowly raised back up, turning to look at them both, and blowing Katie a kiss as she turned 'Wow, that was awesome,' Katie said.

Mené just nodded in time with the music and grabbed Katie's hand, pulling her up, and looked at Emma, reaching out her other hand. *Okay, here we go.* Emma stepped over just as Mené turned to the side, wrapping her arms around Katie and forming a line. Emma knew what she wanted. She pressed right up to Mené, putting her arm around her too just as the chorus began again. They made a sexy little train.

'Voulez-vous coucher avec moi,' all three of them sang. It seemed one of Mené's few failings was a singing voice, but she was having fun with it. Emma took a big breath and came in with a harmony. Mené turned her head, 'You can sing too?'

Emma nodded, liking the impressed look on Mené's face before the three of them started grinding along to the music. Mené led the way, her hands all over her bottom and breasts in a natural way Emma couldn't quite copy. But as they sang and danced she glanced over at Nate and was rewarded with the most loving gaze. *Blowing your mind now, huh baby.*

She slipped her hands around Mené in front of her, who did the same to Katie, and held onto her boobs as they all shook their booties. Kyle's eyes were firmly glued to her too. His cock had pushed out of the top of his underpants now, the tip just peaking out on his tummy. *Damn, that is bigger than I remember.*

As the song came to it's final few stanzas, Emma split off from the girls and went over to the bedpost Nate sat next to. She grabbed the post and sank her bottom down to her heels. Katie saw and split off too, heading over to Kyle, copying Emma's pose. Emma winked at Katie and got her beautiful smile in return. *She's a different person like this.* Katie watched Emma slide her hand up Nate's bare thigh, using it to push herself up and leaning in so as the song finished her chest was right in his face. She laughed, seeing Katie had done exactly the same thing, just as she'd hoped.

Mené let out a whoop as the song finished. 'That was so great,' she exclaimed. 'Katie, you're a diva.'

'Yeah Katie, I think we need lessons from you. You are so good at this.'

Suddenly Stripper Katie disappeared, and the insecure girl Emma had met the night before resurfaced. 'I really don't think so. You two are so beautiful. I'm not even pretty.'

'What, who told you that?' asked Mené.

'No one. I mean, everyone. I don't know.' Katie suddenly looked as if she was about to burst into tears.

Emma rushed over to her. 'Katie, listen to me. You are beautiful. It's lovely you think we are but we think you are too, don't we Mené.' Mené nodded in agreement, coming up and putting another hand on Katie's shoulder. 'How did you feel, when you danced then?' Emma asked.

'I felt so happy.' Katie stood up straight.

'Did you feel beautiful?' Mené asked.

'Yes, I guess so. Yes. I do, when I dance. Beautiful, and sexy. Was I sexy?' Katie looked not to her husband, but to Nate.

Thankfully Nate was on the ball. 'Yes, Katie, you looked amazingly sexy. You are such a good dancer. Kyle is a very lucky guy.'

Katie broke off from the two women and leapt onto Nate's lap. Emma didn't know quite what to think of it, but the pained look on Nate's face made her grin.

Mené walked to the other bedpost and leaned in to Kyle, whispering. 'Kyle, convince your wife she is the most beautiful woman you've ever seen or you'll never get out of your cage again. Are we clear?'

'Oh Kookoo, that was the hottest thing I ever saw.' Kyle declared, somewhat stiffly. Katie's head popped up from Nate's shoulder. A quick kick to his ankle by Mené encouraged him. 'Yes, you look so sexy in that outfit, I just want to do you.'

'See,' said Emma, trying not to laugh. 'He just wants to *do* you. And look, how hard you've got him. Isn't that even bigger than yesterday?'

Apparently, Nate was forgotten. Forsaken for Kyle's cock as Katie slid off his lap and sat by her husband. 'Oh it is big, isn't it. Can you show me some more things to do with it, Emma?'

Emma heard a squeak come from her husband's direction but kept her focus on Katie. 'I'm sure Mené and I can teach you something between us. But first, we have a problem to address.'

'We do?' Katie asked.

'Mhmm. Look at the three of us. We're pretty lousy strippers if we all end up with our clothes on.'

Mené stepped up. 'Don't you have another song on that list, Katie?'

Katie grabbed her phone, all her upset seemingly forgotten as she scrolled through a very long playlist. 'Oh, this one is perfect.'

A deep Latin beat began from the sound system as Katie once again transformed. She spun around, taking the centre of the floor as Mené and Emma moved over near Nate. This time she mimed, '*I know I may be young, but I have feelings too.*'

'Britney Spears, I could have guessed,' Nate said into Emma's ear.

Katie went on, her hands sliding down her side as she wiggled her bottom in time with the beat. She began twerking her bottom and grinned over at the other two women. Mené grabbed Emma by the hand and dragged her next to Katie.

As the refrain '*Get it, get it*' boomed out Mené pulled Emma's hand to her zip and gave her a wink. Emma laughed and slowly pulled the zip down while Mené grabbed both sides of the zip with her hands. As the song hit a high, she pulled the two sides open, swaying her hips inside it seductively before letting it drop behind her.

'Woo, go girl,' yelled Katie over the music. She took centre stage and began teasingly pulling up her skirt, showing more and more of her gorgeous lacy panelled knickers. She had an idea and beckoned in the other two. Mené and Emma listened to her idea and stood by her as she swayed like a belly dancer. 'One, two, three' she said to them and lifted her arms as the two of them grabbed the hem of her dress and pulled it right up in one go. In a flash, it was gone and Nate and Kyle were both applauding. Suddenly in just her beautiful lingerie and heels, Katie seemed to completely forget anyone was even watching. She closed her eyes, lost in the music, performing moves that Emma guessed were probably from the music video.

Nate was mesmerised by the performance. *I can't blame him for that, this girl is something else.* Nate's eyes went wide, and Emma looked back only to see Katie's bra had magically disappeared. With impressive teasing skills, just her bare arm covered her ample breasts as she continued to dance and spin. Kyle had forgotten all about Emma, at least for now – his eyes ate up his wife. *I don't think he's seen this side of her before.* Katie slowly moved towards her young husband, finally dropping her arm, her large, gravity-defying breasts bouncing as she spun and swayed to the music.

Mené snuck up behind Emma. 'Where was I when those tits got handed out?' she complained. She smacked Emma's bottom playfully. 'How come you've still got your dress on?'

Because I'm not as stupidly confident as you? 'I thought it best Kyle kept his focus on Katie.'

'Good thinking. Look at her go.' Mené wrapped her hands around Emma's waist and they both swayed to the music, watching Katie. She had turned away from Kyle and, hanging onto the bedpost, was rubbing herself against his crotch. With every stroke she managed to pull his underpants' hem down, sliding the tip of his cock between her cheeks. She turned, sinking down onto her heels, fingers finding the waistband of his pants, and yanked them down around his ankles. With her hands on his thighs, she swayed to the music, her head dragging her curls over his proud cock.

'Oh, that is a nice one, you were right.' Mené pressed up against Emma's back. 'Look at Nate watching them. Do you think he wishes he was that big?' Emma just nodded in agreement. The music, the smell of sex in the air, and the sight of Katie kissing and licking Kyle all taking her back to the night before. Emma recalled how it had felt in her hand, the rush of pushing Katie's head, the desire, the taste of Kyle on her lips. 'Go help her,' Mené whispered, 'I'll make sure Nate's okay.'

Emma didn't move but just at that moment Katie turned to look at them both, biting her bottom lip, and Mené gave Emma a little shove that carried her over to them.

She looked to Nate, who just managed to drag his eyes away from them to smile at his wife. Emma gave him a little questioning shrug. Nate did the same in return. *Oh Nate, tell me what to do.* She watched Mené sit behind Nate, lean in and whisper something to him. He slowly nodded his head. Emma didn't know what Mené had said but took it as an encouragement. She turned to Katie, crouching down to her level 'You are so sexy, do you feel that still?'

Katie nodded, taking her lips off the tip of Kyle's cock to give her a big smile. 'This makes me feel sexy too. Can you, can you push my head again? I liked that.'

Emma's heart was pounding as she moved onto her knees, one hand supporting herself on Kyle's leg. She didn't even look up. She slipped her fingers under Katie's hair again and grabbed her gently, pushing Katie down onto Kyle's erection. She heard Kyle groan but looked over to Nate, giving him a nervous smile. Mené kept on whispering things she couldn't hear but the look on his face as he watched her was intoxicating.

The music stopped, and besides the whispers of Mené, the only sound was that of Katie's mouth slurping as Emma drove her deeper onto Kyle. His groans matched the hot, sloppy sounds of Katie getting her face fucked. Katie suddenly jerked up, spluttering. 'Sorry, I just gagged a bit.'

'All part of the fun, don't worry,' Mené reassured her. 'Katie?' she said. Emma looked over at her, she knew what she was about to suggest. 'Why don't you let Emma have a go?'

'Oh, fuck yeah,' Kyle said, all too eagerly.

Emma didn't look at Nate, not yet. She first looked to Katie who shifted aside as though this wasn't anything big at all. Nate was biting his top lip, a look she knew well from when he was nervous. Their eyes met and she raised her eyebrows with the unspoken question. He gave a little nod.

With a deep breath, Emma wrapped her hand around Kyle's cock. *God, I think he* is *bigger than last night.* She kept her eyes down and began stroking his beautiful cock with one hand. Slowly she looked up to Kyle. He was watching her with a fire in his eyes. Even her hand on him seemed to be bringing him close. She looked back to the one person whose opinion actually mattered.

Nate was transfixed on her hand. Mené was kneeling behind him on the bed, her hands on his shoulders, taking it all in. Emma kept slowly stroking Kyle, his groans continuing to build, as she watched her beloved husband, watch her. Their eyes met, and she opened hers wide, lifting her eyebrows with a question she couldn't put into words, her lips parting to show what she was asking. Nate took a breath, biting both top and bottom lips now, and with a little smile, nodded his head again.

Emma's heart was in her mouth. She took a moment to refocus, both hands stroking Kyle's cock, knowing Nate would envy even that. She looked at it, proud and hard, trying to enjoy the moment, but the nerves held her back. *I've just got to go for it.* She counted down from ten in her head, each one a long stroke up and down Kyle's beautiful cock. *I'm going to do this, I want to do this* she said over and over to herself between each one. *Five. Four. Three.* She began to lean in, opening her mouth.

She was just a couple of inches from his cock when Kyle made a deep groan. Even the thought of her sucking him was seemingly enough. His cock began spurting out thick ribbons of cum. Emma panicked. What was she supposed to do? She pushed her head forward but a jet of cum spurted right in her eye, instantly burning. For whatever reason she felt obligated to not ruin him, so she stroked him hard and fast with her hand. She could feel his hot cum splatter across her neck and chest and— *Oh God no, the dress!* Too late. She looked down through her one open eye and realised most of his cum had been shot across the beautiful, delicate tassels of the incredibly expensive dress.

She looked up with her one open eye and caught Mené's gaze, clearly trying to not laugh. Nate looked shell-shocked and then slowly his shocked expression turned into a grin. 'You look like a pirate, baby. One-eyed Willy!' he exclaimed, proud of the pun. Mené cracked up and Katie and Kyle giggled too, even if they probably didn't get the *Goonies* reference.

For some reason Emma didn't want to swear in front of Kyle and Katie so she summoned up her frustration in a single word.

'Bollocks!'

Showered

Emma stared at the cum-soaked dress. 'Do you think that is going to wash out?'.

'Nope.' Mené was shaking her head, staring at the delicate fabric.

'Oh shit, the dress,' said Nate, suddenly realising the problem.

'Oh shit the dress, indeed,' Emma agreed. 'Kyle, seriously, didn't you cum a few hours ago. Couldn't you have waited until I got my mouth around it?'

'I'm sorry,' he said, sounding genuinely regretful. 'You can suck it now if you want?'

'I think the moment's passed, but thanks.' Emma finally took her hand off his cock and wiped it on the bedding. She pulled herself up on the bedpost, one eye still shut tight. Nate was there beside her, with some tissues he'd found.

Emma managed a smile. 'Not quite how we'd pictured it.' She took the tissue from Nate and carefully wiped her eye. With her eye back in operation, she appraised the rest of it. She was coated in cum. It was all over her neck, her breasts, and the fucking dress. 'Nate, what are we going to do about the dress?'

'I'm sure it'll be fine, come on, let's clean you up.' He took her hand and led her to the bathroom. Shutting the door Nate turned to Emma. 'I'm sorry I laughed. Even if it didn't go to plan, you were amazing. You are the sexiest, hottest, most beautiful woman in the world.'

Emma took his hands in hers. 'Even covered in another guy's cum?'

'Especially then. Just, fuck. I thought you sucking it would be mind-blowing but watching it get all over you. I can't even—' Nate put his hand behind Emma's head and kissed her. A shiver went through her body. This is what she really needed, her husband, loving her, owning her, needing her.

She pulled back, whispering on his lips. 'Oh God, Nate, I want to suck your cock so bad. How are we going to do this for a year?'

'We could still *not* do this for a year?' Nate offered.

'I know but, it's so hot. And the money, the money would be such a help.'

'Let's not talk about it now. Take the dress off. We need to clean you up.'

Emma stepped back and reached behind her, pulling down the little zip at the bottom of the deep plunging back. Just as she was about to pull the dress off, music started from next door with a whoop from Mené.

Emma paused. 'Sit down,' she told Nate, nodding to the toilet. He shrugged and sat down, watching her the whole time. 'I never got to do my striptease. You're the only one I really wanted watching.'

She started to sway to the beat of the music, lifting the straps of the dress off her shoulders and letting it slide down her body to the ground.

Nate stared in wonder at the incredibly strappy lingerie she'd had hiding underneath. She hadn't tried it on the day before but was delighted by his reaction.

The bra was barely more than straps, even over her breasts. It was like they'd forgotten to put the cups in, and just the framework was left. Very cleverly a middle strap and the lacy trim covered her nipples, making it a perfect tease.

Nate's eyes travelled down to the equally cage-like panties. The thin black waistband went over her hips and dived down to where just a few thin strips covered her mound before a mesh panel preserved whatever modesty she had left.

As the unfamiliar beat pounded through the wall she gloried in her husband's gaze. Emma slid her fingers outside the mesh and started rubbing herself as she moved, more for his reaction than anything but the simple touch reignited the fire inside her. Kicking the deep bathmat over in front of Nate she sank to her knees in front of him.

His gaze kept moving to her breasts, and neck. Emma smiled. 'What do you keep looking at, baby?' she asked, already knowing the answer.

'Cum. All that cum, on you.'

'Did it turn you on, watching that big cock spurt all over my face?' Emma reached behind her and undid the bra. Nate wasn't even able to verbalise a reply. She slipped the bra off, lifting up her chest to put it even closer to Nate. Looking down she grinned. It was still all over her neck, and had dripped down, wetting the bra. 'Gosh there was lots of it wasn't there?' She cupped her breasts with her hands and started massaging it in, her skin shiny with it. 'I'm a very dirty girl.' The musky, earthy smell of cum filled Emma's senses.

She began squeezing her nipples, pulling on them with her fingers and thumbs, lubricated by the load coating them. 'I heard it's good for the skin. I guess with you locked up I have to get it, somewhere else.' Her hands wandered further, rubbing in the trails of cum above her breasts. Nate looked higher, at her neck. 'Did I miss some?' He nodded. Emma took Nate's hand, pulled a finger straight and lifted her neck. 'Get it for me will you, baby?' She led his hand to where she felt the cool trail, and the length of Nate's finger wiped up, leaving it as a shining line from his knuckle to fingertip. 'You always told me it was good for me.' Emma opened her mouth and waited. Nate let out a sexy little sigh and lifted his finger, sliding it into her mouth. She pushed her mouth all the way down, catching every last drop of cum with her lips and pulling back, feeding it all into her mouth. It tasted good. Different, but good. She swirled her tongue around her mouth, feeling it coated with it, then sucked it all to the back, and swallowed. 'I like it. But I prefer yours.'

Without a word Nate pulled her in and kissed her even harder than before. The thought that he could taste Kyle on her tongue drove her wild.

Emma's hand was nearly in her panties when she remembered what was on her fingers. 'Wash me, make me clean, make me yours again,' she begged, deep emotions rising to the surface.

Nate stood, lifting her and walking her with him to the entrance of the big walk-in shower. He reached over and flicked on the water, his hand on her hip, keeping her in place, standing, as he walked around her.

As the steam from the shower started to fill the room she felt his kisses on her shoulder. His hands wrapped around her from behind and grabbed hold of her cum covered breasts, squeezing them hard, almost painfully. Emma cried out as the pain released more of the emotions she'd been holding back. His kisses became hard, hungry sucks under her ear, the place he knew drove her wild. And then they softened, starting at the top of her spine, going down, ridge by ridge, his hands moving to her panties, gently pulling them down, as he went to one knee, stripping her as his kisses nuzzled the base of her spine. Then harder again, biting, sucking on her buttocks. She knew it'd leave marks, and she wanted more. She reached behind, pressing his face against her cheek, feeling the stab of pleasure and pain as his teeth dug into her.

Then his strong hands were spinning her around, his hungry mouth where she needed it, between her legs. She cried out, glad of the music masking it, holding herself steady against the glass entrance to the shower as he went to both knees beneath her. His mouth, his lips, sucking at her clit, emotion overwhelming her, tears coming into her eyes, running down her face as she held onto his head with her other hand. Her hot, salty tears splashed across her cum-covered breasts as she quickly got to the edge, crying for release.

It was too much. She fell to her knees, straddling Nate, who wrapped his arms around her naked, feminine frame and held her. Sharp splashes of water bounced off the floor from the shower jets. Emma sobbed into his shoulder. She didn't know why. She didn't feel sad, just overwhelmed. This is where she needed to be.

'I love you,' Nate whispered. Emma didn't reply. She didn't need to. His hand went down between them, finishing what his mouth had begun. She clung to him as an orgasm swelled inside her and then erupted through her, kissing him deeply and moaning inexpressible words into him.

She let the tears continue to flow, finding peace in them. Nate's arms wrapped around her, keeping her safe. Finally, her breathing began to be less ragged. She sniffed. 'We didn't ever imagine it'd make me cry.'

'No,' agreed Nate. 'Or laugh. I'm very proud of that one-eyed willy joke.'

Emma shook her head against his shoulder. 'You're such an idiot. I love you.'

'I know. And you really need a shower. You're covered in cum you know.' Nate brushed his fingers through her hair.

'So are you now.' Emma giggled.

'Thanks, I was trying not to think about that.

'It was so hot when you kissed me. Could you taste—'

'Okay, shower time!' Nate wrapped his arms under Emma and lifted her up as he rose on his knees. Standing beside her he put his hands under her bare bottom and lifted her, grabbing her bottom hard.

She squealed. He ignored her complaints and carried her into the cascading water. 'Oh shit,' he exclaimed, 'I didn't take my boxers off.' Emma laughed as he put her down, grabbing his shorts and pulling them to the floor.

'Oh, I'm sowwy little guy. If you weren't all locked up you'd be down my throat right now.' She cupped his balls gently; they were heavy in her hand. 'Nate, how are these possibly so full after Mené completely emptied you yesterday?'

'You mean beside you and Mené teasing me mercilessly this morning, and then watching you stripping with her, and Katie.' Nate paused, distracted.

'You liked her didn't you. Little "Pumpkin", dancing around, stripping.' Emma squeezed Nate's full balls, the hot water cascading down her arm. 'She is cute, I'll give you that. You know, I think Fiona's been training her to do stuff to women. Kyle too. Imagine that baby. Imagine if I took them home. Pumpkin and Kookoo, wasn't it?' She laughed. 'Keeping me company while my poor hubby is all locked up.'

Emma turned, rubbing her bottom against Nate's cage. Her tone changed, the dominant washing away in the hot water, and his desperate wife winning back control. 'Oh, I wish you could fuck me. I need you in me.' She pulled his arms around her. Nate grabbed the shower gel, squirting it on his hands and intimately rubbing it all over his wife. He squeezed and caressed her breasts, the slippery soap making them slide from his grasp. He washed her from neck down, fingers slipping through her soapy pubes to push open her lips, rubbing her clit, hard.

Emma leaned against the cool glass, letting him touch, pleasure her. 'More,' she cried. Nate moved to the side of her and as his left hand caressed her clit his right pushed her thighs wider, his middle two fingers finding her slippery pussy, pushing in. 'Oh fuck, yes.'

His fingers worked inside her, twisting so he rubbed against her g-spot, pushing from the inside as his other fingers nearly met them, circling and stroking her clit on the outside. 'That feels…' she just groaned.

Nate formed three fingers into a cone, working the tips of each into her before she pushed back, mounting herself on his hand. His fingers slid inside her to the knuckle, stretching and he worked them in and out as she grabbed his hair with one hand. 'Yes, God, yes, don't stop, don't stop.' He held her there, right on the edge of exploding, her back arched, fucking herself against his hand. 'More!' she begged.

His little finger joined the others, working in and out, judging every reaction, pushing deeper as she pressed against him, keeping her on the edge, dragging out this moment of ecstasy. 'You are so fucking wet, oh my God.' His fingers were stretching her, that aching, primal sensation of being used, being taken, being owned.

Nate slid his fingers out, folded his thumb into the palm of his hand, and pushed. Despite the shower she was drenched with slippery juices. His hand met resistance, the stretch was so intense. Emma forced herself to relax, moaning louder to encourage him to keep going. Nate went down to his knee, kissing her hip, rubbing her clit, and he pushed as she pushed back. She felt the incredible aching stretch, but he began to pull back. 'No,' she cried out, 'don't stop! He pushed again, his hand slipping in and fucking her. She cried out as her climax finally released, grinding herself against his fingers, his whole hand, completely filled with him. Over and over she cried out, the climax feeling like it would never end, cumming on his hand, squeezing, contracting on his fist, over and over, tightening, loosening.

'Oh fuck. Nate, that was, oh my God.' She let out a little laugh, her breath shuddering. 'Is, is your hand still in me?'

'Uh huh. This, well this is new. Should I—'

Emma reached down and gripped his wrist. 'No, don't, just. Oh fuck, that is so weird but oh fuck it feels amazing. I feel like—'

Nate just moved his fingers a tiny bit inside her and with a shout she came again. 'Oh my God, oh fuck, oh fuck, yes, no, I mean, oh fuck do that again.'

He unfurled his fingers a little inside her and she squeezed his wrist tight. 'Oh fuck, that's—'. Emma orgasmed yet again; her breath ragged, incoherent for another twenty seconds. 'Oh my God, how are we even going to get that out without—'.

Nate grinned and slowly slid his hand down just a little, pausing as it stretched her pussy at its widest point, his fingers rubbing her g-spot as they passed. She cried out in pleasure again, but this time clear liquid gushed down her thighs and Nate's arm, splattering on the shower floor. 'Holy shit I just squirted. Take it out, it's so good but I can't take any more.' Nate gently slipped his fingers out of her as the final convulsions of the last orgasm faded. Emma sank down to join him on the shower floor. 'Well that,' she panted, '*was* new.' She leaned into him, hugging him as the hot water cascaded over them, a satisfied smile on his face.

Nate turned her head towards him with his finger, and kissed her gently, cheeks and eyelids shut from the water. Then her forehead, slowly down, little kisses, until his mouth joined hers and they let the water wash away everything it needed to.

* * *

By the time the two of them came out of the bathroom the playlist appeared to have started again. Katie was sitting in bed under the duvet, with Kyle on one side, and Mené on the other. They were all in their underwear but something about Mené's smile made Emma wonder if that had always been the case. Kyle jumped up as soon as they exited and ran into the loo.

'Hallelujah,' said Mené. 'He was about to pee in a plant pot.'

Nate laughed and looked around for his trousers. He'd left his wet underwear in the bathroom. As he pulled them on he did a reverse striptease to the Lady Marmalade song.

'Voulez-vous coucher avec moi?' Nate asked Emma with a grin.

'As soon as you get your cock unlocked, hell yeah.' She laughed.

'What does that mean, the song words, I've always wondered?' asked Katie.

Emma sat on the end of the bed in her underwear, the damp designer dress in her hand. *How have you stripped to it and never looked it up on Google?* 'Would you sleep with me,' Emma actually answered.

Katie looked from Emma, to Nate, to Emma again. 'Okay, but with just you or with Nate too? Isn't he caged though?'

'Wait what?' Nate spluttered, doing up his shirt.

'No I meant—' Emma tried to explain. Nate started laughing and Mené joined in.

Katie looked puzzled. 'Can Kyle watch, Fiona usually—'

Emma stopped her. '*That* is what it means, Katie. *Voulez vous coucher avec moi* means, would you like to sleep with me.'

Katie blushed. 'Oh I thought you meant...'

'Yes,' said Emma, 'we got that.' She paused. 'Fiona usually does what?'

'Doesn't matter. Forget I said anything. Please.' Katie leapt out of bed and started hunting for the panties she apparently wasn't still wearing.

Mené slipped her legs out of the other side, and got up, stretching. Emma noticed something. 'Mené, aren't those Katie's?'

Mené looked down and giggled. 'Whoops, how did that happen?' She whipped the knickers off and threw them over to a still blushing Katie.

Emma shook her head. 'You are incorrigible,' she told Mené.

'I don't know what that means but if you're saying I'm good at teaching blowjobs skills then you're right'.

Katie pulled on her dress. 'I hope you don't mind, you were so long in the shower. Mené offered to teach me some things. She went to the bedside drawer and pulled out a cock cage. 'I don't know what to do, should I lock him back up?'

Emma stood and looked Katie in the eyes. 'Do what do you want to do. Lock him up or leave him out. It's your choice. Nobody else's.'

Katie thought about it as she put on her shoes. 'I think I want to lock him back up but keep the key. Would that be alright? I do love how he treats me

226

and I can unlock him anytime, right?'

'That sounds like an excellent plan. Just don't let Fiona take that key away. It's yours, and so is Kyle's cock. Understood?' Emma picked up the dress. It was still damp, and stained. 'Shit, what am I going to do about this?' Mené came to see, zipping up her uniform. 'That is not coming out in the wash. Can you even wash it? What does the label say?'

Emma hunted around and finally found the care instructions, they were hand sewn into a label. 'Do not wash. Do not dry clean. Well what the hell use is that? I was only allowed one of the dresses, it's not even mine.'

Katie stepped up beside her to look. 'Naeem Khan?' she exclaimed. 'Oh wow, that's amazing. He dresses Michelle Obama. How much is that worth?' Katie grabbed her phone and quickly started searching. 'Wow.' She reverentially reached out and stroked the material.

'How much?' asked Mené.

'£5,322. But there is some good news. It says here you can dry clean it.'

A spark of hope lit in Emma's chest, but then the reality of the situation hit home. 'Not on a Sunday, or within the few hours before we leave. And could they return it if it's been dry-cleaned?'

'No,' said Katie. 'I tried it once with a dress I wore to a wedding. Left the labels in and everything. They knew it had been cleaned.'

Mené started to walk towards the door. 'You could just put it back on the shelf and pretend you never wore it? Maybe Catherine won't notice.'

Emma thought about it but knew she wouldn't be able to. *Sometimes I wish I was that kind of person.*

Nate spoke what she was thinking. 'We couldn't do that. We'll just have to tell Catherine what happened.' He turned to look as Kyle walked back in, drying himself off with a towel. He hadn't bothered to dress and seemed a little surprised but not bothered by the rest of them.

Emma's eyes were drawn to between Kyle's legs where his cock swung between his thighs. *So he's a show-er not a grower.* She was suddenly very aware that she was the only woman in the room still in her underwear, a fact Kyle instantly picked up. She saw his cock twitch and start to rise.

'Honey, we really must go,' Emma said to Nate, dragging her eyes away.

'We have something we have to read, remember?' She grabbed his hand and pulled him towards the door.

Kyle stretched, throwing his towel onto a chair. 'Do you really have to go?' His cock was visibly hardening now.

Emma opened the door, looking back. Mené had stepped between them and Kyle's growing erection. 'I can stay,' Mené offered, stopping Kyle with her hand, and pushing him back so he sat on the bed.

He actually pouted at Emma's departure but was quickly distracted by the hot nurse getting on her knees in front of him. Mené held out her hand to Katie, who understood what she wanted. Before Kyle knew what was happening she had the chastity ring around his balls, and was working his cock through before it got too hard. His complaints were drowned out as Katie turned the music on and started dancing around again, watching Mené force him into the small cage. Emma could see it was going to take a while, but was sure she'd manage it somehow.

Mené turned around and mouthed, 'Goodbye,' to Emma as they slipped out into the corridor.

Emma's mind was still on the dress. Maybe she could find some local dry-cleaners, and get a taxi? The corridor's cooler air made her skin goose bump. *First I need to actually put something on.* She turned with Nate towards their room and gasped.

'Oh, there you are,' said Catherine, an amused smile as she took in Emma's lack of clothes. 'We've been trying to find you.' She paused, her eyes going to the damp, golden fabric in Emma's hand. Half a dozen heartbeats later she smiled, her eyes narrowing. 'Is that...the Khan dress?'

Shit.

Toys and Undies

E mma tried explaining about the dress, but without mentioning the stripping, or the fact it was drenched in semen.

'I see,' was all she got in reply. Catherine led them back to their room and opened the door. 'It's a very expensive dress. They all are. You were only supposed to pick one.'

Emma hung her head; she didn't know what to say. She felt like she'd been hauled before the headmistress, in her underwear. The silence went on.

Finally, Catherine spoke. 'But I'm sure we can work something out. Let's not worry about it, I have some things I want to give you.'

Emma lifted her head, grateful at Catherine's tone, even if she didn't exactly know what 'working it out' meant. She didn't dare ask.

Elizabeth was waiting in their room. She stood as they entered, not making eye contact with them. She was back in an elegant, cream, figure-hugging dress suit. Emma pictured her as she'd been last night, naked, crying, pressing herself against that anonymous flaccid penis. She felt a stirring between her legs, recalling Elizabeth's desperate cries, and then her mind went to Danielle and her deep, gasping sobs of pleasure. *This is the point I am so glad I don't have a penis to betray me. What is wrong with me?* She hurried to the wardrobe and picked out the dress she'd arrived in, slipping it on.

'So what is it you need?' asked Nate, frowning at the invasion of privacy.

'As I said, Nathan. I have some things to give you.' Catherine walked over to the bed where some indistinct mounds lay under a blanket. 'You remember me asking permission to enter your home. This is why.'

With a flourish Catherine threw back the blanket and Emma was instantly mortified. There on the bed were all their sex toys. Nate laughed, seeming to think it was more amusing than anything. But to Emma, these were her most personal things. *Oh no, they didn't find....* Her eyes scanned up and her heart dropped down into her stomach. There at the top of the selection were the toys she'd secretly bought. The ones she'd never dared tell Nathan about. *How the fuck did they find those?*

'An interesting, if small, selection,' Catherine observed. 'So here's my offer. Let me take these, and dispose of them, and you'll get a whole new set of brand spanking new toys.'

Nate seemed happy to agree but Emma was still too caught up worrying about the ones in the top row. *Perhaps if I agree they'll just bin them and Nate won't even notice.* Emma was about to agree but Catherine had sensed her hesitation.

'Perhaps, some of them have sentimental value,' she guessed. 'How about I let you keep one item each?'

Before Emma had a chance to suggest they bin them all, Nate agreed. 'Okay, whatever. Which one do you want to keep, honey?'

'Yes, which one *would* you like to keep?' Catherine was curious, she'd picked up on Emma's discomfort. 'I'd love to know some of the history of these.'

Nate wandered over to have a browse. 'I didn't realise we had that many. It's strange seeing them all laid out.' He picked up a simple plastic vibrator with a screw base that turned it on and off. 'This one was the first toy we got, wasn't it honey, do you remember?'

Nate. Shut. Up. Emma nodded, forcing a smile. 'Yes, when we were engaged. I was so shocked.'

For a moment she remembered that day. Nate dragging her into some seedy sex shop near their university accommodation. He admitted later he'd been planning it for months. Emma hadn't known where to look. Walls covered with porn that was far more explicit than anything on the top shelf of a newsagent. They hadn't dared go through the curtain that separated off the back of the shop. God knows what had been back there, even Nate wasn't brave enough to look. She'd wanted to leave but finally agreed to Nate buying her something, anything, just to go. She remembered her astonishment that a quite pretty lady was behind the till.

She sneaked that vibrator into her room as though it were a stick of dynamite, refusing Nate's offer to 'see how it works'. It was noisy, but it was *so* good. She was soon grateful for it. Reliant on it. Most of all it got her ready for him. Finally, brave, and horny enough to try it inside her. Most of her fantasies were dreams about their wedding night. Not even Nate knew the rest of them. How she'd imagined being the shop girl. Acting out what went on behind the sex shop's curtained doorway.

Emma came back to the present as Nate was waving around a biggish pink dildo. 'This is the biggest one we have, we don't use it much,' he said.

That you know of. Emma couldn't help but smile.

'I, I don't remember these though.'

Shit, shit, shit.

Catherine was suddenly much more attentive. 'Oh really, which ones?'

Nate reached out to the top row of toys and brushed his fingers along a selection of small black leather cuffs. He picked up a delicate black collar with red hearts inset in the leather. Turning back to Emma, he tilted his head, about to ask more when he saw the look in her eyes and paused. 'Oh, wait a minute, these were for that fancy dress party weren't they, now I remember.'

Oh, Nathan Stevens I fucking love you. Emma tried not to shudder as she let out her breath. 'Yep, I think so.' Catherine was looking between the two of them with narrowed eyes, knowing she'd missed something.

'So which are you going to keep?' she finally asked.

Emma mused over the collection. 'Our first vibe. Happy memories.' She looked to Nate who was still swinging the collar in his fingers, biting his lower lip.

'This,' he said. 'The collar. It was a memorable party.' He picked it up, running his fingers over the little hearts, giving her a look that made her melt into a puddle.

'Fine.' Catherine said. Emma enjoyed seeing her frustrated. 'Elizabeth…'

Elizabeth scraped the rest of the toys into a black plastic bag and dropped it outside the door. She returned, struggling to carry a large cardboard box which she put down on the bed with a grunt.

Catherine joined her and with their backs to Emma and Nate they laid out the contents on the bed. When they stepped apart Nate whistled. 'Wow, it looks like Lovehoney just came on the bed.'

Catherine ignored him and began to go over the multitude of toys and objects laid out. There were vibrators of every kind. Luxury models, remote controlled, a mains-powered wand, even ones that looked like a little spout which Emma hadn't seen before. 'It's a clitoral stimulator,' Catherine explained, giving a sideways glance to Elizabeth. 'Like a mouth on you, but it can go for hours.'

'I can go for hours,' Nate muttered under his breath.

Emma chuckled but stopped when she looked at the pained expression on Elizabeth's face.

Catherine continued, showing them the restraints that go under the bed, plus some metal fixings that looked like the one Nate had been tied to that morning. *That's definitely going up.*

There was a selection of butt plugs that grew in size from small to positively eye-watering. 'Why are there two of each?' Nate asked.

Catherine picked up a medium sized one and rattled it. There was a ball hidden away inside it. 'It rolls around as you walk. I'm told it's quite stimulating.' She obviously looked at Elizabeth again.

I wonder if she's wearing one. Anything's possible after last night.

'As to why there are two of each,' Catherine continued. 'I thought you might like to wear a matching set. I do so like matching sets.' She moved onto the dildos, of which there were nearly a dozen. Smooth, realistic, some that looked almost alien. They grew in length from six inches to as big as ten. But nothing ridiculous. Most of them had a suction cup base and it was then that Catherine reached back into the box for an item she hadn't removed yet.

It was a triangular pad with some clips and a rubber ring at the front.

232

From it trailed four straps. Emma knew what it was. 'A strap on harness, oh what fun.'

Catherine showed her how most of the dildos fitted into it via their suction cups and how the size was easily adjusted, 'So either of you can wear it.'

It was much fancier than the cheap one they'd used until now. Emma pictured herself wearing it, and then even more exciting, how it'd look on Nate, a big dildo above his poor caged up cock. *So hot.*

Once more Catherine reached into the box. 'And here's something we made earlier.' She laid it down at the small end of the dildo selection. It was noticeably shorter than the smallest.

'Is that what I think it is?' Emma cried. She lifted it up and turned it around to look at it head up. 'It is, it is. Nate, it's your penis.' Before Nate knew what was happening Emma had put the base of it up against his trousers and was laughing. 'It looks small, but I guess that's just in comparison to these other ones. Oh my God that's so cute.'

Nate took the cloned willy off his wife, looking at it suspiciously. The other women joined in the giggles; Elizabeth seemed to relax at last.

'And finally, speaking of comparisons…' Catherine reached one last time into the box and lifted something heavy. It was another dildo, but this time it was at the other end of the scale. She laid it past the largest in the set. It was a monster, maybe a foot long, at least another couple of inches beyond the biggest she'd got out.

'Well that's ridiculous,' said Nate, 'no one is that big.'

'It's Rex's.' Catherine looked Nate in the eye, and then down to the dildo he held in his hand. He looked over to Emma. Her eyes were fixed on the giant dildo Catherine had laid down.

A quiet, 'Fuck,' was all Nate managed to reply. He sheepishly put his own cock copy back on the bed, as far from Rex's as possible.

Emma slipped her hand into his and squeezed, but she couldn't take her eyes off Rex's cock. Catherine looked at her wristwatch. 'Now, I have one more surprise for you before lunch. If you'd look out of the window.'

Emma and Nate went to the large bay window and looked out over the beautiful grounds. They stretched as far as they could see. Around the house a gravelled section separated from a beautiful lawn, mown into stripes. A ha-ha divided that from the fields and wooded areas beyond, letting sheep graze without wrecking the manicured lawn.

'What exactly are we looking at?' Nate asked.

'Do you see the fire, and Rex?' Catherine said.

Sure enough, someone who Emma had assumed to be the gardener was standing by an incinerator dustbin that was merrily burning away some planks of wood. By him were two black bin bags of what she assumed were leaves.

'I'm surprised we can't see his cock from here,' muttered Nate. Emma shushed him but grinned.

Catherine waved at Rex and he waved back. 'In those two bags are every single item of underwear you own, including the ones from this room you weren't wearing.

Emma suddenly remembered Nate was currently going commando, and from the interest with which he now stared through the window it seemed he had too.

'I will give you up to two thousand pounds if you let me put those bags on the fire.'

'*Up* to two thousand?' noted Nate. 'That's what they say on dodgy sales signs, 'Up to half price. It's never as good as it sounds.'

'And what are we going to wear, you can't expect us to not wear underwear for a year,' Emma complained.

'It can be just as good as it sounds if you'll let me finish,' said Catherine. She walked over to the long built-in wardrobe that had been almost empty when Emma had nosed around the room. 'In here is a complete ensemble of underwear to replace your old ones. Very beautiful, very expensive. Suitable for every occasion.

'Even working out?' asked Emma, conscious that lacy underwear and jogging do not mix.

'Every occasion. And Nathan, the "up to" refers to the fact that should you wish to check the contents of this wardrobe before you agree, you will receive £1,000, cash. If you're happy to let us burn them without checking,

234

you'll receive £2,000. So, what will it be?'

'So wait, let me get this right,' Nate asked. 'You burn our old, cheap, worn out undies. Give us the expensive stuff in that wardrobe, *and* we get a couple of grand on top?'

'Correct.'

'Underwear for *both* of us?' Emma thought to check.

A little smile played across Catherine's face. 'Yes. But it's all you're allowed all year.'

'How would you know if we bought other underwear?' Nate asked.

'Haven't you read the contract yet?' Catherine asked, genuinely surprised. 'It gives us access to your finances, and property, on a spot-inspection basis.'

'What the fuck, seriously?'

'Nathan, if you don't want my money you're free to walk away from here with a selection of wonderful sex toys and one new outfit each.' Catherine looked pointedly at the ruined Khan creation on the chair. 'I suggest you read the contract and make your mind up, the deadline is in a couple of hours and it will not be extended.'

Emma looked at Nate, she knew he was ready to just do it. *What's the catch, there's got to be a catch?* But she couldn't figure out what it was. She looked at the designer dress and caught Nate's eye, nodding towards it. They needed this money in case she got bitchy about the dress. 'Two thousand?' she asked him.

'I can't see why not, sure. You've looked amazing in the stuff you've worn this weekend. Catherine, or Liz, has very good taste.'

Emma saw the first smile of the day on Elizabeth's face. But Catherine smiled too, a cold smirk as she waved at Rex out of the window.

Shit, what did we miss? Emma watched all her and Nate's underwear going up in flames. *That can't be it, what's she so happy about?*

'I must go and get ready for lunch. See you down there in ten.' Catherine left with Elizabeth trailing after her.

As the door shut, Nate twirled towards Emma. 'Two grand baby, let's see what's in the wardrobe.' Nate pulled the sliding door one way and whistled. 'Holy shit, look at this stuff.'

Hung up along the rail was hanger after hanger of the most beautiful lingerie Emma had ever seen. Everything was in matching sets. All of it classier and more expensive than even the set she'd worn on their wedding night, and that had cost what felt like a fortune. She ran her hands along, looking at all the designer labels, stroking the beautiful material. She hadn't realised just how much she'd enjoyed wearing the nice lingerie that had come with the dress this weekend, until now. And here it was, everything she could ever wear, and more.

Teddies, baby dolls, chemises, every type she could imagine. She checked the sizes, they all looked good apart from a box of very girly panties that didn't seem to have matching bras.

She pulled her hand out of the way as Nate slid the other doors across. There was more. This was apparently the racier end. Balconette bras, quarter cups that would support her but leave her nipples exposed. Crotchless panties, thongs, body stockings, even some wet-look basques and bustiers. Everything hung up like in a luxury lingerie store. Good to Catherine's promise, there was a set of attractive sports bras and panties too. And the items at the end made Emma catch her breath. Ten exquisite corsets.

'Oh Nate, look at these, look at these!' She grabbed a couple off the railing, holding them up to herself. Emma had always wanted a corset but could never justify the cost. From shimmering panelled contemporary ones to others she knew would curve her waist in uncomfortably at first, she was in love.

Nate was wide-eyed seeing her hold up something so sexy. 'Those are amazing. Wow, you're going to look incredible in all of these. Are they the right size?'

'Yes, they all look perfect. Apart from that first set, they all look a bit big.'

'Hold up,' said Nate. 'Where are all the fancy designer jockey shorts for me. I was hoping for some that didn't come from TK Maxx. Come on Calvin Klein's, where are you.' He searched around and then pulled back the first door again.

Emma looked out of the window; the fire was dying down now. She had a sudden sinking feeling as Nate got increasingly annoyed. *I know what we missed.* She walked over to the box of unmatched, frilly panties. 'Oh honey...'

'What is it?'

She picked out a pair, putting them against her waist. They were far too big. 'These aren't my size, babe.' Nate's eyes went wide as he started to work out what she was saying. 'They're yours.'

The Dolls Room

L unch was not fun. Nate was still fuming and refused to come down so Emma went and fetched him a plate of food, telling everyone he had a migraine. She felt stupid too, but it was him who was going to have to pay the price for them not spotting Catherine's stupid trick. She left him reading the contract and went to get some food for herself, deciding to take a different route and explore the house a little more.

She'd had a sense Catherine's rooms were at the front of the house, so she headed to the back, past Katie and Kyle's. A thought struck her, if she could get back the pants Nate had left in their shower at least he'd have something. She knocked on the door and went in without waiting, assuming they'd be down at lunch.

They weren't. They were in their room, and Kyle was in Katie. Balls deep. Katie looked up from the far side of the bed where she was lying and smiled. Kyle meanwhile looked up at Emma, and climaxed. Loudly, and looking at her the entire time. He seemed to fuck even harder. Emma could hear his sloppy, wet strokes.

'Oh my God I'm so sorry, I just…I'll leave you be.' She spun around, horrified by walking in like that, and nearly as freaked out by Kyle's unrelenting gaze that followed her as she spun away. She ran through the door, leaning back against it, heart pounding. Apparently, her visit had given Kyle a boost. Katie's cries of pleasure grew as the sound of his thrusts became loud enough to hear even in the corridor.

Despite herself, Emma stayed there, catching her breath and… thinking about his cock, how amazing it was that he could cum, and just keep going like that. *I wish Nate could do that.* Emma couldn't pull herself away from the door. Seeing them like that had brought back the arousal she'd been feeling all weekend. Glancing around she pressed her ear to the door, just to listen for a little longer.

'Oh yes, yes, more, I'm going to cum,' Katie cried.

'You feel so fucking good, did you like her watching?'

'Oh yes, I wish she'd stayed.'

'Me too.'

Emma listened, her breaths short and fast. She fought against the idea of just opening the door again and watching this hot young couple fuck. She found her hand had moved to between her legs, pressing on her dress, pushing, rubbing little circles through the material. This was so wrong.

'Whatcha doing?' Mené's question nearly made Emma scream. She spun around, just avoiding knocking against the door.'

'Mené! Is it your job to catch me doing embarrassing stuff?' she asked in a shouted whisper.

Mené beamed and replied in a quiet voice, 'Well if you didn't keep doing embarrassing things I wouldn't keep catching you at them. Are you listening to something hot?' She pushed past Emma and put her ear to the door. 'So she didn't keep him locked then?'

Emma put her ear to the other door panel, looking at Mené and whispering back 'Definitely not. I just walked in on them.'

Mené lowered her brows and shook her head in confusion.

'I was trying to get Nate some pants.' The explanation didn't change Mené's expression much.

'Kyle?' they heard Katie ask, both pressing their ears firmly on the door. 'Kyle, call me Emma.'

Mené's eyes went wide, covering her mouth to stop herself bursting out laughing. Emma just stared at her open-mouthed. She pressed her ear harder to hear his reply.

'Not Fiona? Kyle asked.

'No, not this time. Emma's hotter.'

'Oh Emma, Emma,' Kyle started shouting in time with his obvious thrusts.

Mené was biting her hand, trying not to cry while still listening. Emma didn't know how to process what she was hearing. The cries of her name got louder and louder. She couldn't get the image of them both out of her head, Kyle, pounding his wife, looking at her, and now, calling her name.

'This is so fucked up,' gasped Mené, tears streaming down her cheeks. 'Oh Emma, Emma…' she mouthed as the cries reached a crescendo and then went quiet.

Emma was in shock. Just like the girl on the till at that first adult store, she felt she was never going to get this out of her brain. She pushed away, not wanting to hear any more.

Mené pulled her hand, her laughs growing louder as they headed down the corridor. Emma slowly got her mind back in gear. 'Well *that's* going to leave a mark.'

Mené bowed over, finally letting go in her distinctive barking laugh. 'That was hilarious. Oh Emma, Emma.'

'Do *not* tell Nate about this. He's in a bad enough mood already.'

'Why, what happened?'

Emma led her further down the corridor and explained about the sex toys and the lingerie.

Mené howled at the punchline. 'He's only got knickers to wear all year? That's hilarious.'

Emma heard Katie's door open and pushed Mené inside the nearest room. 'Will you shut up. If they see us still up here they'll know I didn't leave.'

'Just girly panties. He's going to hate that so much. I can lend him some of mine.' Mené was laughing so hard she started wheezing. Emma led her through the small, dimly lit room to the one chair by the drawn curtains and helped her sit. Mené lay back and opened her eyes, mascara traces down both cheeks. She stopped laughing instantly, looking around. 'Where the fuck are we?'

Emma looked around too. It was the stuff of nightmares. All around the room were small white box shelves. Assorted sizes, various heights, but covering most of the vertical surfaces. And in almost all of them, was a doll. Baby dolls, Barbie dolls, antique dolls, marionettes on strings.

'Did we just walk into a Stephen King movie?' Mené asked. She pushed herself up. 'This is freaky, right?'

They inspected the displays. Some of the dolls were naked, most were clothed. For some reason Emma found the ones that were turned around, facing the wall, the most disturbing. She felt the urge to turn them back, but was scared to touch them, or of what lay on the side she couldn't see.

A few of the boxes were empty, and in about a dozen others were the one exception to the doll collection. Framed photographs. Mené went over to the largest which was directly under the room's single window. 'Oh wow, is that Catherine's husband?' Emma stepped over. Sure enough there was a younger looking Catherine, and next to her a handsome gentleman with his hand on her shoulder. It was a very posed picture, but they looked happy enough.

'Henry, his name was Henry, I think. She told me he died a while back.'

Emma looked for other photos. She looked closely at the first she found. 'That's Rob and Helen, the older couple. They were at breakfast,' she reminded Mené. There were a few more, other couples that she didn't know, but finally she found one of Fiona and Rob. They actually looked happy.

'Is that Elizabeth?' Mené asked. Emma hurried over. She got her phone out and turned the flashlight on so they could see better. The shadows it cast across the white boxes only made the room creepier.

'I think that is Elizabeth. She looks so different. That must be her husband, but I haven't seen him around have you?'

Mené squinted at the picture. 'He looks kind of familiar but no, I don't think so.'

She's right, he does look familiar. 'Look how different Elizabeth is though.' The woman in the photo was only barely recognisable. Her hair was a mousy brunette and badly cut. As was the ugly dress she wore. Gone were the curves of the Elizabeth they'd met this weekend.

'She's had one hell of a boob job,' commented Mené. 'Come on, let's get out of here. This place is giving me the *tz'mar'mret.*'

'The what?'

'You know.' Mené rubbed her arms. 'The cold'

'The shivers. Yeah, okay but first I've got to film this, Nate won't believe me.' She turned on the video, starting with the photo of Elizabeth and husband. She slowly turned, ignoring Mené pulling silly faces.

They both jumped as the door opened.

'What are you doing in here, you mustn't be in here,' Alexandra shouted at them. Emma hid her phone away and the room sank into shadows. 'Get out of here, you're not allowed in here,' the maid continued yelling. The two of them apologised, rushing past her and down the corridor, hearing the door slam shut.

They didn't stop running until they reached the landing, when both of them burst into laughter, releasing some of the tension they felt.

'Oh, my, God. I think I just peed my pants.' Mené was crying with laughter once again.

Emma mimicked Alexandra 'Get out of here, you're not allowed to be in here,' Emma said, copying the maid's gruff yells. She pointed to Mené's open-mouthed expression. 'You look like a doll too.' She cracked up.

'Ah, maybe I'm golem,' Mené widened her eyes.

They began to walk down the grand staircase. 'A golem? Aren't they big and ugly and made of clay?'

'Usually, yes, and can't speak. But there is a story of one that was that special, beautiful. Her creator made her for sexy times because that wasn't a sin.' Mené pumped her hips against the banister.

'A beautiful, living, sex doll. I love it. But she didn't speak?' Emma asked. Mené deliberately stayed quiet and shook her head, still humping the top of the stairs. 'Definitely not you then.' They both laughed. 'I'm starving, I hope there's some food left.'

The food had been cleared away, but they found it in the kitchen, sneaking around like burglars after having been caught earlier. Mené was remarkably good at it. It made Emma imagine her doing her army training.

They split up after they'd shoved some food down, Mené to sort out her make-up and Emma to catch up with Nate before their meeting with Catherine.

The Contract

Emma returned to find Nate on the bed, papers scattered around him. He gave a frustrated sigh. 'I'm not sure I understand all this, can we get someone to look at it, your lawyer friend?'

She sat opposite him on the bed. 'And tell them what, I'm selling your cock off to a rich widow? Anyway, we have to do this today if we want that painting.'

'I know, I know, but the money is set up as a secured loan, until we complete the contract, the money isn't ours. It's secured against our house.'

'But how can she do that, it's got a mortgage on it?'

'This gives her the right to negotiate with them on our behalf, so I suppose it means it's up to her to sort it out,' Nate explained.

'Is there any interest on the loan?' Emma asked. Nate shook his head. 'So that means we just need to be careful, make sure we don't go crazy spending it all,' Emma said.

'I guess so. I mean, we could be looking at half a million for this, that's amazing, right? We could pay off the mortgage. Go travelling - in style! Pursue our dream jobs. This could be life-changing.'

Emma stood up, pacing back and forth. 'Do we trust her though. I think she's into some weird stuff. You've seen what a bitch she can be, with the pants thing.'

'And I'm still mad about that but it's a good lesson too. We can't be blinded by the money. We have to be smarter than her. And we are, right?'

Emma circled the bed, sitting next to him this time, and wrapped her arms around Nate's chest. 'I think she's dangerous. There's some weird

243

stuff going on here. I haven't even told you about the doll room.' Emma explained what they'd seen. It didn't seem so scary here in their room with her hot hubby trying not to laugh.

'Well, she does like pulling people's strings. I'm not surprised. Unlike you. I can only imagine how you jumped when Alex came in.'

'Alex?'

'Alexandra. She must have been away getting me this.' Nate pointed to the cup of tea by the bed.

'Oh, alone with the maid in our room.' Emma giggled. 'I'm glad you're all caged up, that makes it hot.'

'She doesn't really do it for me. She did offer me a blowjob though.'

'What?' Emma sat up straight. 'Seriously?'

'No, you idiot, this isn't a porn movie. She brought me some tea. Speaking of which, pass it over, it's not very nice but it's better hot than cold I bet.'

Nate sipped the tea while reading through the last bits of the contract. 'I think, if we are careful, and not stupid like earlier, we can't lose. It doesn't matter what these check-ups are. We can just say no, right? We can make up some rules, boundaries we just won't break?'

'Safe, sane and consensual,' Emma nodded, repeating the well-known kinky mantra. 'It's twelve months, do you think your cock can handle it baby?' Emma pushed the papers aside and shuffled to between his legs. 'This weekend, it's been pretty crazy. I've nearly done things I might have regretted and...' She leaned her head back on his chest.

'But you didn't. And most of it's been mind-blowing, right? Fantasies come true.'

'What if some fantasies aren't supposed to come true?' Emma curled up, head in his lap as he stroked her hair. 'Some of this stuff, Nate. It's been overwhelming. I don't know who I am when that's happening.'

'You are the woman I love, and trust and who I'd give my whole world for.'

Emma smiled up at him, and then giggled. 'Well you've already given up your underpants.' Nate growled and searched out Emma's nipple, it was already hard. He pinched it. 'Hey you big lummox, that hurts.'

'Is the thought of me in panties turning you on?' Nate caressed her nipple through her dress and sought out the other.

'Maybe a little bit.'

'Seriously?' He stopped playing and cupped her breasts, holding her. 'What about it?'

'I don't know. Maybe I'm so used to it from the blogs. But yeah, I know I'm surprised too but—'. Emma stroked his fingers, '—don't stop playing that feels so good. So yeah, it's hot, I don't know why.'

Nate slipped a hand inside the top of her dress and played with her nipples through just the lacy material of her bra. Emma moaned softly. 'Okay then, that's different,' Nate said.

'What is?' Emma asked slowly, caught up in his finger work.

'I don't mind wearing them if you like it. They're actually quite comfortable.'

Emma rolled away from him and gazed in amazement. 'You're wearing some!' She rolled to the side. 'Show me!'

Nate stood up, stiffly, stretching his legs. He undid his belt and had fun slowly revealing the little red pair of knickers he had on. Emma skidded off the bed and dropped down in front of him. 'Oh my God, that is so cute.'

'That's not what a man really wants to hear, darling.'

Emma looked up at him, her eyes a little teary. 'You'll really wear them for me?'

'Yes. And the money.'

'And the money,' yelled Emma, grabbing some of the paper and throwing the contract pages dramatically up in the air. They drifted down all over the room.

'Those, were in like, an order. Never mind.' Nate pulled Emma up, wrapping his strong arms around her. 'I love you so much, are you ready to do this?'

'Nope, but let's do it anyway!' They kissed, pulling in, finding the strength they needed in each other.

He gave Emma a swipe as she tried to play with the red knickers. 'Do you think she knows you'd do it for much less, you horny little she-devil! It was so hot watching you negotiate for my cock, I'm so proud of you.'

'God Nate, are we actually going to do this?'

'I think we are, baby, and you can ask for the key back, we've still got a bit of time to go and celebrate!'

'I like the sound of that. Who knows when you'll get pierced, we really should have asked about that.'

'Don't remind me, I think I'm most nervous of that.'

'Let's do this! I have plans for that cock while it's still under old management.'

Nate called on the house phone. 'Alex, hi, can you tell Catherine we're ready.' He hung up and had just a few moments to pick up the papers before Alexandra knocked on the door and came in. She collected the mugs of tea and a couple of other things before she led them out and indicated which one was Catherine's door.

Following her directions, they walked to her room, holding hands. They paused, kissed and knocked on it. Catherine opened it, a smile spreading across her face. 'Come in, come in.'

They entered her bedroom. It was more than that, a full suite. The room they were in was clearly where she worked. A giant mahogany desk sitting in front of a bay large. Two luxurious sofas facing each other in front of it. *It looks like the Oval Office.* Emma gazed around. The bedroom was in semi-darkness through a set of double doors. Bookshelves, and awards, lined the office walls. But in the gaps were a series of paintings, distinctive in their style - drawn in just black and red colours.

Catherine caught Emma staring at them. 'Do you like my collection? Come and have a look.' She led them over to a set of four pictures, arranged in a square. Each beautifully framed with a simple white surround and black wood frame. 'Do you recognise them?'

Emma shook her head. She looked closer. Despite the women pictured in the paintings all being classically western looking, and as white as the paper they were drawn on, there were oriental characters along some edges. 'No, are they Japanese?'

'Very good, yes. A lesser known artist called Katou Kahoru. I find them quite delightful.'

Emma's heart began to race as she examined the pictures. They all featured the same young woman, even playing multiple characters in the same picture. And in each one, something depraved was being done to her. Chained, or bound, or in one case, a chastity belt, much to the consternation of the fellow lifting her dress.

'Wow, look at this one.' Nate was examining the next set of drawings further along the wall. Emma came to see. The same exquisitely dressed girl sat at an elegant table, weighing out little food portions. Her double knelt on the floor, the red bow she wore matching her red heels. But her corset, gloves and socks were covered with black splodges, matching the cat that crouched next to her. The little Alice band with cats' ears made it clear she was the pet too.

'This is my favourite.' Catherine interrupted Emma's spiralling thoughts, indicating a larger print nearer her desk. '"The Chess Game" it's called.'

And sure enough, there she was again, the same woman, seated above a giant chess board, waving a baton in her huge red dress, as her doubles, dressed, or rather barely dressed, as chess pieces, were pushed around by a bow-tied servant with a big, spiky stick.

'Why's it your favourite?' Emma asked, wondering what would happen to the girl with the Black Queen headdress, about to be pushed into the White King's space.

Nate answered for her. 'She loves to play games. Don't you, Catherine.'

'When does a game stop being a game, Nathan?' Catherine glanced down at the contract he held in his hand. She seemed to expect an answer.

He thought for a moment. 'I don't know.'

She walked to her desk, her fingers catching the back of Emma's hand as she passed. Looking at them both, she sat, and pulled her chair in. 'It stops being a game, when you have no choice but to play.' She indicated to the two chairs that had been placed in front of her desk. 'Come, sit.'

Emma pondered the riddle's answer as they took their seats. *So is this about to stop being a game?*

Nate waved the contract in his hand. 'Before we sign it, we have a request.'

'Go on.'

'It's not 4pm yet, in fact it's nearly an hour away. If we sign this, we want the key, and privacy until then.'

Catherine smiled, not what Emma had expected after her 'All cocks are locked in this house' speech when they'd arrived.

'I thought you might ask that.' Catherine exchanged a small glance with Alexandra and then looked back at them. 'Okay, sign it and Alexandra will go and fetch the key while you do.' The maid scurried off. 'Did you have any questions?'

'Actually yes, when do I have to get pierced?'

'Immediately.'

'What, here? Now?' Nate asked.

'No don't be silly, not here. In a proper facility. Everything's arranged. The sooner it's done the sooner it's healed and we can get you safely, irrevocably caged up.'

Emma looked at her husband. *Irrevocably sounds very permanent.* She imagined what was underneath his clothing, her eyes travelled up to his. She could see the hunger in them, how horny he was already. She wanted more, *and to not be able to do anything about it.* 'Let's do it' she prompted him.

The contract was laid out on the table. It was a mess and disordered from when Emma had thrown it in the air.

'Oh dear, we can't have that. It's a good thing I have a spare copy.' She reached into the top drawer of her desk and pulled out a neatly stapled version, opening it up to the last page and handing a pen to Nate.

He paused over the signature, looking at his wife. She reached out and touched his hand, thinking through what it all meant. This was suddenly very real. Signing this meant he'd be getting a hole through his cock. Emma leaned close and whispered, 'The thought of a ring through your cock gets me wet.'

Nate shook his head in wonder, and signed his name on the contract. He handed the pen over, 'No going back now.' Emma leaned over, neatly printed her name and felt a hot rush of arousal go through her as she felt the fantasy becoming a reality.

They handed it to Catherine. She pulled out a beautiful fountain pen that had a real peacock feather at the end of it, and added her name with a flourish. 'Excellent, I'm very excited about this, and the two of you.' Catherine's eyes twinkled. 'I hope you've enjoyed the weekend.'

'It's been one of the most interesting weekends of our lives,' Emma said.

'And it's only just the start, I promise you that.'

Alexandra came back in and put the key down on the desk. Catherine picked it up and played with it, looking at them both before she gave it to them. She looked at her watch.

'I make it 47 minutes until the hour. Enjoy.' She gave Emma the key and they stood, not wanting to seem rude but struggling to hold back from running back to their room.

'Thank you, Catherine,' Emma told her. 'We're excited about this too. But, if you'd excuse us.' With that the two of them walked as fast as they could to the door and ran down the corridor, whooping.

* * *

They piled into their room. As soon as he closed the door Emma was all over Nate. Pulling his clothes off as she quickly shed hers.

'I'm so fucking horny, I can't believe we're doing this. I need you inside me!'

Stripping the last of her lingerie off she pushed Nathan to sit on the edge of the bed, and got down, undoing his belt. 'We only have until four so you better be quick,' she laughed.

'I really need to shower. Give me the key. It'll be the quickest one ever, I promise.'

'Okay, but first...' She pulled his trousers down, giggling at the red knickers that were filled up with his caged cock. 'So cute! But hurry up, I need you.' Emma had never meant it more. She gave his thigh a kiss and moved aside as he stood. As Nate dashed to the shower she had an idea. She went to the wardrobe and gloried in the selection of lingerie. She could hear him washing as she picked out a crotchless black teddy that just left her boobs out too. *That screams 'fuck my brains out'.*

She pulled it on, admired herself in the mirror, *I cannot wait to try all these on,* and then jumped on the bed, trying to pick what sexy pose she wanted him to find her in.

She'd just moved from the first pose as she was losing circulation when Nate came back from the shower. His excitement was diminished. Emma looked down, she could see why. 'Oh. That's not what I hoped to see.' His now uncaged cock was hanging down, limp. He sat on the edge of the bed and she slipped off beside him and sank down, taking his still very flaccid cock in her hand.

'I know. It won't get hard, maybe it's the thought of being pierced? Please baby, I'm so horny though, help me!'

'I'm sure we can do something about that.'

Emma wiggled off the side of the bed and Nate properly noticed what she was wearing. 'Wow, that outfit, you look incredible.'

'I know.' She bobbed her head to the side and bit her lip. Reaching out Emma wrapped her fingers around his mostly limp cock. 'Now come on little guy, don't get performance anxiety for the last show.'

'You are wicked.' Nate ran his fingers up Emma's shoulders, sliding into her hair. 'I love it.'

She looked up at him, giving him a hard squeeze and tug. 'You know the last cock I had my hand around wasn't yours. Oh look, *that* got a response.' She felt his cock swell a little in her hand. 'Do you remember it, baby? Watching his cock cum all over my face and chest?'

'I will never, ever forget.' He shuffled his bottom nearer to the edge of the bed, her mouth teasingly close.

Emma slowly stroked him looking up at her husband from her kneeling position. 'Did you think I was really going to suck him? Is that what you're hoping now, that I'll suck you, darling?'

'Fuck, please. We don't have long.' He slid the fingers of both hands into her hair, pulling her closer.

'Of course, he was really hard. And bigger. If you were that big, and hard you'd be in my mouth already.'

'Emma. I'm begging you.'

She looked up and gave him a naughty smile. 'That's so fucking hot.' She leaned in, sucking his still quite flaccid cock into her mouth, pulling on it with her lips. Her tongue rubbing the sensitive underside, sucking it back, filling her mouth. He groaned with pleasure but it wasn't responding the way it should, it still didn't harden up. She kept at it, squeezing his balls, tugging back with her head, using all the tricks she knew.

After a couple of minutes sucking and licking she let it slip out, it was half-erect now, but not what they both wanted. *What is going on?* She searched for inspiration. 'Fuck it, making *me* cum always gets you hard.' She pushed herself up on his knees and sat on the edge of the bed next to Nate. 'My turn!'

Emma lay back and spread her legs, the crotchless lingerie putting her beautifully on show. She loved this, how much he went down on her, barely having to ask. And it felt *so* good. It was *so* good she was surprised every time at how amazing it felt. Maybe by the end of this year she'd finally have learnt to make the most of it. *I guess that's part of why Catherine's making us do this.*

As Nate knelt between her legs the pleasure began. 'Oh God yes, fingers too, fill me up!' she begged, remembering how it'd felt earlier. She grabbed his hair, pulling him in. She was so aroused. *We're actually doing this, we've signed it!* As Nate's mouth brought her closer to orgasm her inhibitions fell even further. 'Oh baby, you're going to be so fucking horny! I'm going to make you suffer my love. Work so hard filling up your balls to make Catherine proud of me.'

Nate moaned into her pussy, she could feel it as much as hear it.

'If she can lock up a cock as huge as Rex's it's only right your little one is secured away, isn't it. You know, the truth is my mouth watered when I held it, is that awful? Is it so bad your wife wants to suck a dick that big?'

Nate's fingers fucked her all the harder, she loved it when she got him like this. She was close to orgasm but started breathing steadily to hold it off. She glanced over at the clock on the wall.

The totally wicked thought of not letting him fuck her or cum fluttered through her mind but she thought better of it as soon as *she* came, hard, on his face and fingers. She ached to have him inside her.

'Baby, quickly, I need you in me!' She was certain he'd be hard. That always worked; he loved making her cum so much.

She was mistaken. He stood, and his cock was still hanging down, much to her disappointment. Emma was filled with sympathy. 'Oh no darling, what can we do? It's just like Elizabeth yesterday.' *It is just like Elizabeth yesterday.* She glanced over at the cup of tea now empty by Nate's side of the bed.

He climbed onto the bed looking a little dejected. 'I don't know what's wrong.'

Emma pushed him back and swung her leg, straddling him. 'Hey, last sex in a year. No giving up, mister!' She started playing with his nipples, grinding her wet pussy forward and back over his cock. 'How's that feel?'

'Good. Don't stop. Oh babe, you look so incredible. That outfit, all those outfits. It's going to be torture.'

Emma ground her pussy back and forth — slick with her orgasm it slid easily over Nate's cock. 'Sweet, sweet torture, every day. You know I think that was the point. Oh Nate, I think it's working!'

Sure enough, his cock was finally starting to grow. Emma humped harder, faster back and forth, teasing his nipples with her fingers. She was watching the clock too. Where had the time gone? There were barely a few minutes left.

She could feel him hardening between her lips at last, sliding herself over him, the head of his cock rubbing against her clit. She was getting close to another orgasm, trying to hold back, to focus on his pleasure.

She reached down and lifted him, sliding him inside her. They both rocked in rhythm, their moans of pleasure merging. Emma looked up, one-minute left.

'Babe, come on.' She said between strokes. 'That bitch is going to walk in that door in one minute, I know it. I want you cumming in me as she does. Let's give her something to remember.'

Nate's face scrunched up in concentration, grabbing Emma's hips. She rode him, treasuring the feeling of him inside her, claiming her, owning her. 'This feels so good but, baby, I don't think I'm going to make it.'

'Then fake it, okay?'

Nathan laughed. Somehow the idea liberated him. 'I love you. Okay.'

Emma let her focus shift to her own pleasure, of him inside her, her clit grinding against his pelvis. She rode him back and forth, his cries of pleasure joining hers. It was all she needed. 'Oh God, I'm cumming, I'm cumming,' she cried. Pleasure exploded inside her and Nate cried out too. She felt him spurting inside, a sudden flow of warmth spilling out as she rode his finally hard cock. He cried out her name just as the door opened, and both of them ignored it, riding each other, riding the orgasm, smiling then sinking down for a kiss.

Finally, Emma looked over at Catherine, and Elizabeth. *Not what you expected to see, is it.* 'Oh, I'm sorry, we didn't hear you come in. Is that the time already?'

Catherine, for once, didn't seem to know what to say. Elizabeth had a wry smile on her face.

Emma kept softly grinding, feeling Nate shrink fast inside her. She didn't want to let him go. 'I'm full of cum, are you planning to help clean up or would you give us a few minutes?'

'I suppose you can have a few minutes, but don't be long.' Catherine spun on her heels and Elizabeth gave a little thumbs up before she followed her out, closing the door behind them.

Nate grinned up like an idiot. 'You've got her number haven't you.'

'Yep, I think I'm starting to learn the rules of the game.'

Nate laughed. 'And the look on her face!' Emma flopped onto his chest, laughing, wrapping her arms under his shoulders. She felt his cock slip out of her. 'What the hell was up with my cock though, I'm sorry that took so long.'

Emma kissed him gently on the lips. 'I have a theory about that. But I'll tell you later. It was hot being caught though wasn't it.'

'It was like that time your mum caught you kneeling between my legs. Do you remember?' Nate chuckled.

'How can I ever forget. Except this time, I won't get a talk about that not being what good girls do.'

'You're the best girl. I promise. But yeah, instead I get my cock locked up. Oh my God I'm still so horny. I can't believe I'm about to be locked up in a cage you can't undo.'

'Is it bad… that really turns me on? I know she's a bit crazy but this whole thing, you being this horny already, being caged, no key, the money, even the piercing. I'm so excited.'

'Fuck me, I forgot about the piercing. That could happen anytime now.'

A knock on the door interrupted them. 'We're just cleaning up, give us a bit longer please,' lied Emma. She waggled her eyebrows and slid down Nate's torso, sucking his flaccid cock into her mouth. She lay there, sucking on him, hands cupping his full balls, and finally let it pop out of her mouth. 'I'm going to miss this little guy so much. Don't you worry, we'll find a way to empty those balls, I promise.' She sucked the tip and kissed it a few more times. 'You know the contract doesn't actually say you can't cum, just you have to be full up for your check-ups. That's a definite loophole.' She climbed back up to kiss Nate and then swung her legs off the bed.

Nate sat up in bed. 'That really is, I hadn't noticed that. Clever you. Okay, time to pay the piper. You want to shower? I'll clean up out here.'

Emma stood, leaning over to kiss Nate. 'I don't care what she throws at us. I'm so excited to be doing this with you.'

'Me too baby. It's not about the money, if you didn't want this, I wouldn't do it.'

'It's a little bit about the money.' She looked at the wardrobe. 'And the clothes, and the toys. Definitely the clothes.' She laughed.

Nate nodded. 'Yeah okay, a little bit. Now go get showered.' He smacked her bottom and lay back, grabbing a towel, cleaning up his flaccid cock, and shaking his head.

The Lock-Up

Five minutes later, they had both cleaned up and pulled some clothes on. They were sitting, holding hands at the end of the bed when Catherine and Elizabeth came back in. 'Good to see you're ready for me this time,' Catherine said. Emma gave Nate's hand a squeeze and she tried not to giggle.

'So then,' she continued, 'time to make good on the deal.' Elizabeth handed her a cage, a different one from before. She walked up to the two of them. 'This, for now, is going to be your chastity device.' She held up a dull silver cage, similar to the one he'd worn over the weekend, but with one key difference: a curved metal rod rose from the forward base of the cage, and finished just in front of the bars that fronted it. Catherine's thin finger traced it. 'This is what makes it inescapable, this is what's going to go through you.'

'But I'm not pierced yet,' objected Nate.

'No, and even when you are this won't be used until it heals. If you look, it can be removed. But only when not worn, of course.'

To prove her point she handed it to Elizabeth who expertly undid a bolt and the shiny metal pin came apart.

'Are you ready, Nathan?' Catherine asked, not expecting an answer. Nate nodded, and stood, about to undo his belt. Emma stopped him, replacing his hands with hers. Tenderly she undid the belt, the button, the zip, and lowered his trousers. He was naked underneath.

Going commando rather than wearing panties, point one to us. Emma gave Nate's cock a tender squeeze and he sat, ready for them. Elizabeth advanced,

255

going down on her knees. She'd picked, or more likely Catherine had, a dress that gave Nate a compelling view right down her top. *I know they are fake but those really are amazing. Oh Nate, seriously, now?*

As Elizabeth rubbed some clear lube around Nate's cock he'd clearly started to get hard. She didn't seem in a hurry, massaging the liquid into his cock and swollen balls. 'Those don't seem too empty I'm glad to see,' said Catherine. Hearing her commenting on it, and watching Elizabeth do what could only be described as playing now stirred complex feelings of jealousy, arousal, and, was it envy?

For the first time ever she was envious of Nate's cock. How easy it was to lock it up. How desperate and sexy it looked, those full balls a marker of how horny he was. She thought back to earlier, and the one secret disappointment when the toys had been handed out. None of them had been what Danielle must have inside her. She had a crazy desire to beg, right now, to be like Danielle, to have that remote control vibe that would prevent her cumming, inside her. She was envious of it, envious of Nate's easily lockable cock, and jealous of Elizabeth's hands on it. *When will I next be able to touch him like that?*

Despite the fact she'd only cum minutes ago it was all making her incredibly aroused. 'Deny me too,' she wanted to cry out. 'Can't I be like Danielle? Do me instead of him.'

But she stayed silent, watching as Elizabeth pulled his full balls through the metal ring, slowly working his semi-hard cock through it too, fingers stroking the tip and deliberately arousing him as finally the smooth, curved ring was pushed to the base of his cock and balls.

With the teasing, and view, it only took the constriction of the ring to turn Nate's semi into a full-on erection. Catherine seemed pleased, watching intently as Elizabeth did her work in a professional but detached manner. Emma suddenly remembered her secret. That under that dress was her pussy, closed with rings, neatly sealed shut. Emma imagined it, a mix of horror and arousal. The idea of being unable to touch, to have your own body turned into a chastity belt. 'I saw your piercings.' Emma said, shocked she'd said it out loud.

Elizabeth paused, one hand gripping the cage she'd just picked up, the other wrapped around Nate's balls. She looked over to Catherine, who stayed silent. Apparently, she wanted to see where this went.

'Why do you have them?' Emma asked.

Elizabeth still didn't reply. She moved the small cage to the tip of Nate's cock, and pushed it down. It didn't cover a quarter of his erect length. 'I asked for them.' Elizabeth said quietly without looking up.

'Why,' Emma asked. 'What are they for?'

Elizabeth pushed hard down on the cage, making Nate flinch, but sure enough the compression started to push his erection down. 'To teach me a lesson. A lesson I needed to learn.'

'What lesson?'

Elizabeth stayed quiet, focusing on forcing the cage shut and remarkably she did. Nate's cock was compressed, and the cage parts came together. Catherine stepped over and inserted the integral lock and key, looking up at Emma as she turned it. 'To be careful what she wished for,' she answered for her.

Something mournful about the look in Elizabeth's eyes made Emma's stomach drop away. She looked up at Catherine, whose eyes sparkled. Was it just Nate's cock finally being under her control, or was it Elizabeth's answers that made her so happy?

Emma reached her hand to Elizabeth in sympathy but she jerked her hand, and her mask, away for a moment. 'I don't need your pity,' she hissed. She paused, gaining control of herself, and elegantly stood, putting the key into Catherine's open palm.

'To be careful what we wish for,' repeated Catherine. 'What a valuable lesson. Thank you, Lizzie, you can go now.'

Emma stood. 'Liz?' She stopped in the doorway and turned. Emma walked over to her and out of Catherine's earshot told her, 'I suggest you tell your husband to be careful who makes his drinks in the future. I certainly will be.'

A look of doubt passed over Elizabeth's face as she looked from her and narrowed her eyes at her employer. She nodded her head up at Emma, turned, and left.

Emma turned back to see her husband, pulling up his trousers over his caged cock, and Catherine tapping the key in her palm. 'I think we're done here. Or just beginning. Thank you both, I haven't been so excited about something in a long time.' Nate muttered something under his breath as he did up his belt.

Catherine slipped the key into a pocket and walked to her at the door. 'And so we begin. Rex is ready to take you whenever you are packed.'

'Home?' asked Nate.

'Yes, with a detour. Your piercing is in a couple of hours.'

Into the Woods

N ate closed the designer suitcase that had been provided to take their new outfits home. All the lingerie had been magically boxed up while they'd been in with Catherine. He blew through his lips. 'Well, we did it. Does it feel real to you yet, baby?'

Emma came close and put her arms around him. 'Nope. This whole weekend has felt like a dream. A fantasy.'

'Yeah, it's been something else. I guess there's no going back now.'

Emma hugged him tighter, one hand going down to cup the cage that she no longer had control over. 'Would you want to? Even thinking about this makes me so excited.'

'I've not seen you this horny since our honeymoon. Do you know how often we've got it on, it's been like a porn movie.'

'Welcome to a new world, darling husband. Honestly, that orgasm just now, as they came in. It was kind of a ruin for me. You know what that does to me darling.'

'Emma.' Nate turned in her arms and lifted her up. She wrapped her legs around his waist. 'You are insatiable. What's gotten into you?' He kissed her neck.

'Well *not you* for the next year.' She laughed as their mouths met, kissing. She broke off to whisper. 'I keep thinking about all those new toys. I can't wait to get you home.' She wriggled, lowering herself down a little bit so she pressed on the cock cage with her bottom. 'Especially that strap-on.' She bit her lip and looked at him, undulating her hips a little.

'Oh really? Anything particular in mind?'

'Mhmmmm, a couple of things. I wanted to wear it...' She paused.

'Okay. Go on.'

She unwrapped her legs and stood, walking around Nate until she was behind him, sliding her fingers up to play with his nipples, relishing the frustrated moan he made. 'And I wanted to put your cloned willy on it.'

'Oh shit, I see where this is going.'

'Do you? You fancy your wife fucking you with your own cock, my love?' She pushed her hips into his bottom, pinching his nipples.

'That is so twisted. I love it.'

'You are so fucked.' Emma whispered.

'I am *so* fucked,' he agreed.

She walked around him again, pushing him back gently until he sat on the bed, climbing up with her knees either side of his legs, straddling him. 'Or maybe you wear it.'

'Me huh.' Nate kissed her shoulders and the tops of her arms, pulling her close as he let her fantasise.

'Mhmmm, at least that way I get to feel your cock in me.'

'You'd be happy with that would you?' He nuzzled into her neck, leaving the bait dangling.

She let out a horny little sigh as his kisses drove her wilder. 'I mean, yes. To start... as a warmup.' She ran her tongue over her lips. 'But then, I'd want something bigger.'

He reached up, squeezing her breast, finding her hard nipple and playing with it to encourage her. 'How big?'

'The... the biggest,' she confessed, not having to say which that was.

'Fuck.'

* * *

They made their way downstairs only to be confronted by someone they hadn't hoped to see.

'Oh look who it is, our special guests.' Fiona left her husband, Dave, who was struggling with too many suitcases, and she sauntered to the bottom of the stairs to meet them.

'Hello Fiona,' Nate said, keeping his distance. 'Have you had a good morning?'

'It's not been what I'd planned, let's just say that. Have you seen Katie around?'

'Oh, we've seen lots of Katie.' Nate chuckled.

Emma grabbed Nate's hand and tried not to laugh. 'And even more of Kyle.'

Fiona's stare was icy. She lowered her voice. 'They're mine, do you hear me? You keep your hands off them.'

Emma bristled. 'They're yours? Who do you think you are? They're not your slaves.'

'Anything can be bought,' Fiona sneered and pointedly looked at Nate's crotch, 'as I'm sure you'll soon find out. I mean it,' she hissed. 'Katie is mine. You don't want to fuck with me.'

'Fiona,' Emma stepped closer, keeping hold of Nate's hand, 'Go fuck yourself.'

The older woman sneered. 'Well Nate won't be fucking you, will he.'

'Oh Fiona, is that the best you can do?' Nate stepped up defensively. 'Go torture your poor husband. Surely living with you must be enough of a punishment.'

Fiona seemed to bite back another retort, making an audible growl as she turned and stalked after Dave, shouting at him to hurry up as she stormed past him out of the door.

Nate pushed his fingers through his hair. 'Well blow me, that came out of nowhere.'

Emma shook her head. 'No, if you had really watched her at dinner, and seen her after. She's been fucking with Kyle and Katie for a while. What a piece of work. I'm so glad we've done something to mess that up, bless them.'

They avoided going out the front door after Fiona, and instead headed through the building to get to the stables, hoping to find Mené. Both of them were quiet, a little shaken up by the sudden attack from Fiona.

The fresh air and sunshine soon helped, as did hearing Mené's awful voice singing something in Hebrew, coming from a window in the stable's loft space.

'Mené, are you there?' Emma called. The singing stopped and the nurse's head popped out of the window above them, a towel wrapped around her chest, and her hair.

'Hello!' she waved enthusiastically out of the window. 'I was just having a shower.'

'Another one?' asked Emma.

'It's the best place to stick suction cups.' Mené made a huge grin. 'Don't be jealous, I was thinking of you.' She blew Emma a kiss. 'And you Nate.' She stuck out her tongue. 'So, are you going home?' She pouted.

'Soon, yes, we just wanted to say goodbye. It's been so lovely getting to know you. You have my number, right?' Emma called up.

'Oh I've got your number.' Mené looked delighted with the joke. 'And I'm seeing you soon, something about checking a piercing?'

Nate made an uncomfortable sound. Emma wiggled into him. 'Yes, Nate's having his cock pierced!' she shouted up unnecessarily loudly.

'Noooo!' Mené leaned out of the window. 'You're kidding?'

'It's so he can't get out of the cage.'

Nate coughed. 'Can we, maybe not shout about this?'

'That's amazing! I can't wait to see it.' Mené yelled down, looking over her shoulder as though she might have another go in the shower.

Emma took her husband's hand again and gave it a squeeze. 'She's awesome, I love her,' she said so only he could hear.

'She's something special, that's for sure.' He waved up at her and then began to turn away.

'Bye you two, see you soon!' They both looked up as Mené vigorously waved both hands, giving her body a shake, almost definitely on purpose letting her towel drop so her small breasts, with their dark nipples, bobbed into view through the window.

Emma laughed, and gave Nate a smack on the bottom for his huge double-take. He shook his head, looking away. 'Something *very* special.' He looked into the woods that were beyond the manicured lawn. 'Want to go for a little walk before we leave?'

'Sure, why not.' Singing started up behind them, and the sound of water. It seemed Mené had been inspired by their visit.

* * *

They followed a path into the trees and soon found themselves surrounded by ancient beeches and oaks, a classic English woodland. Nate gazed around. 'I wish we had something like this in our back garden, isn't it beautiful.'

Emma laughed. 'Well yeah, apart from that burnt-out car, that's more like home.'

Nate followed her gaze and sure enough, in a little clearing was the gutted shell of a car, nothing left but bare metal.

'That's, an Aston Martin I think. Wow, that would have been a classic.' He led the way over to it. It didn't seem to be there by accident. It was carefully placed in the centre of the little clearing, and around it was a selection of flowers that you wouldn't expect to see in a woodland.

Emma touched the bonnet to see if the rust came off but it seemed okay, so she turned and leaned back against it. 'Oh it's nice being away from it all.'

'The house?'

'Well yes, but I was thinking more work, routine, bills.'

'Yeah, it's been a crazy, but wonderful weekend. And it's still sinking in, we've done it, we've signed her crazy contract. How're you feeling about it?' He leaned back next to Emma.

'Well, I mean it's your cock getting locked up, getting pierced. I get the easy bit I think.'

Nate turned toward her, his fingers brushing her thigh. 'Looking forward to all the orgasms, are we?'

'Mhmm, but I have those already. It's...' she let out a little sigh as his fingers pulled her dress up. 'It's the idea of all the benefits of you in chastity, without... oh fuck yes, there...' Nate's fingers were pressing between her legs now, beginning to rub.

'You were saying?'

'Without any of the pressure to be in control, to let you out. It makes me so horny. It's perfect.'

'And we get paid.' He pushed his fingers inside Emma's new knickers, his middle finger sliding down, parting her, pressing in.

'Fuck yes, we get paid. I whored out your cock.'

Nate laughed, moving his finger back to her clit, slippery with her arousal. 'Yes, yes you did. What kind of girl does that huh, to her loving husband?' He rubbed hard and fast, she was already close.

'The bad kind?' she guessed, gasping, 'the good kind?' She turned to him, not able to think now.

'The best kind.' His mouth was on hers, taking her orgasm tally up even higher for the weekend.

'The best kind!' she repeated as she shuddered, her hands falling back on the car, trying to keep herself up. 'This whole thing is so fucking hot. We are so lucky.'

He kissed her breasts through the dress as he slowed his fingers. 'Let's hope so.'

Pierced

T he tattoo and piercing parlour had a 'closed' sign in its window. Nonetheless when Rex rapped on the door it was opened by a giant of a man, 6'5" at least, and pretty much all his exposed skin, of which there was more than you'd expect, was covered in tattoos.

'Hi, come on in, we've been expecting you,' he beckoned them inside.

They walked through to a pristine waiting area and took a seat on an offered sofa. The room's walls were covered with tattoo designs and a cabinet in front of them housed a selection of all kinds of piercing jewellery.

Rex followed the owner to another door. Emma leaned close to Nate, 'Not quite your fantasy is it babes. After yesterday I was kind of looking forward to some pretty piercer. I guess I haven't got Catherine's M.O. down yet.'

'Don't speak too soon,' Nate said, nodding up to the door that was opening. Emma turned towards it, and sure enough a very pretty brunette was entering. She looked vaguely familiar to Emma, but she couldn't place where she knew the face. The woman looked straight to their driver and her face opened into a big smile of recognition.

The woman put her hand on Rex's chest. 'Rex, I had no idea it was you I was coming to see. I wondered why I'd got the offer to come down here, now it makes sense. Is everything okay, no problems?' She looked down at his belt. The look of Rex's large caged cock came rushing back to Emma in an instant, she felt her cheeks flush. This was clearly the woman who'd performed Rex's piercing. *Interesting.*

Emma looked over to her husband and knew something was up. He was sat with his mouth hanging open, eyes wide. *What on earth is going on?* Looking back to the brunette she saw her glance over to them for the first time and to her bewilderment saw the same expression of surprise hit the piercing technician.

'Nathan Stevens, is that you? What on earth are you doing here?'

Nate stuttered something unintelligible before turning to Emma. 'Fucking Catherine,' he muttered. 'Emma, darling, this is Sophie, you met her once if you remember?'

Emma's brain was whirling. *So I do recognise her. Where from though, Sophie...* Suddenly a memory of a party Nate had taken her to when they were first dating came to mind. She could picture him shyly introducing her to this girl, though she'd had none of the tattoos or piercings back then. It clicked.

'Holy shit, your first girlfriend?' Emma snorted. As what was about to happen sunk in she started laughing, harder and harder. She had to put her hand on Nate's shoulder and lean her head against his. 'Oh this is priceless, oh Nate, Catherine really has it in for you doesn't she.'

Wiping a tear on her sleeve Emma stepped over to Sophie and shook her hand. 'Hi Sophie, I'm Emma, Nate's wife. I think we met once, a long time ago.'

'I remember,' said Sophie. 'Good to meet you too?' It turned into a question as she looked to Rex. 'Is this why I'm here, because he's my ex?'

Rex just shrugged.

Sophie awkwardly embraced Nate and he returned the hug while Emma looked on. *A hot nurse, an ex-girlfriend? Catherine really does enjoy messing with people.* But that wasn't Sophie's fault, she decided, and returned her smile as she turned back to face them both.

'Okay, so, you're here to have a piercing?' Sophie said, an eyebrow raised as high as it could possibly go. A thought crossed her mind, 'wait, which one of you?' She looked to Emma, concluding it must be her.

'Nope,' said Emma, pointing her thumb at Nate.

'I need to check my lottery numbers,' said Sophie. 'Nathan Stevens, you are literally the last person on earth I'd ever expect to get a piercing. What are you having done?' She stopped herself. 'Sorry, let's go through first, and you can tell me all about it. It's so good to see you, Nate, even under these surprising circumstances.'

Sophie led the way through to another room that reminded Emma a little of the examination room yesterday with a chair and a medical bed. 'No straps this time,' she whispered to Nate, her hand giving his bottom a squeeze. 'She doesn't know what you're here to have done does she.' She made a little gasp. 'Oh Nate, you're wearing the cage.'

'You just figured that out did you?'

'Oh baby, wasn't she the one who you broke up with because you wouldn't—'

'Yep.'

'Oh boy, is she in for a surprise.'

Rex began to follow them through the door when his phone rang and he excused himself, closing it while he remained in the waiting area.

Sophie turned and indicated a couple of seats for them to sit in, while she leaned back against the padded table. 'So this is weird, isn't it. But it's lovely to see you again. You probably didn't know I got into all this did you?'

'No, that's amazing,' said Nate, trying to remember what she'd been up to when they'd last met. 'Wasn't it, photography you were into?'

'Well remembered, yeah. In fact, I did some work experience with a photographer, ended up with him a while, and guess what he was into…'

'Piercing?' Nate guessed.

'Yes. I got into it too, and then decided to try it out as a career. I love it actually, much better than the shitty jobs I used to do to support my photography. But this has kind of become art for me too now.'

'I'm so glad to hear that,' Nate said. 'It's great to be paid doing something you love.'

Emma turned and whispered, 'Or getting paid to *not* do some*one* you love in our case.' She giggled, starting to relax a little. Nate revealing his cage to someone was something she'd often thought about, but she'd never dared tell any of her friends in case they thought she was crazy. But this, an ex-girlfriend they probably wouldn't ever see again. This could be fun, even if she already felt a twinge of jealousy that she hadn't with Mené the day before.

Sophie folded her arms, pushing her breasts up a little and Emma noticed not only her nipples pushing against the fabric, but little barbells through them. *I wonder what else she has pierced.*

Rex poked his head through the door, 'I'll just wait outside shall I?'

'Miss you already, sugar,' Sophie said, grinning, heading over to shut the door he'd left open.

Emma reached up and kneaded Nate's shoulder, whispering in his ear, 'It's okay honey, it's kind of funny she's an ex-girlfriend. Can you imagine what it's going to be like when she sees you all caged up?'

Sophie returned to the couple. 'I'm afraid I haven't had a full briefing, I just got a call yesterday and was offered… quite the bonus to be here. So, Nate, what are you having done today?'

Nate paused. 'Ummm, well, it's kind of embarrassing.'

'Is it? There's nothing to be embarrassed about, I promise, especially with me. Why don't you pop up here Nate, and you can tell me more.' She patted the padded table and started checking over the equipment laid out already next to it.

Emma came to stand at the end of the table as Nate lifted himself up onto it, his legs dangling down from the side.

'It's okay honey, tell her what you're having,' Emma encouraged him.

'So yeah, it's a cock piercing, a Prince Albert.'

Sophie turned back to face him, a puzzled look on her face. 'You, Nathan Stevens, the boy who wouldn't even let me go down on him, is having a Prince Albert? Seriously?

'It's a hole through my cock. Trust me I'm taking it seriously.'

Sophie paused, looking to the door. 'How do you know Rex? I know he has one. I did it.'

'Long story,' Nate said. 'Weird though, what a coincidence.'

'Hold up,' said Emma. 'You just skipped the interesting bit. I've never known Nate to say "no" when I offered him a blow job!'

Nate turned his head to look at Emma behind him. 'You just couldn't let

268

that go could you darling.'

Emma perched her head on his shoulder. 'You know it. I'm not missing the chance to hear the stories you didn't tell me.' She wrapped her arms around him and hugged him possessively. 'So what happened, if you're happy to say?' she asked Sophie.

'Not that much to say really, I was Nate's first girlfriend, right?' She checked with him and he nodded. 'I was just curious more than anything. Some of my girlfriends were doing it already and I guess I wanted to be part of the cool club. Nate didn't want to. I think I was quite annoyed at the time.'

'More than annoyed, I think it was why we broke up.'

'Well that,' Sophie replied, 'and the super sexy Jamie Alexander.' She got a dreamy look in her eyes. '*He* didn't have any reservations, I can assure you. Anyway, you were a good kisser, I'll give you that. And hey, *now* I get to handle it, isn't that ironic. Speaking of which, can you lie back?'

Nate paused before breathing a sigh of resignation and turning on the table, leaning back against the inclined portion. 'There's something I should tell you first.'

Emma interrupted. 'No baby, keep it a surprise.'

'I'm intrigued. What didn't I discover when we dated?' Sophie said.

'Oh no, this is new,' said Emma. 'Here, let me help.' She slowly undid Nate's belt feeling an erotic rush as another fantasy was coming to life. 'No one who knows Nate is aware of our little secret, I'm assuming this is in confidence?'

'Oh yes, this job is like a confessional at times, piercers and priests, get to hear all kinds of things. Your secret is safe with me. Now what is it, I'm so intrigued.'

Emma slowly unzipped Nate's jeans as he splayed his hands on the table, holding himself in place. Then to his surprise she hooked her fingers under the waistband of trousers and yanked them down to his knees. His suddenly exposed caged cock twitched. They both looked to Sophie.

'Oh, a cage, that's so cool! Wow, Nate, who knew you were so kinky. That's a nice looking one. Neat!'

Emma silently berated herself for thinking a cage would be a surprise to Sophie. 'Do you pierce for cages a lot?'

'Yeah, more and more actually. I've become quite the expert. It seems a lot of men, or couples, like a woman doing the piercing. Okay if I examine you, Nate?'

She waited for him to agree before putting on some black rubber gloves, lifting his cock, and inspecting the set-up.

'I assume you have the key, I can't pierce him in the cage.'

'Actually, no, Rex has it.'

'Wait what? Rex has the key to your cage? Hold on, is this something to do with that Catherine woman?' A look of concern crossed her face.

'You know Catherine?' Emma asked. 'What do you know, we'd be grateful for anything you can tell us.'

'Well, I've only met her twice but if I were you, I'd watch that one.'

'Why?' Emma asked.

'The piercings she came in for, they were weird.'

'Rex's cage you mean?'

Sophie paused from her inspection and looked up. 'Rex's cock is in a cage?' She looked incredulous.

Nate pushed himself up. 'You said you did his piercing.'

'Yeah, I did the piercing but, but... how would you even fit him in a cage?'

Emma laughed. 'I know right.' She saw Sophie's surprised look at her intimate knowledge of Rex. 'It's been a very strange and surprising weekend. Let's just leave it at that.'

'What did you mean about Catherine though, Sophie?' Nate asked. 'What was weird?'

'Well it's common for a partner or friend to come along, but with Rex, and... the other guy, I can't remember his name, the fact she was here was just odd.'

'Well at least she's not here now.' Emma squeezed Nate's hand.

'Amen to that,' Nate replied.

'Let me just go get the keys. Be right back.' Sophie stood, snapped off her gloves and went to the door. She sauntered out, took Rex by the arm and started speaking as she closed the door.' So Rex, how's that huge cock of yours?' was the last thing they could make out.

Emma put her hand on Nate's thigh, squeezing. 'Can you believe we're doing this? How are you feeling?'

Nate put his hand out flat, it was shaking. 'Does that answer your question?'

'Oh honey, it's not too late to pull out.'

Nate looked at his wife, and smirked. 'Is that a piercing joke?'

Emma giggled. 'It wasn't but, honestly baby, this is so hot. We've talked about it for ages. You're doing it for me, if you want to. Nobody else. The idea of it drives me wild.' *That's not totally true yet but it's what he needs to hear.*

It worked. 'That's all I care about.' He leaned in and kissed her.

'Aww you two are so cute.' Sophie walked back in, dangling the keys and pulled up a stool. 'Okay, let me run you through what happens next.'

Nate and Emma listened carefully as Sophie explained what was involved, how she had some topical anaesthetic to dull the pain, and what would be involved afterwards. 'It's actually the least invasive of the piercings, as there's just one hole to make. Most of the ring, or cage attachment, is just using the hole you've already got,' Sophie explained.

She fetched several curved barbells, each larger than the last, and explained how these would help stretch the initial piercing so that it would fit the cage fixing comfortably. Sophie glanced at the closed door. She dangled the cage keys in front of Emma. 'Want to do the honours?'

'Oh yes, thank you.' She skilfully unlocked him and pulled the new cage off. Nate's cock began to grow. 'The ring too?'

'Yes please, we don't want any restrictions to the blood flow.'

Emma wiggled his bits through the ring and gave his cock a squeeze. 'Poor Little Nate, I'm sorry for what we're about to do to you.' She smiled at her husband.

'Fab, thanks. Nate, I'm going to just clean you up a bit, this may feel cold.' She took hold of his cock, Emma somewhat reluctantly handing it over, and wiped it down with something that smelled of dentists. 'This isn't strange, seeing an old girlfriend handling your husband?'

'Honestly, after this weekend nothing feels too strange,' Emma replied, keeping her eyes on Nate.

'I won't even ask. Okay, Nate, think you're ready for this? Lie back again.'

Nate swung his legs up and settled onto the angled table. 'I'm not sure this is something I can ever be ready for but let's just get this over with.'

'Oh sweetheart,' said Emma, taking his hand. 'I know it's a bit scary but we've played with this fantasy for a while now. It's so hot to imagine you can be caged and have no way of getting out, don't you think?'

'Depends who has the keys,' replied Nate, not wanting to give too much away to Sophie.

The familiar snap of gloves made Nate jump a little as Sophie put on some new ones. 'If either of you would like to rub this in we can give it a few minutes to take effect. You'll need a glove on too unless you want numb fingers though.'

Emma took the small tube of anaesthetic gel, pulled a glove on her right hand, *Oh I like black rubber gloves, I'm gonna get me some of these.* She began rubbing it where directed.

Sophie handed her a little cotton swab on a stick, 'You've got to put some, inside, too,' she explained.

Nate tensed up as Emma wiped some of the gel onto the cotton tip. 'Oh honey,' she said,' don't be a baby, this is the least of what's going in here today.' She slipped the tip in while he clutched at the paper towel covering the table. 'There we go, all done,' she announced.

'Wonderful, we'll give that a little while to take effect, I'll do a final antiseptic swab and then we're ready to go,' Sophie said. She held up a little curved barbell. 'This is what we're using at first, your starter jewellery. This needs a few weeks to heal, although it can take longer, before you can stretch it enough to work with the cage attachment.'

As the numbing gel took effect, she explained the aftercare involved, the saltwater washes, eating and sleeping well to encourage healing, and most importantly no sex.

'Well that's hardly an issue in that thing,' said Nate, pointing to the cock cage.

'Sure, that'll help, but it doesn't stop everything, does it. So no cumming. Pee, as long as you're drinking lots of water, is a good thing, and you can't stop that anyway. But semen in there doesn't help it heal, okay?'

'Oh wow,' said Emma, 'so really no cheating while in the cage. That was your last orgasm for a while.' She patted his leg and gave his muscular thigh a squeeze.

Nate kept the conversation going. 'Why's it called a Prince Albert, is it true he had one?'

Sophie began setting things up for the piercing as she replied. 'That's the rumour. There was a craze in the 1800s for super-tight trousers, and to minimise bulges men's cocks were held to the side. Like many fashions, it got a bit extreme. Men began to get cock rings so they could hook it in place. They called it a "Dressing ring" at the time.'

'My goodness, I thought women were on the receiving end of all that nonsense with corsets and girdles,' said Emma.

'Yeah, no. It's kind of nice to know men went through some of it too, isn't it. So the rumour, and name, is that Prince Albert had one before he even got married. Must have had a big cock. No wonder Victoria missed him so much.'

Emma's eyes lit up at the topic, seeing an opportunity. She wandered around to the other side of the table, facing Sophie across it, and put her hand on Nate's cock. 'But, they're okay on little cocks too are they?'

Sophie looked to Nate for his reaction. He just bit his lip and looked at his wife's hand, gripping his flaccid cock. It started to grow in her hand. Sophie grinned, meeting Emma's eyes. 'Yes, I mean you get the most benefit on a big cock.'

'Oh? How so?'

Nate looked in disbelief at his wife and first girlfriend discussing cock size. Emma gently squeezed him.

Sophie replied, 'Well the big benefit to us of course, is how it rubs on our g-spot, when we're taken from behind you know?'

'Doggy style you mean?' Emma had a naughty grin growing on her face.

She squeezed his growing cock harder.

'Yeah, on all fours, getting really pounded. It feels so good,' Sophie added, putting her hands on the table and leaning closer to Emma.

'I have to be honest, that's never done much for me. I don't get why so many women say it's their favourite. Will the piercing help that?' Emma was fishing for a response. She got it.

'It might, but not much I'm afraid. It actually has to be able, you know, to reach the g-spot from behind. You want a nice long cock for that.' Sophie glanced down at Nate's penis filling Emma's hand now. 'Some just aren't big enough. A cock ring can't help with that.'

'Oh no, what a shame, I'd love to feel that.' Emma was squeezing Nate's cock with tight pulses now, he was so hard under her hand. He let out a frustrated moan but the girls ignored him. 'What's it feel like?'

'Oh there's nothing like it. I love to just put my shoulders down, hug a pillow, feel him impale me. Slowly at first, stretching me. But it feels so good, soon he can pound me so hard, so deep. Just feeling it. Completely filled, pleasures inside you didn't even know were possible.' Sophie leaned across Nate's legs, close to Emma, caught up in what she was saying. 'And knowing he's feeling it too. Every inch sliding in and out bringing him closer to exploding with pleasure inside you.'

'Shit,' was all Emma could say in response. She'd started this as a game but Sophie's description had turned her on more than she had been prepared for.

Sophie looked down at Nate's full erection. 'I mean, he's not that small. If you did the shoulders down thing it might help.'

'A year is starting to feel like a very long time,' Emma confessed.

'A year? You aren't going to have access for a whole year?' Sophie glanced towards the door but couldn't see Rex through the frosted glass. 'If I distracted Bigus Dickus through there you want to make the most of your last moments?'

'You would? Oh God, yes please, thank you,' Emma said. Nate was already pushing himself up, delighted at his unexpected luck.

Sophie headed to the door. 'I can't give you long though.' She went through, and they could hear her start to talk to Rex.

Emma's head was down before the door was shut, pulling Nate's cock into her mouth. 'Eugh oh no, you taste funny.'

'Oh shit, the anaesthetic! He pushed his hips up but gave a frustrated moan.' Oh no. The gel, the anaesthetic. I can't feel you. No, no, no!'

Emma pushed her tongue out trying to get rid of the taste. Shit, I forgot that, this is our last chance. Dammit.' She went down, sucking him again, and giggled on his cock. 'I fink my mouf is getting nump.'

Nate slid his hands into her hair. 'At least I can remember how it looks.' Ignoring the lack of sensation he pushed his cock in and out of her mouth, stroking her cheek with his thumb. Emma worked her way down, so he was as deep as he could go, slowly pulling back up with a sucking noise.

She held him with her hand, her lips and tongue tingling. Kissing and sucking on the numb tip she whispered, 'I'm going to mith thith tho much.'

Nate's face was a mix of arousal, frustration, and hilarity. '*You're* going to "mith" it huh. How do you think I feel?' He laughed. 'I love you so much.'

She gave his cock head another suck and then a kiss. 'I love you doo,' she managed to say nearly normally, turning to the door as it opened.

'I'm coming back in,' Sophie warned from the doorway. She entered, thankfully alone. 'Sorry guys, couldn't distract him anymore, I hope you had long enough?'

Nate pushed up on his elbows. 'We appreciate the time you gave us, don't we Emma?'

'Mhmmm,' was all Emma managed to get out.

Nate wasn't letting her get off that easily. 'Don't you want to say "thank you" to Sophie?'

She gave him a glare then sighed. 'Dank ooo.'

Sophie looked puzzled for a moment and then broke into a high-pitched laugh. 'Oh no, the numbing gel, in your...?'

Emma just bit her lip and nodded, rolling her eyes.

'That is hilarious! I'm so sorry, I didn't even think of it. It'll wear off soon, don't worry. Speaking of which, I better get to work. It actually makes it a bit easier to do when it's hard, do you mind if...'

She grabbed the antiseptic and got to work giving him another quick but thorough clean. 'I suggest you look away, it doesn't take long, and with the numbing it'll hurt a little but be more of a strong tug.'

Emma took Nate's hand as he tried to calm his breathing, looking up. 'I love you.' She mouthed, leaning in and kissing his cheek as he suddenly twitched.

'It's done,' Sophie announced. 'Okay, just give me a minute here, this will feel a bit weird.'

They both resisted looking down. Nate kissed his wife again. 'I love you too. That was quite a last memory.'

'Wasn't it.' Emma looked surprised. 'Oh, it's fading already. Still tastes yucky. But yeah, sucking you made me realise how much I'm going to miss it. I'm kind of excited about the Prince Albert, for after you know?' Emma stroked Nate's cheek.

'Oh you like the thought of a ring through my cock do you?'

'Way more than I thought I would. Although I can't stop thinking about the real Prince Albert. I wonder if how big he was, bigger than Rex do you think?'

'No one is bigger than Rex, trust me,' Sophie chimed in.

'Oh really?' Emma asked.

'Huge, biggest white cock I've ever seen. The fact it's caged is hilarious. Sorry, I shouldn't say that should I.' She stood back. 'Okay, there you go, what do you think?'

They both looked down at the small curved metal bar poking out of the tip of Nate's penis. 'That is *so* weird,' he said. A thought suddenly struck him. 'How do I pee?'

'Regularly, and sitting down. Seriously, drink lots. It'll sting at first but it helps it heal. Some guys learn to pee standing up with them, you'll just have to see how it works out.'

Sophie took the cage assembly, carefully and expertly putting the ring back on and then fitting the cage back on top. 'You see how it works with the piercing? This cage design gives it space. It's not ideal, it'd be better to just be free, but this protects it a bit too. And when you're healed, see how it'll hook through from underneath?'

They both nodded, and thanked Sophie for looking after them so well. She smiled, and handed Emma the key. 'Why don't you lock it, remember, no matter who has the key, he's still all yours, okay?'

Sophie's slightly ominous words rang in her ears as she slid the lock into place and gave it a turn. She kissed Nate on the lips and she slid it out. Sophie took it from her. 'Okay Rex, all done here, thanks honey,' she yelled. She handed Emma a box with all the parts in, along with detailed aftercare instructions. 'My number is in there if you have any problems, and it'd be nice to hear how you guys get on. So lovely to see you again Nate, but I must dash. Emma, you've got a good man here, keep hold of him, okay?'

With that she rushed to the door, picking up a bag and jacket, and let herself out. They watched her hand the keys to Rex who'd been waiting patiently outside. 'Ready when you are,' he told them.

Nate breathed a sigh of relief. 'Well that was more interesting than I'd expected.'

'Are you okay honey, does it hurt?' A little bead of blood had welled up on the piercing.

'No, it's still numb, but I should take some of those painkillers I think. That is going to be sore when it wears off.'

He slowly sat up, a little dizzy, while Emma grabbed some water and ibuprofen that Sophie had left in their kit.

After a minute he pulled on his trousers with a wince. 'Yep, that's going to take a while to get used to. So it begins. I wonder what else Catherine has in store for us?'

Emma took his hand. 'As long as I'm with you we can handle anything.' They walked slowly to the door. 'No going back, let's do this.' They pushed through the door where Rex was waiting to drive them home.

Going Home

Emma and Nate curled up in the back of the car and didn't talk for most of the journey. Nate kept nodding off on her shoulder, occasionally stirring to readjust his hold on her hand. *Poor baby, I think this must have been quite a shock to his system.* She decided to see if Rex would be any more talkative this journey.

'How long have you worked for Catherine?'

He seemed about to give his standard answer but caught Nate sleeping in the mirror and paused. 'A few years.'

'And you are caged as part of the job?'

'Not originally, but yes.'

'Can I ask why?' Emma pushed.

She thought she'd pushed too far but then he answered. 'I get paid more doing this than I did working as a private military contractor. It's my pension plan. It's just part of a very well paid job.'

Wow, I've never heard him say so much. 'So how have you found having a cock piercing, Rex?'

'Restricting,' was his taciturn reply.

'Is the piercing only used for keeping you in the cage?'

'No.'

'Come on Rex, help me out here. Nate just got pierced, is there any advice you'd give?'

He paused this time. 'Be careful what you wish for.'

His echoing of Elizabeth's words sent a shiver down her spine. She thought that was all he'd say but to her surprise, after a long pause, Rex volunteered some more information.

'It's hard to express. Once it's healed. Once it's in place. It changes things. No escape.'

Emma brushed her fingers over Nate's thigh. She still couldn't believe they'd done it. That under there his cock had a piercing through it. *No escape, that's so hot.* She couldn't wait to look at it up close, without Sophie or anyone there. Despite herself the thought turned her on. She felt her nipples hardening against her top, and peeking up to make sure she wasn't being watched she slipped her fingers under Nate's shoulder, which handily covered her, and massaged her breast through her top. Instantly she felt the response between her legs.

Feeling very naughty she pushed her other hand down there, subtly pushing the palm of her hand against her pussy. Even that felt so good. She felt a desperate urge to do more. She imagined Nate's cock, with the piercing through it. How it would feel in her mouth, inside her. She imagined a big thick ring through it instead of the little barbell at the moment. *A ring, just like Rex's.* Here she was, with two pierced, caged men. She remembered his cock, through the wall, the offer of the key. Before she knew her thoughts were turning to his cock, free and hard, in her hand, in her mouth. Without realising it she had opened her mouth, and in embarrassment, pretended to yawn to cover it up. Rex looked at her in the rear view mirror.

Arousal and curiosity getting the better of her, Emma caught his eye in the mirror. 'Rex, what's it like having a big cock?'

Rex smiled, and then let out a little chuckle. 'You don't realise you do, at first.'

'Really? Surely someone must point it out?'

'It's not what guys tend to do. And you watch porn, and just think it's normal.'

Emma laughed, but stifled it, trying not to wake Nate. 'When did you realise it wasn't, normal?'

'Well playing sports you get some idea, but it was women's reactions. After I'd been with a few word got around. Girls would ask to "see it". I just figured women loved sucking guys off but it was my dick they were interested in. Don't get me wrong that was great but it's just as much a curse as a blessing.'

'Wait, women drop to their knees to see it and suck you off and it's a curse. How?'

'Actual sex hurts a lot of women. I don't know if it meant I lasted longer but I was always asked to stop. I couldn't keep a girlfriend for a long time. A few had to go to a doctor because of it.'

'They got injured by it?' Emma asked.

'Yeah. And forget about anal sex. I actually tried with some escorts and they wouldn't even for money.'

'Oh no, that's awful, I guess? But you must have found some who liked it, just normal sex, girlfriends I mean.' Emma blushed as she failed to avoid moving beyond him using escorts.

'I did, but even then it makes them cum so quickly it's not much fun.'

'For you,' Emma clarified.

'Yeah, but it meant they'd get bored and not put much effort in. It makes you think that's all they are interested in.'

'That's extraordinary. I'm sorry about that Rex, it can't be nice to be treated like that. But—you're saying they all cum from sex with you, just, you know, fucking?'

'Everyone it fitted in, yeah.'

Emma couldn't help but imagine Rex's pornstar cock and all the women it had made orgasm. The thought of it made her clench. She tried to focus, she was amazed at how Rex had opened up. 'Do you ever wish yours was smaller?'

'It kind of is now, isn't it.' He actually chuckled. 'But no, it's good. Despite all the hassle, all the broken condoms and painful erections, it's good having a big cock.'

I can only imagine. Emma shifted in her seat, her knickers were definitely damp now. She remembered back to examining, holding Rex's caged monster. *God, was that only Friday?* She pressed her palm harder between her legs, grinding it down over her mound, her breath giving a little shudder.

She thought about the dildo Catherine had given them. 'How big are you,

Rex?'

He stayed quiet, then looked again in the mirror. 'Maybe you'll find out.'

Emma wasn't sure whether that was hot, or creepy, or maybe both. Either way she couldn't think of a clever retort so she stayed quiet, and shut her eyes. Maybe she could catch a bit of sleep too. *I'll probably dream of snakes. Big, one-eyed snakes.*

* * *

It was getting dark when they pulled up outside their house. It seemed like a different world. Was it really only the weekend that had passed?

Emma gently woke Nate who'd slept the whole way. 'We're home baby, how are you feeling?'

The painkillers were still working it seemed, so the two of them went to the house while Rex unloaded the car. They opened the door and watched Rex carry the big box of toys into their hallway. *I'm glad the neighbours don't know what is in that.*

It took a few more trips ferrying designer labelled bags and boxes. 'Well that's your underwear sorted,' chuckled Nate, looking at the almost filled corridor.

Emma squeezed his bum. 'And yours.'

'Don't remind me, oh my God that was so embarrassing with Sophie.'

Finally, Rex ferried in three suit bags. 'Looks like we got the second dress,' Emma whispered.

Rex stood in the doorway, filling most of it. Nate reached out his hand and Rex shook it, nodding to Emma. 'Thank you,' Emma said, 'it's been nice getting to know you.'

Rex nodded, and just about cracked a smile. He patted his jacket and brought out a large envelope. 'A copy of the contract for you, and your current balance I believe.'

Nate took it, not looking too pleased at what that might mean.

'I'm sure I'll be seeing you soon. Good luck to you both.' He looked to Nate, and then his eyes lingered on Emma.

Why does my brain fill in 'You'll need it' after he says that?

Nate closed the door and the two of them wove their way through the boxes and bags to the kitchen.

He sat at the table and opened up the letter. 'Shit. This isn't good.'

Emma looked at the balance. 'What, how can that be, how can we owe *her* over four thousand pounds? Why are there two cages, and the piercing on here? What about the two grand for our underwear?'

Nate was checking through the contract. 'Damn it. Look, here, the costs associated are advanced to us, that doesn't mean they pay. So the toys were free, but the cages, the piercing, and the extra dress. That total includes the two thousand we got.'

'This is awful, it was supposed to help out finances, now I've made it worse.' Emma began to cry.

'Baby, it's going to be okay. We don't have to pay this back now. And we're getting £2,500 a month AND that painting, plus more.'

'If we stick it out.'

'We'll stick it out.' Nate sat next to Emma, rubbing her hand. 'This is just more of her messing with us. Don't let it get to you. We'll make her pay, literally. And make it super hot too.'

She sniffed, and wiped her eyes on her sleeve. After a big breath in and out she turned to him and smiled. 'It *is* super hot. Oh my God, Nate, you just got your cock pierced! I can't wait to see it later.' Emma squeezed his hand, and gave him a smile. 'But you know what I need?' Emma said.

'A cup of tea?' Nate raised one eyebrow, a move that always made her tingle. 'Or an orgasm?'

Emma sniffed again, then giggled. 'A cup of tea,' she nuzzled into his cheek, 'for now.'

Epilogue

Nate lay snoring next to Emma as she sat up against the headboard, trying to process some of what had happened. She'd come to terms with Catherine being a conniving bitch, and that the money situation would be fine if they just didn't do anything else stupid.

But it was that room, that doll's room that she couldn't stop thinking about.

She pulled out her phone, blinking as her eyes adjusted to the brightness. Bringing up the video she watched it through, trying not to let it freak her out. It was strange, but she couldn't pinpoint what was troubling her. *Maybe if I watch it again.* Emma set it back to the beginning where it paused, the photo of Elizabeth filling the frame. She looked closer. This was it, what had her brain figured out?

Suddenly she saw it. 'Nate, Nate, wake up. Look.'

He stirred, scrunching up his eyes against the bright screen. 'What is it?'

'It's Alexandra.' Emma shouted as though it was obvious.

'Huh?' he tried to focus on the screen. 'What about her?'

Emma shook the phone in front of his face, he could finally make out the couple, Elizabeth with her husband next to her. 'She's not a "her", can't you see?'

'What do you mean? Who isn't a "her"?' He squinted up at Emma.

Emma stared wide-eyed at her husband, her face lit by just the picture on the screen. 'Alex. Oh my God, Nate. *Alexandra is* Liz's husband!'

Looking for more? Try 'The Dead Bedroom Remedy'

A new chastity series by James AND Jane Hardcourt!

The Dead Bedroom Remedy

Get it on Amazon

Enter the following link or scan the QR code below to go straight there.

https://smarturl.it/dbr1

Kirsty's marriage is in trouble. Can her best friend's kinky secret be the inspiration to turn everything around?

When mother of two, Kirsty Nelson, gets over her shyness to confess her dead bedroom desperation, it frees the two friends to finally talk about sex.

The ever-positive Jennifer shares that she and her husband, Tom, have an erotic secret that keeps their passions aflame. But before she divulges that, there is a more pressing concern – Kirsty isn't fully aware what she is missing out on, and Jennifer has the perfect solution.

And then? Kirsty is going to be the one peeping at Tom. And her best friend's big kinky secret will ignite passions she didn't even know she had.

Can she take what she learns and use it to save her own marriage to a man she loves, and bring their dead bedroom to life?

This is part one of a second-chance kinky romance series, published in parts by Jane Hardcourt, real life mother of two and accidental sex educator, along with James, her husband and author of the international chart topping Kink by the Numbers and Chastity Contract series.

As with many of James's works, it's written not just to entertain and titillate, but to educate too. Read the *Dead Bedroom Remedy* and get inspired and encouraged some new ideas to spice up your love life.

Read it now on Kindle Unlimited

Friends with Kinky Benefits

Here's the start of the first book in a new series I've been working on. It's my first book written in first person, from both the female and male main characters' perspectives. The main themes are sexual discovery, tease and denial, and chastity play.

It's available from Amazon now. You can read the first few chapters below.

FROM THE BESTSELLING AUTHOR OF *KINK BY THE NUMBERS*

Friends
With
Kinky
Benefits

HE WANTED LOVE,
BUT SHE'S OFFERING
SOMETHING ELSE
ENTIRELY...

A New Adult Kinky Romance Novel by
JAMES HARDCOURT

* * *

Amy

'You know he's into you, right?' Callie grinned at me over her caramel latte.

I nearly spat out my coffee. 'Are you crazy? Dylan's like a brother to me. We virtually grew up together. I love you, but he's my best friend. And you're wrong, he isn't *into* me.'

'Amy, he is,' she insisted, 'you just can't see it because you're too close, or you don't want to.'

'I absolutely don't want to. I don't want to even think about it.'

Callie laughed, 'Think about what? How Dylan gets a boner when you hug him?' She opened her eyes wide, waiting on my reaction. It didn't disappoint.

'Stop. Oh my God, I hate you, I'm never going to get that image out of my head.' I shook it as though trying to jolt it out. *It can't be true.*

This was not the catch up with an old friend after getting home that I had imagined. Callie put her coffee down and looked at me. 'He's cute, you know, and such a nice guy. Very different from the ones you go for.'

I sighed, 'Not as if I have had any success with them. But yeah, he's just not my type, and I can't believe we're even talking about this.'

'Not everyone's an alpha male, Amy. And those that are tend to be assholes.'

'Well, you're not wrong there,' I said. I thought back to the few disastrous dates I'd had during my first year at university. I'd imagined it'd be easier, being away from home, a new setting. The guys had seemed so attractive, but they'd all seen a single date as an invitation into my pants. And as much as I was keen to do more, I wasn't prepared to give it up *that* easily, especially if they weren't exactly what I was looking for.

I paused, took another sip of coffee. *Is she going to understand? Now's as good a time as any to find out.* 'It's not just an alpha male I want,' I paused for her reaction.

'No?' She waited on me, letting me stew until I confessed.

'It's more than that,' I finally said, my foot tapping as the nerves kicked in. 'This is between us, right?' Her eyes lit up. Callie was a complete sucker for secrets. She nodded enthusiastically and shuffled her chair closer so that no one might hear us in the busy cafe. 'I'm looking for someone…' I paused, there was no going back if I said it, '… dominant.'

'Oh, *really!*' The grin on her face told me she was delighted with the quality of my secret. She tried to hide it and look all nonchalant, 'I'm not surprised, I figured you were a bit kinky.'

'What the hell? How?' This was not the response I'd imagined.

She shrugged and sat back, drinking more coffee. 'I don't know, you give off that vibe. And then, of course, there's Halloween.'

My drink had just about got to my lips, but I paused. 'What about Halloween?' I could guess what she was going to say, but I didn't want to admit it.

'You think I haven't noticed you always take it as an excuse to dress up like a slut. I don't even know how you walked in those platform heels. And didn't you wear a collar last year?'

I could feel my face burning up. 'Everyone uses Halloween to dress slutty. You didn't say anything! Is that what everyone thinks?' *I'm such an idiot, of course it was obvious.*

'I mean, most of the guys are probably jerking off to the pictures they took of you. But yeah, it doesn't do great things for your reputation, although maybe they just think you're quirky and it is a Halloween thing.'

I didn't really hear the second bit of what she was saying. 'Jerk… jerking off?' The image of it made me feel dizzy. I hadn't even considered it. I was starting to shake a little, so put my coffee down.

'Hell yeah, girl. I know for sure Justin had at least ten of you on his phone.' Callie was still sipping her drink, clearly having fun at the torment she was putting me through.

'Shut up. Your ex was not jerking off to me.'

'Well, it wasn't to me, that's why he's my ex.' She didn't seem bothered. 'I can't blame them. You realise how sexy you are, right?'

'I...' I didn't know what to say. 'I am?'

She tilted her head at me. 'Girl, come on. You might have been a late bloomer, but now you're one of the hottest women I know. It's only the fact you keep yourself all covered most of the time that hides it.' She chuckled, 'Well apart from Halloween. What are you going to be this time?'

'Maybe an angel?' Halloween was months away, but I'd already had fun planning and gathering items. I hoped my choice disproved her theory.

'Oh, an angel. Let me guess, it's a white corset that shows off your boobs, maybe a tiny skirt, and super high heels?'

Shit, she's got me pegged. 'And thigh-high stockings.'

She laughed so loudly people around stared for a moment. 'So a slutty angel. You see? Don't get me wrong, I think you look amazing. It's just hilarious you're so unaware.' She sat back and bit into the stroopwafel she'd bought with the coffee. 'So how kinky are you?'

I looked around, horrified, but no one seemed to have heard her. 'I don't know. Is there a scale?' It wasn't what I wanted to say of course. *Really, really kinky, it's all I think about.*

'Well, how serious are you about finding a "dom"?' She made air quotes, showing off she knew the language.

'It's all I dream of,' I said. It was true, the search for the perfect dom felt like the focus of my life; and how hard it was, my biggest disappointment. 'It's really difficult. Like you say, so many of these guys are assholes, the ones online are even worse.'

She sat up. 'You do this stuff online?' *I've definitely said too much. She's never going to find out about that.* 'What do you do?' she prompted.

'Umm, you know, like explore what's out there. But it's a complete shark pit, you have to be super careful.' I recalled all the frustrations, the disappointments, the 'doms' who just ghosted me because I wasn't prepared to fall to my knees and strip naked before we even talked properly. I guess my face showed what I was thinking.

Callie took my hand. 'Hey, it's okay. I get it, even the online dating stuff is a minefield, I can only guess what it's been like.'

I sniffed, 'I want to try so much, but I'm still a fucking virgin and all they want is to take advantage of me.' I was getting emotional now. This was *not* how I'd imagined telling someone I was kinky would go.

Callie rubbed my hand. 'You know, Dylan wouldn't take advantage of you, I'm sure of that.'

That *was* for sure. He was the loveliest, sweetest guy. I was so lucky to have him as my best friend. I'd never even thought about him sexually. 'Are you sure he's into me?'

'Hon, he follows you around like a puppy dog. You heard Kara asked him out on a date last year and he said no?'

'What, Kara? Seriously? He never told me that.'

'That's because *you're* the reason he said no.' She got a wicked look in her eye. 'I bet he has way more than ten photos of you in your Halloween costumes.' She sniggered.

'Callie, no, oh my God. Wasn't the thought of his boner enough!'

She leaned in, a salacious grin on her face. 'I bet he jerks off looking at them every day.'

'You're twisted, stop it.' I covered my ears with my hands but I couldn't unsee the picture of what she'd described. She laughed, pleased with my reaction. I wasn't sure if Callie was right, but it didn't matter, I'd never think about Dylan the same way again.

* * *

Dylan

My phone vibrated. I ignored it for a moment until I saw it was Amy. I grabbed it, staring at the screen while the messaging app took forever to open. 'Hey Dylan - I miss you, wanna hang out tonight?' it read.

Play it cool, play it cool. I typed out, 'Yeah, sounds great. Can't wait to see you, I've missed you.' *That is not playing it cool...* I deleted it and tried again. 'Sounds great, be at yours at 8?' *Yeah, that was better.*

'Awesome, I'll pick a movie. What do you fancy?' she wrote.

You. You, you, you, you. 'Whatever works, just looking forward to seeing you.'

'Aww you big sap. Me too. Love you bestie xxx'

'Love you too.' She had no idea how much I meant it.

I stood up, exhilarated at the chance to see her this evening. We'd grown up together; she meant it when she said best friend, and I did too. But the last few years she'd become even more to me. Just whenever I tried to tell her it went wrong.

I thought back to my disastrous first attempt, a Valentine's gift that she'd assumed I gave her out of pity. She'd been so cross, throwing the necklace I'd chosen so carefully and saved up for, in her bin.

That had put me off saying anything for a long time. Then each time I built up the courage, it came out wrong. Or maybe she just didn't want to hear it. That was the risk. What if I ruined our friendship? *I couldn't cope with that, I need her in my life.*

I looked at myself in the mirror. There wasn't much to look at. I wasn't like the big, strong guys I could see Amy was attracted to, and it killed me. I'd been working out this year, trying to bulk up, but it didn't seem to make much of a difference.

But I couldn't go on like this. Her heading off to college had been torture. I'd taken a gap year to do a bit of travel, and get some work experience and money together while she'd gone straight on to study. My dream had been that she'd join me on my travels, but she'd assumed I was joking when I suggested it. By then, I'd deferred entry. I ended up having a good year, but not the one fantasised about, travelling around Europe with Amy by my side. *And in my bed.*

For most of the year all I could imagine was her finding some hunk of a boyfriend, and I knew it was going to break my heart. *I need to tell her how I feel, while she's back for the summer.*

No. Tonight. I'm going to tell her tonight.

* * *

Amy

I rifled through my wardrobe. 'Oh my God, what am I going to wear?' I'd never even considered that question for a night in with Dylan before. *I do not need this stress, eugh, why can't he not fancy me? Is it that hard?*

The more I thought about it, the angrier I got with him. Why did he have to be so stupid and take what we had, a great, deep friendship, and mess it up like this? And even worse, that he hadn't told me. He had cute girls like Kara going after him. Okay, she wasn't the smartest, but she was sweet and pretty. If I was the reason he'd turned her down then he was just an idiot.

I looked at myself in the full-length mirror inside my wardrobe, remembering what Callie had said. 'Does she really think I'm sexy?' I said to mirror image me, but all she did was shrug and check out my butt.

'Okay, maybe I am a bit.' I turned back to face myself and cupped my boobs with a smirk. *I sure did grow into these.* I laughed and a wicked thought came to mind. If Dylan is so secretly into me, let's see what impact I can have on him.

I stripped off what I was wearing, avoiding looking at myself in the mirror. A *few nice comments do not undo a lifetime of body issues.* I got excited as I began reaching in for the secret stuff I kept in the back of the wardrobe. My parents were pretty good about not going through my things, but my little sister, not so much, so I kept the sexier outfits out of sight.

First out of the box was my hottest set of lingerie. To be fair, it was my only actual *set* as everything else was random panties and bras. It was my ambition one day to only have rows of matching lingerie sets to pick from. *Or even better, to have someone else pick for me.* Wearing this always made me feel extra sexy, even if no one else saw it, and I certainly didn't plan on Dylan seeing it, but it made my boobs look fabulous.

I pulled out my short skirt options. I sometimes wore them with leggings but never without, besides as a costume. School girl tartan, a very tight black one, or my new white one I'd already picked out for the angel outfit. *Maybe Callie has a point about Halloween.* I decided against them and instead chose a pair of tight jeans — sexy without trying too hard. *Anyway, my top will do the work for me.*

I picked out what might have been a cute little cardigan — it turned into a very low-cut v-neck top if worn with nothing but the bra underneath it. It was also cropped enough to show a bit of skin above my belt too. Dylan was going to be surprised.

I looked at myself again, gave a little spin. *One thing missing.* I searched through my necklaces and picked out a choker that reminded me of a collar, smiling as I clasped it around my neck.

There was an old picture of Dylan and me I kept pinned on my poster board. *Oh Dylan, I'm going to make you suffer for not telling me how you felt, if it's true of course. And if it isn't, then this won't do anything to you, so it's only your own fault.*

'Now, what are we going to watch?' I let out a little gasp as an idea took hold. *Is that too mean?* I grinned, I was feeling naughty now. I reached up for the DVD that I'd only ever watched once and sworn never to again. I was about to break that promise, but it was all for a good cause.

'This could actually be quite fun.'

* * *

Dylan

'Amy, I love you.' *No, she'll just say she loves me too, that's no good.* Despite a thousand times having imagined my declaration of love, and her delighted response in kind, I still needed to figure out what I was going to say.

'I want to be more than just good friends,' I practised. *Eugh no, such a cliché.* How, how do I tell this incredible, beautiful, sexy girl that I love her and want to be with her?

As with most things I didn't know, I Googled it. 'How to tell a girl you like her'. It even had pictures. 'Keep clean and well dressed' I read. 'Keep calm'. *Okay, but what do I say...*

When I found their suggestions, it wasn't much help. 'I think you're awesome and I really like you.' *Seriously? She knows that already.* I read the next suggestion, 'Hey Amy, I don't usually go up to girls and say this, but I really like you.' Eugh. Okay, this clearly isn't meant for me. *That might get me killed.*

I scanned other suggestions, and one stood out. 'Do you want to go out on a date?' *That might actually work.* A date, that would show it's more than just hanging out. I pictured myself saying it, and of course, her saying 'yes, I've been waiting for you to ask for so long.' Okay, that's probably unrealistic but I couldn't help myself.

I soon got caught up speculating where I'd take her. It should be somewhere new, maybe a nice restaurant, or was that too obvious? I'd earned money during the year, I could definitely afford to impress her.

Maybe a walk and a picnic, that could be romantic. We could go somewhere secluded. I was picturing Amy in one of her super cute summer dresses, leaning in towards me, 'Why did we wait so long, Dylan?' before she kissed me, the thin strap falling off her shoulder, I looked down, and my suspicions confirmed, she's braless under the top.

'Fuck yes,' I whisper to my fantasy as I cup her breast through her top. The thought of it makes me ache. I have to do something about it.

I lie back in bed, my jeans quickly pulled down, my cock in my hand. I imagine the feel of her perfect breast, kissing her, touching her, unbuttoning her top and at least seeing what I'd only dreamed of for so long. She moans her devotions to me as I climax in real life, emptying my balls on my fresh t-shirt, too caught up in it all to even grab a tissue.

You're worth it, Amy.

I couldn't wait to declare my love. A new t-shirt and some body spray and I'd be ready.

* * *

Amy

I was nervous as 8pm came around. My dad raised an eyebrow at my choice of top but my sister said it looked good on me. I did have second thoughts about what I was wearing, but I was curious to see how Dylan reacted. As much as I fantasised about pretty much *everything*, I'd never imagined him in any of them. The concept he might not feel the same about me had me more than curious.

My mum let him in and soon sent him up. I could hear them having a brief chat at the front door. My parents loved Dylan. I padded around my room, ensuring that when he walked in I was bent over, rearranging something. I heard him pause at the door, looking at me for an extended pause before he said, 'Hey.'

I feigned being startled and turned to him, my cardigan bouncing, giving him a glance at what I had on underneath. He stopped, he stopped hard. He didn't quite drop his mouth comically open, but his eyes didn't lie, nor did his silence.

I stared back at him. 'Helloooo? Earth to Dylan?' *Fuck my life. It's only a cute top. Damn it, Callie's going to be so smug.*

'Hiya', he eventually managed.

I reached up to hug him and felt his hands on the small of my back linger just a little longer than they normally would. We pulled away and he eyed the choker around my neck. I tried not to smile too hard. 'Are you alright?' Teasing him like this was easier and more amusing than I'd imagined. I kept close to him, my bra and the v-neck top giving a view I was intrigued to see if he could ignore.

He couldn't. His eyes flicked down and lingered. 'Yes, fine, thanks.' He realised finally that I could see where he was looking.

'Are you sure? You look a bit flushed.' I tried not to laugh. *Keep it together, Amy. Man, this is too easy.* I stepped back. 'Come sit down, how're you doing? I haven't seen you all week, what have you been up to?'

Dylan perched on the end of the bed. As we had a proper catch up about the rest of my week since I got back home he seemed to relax a bit. But something was up. He was definitely nervous, and I don't think my outfit could be entirely to blame.

'So what movie have you picked?' he eventually asked.

My plan had evolved since I'd come up with it earlier. I pulled out a couple of DVDs. Normally we'd find something on Netflix, but this time I wanted to see what he did. His first test. On top of the two was *Aliens*, the Special Edition, of course–one of his favourite movies–and something he'd made me watch a million times. Gaining Sigourney Weaver as a badass role model wasn't a terrible outcome.

I watched his eyes as I uncovered the second DVD. Let me make it absolutely clear, I hate this movie. It was a tremendous disappointment. I didn't think the two main actors had any chemistry, and now I know more about consent, much of the story line is hugely problematic. But I'd never told Dylan any of this, I figured he'd only know it by its reputation.

'Fifty Shades of Grey,' he said, looking up at me, eyebrows raised.

'Yep.' I didn't want to give him anything more to go on.

He seemed to take a while to think about it. I reckon he was trying to play it cool. 'We've seen Aliens so much, let's try that instead,' he suggested, trying to be nonchalant. It wasn't convincing. I bit my lip to stop myself grinning.

Oh really, now *we don't have to watch your favourite. I see.* 'Okay.' I shuffled off the side of the bed and bent over to put the disc in and get it playing. I glanced back at him. He was totally checking out my butt. *Men, is that all you can think about?* I hit play, and walked back to the bed. *Actually, I'm hardly one to talk. Maybe this means we can talk about some stuff at least.*

That had been the other part of the plan. To use the film as a way to talk about some of the stuff I'd admitted to Callie. It had felt good to tell someone, and Dylan was even more important to me.

Unfortunately, I had forgotten how painful some of the movie plot problems were.

Once we'd watched a little I couldn't keep quiet. 'She doesn't have an email address, are you kidding, what century is this set in?'

Dylan laughed at me, but soon he was joining in. 'Is it me or is this guy basically a stalker?'

'I forgot how creepy it was,' I admitted.

I'd mostly been thinking about the kinky sex scenes, and the bondage playroom. When Christian pulled out a BDSM contract Dylan seemed shocked. 'Why would you need a contract? That's dumb.'

'Nothing says I love you like a non-disclosure agreement.' I laughed. 'But the idea of setting out rules, that's not a bad idea.' I tried to educate him but it fell on deaf ears.

'But what about being spontaneous, and what kind of things would you even have to agree?'

I wasn't certain if he was just unsure, but he sounded pretty judgemental. I tried to explain. 'You know, rules, boundaries, safe words, limits of what you were prepared to do, punishments too.' I looked at him, hoping for a glimmer of understanding.

'You seem to know a lot about it.' If he'd smiled, softened it, I'd have known what to do, but he gave me nothing. And then he said it. 'All seems pretty weird to me.'

I realise he didn't appreciate how much this stuff meant to me but I couldn't help but take it personally. 'It's not weird. Sure the film, and the book aren't a good example, but lots of people take this stuff very seriously.' I sat back in the bed, crossed my arms, and we watched the rest of the film in silence.

The fact the movie ends with Ana concluding that Christian is a perverted deviant didn't really help my cause. 'Stupid movie' I muttered under my breath. *That was the worst plan ever, what were you hoping to achieve?* I chastised myself as I headed to the loo. Even the sexy bits had been ruined by Dylan's judgement hanging over me. I pondered how ironic that was given what Callie had told me he liked to think about. It was time to find out if it was true.

* * *

When I came back into the bedroom, he'd shifted position, perched on the edge of the bed. 'So, Amy, I had something I wanted to ask you.'

I sat down back on my side of the bed, legs stretched out. 'Oh cool, actually I had something I wanted to ask you too.'

Dylan looked like I'd put him off his stride a bit. I stayed silent, not asking him what his question was. It didn't take long for him to fold.

'So, umm, what did you want to ask me?' he said.

I looked at him with a confusing mix of love and anger. I leaned forward and his reaction pushed me over the edge — he looked down my top without the slightest attempt to be subtle. *Fine, if that's how he thinks about me, let's see what he has to say about it.*

He saw me watching his gaze, and looked up guiltily. 'What did you want to ask?' he repeated, trying to distract me.

Here we go. 'Do you think about me when you wank?'

His eyes went wide. It's awful, but I found the shock on his face funny. I bit my lip again to stop myself laughing.

'What?' he cried. 'W…what do you m…mean?' *Oh boy, he only stutters when he's really flummoxed.*

I smiled sweetly, but my gaze was stern. 'Do you fantasise about me when you masturbate?' It was only at this point I realised that I wasn't sure *I* wanted to know the answer, but it was too late now.

He looked at me in disbelief. 'Why would you ask that?'

I huffed. 'That's not a "no". It's a simple question, Dylan.' *Shit, he does do it, he's not denying it. Bollocks, Callie was right. Now what do I do?*

He was confused, I could see it. I began to feel a little sorry for him but then the image of him actually wanking got in my head, no longer a crazy theory but apparently, reality. 'Yes, or no?' I demanded.

He frowned, leaning on the bed on one hand, and then raised an eyebrow. It was always cute when he did that. But this was so the wrong time. 'Do you really want to know the answer to that?' He seemed a little more confident.

Oh shit, does he think I like the idea? Shit, shit, shit. 'Answer the damn question, Dylan. Do you?'

He looked down at the floor. 'Yes, sometimes.'

'Oh my God,' I whispered. I looked down too, feeling my chest tighten.

That sent him into a renewed panic. 'I'm sorry, I try not to, I feel bad about it.'

'Well, that makes two of us. Do you know how that makes me feel?' I paused, I wasn't sure I knew.

He must have seen my confusion. 'I'm so, so sorry.' Dylan reached out, but I jumped up, taking a few steps back.

I looked at my best friend, he was clearly distraught. I felt bad about that, but I was angry that he'd not told me anything about this. I went back to my question. *How do I feel about this?* I didn't know, but I was curious.

I turned and leaned my head against the wall, trying to calm my breathing. 'What do you think about?' He stayed quiet and I turned to look at him. He'd been blushing before from my challenge, but that question made him go bright red. *What the hell?* 'Oh my God, Dylan, what *do* you think about?'

'Please, don't ask me that.'

What the fuck? My anger was quickly transforming into deep curiosity. Was he secretly kinky too? I'd talked to him about my submissive leanings a few times, maybe a little coded now I consider it, but I realised that he'd never opened up about what kind of things turned him on. *Maybe the fact that I'm what turned him on made that understandable.*

But now, I had to find out. I'd opened the can, the worms needed dealing with. 'Tell me, help me understand.' I sat back on the bed, opposite him. He stood, wanting to come closer and walked awkwardly to perch on the near corner of the bed. *What's he... oh God, he's got a boner.*

It wasn't that I'd never seen Dylan get one. We were on a train one time and he'd had an obvious bulge when he reached up to get our bags down. I'd teased him about it. But this one was because of me. That made me feel strange. I didn't tease him this time, although, I have to admit, I was tempted. The situation was getting ludicrous. He sat back down beside me, trying to casually rearrange himself. I managed not to giggle.

'Are you sure you want to know?' he repeated. There was that strange mix of fear and, what was it... surely not arousal? *I mean he does have a hard-on.*

'I do,' I answered.

He didn't look me in the eyes. 'I think... about being with you.'

'Fucking me?' I said, purposefully raw about it.

'No.' He paused and reconsidered. 'I mean, yes, sometimes, but more, I mean being *with* you. Your boyfriend.'

'But fucking me too?' I was determined to ignore the boyfriend thing. This was not the way to ask me.

'Yes,' he said, looking defeated. I kind of felt sorry for him, but if I was going to get more details, this was the time.

My eyes met his. 'Tell me.'

He tilted his head. 'Kissing you, I think a lot about kissing you.'

'Oh.' *Okay, kissing, that was cute.* I could handle that.

'Kissing you everywhere.' He looked up at me, eyebrows lifted. Suddenly it was me who was blushing.

Everywhere? That just went from cute to something very different. *Everywhere!* I looked at him. Shit. I could see it in his eyes. He was about to do something stupid. Before I knew it he was leaning towards me.

'Dylan…' I said, trying to warn him off. He kept on leaning in. 'Dylan…' Seriously, was he not picking up on my tone. *Oh God, he's shut his eyes.* I shied away but he kept on going, opening his eyes when I wasn't where he obviously expected my mouth to be. But even that wasn't enough, he leaned further, awkwardly trying to get to my lips. I jumped up from the bed. 'Dylan!' I shouted. 'No!'

Thankfully, that was enough. More than enough. I saw it, his fairytale story burning before his eyes. He rolled back to where he'd been sitting, gazing at his floor, looking utterly defeated. I felt awful. 'I'm sorry,' I said, 'but I just don't… I never have. Eugh, I….' I was lost for words.

I paced back and forth, trying to work out what to say. 'What was it you wanted to ask?' I hoped the change of subject might get us out of this mess.

He gave a sad little laugh. 'I was going to ask you on a date.'

You're kidding me. I stood still. 'Oh. Gosh.'

'I guess you answered it, anyway.' He sounded like he was about to cry. Suddenly all my anger evaporated.

I wanted to go to him, to hold his hand, but I stayed standing. 'Dylan, I'm so sorry. I just… had no idea. I was cross, confused.' I tried to make him feel better. It didn't look like it was working. 'I love you, but not like that.'

His silence was worse than anything he could have said. It seemed to go on forever. He didn't look up. 'I... I should go,' he finally said, standing too.

'Okay.' I didn't know what else to say. I watched him gather his things and leave.

* * *

Dylan

I walked slowly back to my house, feeling like shit — entirely wrapped up in my thoughts.

'How did that go so wrong?' I'd rehearsed what I was going to say a thousand times, and I don't think I'd managed to say a single sentence of it. *What was up with that movie, and that outfit,* 'And her question?' I finally said aloud.

'Do I think about her when I wank?' I mean, why did she even ask? And how do I answer that?

I tried a possible response out loud as I walked down the road. 'Of course I do, you're the most beautiful woman in the world.' *Fuck, even that would have been better than my stupid silence.* 'Oh God, what have I done? I've messed up everything.' The cat passing me in the street didn't seem to have any sympathy.

I went back to her words, 'I love you, but not like that.' Was there ever a more awful thing to hear? But who could blame her, after the bumbling, judgemental way I'd acted. Surely she was trying to tell me *something* with that movie choice. And her top. I just had no idea what.

I felt like such an idiot. She was supposed to be my best friend, but it seemed like I hardly knew her tonight. And why on earth had she asked that question?

For a moment, just a moment, I imagined she was coming onto me. I know, hardly a conventional technique. And then what had I done, only tried to kiss her. *Fuck, how am I ever going to get past this? I've ruined our friendship. I'm so stupid. I have to do something. I have to fix this.*

I jumped the fence of the playground I was walking past, and sat down on one of the swings. It was too late for any kids to be there, and none of the gangs of teenagers who sometimes hung out here in the evening seemed to be around.

I pulled out my phone. 'Amy, I'm so sorry. I didn't mean to upset you. It's okay you don't love me that way...' I didn't finish the message. *Is it okay? Is this it? Have I just lost my best friend?*

I deleted most of the text. 'Amy, I'm sorry about what happened tonight. Can we talk?'

I sent it, watching for the read notification. Finally, after what seemed like hours, the little symbol changed. It told me she was typing. I waited. And waited. I didn't dare reply, not even type a letter in case it gave her an excuse to not say what she was thinking.

Still, nothing from her. *If she still hasn't replied by the time I've got home, I'll message again.* I began walking, faster now. I checked my notifications were on, that it would ping, and vibrate, when... if, she messaged.

It still hadn't by the time I'd reached my front door. I pulled my phone out, standing in the porchway. I gave in, but as I was about to write more, it showed her typing again. I waited, my heart racing. Finally, it appeared.

'I'm sorry too. I have lots to think about. I'll call you tomorrow.'

A spark of hope ignited in me. Could that mean, something positive? *She's sorry, that's a good start, right?* My thoughts vacillated from positive to negative. Every time more convinced the message was a good, or bad thing.

I had to reply, just something. An emoji? They were always safe, but I'm not sure one could quite capture how I was feeling right now. I decided to take a risk. 'I love you,' I typed. My finger hovered over it. *Fuck it, it's true. She needs to know.*

I hit send, and waited. I wished I had stayed, that we could have talked this out. Waiting on her replying was such torture. But I didn't have to wait long.

'I know you do. I just didn't realise quite how much. I love you too.'

That has to be good? Maybe I haven't totally messed this up.

I managed to feel slightly less freaked out. Which let me reconsider that damn question of hers. I pictured her saying it again, 'Do you think about me when you wank?'

Even in my distressed state I couldn't help appreciate the irony. I crept upstairs, still thinking about how incredible she looked tonight, my cock taking charge of my thoughts, helping me to worry less about the stress of the evening. *You're all I think about when I wank.* I slipped into my room to prove how true it was.

* * *

Want to know what happens next?
Visit smarurl.it/fwkb

You can buy the book on Amazon. Simply search for James Hardcourt, enter the following link or scan the QR code below to go straight there.

https://smarturl.it/fwkb

If you liked this book

Thank you so much for reading my story. I hope you've enjoyed reading it as much as I enjoyed writing it. **The best way to let me know you did, is to leave a review on Amazon.** The only reason I didn't just leave *One-Bar Prison* as a standalone short story was all the reviews encouraging me to write more. And now we have four books!

I read every single review I get. They mean a tremendous amount to me. **If you want more of Emma and Nate's adventures then please, if you possibly can, leave me a review on Amazon.**

How to leave an anonymous review

There are something like 60,000 new books published on Amazon every day. As a new author, it's very hard to compete - to stand out from the crowd.

One of the biggest helps in getting this book noticed is to have reviews. It would be so helpful if you'll take the time to go onto Amazon's site and tell others what you think of it.

If you're worried about leaving a review for a book like this, I have good news. The reason I recommend going to Amazon to leave your review, and not just using the option at the end of the Kindle or other device, is because **you can make it anonymous:**

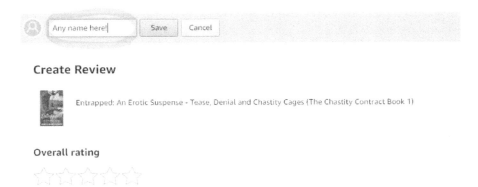

Create Review

Entrapped: An Erotic Suspense - Tease, Denial and Chastity Cages (The Chastity Contract Book 1)

Overall rating

Just click 'Edit' next to your name and you can put anything you like for your review

Thank you! I really want to write more, in this series, and others - knowing you like the book and letting others see they are good quality and well written is a huge help and encouragement for me to do that.

Thanks so much for your
review. I read every one
and really appreciate you
taking the time to leave
one for the book.

https://smarturl.it/entrappedreview

Click this link to go to the book page on Amazon

Get early access

Would you like early access to my writing, and to help shape where it goes? Then my SubscribeStar might be for you.

As a **Fan Club member,** you'll get early access to stories, edging tasks, and the stuff too hot for Amazon or Tumblr to handle.

Book Club members additionally get to vote on stories, contribute ideas, and receive Advanced Reader Copies.

And if you're an aspiring erotica writer there's even the **Writer's Club** - benefit from encouragement and feedback on your writing, exclusive membership of the Edging Space Writers Discord group and more.

Find out more at subscribestar.adult/edgingspace

Also by James Hardcourt

The #1 Amazon Bestselling Kink by the Numbers series...

The One-Bar Prison

A kinky fantasist, a hot, dominant neighbour, and the toy of her dreams. How could it go so wrong?

Natalie is very kinky, at least in the safety of her bedroom - too bad in real life she is shy and regrettably innocent. That is until hot new neighbour, Brandon, moves in next door, and is kind enough to hold a delivery she's missed. That delivery, and the super kinky toy it contains, is about to propel Natalie's fantasy very hard and very fast into reality.

The predicament she gets herself into will either be the most embarrassing experience of her life, or the start of something hot and beautiful. The choice is hers.

THE ONE-BAR *Prison*

Kink by the Numbers - Book 1

A kinky fantasist, a hot, dominant neighbour, and the toy of her dreams. How could it go so wrong?

A First Time Maledom BDSM Novella by
JAMES HARDCOURT

You can buy the book on Amazon. Simply search for James Hardcourt, enter the following link or scan the QR code below to go straight there.

https://smarturl.it/onebarprison

Full of kinky play, humiliating but adorable scenarios, and the hottest consent you'll find in any erotica - dip into this first book in James Hardcourt's Edging Erotica Series - **now with special edging instructions and author's note**

Get it on Amazon today

About the Author

James has been creating kinky smut for a couple of decades - it's mostly been in his head until now - and more recently on his unexpectedly popular Tumblr blog. He writes erotica and non-fiction about edging, orgasm denial, chastity play and anything else kinky he can come up with. His books explore the twists and turns of BDSM power dynamics, hot consent and erotic predicaments. He's married to Jane, who runs her own blog too, and somewhere in the mix they've managed to produce a couple of wonderful kids. They live happily just outside of London, England, and their friends and family are entirely oblivious to just what avid kinksters they are. You can find out more at Edging Space Publishing: https://edging.space

Twitter: https://twitter.com/edgingspace
SubscribeStar: https://subscribestar.adult/edgingspace
Sign up to the newsletter: https://www.subscribepage.com/w8h2j5

Books by James Hardcourt:

Kink by the Numbers Series:
> *The One-Bar Prison*
> *Tease for Two*
> *Three-Line Whip*
> *On All Fours*
> *Five by Five (coming soon)*

Friends with Kinky Benefits

The Chastity Contract series:
> *Entrapped*
> *Enticed*
> *Encased*

The Dead Bedroom Remedy

Printed in Great Britain
by Amazon

20940722R00192